THE FIRST
BETRAYAL

Patricia Bray

BANTAM BOOKS

THE FIRST BETRAYAL
A Bantam Spectra Book / June 2006

Published by
Bantam Dell
A Division of Random House, Inc.
New York, New York

Bantam Books, the rooster colophon, Spectra, and the por-
trayal of a boxed "s" are trademarks of Random House, Inc.

ISBN-13: 978-0553-58876-7
ISBN-10: 0-553-58876-1

Printed in the United States of America
Published simultaneously in Canada

www.bantamdell.com

OPM 10 9 8 7 6 5 4 3 2 1

Also by Patricia Bray
Published by Bantam Spectra Books

THE SWORD OF CHANGE TRILOGY

BOOK 1: DEVLIN'S LUCK
BOOK 2: DEVLIN'S HONOR
BOOK 3: DEVLIN'S JUSTICE

Acknowledgments

I want to thank the following:

My editor Anne Lesley Groell, who liked the lizards.

My agent Jennifer Jackson, who pushed me when I needed it.

And the folks at The Lost Dog Café and The CyberCafe West, for providing good food, good drink, and a waitstaff that doesn't flinch when they overhear writers plotting mayhem.

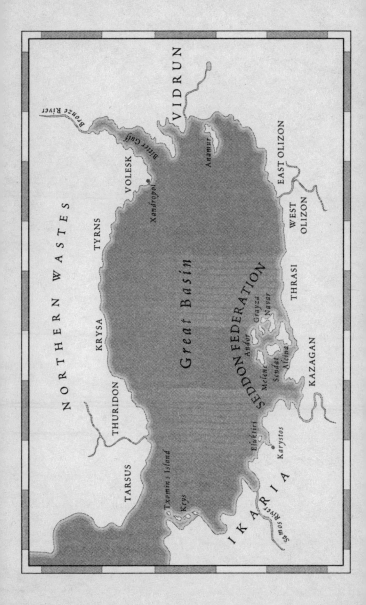

Chapter 1

The lantern flickered as a gust of wind blew through the lighthouse tower. Then the flame died, plunging Josan into darkness. His right hand searched the floor beside him till he found the sparker, then he groped for the base of the lantern with his left. Using the edge of his cloak to protect his hand from the heated glass, he removed the chimney. His hand trembled so much that it took three tries before he was able to relight the wick. Finally, it caught, and with a sigh of relief he carefully replaced the glass. The soft light illuminated the small platform for a few brief moments before succumbing to another draft. This time, Josan did not bother to relight it.

He told himself that he did not need to see, but could not repress the shiver of unease as the darkness engulfed him. Before tonight this had always been a place of light, the large windows letting in the daylight, and at dusk the three great lamps would be lit, powerful beacons that filled the platform with their radiance as they guided ships far out at sea. But tonight the signal lamps were dark, for not even the most sheltered flame was proof against the howling wind. Now darkness had consumed the light, just as the sea outside threatened to devour the tower.

In the dark, every sound was magnified as the rain lashed against the wooden shutters, and the merciless wind sought the cracks in his defenses. Strange drafts swirled inside the tower and he drew his knees to his chest, pulling his coarse woolen cloak more tightly around him. The wind outside intensified, howling until he could scarcely hear himself think. From far beneath him, he heard a crash. Startled, he began to stand, then common sense reasserted itself and he resumed his seat. There was nothing he could do until the storm passed. Instead he listened intently, and underneath the sound of the wind and rain he heard the relentless crashing of the waves. It sounded as if they were breaking all around him, and he knew the lighthouse was being swallowed by the angry ocean.

He wondered if the ocean would eventually release its prize, or if the stone tower would crumble beneath the fury of the storm. He tried to view his situation dispassionately, the question of his survival as a mere intellectual exercise, but none of the tricks he had learned in his years of study could dispel his fear. He could almost taste the terror as it rose up and threatened to overwhelm him, just as the sea threatened to overtake the tower.

It would be easier if he could pray. If he were one of the fishing folk, with their simple faith in the gods of the sea and storms. Gods that could be placated by offerings and rituals. Gods that were petty enough to care if a single man lived or died.

Josan's faith allowed him no such comfort. He served the true gods: Zakar, the giver of life, and his brother Ata, the giver of knowledge. The twin gods concerned themselves with the affairs of the heavens. They were far too lofty to care about the fate of a simple monk.

He recalled the face of Brother Thanatos as he lectured

his young pupils. "Remember, we serve the gods. The gods do not serve us." It was the first lesson he had learned from the monks, and the most important one.

The true gods were the masters of all knowledge, and the Learned Brethren of the collegium served their gods through scholarship and the accumulation of wisdom. Before his exile Josan had served them well, but he knew better than to expect that this had earned him any favors. The gods were indifferent to Josan's peril, as indeed they were indifferent to the fate of all men.

Instead, Josan must put his trust in the skills of those who had built the tower. Two hundred years ago, Prince Txomin's ship had run aground on a nearby sandbar, then broken apart under the relentless pounding of the waves. Forced to swim for his life, the prince had promised his gods he would build them a great monument if he survived.

The lighthouse had been built near the spot where Txomin was said to have come ashore. Nearly a hundred feet high, it was made of massive granite stone blocks quarried far in the south. Wide enough at the base to contain a small storeroom, it tapered as it rose until you reached the platform at the top, which was barely twenty feet across. Starting at the base of the round tower, a steep staircase wound three times around until it reached the first course, which consisted of a half-circle wooden stage and the lowest rung of the iron ladder. As you climbed there were two more courses, each progressively smaller, which were used for storage and as a place to rest for those wearied by the climb. Finally, at the top of the ladder a trapdoor led up to the platform, with its three great lamps. Pulleys at the top allowed a man to hoist heavy or bulky objects up the long shaft, though Josan had seldom found a need for this.

The repetition of threes was a sign that the builders had been followers of the old Ikarian religion, with its belief in the mystical powers of that number. Josan, of course, knew that the only number with true mystical significance was the number five.

Still, despite their quaint beliefs, the builders had constructed a solid structure that had endured for centuries. In some ways the tower was a relic of past glories, when such an extravagant undertaking could be commissioned on behalf of one who was merely sixth in line for the throne.

In the beginning, the priests of the old religion had served as lighthouse keepers, then when Emperor Aitor had assumed his throne, the old religion had fallen out of favor and the Learned Brethren had taken over the task, in return for imperial consideration. Chanted prayers had given way to meticulously recorded observations of the weather and the tides.

Before he had come to this place, Josan had paid no heed to the weather. And why should he? Most of his life had been spent indoors, studying in the great library or visiting with scholars when he had journeyed to Seddon and Xandropol. But since his transformation from scholar to lighthouse keeper, he had developed an uncanny sense for the weather.

He had known this storm was coming since yesterday, when the dawn had revealed long waves breaking on the shore against the direction of the wind. The very air had felt strange against his skin, and he had known that the clear sunshine was a false prophet, giving no sign of what was to come.

Josan spent that morning making his preparations, moving what supplies he could from the storeroom to one of the three courses that bisected the tower, filling every inch of available space. His duty done, he'd then made the long trek to warn the villagers who lived on the island during the summer and autumn. But with the skies still clear, they'd eyed him askance. It seemed incredible that these folk, who had lived here all their lives, could not see the danger signs. They had been polite but skeptical, trusting in their own instincts and the bright sun that shone above.

At last, he'd reminded them that he was a servant of the twin gods. When asked if the gods had sent him this warning he had not agreed, but neither had he denied it. He had salved his conscience with the thought that in a way the gods were responsible for his knowledge, for they had given him the wits to study the weather and read the messages of the wind and tides.

By the time he'd returned to his lighthouse, clouds had covered the sky. The tide that night had been unusually high, and when the dawn came, so too came the first drops of rain. The storm had grown during the day until the skies were so dark that he could not tell when the sun had set. The winds raged so fiercely that there was no point in trying to light the great lanterns. He could only hope that there were no ships caught in the storm.

He wondered how the villagers were faring. Had they heeded his warning and moved to higher ground? They, at least, could flee the storm, leaving nothing behind but their fishing shacks.

Josan had chosen to remain in the lighthouse, despite its proximity to the sea. But what had seemed an admirable devotion to duty was now proven sheer folly as the waves broke around the tower and he swore that he could feel the massive stones trembling under the onslaught.

He realized that he would die here, a victim not of the storm but of his own miscalculation in thinking that the massive tower would be proof against the forces of wind and water. Anger mixed with fear, as the irony of his situation sank in. His life had been spared once, when against all odds he had survived a disease that was nearly always fatal. He had been given a second chance, and now even that would be taken from him.

With morbid fascination, he wondered if he would be crushed to death by the stones as the tower fell, or if he would be swept out to sea and drowned. It was a puzzle that required far more knowledge of engineering than Josan possessed; nonetheless, he began calculating the odds of each event, as if this were an exercise given to him by his tutors.

As minutes turned to hours, he came to the conclusion that it was most likely he would be injured when the tower fell—perhaps even trapped under debris—and only then would he drown, unable to free himself.

Having reached this conclusion, he settled himself to wait until events would prove or disprove his hypothesis. But as he listened, he realized that the wind had changed direction, and had become merely loud rather than deafening. Gradually the wind calmed, and only the occasional wave broke around the tower. He could still hear the rain, but it fell more softly, as if this was an ordinary storm. This time when he relit the lantern, it stayed lit. Cautiously he made his way to the edge of the platform and peered down the shaft, but it was too dark to see what lay beneath him.

He was forced to wait until the rays of the sun crept through the broken shutters on the eastern face of the platform. Rising to his feet, he pushed aside the damaged boards and looked outside.

The ocean still churned, frothy whitecaps dotting the broken swells. But the rain had stopped, and the sky above held only scattered gray clouds. He looked down and saw that the waves had retreated, now breaking on the sandy shoreline a good sixty paces from the base of the lighthouse tower. The ocean had given back the prize it had so briefly claimed, but it was only a temporary victory. Before the storm, even at high tide, the waves had come no closer than a hundred paces. Now that distance had been cut nearly in half. The next storm might well claim the tower permanently.

But that was a worry for another day. Josan made his way to the ladder and began the long climb down, to see what damage the storm had wrought.

There was not a single trace left of the wooden cottage that he had called home for the past five years. Even the very impression of its foundation was gone, and Josan felt strangely saddened by its loss. As a member of the brethren, it was not fitting that he had become attached to a mere dwelling, but the cottage had been his home from his earliest days on the island, when the waves had seemed so loud that he could not sleep unless he stuffed thistledown in his ears.

He felt empty, almost numb, as he observed the destruction. The beach was dotted with strands of sea kelp, broken shells, and a few bits of driftwood that might have been from his cottage, or from some long-ago sea wreck only now being washed ashore. Seabirds quarreled over the carcasses of fish that had been stranded by the high waves, their familiar calls sounding strangely loud in the absence of the wind.

The sea itself was dark, murky with all that had been churned up. More bits of wood were scattered on the waves, including a large pine bough that made him wonder just how far inland the storm waves had reached. He had done his part in warning the villagers; still, he could not help thinking of them, even as he set about cleaning up the mess the storm had left behind.

The lower stones of the tower were still damp, showing that the waves had reached twice the height of a man before retreating. The wooden door at the base of the tower had held, but the glass that had once lined the window slits on the lowest level was gone, which had allowed the storm waters to pour into the tower, leaving several inches of brackish water in the base and the adjacent storeroom. The wooden barrel that held his freshwater was contaminated by brine, and two of the empty oil jars had tipped over and smashed, but the full jars had remained unbroken, their wax seals intact.

The loss of the cottage was a blow to his comfort, but he would be able to survive with what he had stored.

Freshwater would be more of a problem. He had a small firkin on the third platform, which would serve him for a day, but soon he would have to make the trek up over the dunes to the nearest clean well. It was a long walk, and he spared a moment to hope that the dunes had been enough to shelter the well from the storm waters. Checking on the well would be his first priority, once he had set the lighthouse tower to rights.

He began by bailing out the seawater from the base of the tower and mopping it dry with a rag that had once been his second-best tunic. Behind one of the jars he'd found a dead fish, and so he'd carefully moved each jar in turn to be sure there were no other hidden surprises. Then he'd climbed back up to the lighthouse platform. He was no carpenter, but he did manage to repair one of the broken shutters. It was a trifle crooked, and it took two leather cords to hold it in place. The other shutter was too damaged and he set the scraps aside for later.

Then, because this was a seventh day, he carefully disassembled the three lamps and washed their globes using his precious supply of freshwater. Keeping the lights burning brightly was far more important than his comfort.

Each silver mirror was polished with a leather cloth kept solely for this purpose. The wicks were trimmed and the oil reservoirs filled, then finally he replaced the glass globes. He took comfort in the routine tasks and their familiar rhythms.

There was less than a month before the arrival of winter; then he would be free from his duties till the spring. It was unlikely that any ships would pass by so late in the season, but that did not matter. The lighthouse lamps would shine as brightly this night as they had during the height of the summer shipping season. He could do no less.

Finally, satisfied that all was in readiness for the evening, he glanced through the open shutters at the sun, noticing that it was early afternoon. There was time for him to check on the well and return before sunset. Or it might be wiser if he took this opportunity to rest and saved the trip to the well for tomorrow. He had a long night ahead of him, and it had been days since he had slept.

But even as he hesitated, he caught sight of two figures trudging along the sandy beach, making their way toward his tower. Coming to see if he had survived the storm, he supposed. It was a long walk, so he descended to the middle course and filled a small earthenware pitcher with his fast-dwindling supply of water. He tucked two wooden cups into a pouch that he slung around his neck. Holding the pitcher in his left hand, he stepped onto the ladder, wrapping his right arm around the iron frame for balance. Carefully he descended, feeling a faint flicker of pride as he reached the base without spilling a drop.

By this time, he could recognize Renzo's white hair, and surmised that the smaller figure next to him must be his niece Terza. He waved and they waved back, then he sat down on the steps of the tower to await their arrival.

"Brother Josan, I give thanks to the gods that you are well and unharmed," Renzo said, holding out his two hands palms upward, in the traditional gesture of thanksgiving.

"I live to serve them," Josan said. He handed them each a cup of water and waited while they drank.

Renzo appeared unchanged. He looked much the same as he had when Josan had first arrived on the island over five years ago—his skin leathered with age and deep wrinkles around his blue eyes from squinting at the sun. He was a good man, and had been endlessly patient with the city-bred monk and his never-ending questions.

His niece Terza was a different matter. She had grown from a girl into an adult in the past years, and while she was quick-tongued enough with the men of her village, she still blushed and avoided his eyes when in Josan's presence. As a child she'd been infatuated with him, not understanding that his vows included an oath not to take a female lover. Eventually he'd taken pity on her and explained, but his efforts to spare her feelings had unforeseen consequences. Rather than seeing this as a polite dismissal, she'd convinced herself that it was only his vocation that kept them apart. He supposed there was some comfort in knowing that your rival was the twin gods, rather than another woman.

Nothing he had said or done since had served to change her opinion, so he treated her with formal politeness and was careful never to be alone with her.

"And your people, they are well?" he asked, as Renzo lowered the cup and wiped his mouth with the edge of his sleeve.

Renzo nodded. "Most of the folk went back to the mainland. Those of us who remained took the traps and the boats up to the highest ground and waited out the storm. We came through fine, but the fishing shacks are gone, and coming here we had to wade through a new channel that's cut through the island just south of the bayberry bluffs."

The fishing shacks were no great loss, since they were rebuilt every year after the winter storms. But if the villagers had been taking shelter in their shacks, as they would have been during an ordinary storm, then they might well have perished.

Terza raised her eyes and looked him in the face. "It was thanks to your warning that none were harmed. If the gods had not told you there was a great storm coming, by the time we realized our peril it would have been too late."

Now it was Josan's turn to look away, made uncomfortable by the reminder that he had used deception to gain his way.

"I see your cottage is gone," Renzo said. "It will take some time for us . . ."

"No need," Josan interrupted him. "We can rebuild it in the spring."

Renzo knew him well enough not to conceal his relief. Rebuilding the cottage would have taken precious days of labor at a time when all efforts had to be focused on preparing for winter.

"Of course we will replace whatever you lost, but most of our folk will stay in the village," Renzo said. "Time enough to rebuild here when spring comes."

Some of Renzo's people lived on the mainland year-round, tending crops or fishing in the protected waters of the sound. Others came to the island for the summer months, catching shellfish from the ocean beds. In the fall, they hunted the birds that rested in the thickets and marshes before resuming their journey south.

Each year as winter approached, the villagers retreated to the mainland, leaving only the flimsy fishing shacks at the mercy of the harsh winter storms. Josan would join them there when the first moonrise of winter relieved him of his duty.

"Now that we see you are well, I have a favor to ask," Renzo said. "During the early hours of the storm, a foreign ship sailed into the Angry Bay. The captain sent his noble passenger ashore in a dinghy, and we gave her shelter during the storm. Trouble is, we can't understand a word that she is saying, nor she us. I think she wants us to go look for her ship, but . . ." Renzo's voice trailed off.

The ship was most likely sunk. Someone would have to explain this to her. It was fortunate that Josan's training had included the language of both the Ikarian and Seddonian courts, as well as a smattering of the low tongue used by sailors. Pantomime and drawings scratched in the sand could only convey so much.

"I will keep the watch for you this night," Terza said.

After a moment's consideration Josan nodded. He disliked leaving his duties to another, but this would not be the first night that Terza had spent as keeper. After the death of Brother Hakim, the previous keeper, Renzo and Terza had taken turns serving at the lighthouse until Josan had arrived to take the post.

Terza accompanied him as he climbed to the top course and showed her where he had stored the supplies that she would need. Then he grabbed his robe, and after a moment's thought, his waterproof writing case.

Renzo was waiting for him at the base of the lighthouse.

"Come now, we must hurry if we are to return before full dark," he said.

As Josan and Renzo set off, he found his thoughts turning to the stranded noblewoman. His curiosity stirred as he wondered who she was and what had brought her to this wild place. It had been years since he had spoken with a person of education, and he was looking forward to whatever news she had to offer of the civilized world.

Perhaps there would even be news of the collegium, and of those he had left behind. Unconsciously his steps quickened, until a quiet word from Renzo reminded him to save his strength, for they still had a long way to travel.

Chapter 2

It was fortunate that he had Renzo to guide him, for on his own Josan would have been lost, which was quite a feat when you considered that this was the smallest of the barrier islands. But the power of the storm had changed the landscape almost beyond recognition. Paths through the dune grasses had disappeared, covered by sand sculpted into strange shapes by the wind. Pools of standing water made ponds and marshes out of what had been dry land, and necessitated frequent detours. Familiar dunes had disappeared or been reduced to mere shadows of their former selves, while others had appeared as if out of nowhere.

When they reached the new channel, Renzo told Josan to wait on the bank as he lowered himself into the water. The muddy water came up to his waist as he made his way slowly across. Only when he reached the far bank did he motion for Josan to follow.

Josan took off his sandals, tying their straps around his neck, before he slid down the bank into the water. He stood, his feet sinking into thick mud, as he tried to brace himself against the current. The chill water bit through his flesh into his bones, but even as he shivered, a part of him wondered at the source of the flowing current. Did it obey the pull of the tides? Or was there some imbalance between the water of the deep ocean toward the east and the water of the protected sound to the west?

As Josan reached the far bank, Renzo leaned down, extending his right hand. The old fisherman had lost none of his strength, and he pulled Josan up the bank with ease, as if he were a child instead of a man grown. As Josan sat down to retie his sandals, Renzo stood gazing at the channel and shaking his head.

"It's nearly half again as wide as it was when Terza and I came this way," Renzo explained. "No telling how big it will be by tomorrow. You may need to swim across until we can build a rope bridge."

Josan nodded. Swimming was another of those skills which he had learned since he had left behind his sheltered life in Karystos. He was a fair swimmer, but at this time of year the seawater was too cold to endure for long. Still, he would do what he must.

He stood and stamped his feet, trying to restore warmth and feeling to them. The waterlogged hem of his robe slapped wetly against his shins as they walked. When his feet began to stumble, he forced himself to clear his mind and pay attention to each step. He was all too conscious of his empty belly and parched mouth for there had been no freshwater to spare for the journey. Yet he did not complain, for how could he, when Renzo—who was more than twice his age—bore such discomforts without complaint and showed no signs of fatigue even though this was the second time he had made this difficult trek that day?

The sun had set and the last of the twilight was fading when they crested a dune and saw the glow of fire pits just ahead. Their arrival had been noted, and cheerful voices hailed them as they approached. Young Piero brought two rough wool blankets, draping one around Josan's shoulders and the other over Renzo's back. Josan clutched the blanket around him like a cape with one hand, while with the other he accepted a wooden cup filled with warm tea. He drank it down in quick gulps, eager to slake his thirst. When it was emptied, Young Piero returned and refilled it. This time he drank a bit more slowly, pausing to look around. A dozen men sat around the largest of the fire pits. They looked weary, but content. And well they might be, having passed through the storm with no harm.

To his right he glimpsed the rounded outline of dark shapes, which he assumed were the prized boats. Ahead of him he could see a handful of low tents, each with a small fire in front. The tents must have been erected after the winds had died down, and he wondered what the villagers had done for shelter during the height of the storm. Had they hidden under the boats? Trusted their safety to one of the shallow caves that dotted the bluffs? Or had they simply huddled together in the scrub forest, using tarps to shelter themselves from the worst of the rain?

Having safely delivered his charge, Renzo took a seat near the fire pit and accepted a square of dried fish, unwrapping the seaweed wrapper so he could gnaw on the salty contents. Josan's own stomach rumbled with hunger, but there would be time for food later. He had not been brought here simply to share their hospitality.

He drew himself erect as Old Piero approached. Old Piero was not truly aged—indeed his hair was still straw-colored—but since his son had been old enough to cast a net, he had borne the name of Old Piero. At his side was a diminutive woman, wearing an embroidered woolen shawl over a dark-colored dress.

Josan handed his cup to Young Piero, then began a bow of greeting, but the courtly gesture was cut short as the blanket threatened to slip from his shoulders.

"Piero, I was pleased to hear that your people survived the great storm unscathed," Josan said.

"That we did, and were grateful for your warning. And you? Is the lighthouse still standing?"

Josan nodded. "Yes, though the shoreline has shrunk. Another storm of this size and it will be in the sea rather than next to it."

"May the gods grant us years before such a thing comes to pass. One such storm is enough for any man's lifetime."

Josan then turned his attention to the woman who had waited patiently throughout this exchange. Her dark eyes and golden complexion marked her as a foreigner, and the gown she wore was in the style of the Seddonian court. She held herself with grace, as if daring anyone to notice that the hem of her gown was crusted with sand and dried sea spray.

"Noble lady, how may I serve you?" he asked, the fluid syllables of Decanese coming as easily to his tongue as if he spoke them every day.

"At last, a person of civilization," she exclaimed, her face brightening. "I was beginning to despair of ever making myself understood."

"I am Brother Josan, who tends the lighthouse on the south point," he said, giving a second shallow bow.

"I am Lady Ysobel Flordelis of Alcina," she said, naming one of the islands in the Seddonian Federation. "We were sailing to Karystos when the ship encountered a great storm at sea. The ship was gravely damaged, so the captain sent me, my maid, and four of his sailors ashore in a small boat, while he planned to anchor in the cove to ride out the storm. One of these folk found our party and convinced us to follow him to shelter. But now they will not take us back to the shore so we can rejoin the ship," she explained. "I am grateful for their care, but they simply must take us back in the morning. Captain Tollen will be frantic searching for us."

It was late in the year to be making such a journey, but the Seddonians were renowned as expert navigators and ship handlers. It was rare that you heard of one of their ships coming to grief. Still, he supposed the storm could well have caught them by surprise, and there was no telling how badly the ship had been damaged before the captain spotted the island and managed to set his noble passenger ashore.

Josan turned his attention back to Piero. "Was there any trace of her ship found?"

"Not even a scrap of wood, so it's likely the ship was dragged out to sea before it wrecked against the shoals."

"They may have survived," Josan said, though he knew it was unlikely.

"My son saw the ship when they sailed into the bay. One of the great masts was snapped clean off. And only a fool would anchor in the Angry Bay, where even on a calm day the tide is likely to rip an anchor up by its roots. If we'd had more time, we would have tried to warn them, but the waters were already choppy and none of us were going to risk our lives for theirs," Piero said with a fatalistic shrug.

If it had been an Ikarian ship, they might have risked their lives to pass on a warning. Then again, they might not have. The villagers believed that every time a man ventured out on the sea, he was putting his life into the hands of the gods, and if the gods decided it was time to take that life then there was nothing anyone could do.

It was left to Josan to pass on the grim news. "The headman has already sent men to the bay where you landed, but found no trace of your ship, nor of any survivors. It is possible that they were blown out to sea, but if so, they will be far from here."

"Or it is possible that the ship foundered and all are lost," she said.

"That is likely the case."

Her face looked grim, but she did not weep, for which he was grateful. His life among the brethren had made him wary around women, and he would not know how to comfort one in distress. The questions that he had prepared during the journey dried up in his mouth. His own curiosity was a petty thing when balanced against her loss.

"It seems I must make my own way to Karystos. When is the next ship expected?"

"There will be no ship until spring," Josan said. The shifting sandbars around the island that were the reason for the lighthouse also made the island treacherous to approach. Ships passed up and down the coastline during the sailing season, but trading ships stopped at the island only twice each year, to deliver cabbage-seed oil for the lamps and other precious supplies from the capital. For the rest of their needs, the villagers sent their goods along the mainland road that led to the town of Skalla, with its sheltered harbor where ships could safely anchor.

"Tell her that tomorrow I will take her and her folk to the mainland," Piero said. He must have guessed what her question would be, having recognized the word for ship, which was the same in pidgin as in Decanese. "We'll set them on the trading road, and once they reach Skalla they can either find a captain still willing to brave the autumn storms or take the coach road down to the south."

Josan translated his offer.

"Please tell the headman that I accept his kind offer. And now I must bid you good night, for I should tell my companions what I have learned."

"Of course, my lady," Josan said. He watched as she turned and made her way toward the largest of the tents.

"Sensible enough, for all she's a noble," Piero observed.

Then he clapped Josan on the shoulder. "Come now, there wasn't time for a hot meal, but there's plenty of salted yellowtail, and I reckon you wouldn't say no to another cup of tea to warm your bones."

Josan nodded and followed him to the fire pit. The warmth of the flames had dried out the surrounding sands and he sank down, grateful to finally be able to rest. It had been more than two days since he had slept, and exhaustion had dulled the edge of his hunger, though he gnawed absently at the strips of salted fish. Well used to his silences, the villagers did not press him for conversation, so he was left in peace to listen as they recounted what damage they had seen from the storm, and whether it was likely to have disturbed the shellfish beds. A few of the men fretted over their families, wondering what they would find when they escorted Lady Ysobel to the mainland. When Josan could keep his eyes open no longer, he wrapped the blanket tightly around himself and curled up to sleep on the sand.

Morning came, the dawn revealing clear skies with only a few wispy clouds scattered overhead. Sleep had restored both his body and wits, and he felt confident that he could find his way back to the lighthouse without too many detours.

There was fresh tea and salted fish left over from last night. After eating his fill, Josan opened his writing case and unrolled the scroll that he had previously written to the head of his order. He penned a quick postscript describing the damage done by the storm, assuring the brethren that he was well, but that the lighthouse would likely not survive another such tempest.

He hoped his words did not sound too much like begging.

He tied the scroll, then gave it to Piero, who assured him he would see that it was sent along to Karystos.

Then he waited impatiently for Lady Ysobel to arise. It would be a long journey back to the lighthouse, and he was impatient to get started. But courtesy dictated that he not leave until he had bade Lady Ysobel farewell and ensured that there was nothing else he needed to translate for her.

Though he had been anxious to meet her, he no longer had any urge to prolong their encounter. There was something about her that had made him uncomfortable, far too self-conscious to ask her any of the questions that he had stored up. He wondered if it would have been different if the stranger had been a nobleman. Or perhaps it was simply that after so long spent alone, he was no longer in the habit of making civilized conversation.

The lady emerged from her tent only an hour after dawn, showing commendable promptness. Josan made his way toward her and bowed.

"Lady Ysobel, the greetings of the day to you," he said. This time, with no blanket to encumber him, he managed a credible version of the bow appropriate for a freeman conversing with a member of the nobility. "If there is anything you wish to ask Piero, you must tell me now, for soon I must take my leave."

She arched her eyebrows in surprise. "You are not coming with us?"

"My duty binds me here," he said. "Do you or any of your party speak Ikarian?" he asked, switching to that tongue.

"Of course," she said, answering him in his native tongue.

"Then once you reach the town of Skalla you will be able to make yourself understood."

"And how is it that you speak my tongue as if you were born to it, and Ikarian as if you were a member of their court?"

"My home was in Karystos for many years. But now I live here and serve my order by tending the lighthouse."

She studied his features for a long moment. "I feel as if we have met before," she observed. "Perhaps in Karystos, a half dozen years past? Though I do not recall meeting any monks when I was last there. . . ." Her brow wrinkled in thought.

"I am of the Learned Brethren." He waited, but there was no trace of comprehension in her face. "A son of the collegium," he added.

The wrinkles cleared as her face resumed an impassive mask. "Of course. My pardon, but I did not expect to find one of the brethren so far from civilization."

Her response was a masterpiece of tact, as was to be expected from one of the court. Though no one ever spoke of it aloud, somehow it was common knowledge that the noble families of Ikaria disposed of their bastard sons by leaving the infants on the steps of the collegium, along with a purse of gold. It was not Josan she had recognized, but rather some trait he had in common with his unknown sire, or perhaps an uncle or half brother who frequented the court.

"There is knowledge to be found everywhere," Josan said.

Though in truth there was little on the island to occupy one from a scholarly order. He kept a journal of his days, as his predecessors had done. But he could pursue no great work, and no scholarly discoveries would be credited to his name. Once he had been a rising star, and some had whispered that in time he would take his place as head of the collegium. But the breakbone fever that had nearly cost him his life had robbed him of something almost equally precious. His mind had been damaged, and he knew that he was only a shadow of the man he had once been.

In the collegium, he had been angry and frustrated by

his newly clumsy body and fragmented memories. It had been kindness on the part of the brothers to send him here, where he could slowly retrain his body and wits without the constant reminders of what he had lost. He knew he had come far from the broken man who had first arrived at the lighthouse, but without other scholars to measure himself against he had no true way of gauging his progress.

It was seldom that he allowed himself to reflect upon his loss though he could hardly blame Lady Ysobel for stirring up feelings best left forgotten.

He smoothed his face into a pleasant mask, letting none of his unhappiness show through. "Is there anything else I can do my lady?"

"If you would be so kind, please inform the headman that we are ready to depart," she said.

"I will do that. And I wish you a fair journey and safe passage."

"Fair journey to you as well, Brother," she replied.

Fortified by a night's rest, the journey back to the lighthouse was swifter than it had been the night before. Only twice did he find his way blocked and have to retrace his steps. Renzo's dour prediction had come true, and the inlet had grown wider and deep enough that Josan had to swim across, though it was only a few strokes. He noticed that the flow of the water had indeed changed direction with the tide, answering his question from the night before. Perhaps the inlet would continue to grow, fueled by the power of the tide, until the small channel widened and the two halves of the island were permanently separated.

He recalled the map of the barrier islands and how their curved chain seemed to echo the curve of the mainland they sheltered. Was it possible that the islands had once been a single solid mass, before centuries of great storms and the relentless action of waves and tide had carved them into ever-smaller chunks of land? It was an interesting hypothesis, and there must be some way to test his theory. The library of the collegium had the accumulation of centuries of knowledge. Surely somewhere deep in the bowels of the library were maps of the islands, from the time that they were first conquered. Comparing these maps to the present form of the islands would be an interesting exercise.

His pulse leapt with excitement, for if his theory was correct, then this was surely a discovery of some note. His steps quickened, then lagged as the lighthouse tower came into view and he recalled where he was. He was a hundred leagues away from the great library of the collegium. In fact, he was as far from the capital as one could be and still remain within the Ikarian Empire.

Still, he could write to Brother Nikos and tell him of his theory. Brother Nikos would assign one of the young acolytes to research the maps, and if Josan was proven correct, no doubt his name would be mentioned when the acolyte wrote up his conclusions to share with their brethren. It would not be the same as if he had done the research himself, but it was still a way to contribute to the great work of the order and prove that he was still a truth seeker.

And surely such a discovery would be a demonstration that he had healed and reason enough for them to recall him from his exile.

Chapter 3

The collegium of the Learned Brethren in Karystos was
home to over four hundred scholars and tens of thousands
of scrolls, containing the accumulated knowledge of the
ages. As head of the order, Brother Nikos presided over an
empire of knowledge, guardian of secrets that were un-
dreamt of outside the collegium's walls. True, the brethren
in Xandropol had a far larger library—and a collegium to
match—but they were mere scholars. In Karystos, the brethren wielded power far beyond their walls. Nikos was a personal confidant of Empress Nerissa, something no other
abbot could claim.

Ordinarily he reveled in his position, yet on this day his
thoughts were troubled by a single scroll, and the scholar
who had penned it. He had read the scroll once, when he
had first received it, then locked it in his desk while he
pondered his response. Three days had passed, and he was
still no closer to an answer. All paths were fraught with potential peril, and he reluctantly decided to seek counsel.
There was risk in sharing this information, but even more
risk if he miscalculated his next move.

It took time for Brother Thanatos to respond to his

summons, and when the elderly monk arrived in his office, his slack features and blinking eyes hinted that he had been roused from an afternoon nap. Leaning heavily on the arm of the novice who had escorted him, Thanatos limped into the study and was helped to sit in the high-backed chair set aside for visitors.

Nikos dismissed the novice and waited until the door closed behind him before speaking.

"Brother Thanatos, I thank you for coming so swiftly."

"Not at all, I am happy to serve. My days are not as full as they once were," Thanatos said with a half smile.

Thanatos was in his eighties, and had retired from teaching novices over a decade before. Still, his mind was sharp and his memories seemingly clear, and it was these two things that Nikos needed from him.

"What can a student of mathematical mysteries do for our esteemed leader?" Thanatos asked.

From another his tone would have been judged impertinent, but Thanatos was too old and set in his ways to remember to pay Nikos the proper deference. In his mind, the abbot was still the youth he had taught nearly forty years before.

"I need your opinion on one of your students," Nikos said, reaching into the desk to pull out the troublesome scroll. "Tell me what you think of this letter from Brother Josan."

"Brother Josan!" Thanatos exclaimed, as he eagerly reached for the scroll.

Nikos watched as he read the scroll, at first swiftly, his fingers fumbling as he unrolled it in his haste. The second time he read it more slowly, considering the import of each line. It was not a long missive, but Thanatos studied it as if it were a tome of his precious logic.

Nikos waited with seeming patience until Thanatos rolled up the scroll and handed it back to him.

"He seems well, if unhappy with his circumstances," Thanatos said.

Besides himself, Thanatos was the only other person who knew that Josan had been sent to serve at the remote outpost of Prince Txomin's lighthouse. And even Thanatos did not know the full story behind Josan's exile. Only Brother Giles had been privy to that information, and he had died two years ago. As far as the rest of the monks were concerned, Josan was on pilgrimage, and his name was no longer spoken.

"The letter, does it sound the way you remember him?"

"His letters to me were written in a more pleasant frame of mind, but yes, I recognize his turn of phrase. And the logic of his argument to return here follows the classic form of five parts. Flawless." Thanatos beamed, as if he were commending a pupil.

He wondered what Thanatos would say if he were to show him the letters from when Josan had first been exiled. Childish scribbles; he had barely been capable of holding a pen. Now he had recovered enough of his wits that he could argue in the tongue of scholars. But Nikos could not show Thanatos Josan's earlier letters, any more than he could share with the monks the careful observations that Josan had made during his time as lighthouse keeper. Everything that Josan sent was carefully locked away, too dangerous to be seen by any except himself. It was vital that no attention be drawn to Txomin's Lighthouse, nor to the man who lived there.

It was a shame that Brother Giles had not lived to see proof of his success. Both he and Nikos had been certain that Giles's efforts had failed, leaving a witless child in the body of a man. But as time passed, Josan had reclaimed more and more of his former knowledge. The question was just how much did he remember? And what would he do with this knowledge?

"If you want my advice, I say that the time has come to bring him home. I know you told me that his wits were damaged, but the man who wrote this letter is a scholar of the first order. We need him here, not moldering away on some cursed rock pile," Thanatos said.

"If only matters were that simple," Nikos began. "But as I have told you before, it is not safe for Josan to return to Karystos."

"Five years have passed; surely it no longer matters what he might have seen? He is a monk, hardly likely to be a threat to anyone."

In this, Thanatos was being deliberately disingenuous. Knowledge was power, as both men knew, and a man with power was most definitely a threat. Still, he was not surprised that Thanatos was arguing in favor of the return of his favorite pupil.

"On the contrary, it matters a great deal. Josan would not be safe if he were to return."

And neither would Nikos, though he kept this knowledge to himself.

"Then let him go to Xandropol instead. Brother Xavier would welcome another mathematician. It is not fair that Josan should waste his talents in that place."

Nikos shook his head. "With all respect to our brothers in Xandropol, I do not trust them in a matter so delicate. For his own sake, Josan must remain where he is."

"Then why did you ask for my advice? If you've already made up your mind..." Thanatos grumbled.

"I need your knowledge of his character," Nikos said. He had known Josan merely as one face among the other novices, listening to the praise of his teachers, but his duties had kept him too busy to pay personal attention to a mere novice. Later, they had met only infrequently as Josan had traveled, bringing back riches of knowledge for the order. He did not know Josan well enough to predict what he would do next, which was why he had been forced to confide in Brother Thanatos.

But Nikos was caught in a dilemma. The reasons he had given Josan for remaining on the island were no longer valid, yet he could not afford to commit the true reasons to parchment. The risk that it would fall into unfriendly hands was too great.

"If I write Josan and tell him that he must remain on the island, will he obey? If he decides to leave, will he inform us or will he simply run away?" he asked.

"He's a good lad," Thanatos said, as if they were speaking of a youth and not a man approaching his thirtieth summer. "He will not like it, but he'll do what you tell him to."

"I hope you are right. For his sake, as well as ours," Nikos said.

Brother Thanatos could be sentimental about the fate of one monk, but Nikos could not afford such indulgence. He had a far greater duty to the brethren, and the preservation of the collegium. Five years ago, Josan had been a broken tool in his hands, unfit for any purpose, a danger to both himself and those who sheltered him. It would have been wiser to let him die, but Nikos had exiled Josan instead on the slender chance that he might one day be able to return. But that day had not yet come, and one monk could not be allowed to jeopardize all they had worked for. If Josan could not be trusted to obey orders, then he would have to be dealt with. And this time, there would be no second chance.

Three weeks after the great storm, Josan shivered on the lighthouse platform, a blanket wrapped around his heavy robe as the first full moon of winter rose in the sky, signifying the final watch of the year. When dawn came, he blew out the lamps, then began the long climb down to the base of the tower. Supplies were low, but he had saved a handful of tea leaves for this day. He sipped the bitter drink slowly, savoring both its warmth and the clarity it brought to his tired mind.

By the time he had finished his breakfast and climbed back to the top of the tower, the lamps had cooled enough so they could be touched. Carefully he removed each glass globe, giving it a final cleaning and polish before wrapping it in linen and storing it in a straw-filled crate. The reservoirs of oil were emptied back into a cask, while the silvered mirrors and metal frames were wrapped in oiled leather to protect them against the damp winter winds.

His hands moved without conscious direction, though that had not always been the case. When he had first come to the island, he had been so clumsy that he could barely walk. Whenever he had tried to move quickly, he had tripped over his own feet, and objects had slipped from his grasp. It had been weeks before Renzo had trusted the new lighthouse keeper enough to allow him to care for the most fragile objects.

Gradually Josan had gained control over his body until he no longer felt as if he were living within a stranger's skin. Gaining control over his fragmented thoughts had been harder, but here, too, patience and discipline had been the key.

Remembering the frustration of those early days, he now took pleasure in the deft movements of his hands as he carefully packed each object away. He observed that the globes were showing their age, for despite the care of the monks who had tended them, each globe had a network of fine scratches. If they were not replaced, in time the damage would render the globes opaque, dimming the light and weakening the strength of the beacon.

Fortunately, the silvered reflecting mirrors had fared

better, and were still unmarred despite decades of use. The royal treasury could replace the fragile glass globes if it chose, but the magically crafted mirrors were another matter. And without the mirrors, the lighthouse would be useless. By the time a ship saw the beam cast by an ordinary mirror, it would already be among the shoals. Only these specially crafted mirrors could reflect a beam far enough to serve as a warning, and he doubted very much that there were any left in Ikaria with the skill to manufacture a new set.

Morning turned to afternoon by the time he was satisfied that all was in order. At last he closed the wooden shutters, nailing the makeshift boards in place. He had done his best to repair the damage caused by the great storm, but he lacked the tools needed to craft wood into the correct shape and fit it onto the heavy hinges. Instead Josan had salvaged the last pieces of wood from the broken shutters, reinforcing them with staves taken from the empty oil barrels. Crude they might be, but they would serve to keep both birds and the winter weather out of the tower until he returned in the spring.

Descending to the base of the lighthouse tower, he picked up a waterproof pack that held his clothes, a writing quill, a half-filled bottle of ink, and the two books that chronicled his experiences since he had come to the island. The rest of the logbooks were too heavy to carry, so instead they were stored safely on the lowest course, along with the other tools of his trade. As he left the tower, he barred the door shut to prevent any animals from trying to turn the lighthouse into their winter den.

The sun was already low in the sky by the time he reached the sheltered cove on the northwestern side of the island and the small boat drawn up on the sandy beach. The villagers had returned to the mainland a fortnight before, but by custom they sent someone to fetch the lighthouse keeper on the first day of winter.

Young Piero rose to his feet as Josan approached, his thin face breaking into a relieved smile. "I was beginning to fear that you weren't coming today," he said.

Josan shook his head. "Took longer to close up the lighthouse this year. Come spring I will need your father to lend me one of his carpenters to craft proper shutters."

"I'll tell him," Piero said. "And the new inlet, has it grown? I thought to take a look at it myself, if there was time, but the day is rapidly fading."

"The inlet is no wider than it was on that second day, perhaps fifty feet across, and the water is calm, more like the sound than the sea. But it's too deep to wade."

Josan shivered as he remembered the uncomfortable crossing. This time he'd placed his robes and sandals in the waterproof sack before venturing into the icy-cold water, so he'd have dry clothing to don on the other side. But the chill had sucked the air from his lungs, and it had taken a long time for him to warm up again.

"Some changes on the mainland as well," Piero said. "The storm brought flooding, and we lost the granary down by the commons, but your place is still there. Terza spent the last two days getting it ready for you."

Josan grimaced, and Piero laughed softly at his expression. Josan was the elder by at least a half dozen years, and had the advantages of one who had been educated by the finest minds in the empire. But when it came to the ways of young women, it was Piero who was the master, while Josan constantly displayed his ignorance.

Piero watched him for a moment, then softened. "You need not worry about Terza. When Marco returned from escorting the noble lady to Skalla, he brought Terza a fine necklace of glass beads, and she invited him to share her hearth."

"I am pleased for them both," Josan said.

Indeed he had been concerned over Terza, and how he could deflect her attentions without giving insult to her and thus insulting the villagers who provided him with both food and shelter. By law, they could not deny him what he needed to survive, but they could make his life extremely difficult if they chose.

Terza was not the only woman of the village who flirted with him, but she was by far the boldest. Some might have felt flattered by her interest, but Josan knew that she would have behaved the same toward any young man who had come from the heart of civilization. She had not realized that the man she had set her sights on was damaged.

He shook himself to clear such dark thoughts from his mind.

"Come now, let us make our way. You'll never warm up standing here." Piero had mistaken his gesture for a sign that he was chilled, and Josan saw no reason to correct him.

He loaded his belongings into the center of the small rowboat, then helped Piero drag the boat into the water. The waters of the protected sound were calmer than those of the open ocean on the other side of the island, but Josan's late arrival meant they were fighting the tide. After a few minutes pulling at his oars, Josan was sweating freely. Still, with two sets of oars pulling, they made fair progress and in less than an hour they had crossed the sound, arriving just as the sun slipped below the trees.

The sandy beach where they came ashore was larger than Josan had recalled, and he wondered if this was another legacy of the storm. They pulled the rowboat ashore, dragging it far above the tide mark and storing the oars carefully under the plank seats. It was too heavy for two men to lift, so tomorrow Piero and others would return to place it on the boat rack, then cover the rack with tarps to protect the boats from the winter storms.

By the time they finished, dusk had fallen, but the rising moon provided enough light for them to make out the rocky path that wound up the bank of the hillside. Josan followed Piero as he strode along confidently, showing no hesitation even when trees shaded the path. Skirting the edges of the village, he led Josan to the keeper's cottage, which was set some distance apart from the rest of the village, then bade him good night.

Yawning with tiredness, Josan opened the door to the cottage, blinking a bit as the light spilled out through the doorway. The scents of fresh bread and fish chowder greeted him, warming his spirits as much as the brightly burning fire. Terza had even thought to stack fresh kindling by the fire. Placing his pack on the table by the brightly burning lantern, he shrugged off his robe and filled a bowl with the rich chowder. It took two bowls to satisfy his hunger, then, without even bothering to unpack, he kicked off his sandals and crawled onto the cot, where a cedar-scented woolen blanket covered a feather mattress.

He would have to find a way to repay Terza for her kindness, he thought, as he slipped into sleep.

But despite his weariness and the fine mattress he slept fitfully, for his body was still accustomed to the schedule of working during the night and sleeping during the day. Long before dawn he found himself awake, so he stirred up the fire and lit the fish-oil lamp. Opening his journal, he recounted what he had seen the day before and the changes wrought by the storm.

When dawn came, he reheated what was left of the chowder, then washed his face and hands and combed his hair. Changing into the better of his two winter robes, he made his way to the village and called upon Old Piero. He gave Piero the scrolls to be sent to the order, then listened as Piero recounted the latest news from Skalla. He stayed long enough to drink two cups of tea as custom required, then returned gratefully to the peace of his own dwelling. His years as lighthouse keeper had accustomed him to solitude, and now even a small gathering made him nervous. To a man who spent weeks at a time seeing no other face and hearing no voice but his own, even a handful of people could seem like a bewildering crush.

Fortunately, the villagers respected his wish for solitude. If a hunter had a good day, then Josan was given a share of the fresh meat, and when the weekly baking was done a wrapped loaf was left at his door. Other than that, he cooked for himself and split his own wood, and accustomed himself to the rhythm of winter life.

When he found himself craving the company of others, he sought out Renzo. Unlike the younger men, Renzo saw no need to fill silence with empty words. Renzo was not an educated man, yet there was something in him that reminded Josan of the gray-haired monks who had been his tutors. Perhaps it was his kindness, and the memory of how patient he had been in the face of Josan's endless questions during the first months of their acquaintance. Or perhaps it was Renzo's curiosity about the world beyond the borders of this village—that same curiosity that had led him to take up the life of a sailor in his youth. Whatever the reason, he was the one person that Josan could call a friend in this place.

During Josan's first winter there, Renzo had taught him how to weave the snares that were used to trap birds, and now, when Josan joined him at his labors, he used his younger eyes to inspect the snares, mending those that could be salvaged and weaving new ones to replace those whose cords had rotted from age or hard use.

Winter wore on, and one day blended into another so he could no longer tell them apart. Midwinter's Eve came, and Josan made the mistake of joining the villagers for their celebrations. Unaccustomed to strong drink, he awoke the next morning with a pounding head and no recollection of what had transpired the night before. Renzo later told him that he had lapsed into a foreign tongue, peering at the villagers as if they were strangers until he had been persuaded to lie down to sleep off his drunken folly.

It was no comfort that others had apparently behaved far more outrageously than he had. They were uneducated peasants and could be forgiven their follies. He was a scholar and knew better than to let his intellect be overwhelmed by strong drink.

As spring approached, Josan returned to the island, along with two men from the village—skilled carpenters who made swift work of mending the wooden shutters. Replacing his living quarters had been another matter. Only a narrow ribbon of sand now separated the tower from the lapping waves at high tide. Even an ordinary storm might flood the gently sloping beach, so instead they constructed a small cabin up over the dunes, next to the newly redug well. Hidden in the shelter of the dune thicket, Josan could not see the ocean from where he slept, but he could still hear the rhythmic pounding of the waves.

A few days after the men had left to return to their village, a ship sailed cautiously up the coast and anchored well offshore. A pair of longboats rowed the long distance to shore. In addition to the cabbage-seed oil and other expected provisions, they brought three new glass globes for the lamps, carefully packed in straw. It took four trips to bring everything ashore, and the sailors sweated as they stacked the goods in the storeroom under Josan's supervision, making haste so they could leave before the tide turned.

On their last trip they brought a leather document case, and in turn Josan gave them a sealed letter to the head of his order, and a copy of his logbook to be delivered to the collegium.

The case contained a letter from Brother Nikos. There was no mention of Lady Ysobel in the missive, and Josan spared a moment to wonder if she had indeed reached Karystos safely. But surely if she hadn't, Brother Nikos would have seen fit to mention it.

Brother Nikos expressed concern regarding the condition of the tower and urged Josan to be mindful of his safety as he went about his duties. In case the tower fell or had to be abandoned, Josan was to send word to the brethren and await instructions. He was not to return to Karystos under any circumstances.

This phrase was repeated twice, as if Josan were a willful child who needed to be reminded of his responsibilities.

Josan swallowed hard as he realized that he would never be allowed to return to the collegium. When the sea reclaimed this stretch of beach, as surely it would during the next great storm, the brethren would find somewhere else where he could end his days.

He had thought of this as a place of exile, but only in his worst nightmares had he imagined that it might be permanent. When he had first arrived, he had been certain that, given time, his mind would heal itself, just as his body had slowly recovered from the ravages of the fever.

And indeed, within months his coordination had returned so instead of jerky scrawls he could once again write with the precise script of a scholar. True he had forgotten much of what he had once known, but he had taken comfort that he was mastering new skills. After all, he had learned the language of the villagers with relative ease.

But Brother Nikos's letter made it clear that Josan had been clinging to a foolish dream. The brethren did not need him. Nor did they want him. He was no longer their equal but merely an obligation, no different from the brothers whose wits had grown feeble with age and had to be confined to the pensioners' ward lest they cause injury to themselves.

It would have been far kinder if the fever had killed him.

Chapter 4

My dear Lady Ysobel, you must be exhausted from your ordeals. There is no need to stand on formality. Surely you will want to rest and refresh yourself," Ambassador Hardouin declared. A polished courtier, his eyes remained firmly fixed on her face, but she had no doubt that he had taken in every detail of her appearance.

In deference to the winter chill she wore a soft wool mantle over a calf-length chiton. Her legs were covered with stockings so sheer that her sandals buckled over them with nary a wrinkle. Though her only visible jewelry was a strand of pearls woven through her hair to hold the coif in place, the pearls themselves were of fine quality.

In short, her appearance was eminently respectable— for the wife of a merchant or provincial bureaucrat. But she was neither, and therein lay the source of Ambassador Hardouin's discomfort.

"My ordeal was weeks ago," Lady Ysobel pointed out. "Since then I have endured no more hardship than any other traveler. I have lost enough time as it is; I do not intend to lose any more."

"Of course."

With that small skirmish won, she took her seat, and the ambassador followed suit. Because it was still morning, a servingman brought a tray of nut pastries and crystal glasses filled with tipia: a mixture of fruit juices and pale wine. She took a sip for politeness' sake, repressing a grimace at the overly sweet taste.

She had missed many things in her absence from Ikaria, but tipia was not one of them.

She took advantage of the ambassador's distraction with the rituals of hospitality to study him. He had changed little in the five years since she had been here last. Still portly, the good humor implied by his round cheeks was belied by his shrewd gaze. What gray hair he had left was cropped close to his skull—a local custom that he had adopted. He had served as ambassador to Ikaria for the last dozen years, and by all accounts he was good at his job.

When she had first met him, she was a novice at this game, as green as any landsman heaving his guts over the side of his first ship. Then he had been the one with power and she the junior anxious to impress, and to curry his favor.

Now the balance had shifted. He was still ambassador, but she had returned as a trade liaison, which meant that in many ways she was his superior. Even the Ikarians, who were not known for their sensitivity to cultures that differed from their own, knew that the Seddonian ambassador was a mere figurehead. The ambassador, after all, dealt with matters of government. A necessary position, of course, but hardly crucial, not when compared against the importance of the trade liaison. In the federation, trade was everything. Mere governments rose and fell, but a canny trader could outlast them all.

Not for the first time, she wondered what role Hardouin had played in her recent misfortune.

"Has there been any news of *Seddon's Pride*?"

Hardouin shook his head. "None. As soon as I received your letter, I sent word to all the ports along the coast, but no one has seen her. I fear you were correct, that she was lost at sea."

"A sad loss for us all. I am sure that Captain Tollen did his very best, and I will inform the guild so they may make appropriate compensation to his family."

"I have already sent word back to Seddon. Though a personal letter from you would surely be prized by his family," he added.

It was the least she could do. After all, she was certain that Captain Tollen had done his best. She had spent enough time at sea to know that *Seddon's Pride* had been a well-run ship, the captain respected by his crew. It had taken great skill to survive the first storm they had encountered and to guide the ship to a safe landfall. She owed her survival to Captain Tollen and his insistence that she ride out the storm on the island rather than staying with the ship.

But just whose orders had the captain been following? The course he had followed had been unusual, but explainable as a need to avoid the dangers of an autumn storm. At the time, she had not argued. The *Pride* was a federation ship, built for transporting important passengers in comfort, rather than the swift trading vessels with which she was familiar. And Tollen was a government captain, not a merchantman. It had not been her place to interfere with how he ran his ship.

Still, she could not help wondering if his orders had included delaying her arrival in Karystos. Perhaps he had left her on that island not out of concern for her safety but because it was the perfect opportunity to delay her. And if ill fortune befell her after her landfall, the captain could hardly be blamed.

Where was Tollen? Did his body lie on the ocean floor, along with that of his ship? Or was the *Pride* anchored in a foreign harbor, its timbers repainted and the distinctive gold figurehead replaced with a plain wooden pole?

It would have been better if she could have arrived unannounced and seen for herself Hardouin's reaction to the news of her survival. Even an experienced diplomat could let things slip in the first moments of shock. But such a course had been impractical. It would have shown that she believed Hardouin might have been involved in her trials, and that would have meant tipping her hand. Let him think that she trusted him and hope that he would trust her in return. In the meantime, she would make her own inquiries.

She took another sip of the tipia. "As you can see, most of my possessions went down with the *Pride*. There was not time to gather anything more than the documents chest and a few trifles."

The holds of the *Pride* had contained chests of coins to be used for bribes and samples of the newest and rarest trade goods with which to tempt Ikarian merchants. And weapons, of course—deadly daggers and short, curved swords manufactured in Vidrun, favored by mercenary troops from one end of the great basin to the other. Not to mention a wardrobe fit for the second-highest-ranking member of the Seddon Federation's mission to Ikaria. All would have to be replaced. Some openly, some less so.

"There are many fine garment makers in this city. I will have my wife send over her own tailor this afternoon."

"I will provide a full accounting of what was lost, so you may account for the expenditures in your report."

Hardouin winced, but did not protest. She had expected him to argue over replacing her clothes, since the cost of a new wardrobe could vary from merely expensive to ruinous.

The fact that he did not protest might be a sign of his guilt over her ordeal. Or perhaps it was merely a sign that he recognized where the true power lay.

Not that Ysobel had any intention of bankrupting the embassy. She had several lines of credit that she could draw on, including her own line with the merchants' guild, and that of her house, which could be tapped into for an emergency. But there was no reason to spend Flordelis funds when the federation could be held liable. She would let Hardouin replace the goods that she needed for her mission and provide her with a basic wardrobe for court functions. Then she would use her own funds for luxuries... and for those purchases requiring the shroud of secrecy.

It took some time for her to escape from the ambassador, but at last she was able to make her way to the rooms set aside for her use within the embassy. There was a sitting room for entertaining visitors, which flowed into a private dining room, furnished with couches to host dinners in the Ikarian style. A door from the sitting room led into her office—a narrow room, but long, with one wall filled with files and books. She glanced idly at the books, noting that her predecessor had left her a catalog of Ikarian vessels, along with a nearly up-to-date copy of the registry of merchants. Her own copy, safe in the documents box, had been printed just prior to leaving Seddon. On the wall opposite the files, a large map portrayed the harbor of Karystos, with each anchorage, dock, wharf, and warehouse clearly labeled.

She would take inventory later, but it seemed she had everything a trade liaison would need. Her public role was assured.

Her other role would require privacy, and there would be nothing committed to paper.

Passing through the office, she entered her bedchamber; beyond that lay a private bathing room. While soaking in the baths, one could admire the exquisite views of the city or the equally exquisite glass mosaics that covered the walls. The two baths—one hot for soaking, and the second tepid for bathing—were large enough that she could share, if she so chose. In that, too, it would be wise to be discreet. It was not just Hardouin who would know of anything that went on within these walls. She must assume that the Ikarians would know as well.

A glance into her wardrobe showed that her maid Anna had already unpacked the few clothes that Ysobel had acquired during her journey. No doubt Anna was also responsible for ordering the charcoal braziers lit, to chase off the damp chill of the winter's morning. Of the ever-efficient Anna there was no sign. Hopefully she was obeying Ysobel's instructions to relax, for she had certainly earned a holiday. Ysobel had retained enough gold to smooth their journey, but traveling the length of Ikaria in winter would never be anyone's idea of a pleasure jaunt. Anna had earned herself a rest.

Her mistress, on the other hand, was eager to get started on her tasks. Ysobel gave one last glance at the bathing chamber, promising herself a long bath later. Then she returned to the office and sat at the desk.

There she wrote three letters, each with its own cipher. The first letter was to Lord Quesnel, the head of the ministry of trade. There was very little difference between the surface letter, which contained an account of her arrival and praise for Ambassador Hardouin's hospitality, and the hidden message beneath. The cipher in this letter was simple, and meant to be broken, to lull the Ikarians into a false sense of ease.

The second letter was to the house of Flordelis, using the house cipher. On the surface this letter informed her family of her safe arrival in the Ikarian capital and offered her assurances that she would bring honor to her house by her diligent performance of her duties. Encoded within the letter was the news that she might need to draw on the Flordelis line of credit at the merchants' guild. And, of course, that she would pass along news of any opportunities to their trade representative here in Karystos. For while civic duty was important, there was no reason why one could not serve the federation and improve the fortunes of one's house at the same time.

The final letter was to Captain Zorion, the senior of her three captains. With luck, this letter would reach him before he took his ship on its first voyage of the spring. She informed Zorion of the presumed loss of *Seddon's Pride* and asked him to pass along any news of Captain Tollen or his officers. This letter was encoded with a cipher of her own devising. To the uninformed it appeared to be a list of cities and trade goods, along with firm directions on where the captain should plan his next voyage. Typical correspondence between a trader and a captain in her employ, there should be nothing here to rouse suspicion. Only Zorion would be able to read the contents, and she could trust both his instincts and discretion. If Tollen or the *Pride* had somehow survived, Zorion would find them and send word.

She folded each letter into a square, sealed it with wax, and wrote the direction with a firm hand. Then she summoned a servant to bear them off for delivery.

The letters would be read, of course. The carefully applied wax seals would be pried off, the contents read and perhaps copied, then the seals carefully reapplied. She must assume that the Ikarians had spies planted within this embassy, as well as at the docks, where the letters would be taken for dispatch. If the ambassador were a cautious man, he would read them as well.

It would take weeks for the letters to arrive in Seddon, and weeks more before she could expect a reply. Pushing back her chair, Ysobel rose to her feet. It was time for a light meal and to find out just when the tailor was expected. The sooner she had proper clothing, the sooner she could present herself at court. And then her true mission would begin.

It took a week for the first of her court outfits to be ready, and another week before the empress was ready to receive her. Ysobel used this time to her advantage, reacquainting herself with the city and studying the documents left behind by her predecessor. Protocol dictated that Sir Aleron should have waited until his successor arrived, to ensure a smooth transfer of authority; but the unfortunate events that had dictated his sudden recall to Seddon also meant that he was unable to wait for her. He had sailed on one of the last ships to leave before the winter season. If she had arrived on schedule, she would have been mere days behind him. As it was, the post had been vacant for nearly two months.

A long time for Seddon to have no trade liaison. Hardouin and his staff had filled in to perform the public roles of the liaison, but there had been no one to take up the post's private duties.

Fortunately, Sir Aleron had been a methodical man. The files he left for her were enlightening, but she was certain they contained but a fraction of his knowledge. There were some secrets, after all, that were too dangerous to commit to paper, no matter how strong the cipher.

Ysobel was starting this assignment weighed down by the lateness of her arrival and the absence of her predecessor. Ill luck some might say, and perhaps that was all it was. Or perhaps not. After all, should Ysobel fail in her tasks, it would deal a severe blow not only to herself but to the ambitions of her house. Flordelis had its share of enemies, and there were many who would be pleased if the house never regained its former stature.

Ysobel was determined not to fail. She quizzed the ambassador and his staff, and read Aleron's files until she had memorized the biographies of all the key players in the realms of both politics and business. Many of the names were familiar to her from her earlier assignment in Karystos, but it was the ones who had come into power in her absence that she would have to pay closest attention to. The empress had a habit of playing her favorites off against each other—elevating one courtier to a position of power, then, when she judged him having grown too secure in her favor, she would dismiss him and elevate one of his opponents in his place. Mere names and titles were not enough to tell Ysobel who was currently in power and who was not. She would have to observe the interactions of the court and judge for herself—to see who was close to Nerissa and who might be feeling disgruntled and open to persuasion.

Finally, the day arrived on which Empress Nerissa had declared that she would be pleased to meet the newest members of her court, including the newly arrived trade liaison from the Federated Islands of Seddon.

Ysobel dressed in her formal court attire, standing patiently as her maid fussed with the draping of the overrobe, until the folds lay just right. It had taken some time to explain what she wanted, and even longer to convince the scandalized tailor that she could not be dissuaded. The unwritten rules of Nerissa's court dictated that during official functions all ministers and government functionaries wore a uniform that had not changed in the last one hundred years. Tunics of unbleached linen were worn next to the skin to symbolize humility, and over these the ministers wore knee-length robes of silk or wool, depending on the season. The sleeves and hems of the robes were trimmed with colorful ribbons or embroidered in elaborate patterns.

There had been no time for embroidery, but a search of the warehouses had yielded six ells of patterned gold ribbon, which was a perfect complement to the rich red silk. It was a fine outfit—for a nobleman, and therein lay the source of the tailor's distress.

No formal court outfit had been designed for women because there was no precedent for a female minister. With the exception of the reigning empress, all members of the Ikarian government were male, as were the empress's official advisors. Women might be found in the lower ranks of the professions, but it was universally acknowledged that they were not the equal of men and were therefore unsuited for public responsibilities. The empress was the sole exception, her imperial lineage outweighing the presumed weakness of her sex.

It was a curious blind spot to have and a weakness that could be exploited. In the federation, women had long been acknowledged the equals of men. A man's muscles might be more suited for the labor of hauling deck lines, but men and women had been equally gifted with intelligence and cunning. Only fools would ignore the talents found in one-half of their subjects, and those in the federation prided themselves on their practicality above all else.

In deference to Ikaria's peculiar sensibilities, the Seddon ambassador was almost always a man, as was the trade liaison—though the junior members of the delegation were both male and female. Ysobel's sex would lead many in the court to dismiss her importance, which was precisely what she needed.

Twin litters carried herself and the ambassador through

the crowded streets to the palace. Landsmen had been heard to compare the jolting, swaying motion of the litters to that of a ship, but Ysobel had never understood the comparison. Besides she was perfectly at home on a ship, while a ride in a litter always left her feeling vaguely queasy, and this day was no exception. Not that she had a choice. Her delicate court sandals were wholly unsuitable for walking any distance, and at least the closed curtains of the litter prevented the winter rains from damaging their attire.

A shaven-headed functionary, his features nearly obscured by heavy black tattoos, was waiting at the portico to escort Ysobel and Ambassador Hardouin to the main audience chamber. Sworn to serve the imperial household since childhood, by law the functionaries forsook their own names and instead were called by their assigned task. This one introduced himself as Greeter.

The masking tattoos and lack of individual names were meant to ensure that the functionaries had no private identities. They had no families, no names, and no role other than to serve the imperial household. As Greeter led them through the arched corridors toward the audience chamber, Ysobel stole a glance at his features. Surely, Greeter was still a man. And the first lesson of trade was that everything was for sale.

Such a highly placed set of eyes and ears within the palace could be of tremendous use to her. If she could discover how to corrupt the supposedly incorruptible . . .

Such speculation occupied her mind while she and Ambassador Hardouin waited their turn. At the far end of the room was a dais on which Empress Nerissa sat on a backless throne carved from ivory and inlaid with gold. Below the empress and to her right sat the Proconsul, Count Zuberi. Five years ago he had been a minor court functionary—the second minister in charge of the city grain stores, as she recalled. His rise since that time had been rapid, driven as much by his blood ties to the empress as to his abilities.

Four imperial guards stood watch from the back of the dais, and two stood at the front, ready to prevent anyone from approaching the empress without her express command. These, too, were new since Ysobel's last visit.

The audience chamber could easily hold five hundred, but there were fewer than a hundred in the room—presumably those with an interest in the day's proceedings. Ministers in their formal court robes mixed with an audience of fashionably dressed noblemen and -women. And while Ysobel's attire was far less revealing than the tightly corseted gowns of the women in attendance, the sight of her bare calves caused more than one eyebrow to rise.

The scars from the aborted uprising five years before could be seen in the audience that awaited the empress's pleasure. Five years before, the court had still contained a substantial number of the old Ikarian nobility, but now each fair head stood out like a beacon.

There were other changes as well. She spotted a plainly dressed man standing at the front of the room, where he could hear each whisper between the empress and her petitioners, yet was still somehow apart from the gathered watchers.

Ysobel put her hand on Hardouin's sleeve to draw his attention. She let him see the direction of her gaze, then turned her head away. "Who is that?" she murmured softly.

"That is Brother Nikos, head of the Learned Brethren," Hardouin said. An old hand at court games, he, too, had his gaze fixed on the ambassador from Vidrun, as if he were the topic of discussion. "Once tutor to the empress's children, he is now counted chief among her unofficial advisors."

"Of course. I was expecting him to wear the robes of the brethren. . . ."

"He wears them when he is acting as religious leader. But when he is playing the role of advisor, he wears the clothes of the common man. Or so I am told."

Interesting. Not that there was anything common about Brother Nikos's attire. Plain, yes; his robe was unadorned, as befitted a man of humility. But raw silk was hardly the garb of a commoner. He would not be the first priest to discover a taste for luxury. She would have to reread the file on Brother Nikos tonight.

They waited patiently as a provincial duke offered his oath of loyalty to the empress, and she confirmed his inheritance. A young boy was brought forward to make his obeisance to the empress. The nine-year-old heir to the throne of Kazagan, he would spend the rest of his youth being schooled in Ikaria, hostage to ensure that his father's ambitions remained in check. Ysobel was impressed by the boy's self-possession, and the empress spared a smile for the young prince, expressing her hope that he would become friends with her sons.

Of more interest was the appointment of the new minister in charge of the Karystos harbor. As Hardouin had predicted, young Septimus was named to succeed his father in the post. These days it was rare to find one of the old purebloods granted a ministerial position, and from the relief on his face it was clear that Septimus himself had not been sure of his promotion. He expressed his gratitude at length, until the empress's smile grew fixed, and Count Zuberi switched from clearing his throat to glaring at the newly named minister.

And then it was their turn. Ambassador Hardouin advanced toward the empress, with Ysobel trailing one pace behind as was proper. As they reached the point four paces from the dais, Hardouin stopped and bowed. As an ambassador he was not required to make obeisance.

Ysobel, however, was expected to pay her full respects. She sank down on her right knee, then bent forward, her back straight, until her palms were flat on the floor. She held the position for four heartbeats, then rose.

"Most Gracious Empress Nerissa, Heir to the Wisdom of Aitor the Great, Defender of Ikaria, and Blessed Protector of Her People, may I present Lady Ysobel of the house of Flordelis, with your leave the new liaison for trade between our two great countries."

"Lady Ysobel. You have visited our empire before, have you not?"

Ysobel's palms were damp, and she felt a chill sweat break out. Fervently, she hoped that none could sense her nervousness. Or if they did, she hoped they would ascribe it to the awe of being face-to-face with such a powerful ruler.

"Yes, your graciousness. I had the privilege of visiting Ikaria several years ago, as part of my education," Ysobel said carefully.

Back then, she had seen the empress from time to time—on those rare occasions where even the juniormost members of the embassy staff were invited to the imperial palace. But she had never been formally presented to her. Somehow that had made her task easier. She had been working to bring down an empire—to destroy a figurehead, not a living woman.

From this short distance, she could see that the empress had changed in the five years since she had crushed Prince Lucius's rebellion. Her figure remained plump and curved, as was to be expected from a woman whose sons were grown men. But there were deep lines on her face, and if this audience was any indication, her once-ready smiles had disappeared.

"I understand you had difficulties on your journey here," the empress said.

"The ship I was traveling on was lost at sea, though through the wisdom of its captain I was spared. And your subjects offered every kindness to myself and my companions on our journey here."

"I am pleased to hear that," the empress said. Her gaze lingered on Ysobel, taking in every detail of her features and attire.

Ysobel struggled not to hold her breath. It was unlikely that the empress had any inkling of the role that Ysobel had played in the rebellion five years before. If she had, she would have ordered Ysobel's arrest rather than arranging to receive her at the palace.

Unless, of course, this was all a trap. Perhaps the empress had waited, in order to ensure that the maximum drama would be achieved.

It was difficult to believe the matronly woman in front of her would be capable of such cunning. Then, again, appearances could be deceptive. This was the woman who had decisively put down the rebellion against her. Prince Lucius, who had been a foster brother to her sons, had died in her torture chambers, at Nerissa's express command. It would be folly to underestimate her.

Hardouin had been confident that the empress suspected nothing. If any had whispered about federation involvement in the failed coup, their stories had been given no credence. After all, if Nerissa or her ministers had suspected their complicity in the plot, the very least they would have done was to dismiss Hardouin from their empire and demand that Seddon send a new ambassador. For her part, Ysobel hoped he was right.

"It will be pleasant to have a woman in our court," the empress said at last, when it seemed the silence had stretched on forever. "I accept your credentials and acknowledge you as the new trade liaison."

"It is my privilege to serve, your graciousness," Ysobel said.

This time, both she and Ambassador Hardouin bowed. The ambassador handed a scroll listing her credentials to the waiting official, then they backed away into the crowd.

It was over. She took a deep breath, then another.

"As you see, she has changed greatly since when you were here last," Hardouin said, when they were far enough away from the empress that their conversing would not be taken as a sign of rudeness.

"Yes," Ysobel said. "But so have I."

Chapter 5

Here is the list of merchant houses that you requested. Those of the old blood are listed on the left, and those with ties of blood or marriage to the newcomers are listed on the right."

Ysobel took the scroll from Perrin, but did not immediately unroll it. Instead she kept her attention focused on the young man who had been assigned as her clerk.

"These houses are in decline, but not yet bankrupt, correct?"

Perrin nodded. "As you requested, these are houses that have experienced losses or stagnation while their peers have prospered. I excluded all those whose debts outweighed their assets, or whose losses stemmed from reverses at the court rather than bad luck and financial miscalculations."

"Very good," she said. She had her own guesses about which names would be on the list, and was interested to see how closely her conclusions matched the results of Perrin's meticulous research. The houses in question were ones that should be open to new trading ventures as a way to rebuild their fortunes. A risk shared was a risk halved, and there were a number of ventures in which an Ikarian partner might well prove advantageous. Her predecessor had been competent enough, but he had favored the status quo, seeking to preserve existing relationships rather than forging new ones.

And indeed such caution had been appropriate, in the days when Ikaria had been reeling from the aborted rebellion and all foreigners had been looked upon with suspicion. But the time for change had come, and Ysobel had been chosen as the instrument of that change.

"I will let you know which houses are of interest, and you will arrange for me to meet with the senior trader of each, at his earliest convenience."

Winter was more than half-gone. Spring was coming, and with the arrival of spring the Ikarian merchant fleets would set sail from their harbors. Now was the time for deals to be struck, before the merchants committed themselves to less adventurous routes and cargoes.

"Of course. Is there anything else you require?"

There were many things that she required, but Perrin was an unknown quantity. A young man, he had been sent to Ikaria to gain seasoning in the ways of the world. As a clerk he seemed competent enough, and she had yet to catch him committing either an error or deliberate omission. Yet neither did she delude herself that she had first claim on his loyalties.

If Ansel had survived, then she would have been certain of the loyalty of at least one person in Karystos. But someone had had to remain on the *Pride*, as steward of its cargoes both open and secret. Sworn to serve the house of Flordelis, Ansel had paid for his loyalty with his life. For even if the *Pride* had survived, then Ansel would surely have been murdered to keep the plot secret.

So instead of Ansel's loyalty, she had this diffident

stranger, with his ink-stained fingers and the sure knowledge that whatever she told him went straight to Ambassador Hardouin.

"Yes, there is one more thing. I require a residence in the trading quarter."

"But—"

"Nothing grand. A parlor suitable for gatherings of up to two dozen, and a second story with three or four bedrooms. Oh, and a largish bathing chamber in the Ikarian style. Somewhere in the merchants' district—respectable, but no longer fashionable so that no one will pay strict attention to my comings and goings."

"But—"

"I will pay for it myself," she said, pretending to misunderstand his protests. "I just need you to find a suitable place."

"But why do you need your own residence? Surely the embassy is far more suitable than any merchant's house?"

"The embassy is not suitable for my needs."

Perrin's open mouth indicated his confusion.

"Pretty boys," she elaborated. "I enjoy the company of pretty boys, and I'm sure I would enjoy myself far more if I did not have to fear interruption."

Perrin flushed a deep red that extended from the tips of his ears down to his neck.

"Um, yes. Of course. I will ... see what I can find," he said, then, at her nod, he fled the room before he could embarrass himself any further.

Hard to believe that he had been serving in the embassy for nearly a year if he could still be shocked. His family would have done far better to send him on a long trading voyage with a strict captain to wipe away such signs of a sheltered childhood. He would never rise in the ranks of his house if he could not learn to conceal his emotions.

Ysobel remained at her desk, finally opening and studying the scroll that Perrin had prepared. She was not surprised to see that the list was heavily weighted toward merchants from the old Ikarian families. Just as at court, where the newcomers dominated the positions of power, it seemed the merchant houses with ties to the newcomers had prospered at the expense of those too hidebound to align themselves with their former rivals.

She was surprised to see Septimus the Younger included on the list. Surely the minister of the harbor would be in the position to use his knowledge to advance his house, and Septimus the Elder had held that post for over twenty years. According to Perrin's notes, their fortunes had stagnated in recent years, which might indicate a lack of imagination or merely that the father had been failing and the son had not yet asserted his control. Perhaps now that he had succeeded his father, Septimus would be open to new opportunities. She made a note to meet with him in his official capacity, so she could judge his qualities for herself before she turned the discussion to matters of trade.

She studied the rest of the list, and from the three dozen houses she selected eight to be interviewed—three of the newcomers and five from the natives. It would not do to make her bias too obvious.

As if on cue, there was a knock at her door and Ambassador Hardouin entered her office. He waited for a moment, but she did not rise. The office was an uncomfortable place for a discussion, since there was just the one chair at the desk and a stool suitable for a clerk pushed in the corner. Politeness dictated that they remove themselves to the sitting room, but politeness wouldn't serve her goals. Hardouin had already conceded power by seeking her out rather than summoning her, and she was in mind to press home that advantage.

"You have scandalized your clerk. Poor Perrin is convinced that you will bring disgrace on the good name of the embassy."

"I see he lost no time in reporting to his master," she said.

"Can you blame him? He is rather young, after all, and new to his responsibilities."

"He is not that young. And you yourself recommended him to me," Ysobel pointed out. At Perrin's age, she had been entrusted with details of a conspiracy that could have cost her life, as well as the lives of all those involved. If Perrin did not mature swiftly, he would never be fit for more than a position in his family's countinghouse.

"Perrin is a very able clerk, if a bit naïve," Hardouin said. "Still, he is loyal and discreet, which will serve you well."

Loyal, yes, but it was clear that Hardouin had first claim on those loyalties. Which was as it should be, assuming the ambassador was trustworthy and not playing his own games. But it was not an assumption Ysobel was prepared to make.

"There are those I must meet that require discretion, and the embassy is far too public a venue for our discussions."

"And thus you spun Perrin a tale of pretty boys?" Hardouin smiled indulgently, as if amused by the jest she had played on her clerk.

"I will need pretty boys as well. Though from his reaction I doubt Perrin will be much help in finding them. . . ."

She let her voice trail off suggestively, enjoying Hardouin's discomfort. Then, at last, she relented.

"We must assume that the Ikarians have me under observation. At least until they are satisfied as to my mission here. They are already scandalized by my sex, and will have little difficulty believing that I have strange appetites that must be satisfied in private. The young men will serve to deflect their interests from my activities."

"Of course. I should have thought of it myself," Hardouin said. "I will remind Perrin that he is to follow your orders even if he does not understand them."

"Thank you. I would hate to have to replace him," she said.

Then, convinced that she had won this round, she rose to her feet and asked him to join her for lunch, which he accepted. She had, after all, confirmed Perrin's loyalties. And more importantly, she had let Hardouin know that she knew that Perrin was assigned to spy upon her. Which was, of course, another reason why she required a separate residence, one not under the ambassador's direct control.

She would have to investigate her new household carefully, for surely both Hardouin and the Ikarians would attempt to introduce spies among her servants. But she had ways of dealing with that eventuality when it arose.

Perrin's loyalty might be questionable, but his efficiency was not. He took the list she had left for him and arranged the first meeting for the very next morning. Over the next days she met with representatives from each of the eight merchant companies and toured a half dozen properties.

It did not take her long to find a house suitable for her needs. The former residence of a silk trader, it was being offered for rent while his purported heirs wrangled with each other and the civil magistrate, trying to prove who was the rightful inheritor of his property.

Located in the southern quarter of the fifth tier, the district was home to successful merchants and the lesser sons of minor nobles. A respectable district, and one where no one would pay particular heed to her comings and goings, or that of her guests. The two-story limestone house was a bit smaller than she had wanted, but the bathing chamber was superb, and while most homes pressed cheek and jowl against their neighbors, this house came with a walled patio and garden in the back, providing a private space to enjoy the fine weather or meet with callers who could not be acknowledged in the light of day.

Perrin made arrangements with the magistrate to lease the house for a year, while Ysobel called upon the local agent of Flordelis and used his recommendations to hire a small staff to look after it.

For a house that had been vacant for six months, it was in surprisingly good shape, requiring merely a good cleaning and the purchase of new linens and draperies. The only difficulty was a nest of large lizards that had taken residence in the garden. While not the bane of a merchant's life in the way of rats or insects, lizards were destructive enough in their own way, and she wanted them gone before she moved in. Under the former rulers of Ikaria it had been forbidden to harm the so-called royal lizards, but with Aitor's ascent to the throne the lizards had been seen as the nuisances they were. Now they were called common lizards, and a freeman with a trained hunting cat took care of the problem in a single afternoon.

Finding a residence had been easy. Finding trading partners proved far harder.

The traders she met with fell into three categories. The first were the figureheads who had no real experience and probably had never ventured farther than their own dockyards. These were the ones who were visibly uncomfortable with the presence of a woman in their places of business. Any merchant worth his salt had learned to overcome such prejudices, or at least to hide them to deny his opponent an advantage.

The second were those whose misfortunes were the result of incompetence, lack of imagination, or both. They were the ones who refused to consider new trading opportunities, insisting that the best course was to continue to serve markets that had proven themselves over time. A prudent course, but one bound to yield diminishing returns. One trader went so far to lecture her on the folly of taking on unproven cargoes, and suggested that as she matured she would see the wisdom of her elders' prudent ways. Lady Ysobel had listened courteously, pitying the shareholders who looked to this man for leadership. In ten years' time, she'd turned a single aged ship into a fleet of three swift vessels, while this same trader had squandered the advantages he'd been given.

There were two houses that seemed receptive to the idea of a joint trading venture and promised to study her offer carefully. A modest start, but progress all the same. And even those traders who had disdained her offer still provided valuable information about the political climate of Ikaria, under the guise of educating the new trade liaison. It was amazing what a man would reveal, even one as normally tight-lipped as a trader, when he was trying to impress a woman.

Her final meeting was with Septimus, the newly named minister in charge of Karystos harbor. He had agreed to meet her not in his imperial office, which was buried within the labyrinth of the palace complex, but rather in the harbormaster's office adjacent to the central wharves. Much to the dismay of the guard assigned to her, Lady Ysobel refused a litter, choosing instead to enjoy the crisp morning sunshine. She walked briskly through the streets, noting that the people seemed cheerful, and while those who showed obvious signs of wealth or status were accompanied by one or more retainers, that was a prudent precaution to take in any large city, regardless of how law-abiding its citizenry was reported to be.

Karystos was built on a hill that sloped down to the

sheltered harbor that had first brought it wealth. Over the years that hill had been sculpted and transformed by the inhabitants into a series of terraces, erasing any trace of the original landscape. The palace dominated the highest terrace, and from there its inhabitants literally looked down upon their subjects. Wealth and status were counted by proximity to the palace, and as each level descended from the next, so too did the aspirations of its inhabitants.

As she passed through the lowest tier, which led down to the docks, her eyes lingered on the brick buildings that had replaced the wooden ones burned down during the riots. She wondered who had paid for the rebuilding, and whether the new structures were an attempt by the empress to bribe her people into forgetting their past grievances? Or was it simply a matter of civic virtue, to lessen the damage that any future riot might cause? After all, the fires had not stopped with the homes of the dissenters.

She very carefully did not think of those who had been killed in the riots.

At first glance the harbormaster's office appeared to be a mere wooden shack at the end of a pier, with mismatched wooden walls showing signs of having been repaired after more than one severe storm. Though small, it rose two stories in height, with a balcony that circled the second floor providing a view of the harbor.

Ysobel paused for a moment to drink in the sights. Since it was winter, the sailing ships were safely moored in the harbor, protected by the great moles. Only a handful of coastal barges were drawn up to the piers to unload their goods. Overhead she saw gulls wheeling in the sky, circling the southern end of the harbor where fishing boats unloaded their catch. The air was heavy with a mixture of familiar smells: sea spray, kelp drying in the low tide, pine tar, rotting wood, and the faint tang of spices as a dockhand brushed by, his shoulders bowed under a heavy sack.

Sailors called out to each other in the pidgin of their trade, and for a brief moment she was homesick.

This was what she missed most. When she closed her eyes and thought of home, this is what she saw. She longed not for a glimpse of the brilliant white of Alcina's buildings against the pure blue of their sea, but rather for a ship beneath her feet and the thrill of making landfall in a foreign port. She was a trader, and she had been born to that life. It was in her blood.

She shook herself from her reverie. She was still a trader, though these days she played on a bigger stage. This posting in Ikaria was a test, and she would never prove herself if she insisted on daydreaming like a foolish child.

The door to the harbormaster's office was open, so, motioning her guard to wait for her outside, Ysobel walked in.

She found Septimus seated at a large table that dominated the room. The table was covered with layers of charts, the topmost of which appeared to be a map of the harbor, similar to the one in her own office.

"Tell Captain Menkaura that his cargo is still impounded, and if he wants to argue, he'll have to take it up with the magistrate," Septimus said.

"I would, but I'm not certain where to find him," she said.

Septimus's head shot up, and he scrambled to his feet. "Lady Ysobel, my pardon. I must have lost track of time."

He extended his hand in the clasp of friendship, and she took it, returning the firm pressure. If he were surprised by her strength, or the calluses on her hands, his face gave no sign.

During the presentation to Empress Nerissa, he had appeared both awkward and young, but away from the imperial shadow he was more confident, and older than she had thought. He had the broad-shouldered build of a dock laborer rather than the slenderness of an imperial official who made his living with the stroke of a pen. But it was his light blond hair and blue eyes that marked him in Ikarian society and would govern the first impressions of any who met him.

The Seddon Federation was a mélange of races, as befit a country of sailors who had brought back with them more than mere trade goods. The only unifying characteristic of the citizens of the federation was their diversity. Ysobel's dark hair and golden skin was not common, even within her own family, but neither was she unique.

In Ikaria it was a different matter. The original Ikarians had been a ruddy-skinned race, with fair hair and light-colored eyes. The newcomers were a race apart, with their porcelain skin, ink-black hair, and dark eyes. It was possible to tell an Ikarian's heritage by their coloring, and from there to infer their likely politics and status. Septimus, for example, was clearly one of the purebloods. So far unmarried, according to her files, if he wished to advance any further in the imperial ministries, he would be wise to consider taking a wife who was at least a half-blood.

"Please take a seat," he said. "I beg your pardon for asking you to meet me here, but I am so busy that I rarely make it to my office in the ministry before nightfall."

"Not at all. I understand that your duties must come first, of course." She took a seat across from him and waited while he summoned a servant to bring them the ritual drinks that accompanied any important meeting. The servant brought them both red tea, which was a marked improvement from the tipia that the other merchants had thought suitable for a female.

Septimus waited until she had taken a sip of her tea before speaking.

"Lady Ysobel, may I be so bold as to ask if the title is a courtesy of your position or was it earned in trade?"

"The title is mine."

He nodded, as if she had confirmed his private theory. "My congratulations. It seems the federation chose wisely when they named you trade liaison."

"Some of your fellow traders would not agree."

"And few of them were sole traders at your age. I would not pay heed to their mutterings. Becoming a named partner is an accomplishment to be proud of."

It was not a thing that she had hidden, but Septimus was the first to have done his research and tally his sums correctly.

Born into the house of Flordelis, Ysobel had been destined for a place in her family's trading company. Like her siblings she had spent time in the countinghouses and the markets, and as she grew older she went along on short trading voyages so she would learn all phases of the family business. Flordelis, though no longer as prestigious as it had once been, was still a force to be reckoned with, with over a hundred ships and trading representatives in every major port. But fate had intervened in the form of an aunt, who had chosen Ysobel's fifteenth name day to gift her niece with a ship. It was not a new ship, nor a particularly fast one, but it was seaworthy. And with it Ysobel went from a dependent of the house of Flordelis to a trader in her own right.

Promptly leasing the ship back to her aunt, she invested the profits in leasing a second ship. Now, ten years later, she was full owner of three swift trading vessels, and she would match those ships and their captains against any who sailed.

Her title of "Lady" was recognition that she was a named partner, entitled to vote in the council of the merchants.

She was still loyal to Flordelis, of course, but when the time came she would found her own house.

"My skills as a trader are clearly rusty, for I have approached several of your merchants with a business proposition and found no takers," she said, turning the conversation to the stated purpose of her visit.

"I believe Clemence is still considering your proposal, and Jhrve is biding his time so as not to appear too eager, but I would wager that he will say yes before too long."

It seemed Septimus was well-informed, which reinforced her decision to cultivate him.

"Tell me though, why is Seddon so eager for partners in this venture?" he asked.

"A risk shared is a risk halved."

"And the potential profits are halved as well."

"True." She paused to take a sip of tea, refusing to be hurried. "But the opportunity is limited. Last year's failed harvest in Tarsus means they will be desperate for grain this spring, both to feed their people and for seed to re-plant their fields. There is profit to be made now, but none if we wait."

"So all can agree upon. What do you need us for?"

If he knew the names of the merchants she had already spoken with, then surely they had also informed him of her proposal. But she played along, explaining as if for the first time.

"To transport grain in this quantity, barges would be ideal. Lacking those, one would need broad-beamed coastal trading boats such as your merchants possess. We have few such craft in our fleets, and there is no time to build more. In return for the use of your crafts, we will supply the capital to purchase the grain and pilots to guide the ships through the winter seas."

Septimus's family possessed at least six vessels that would be ideal for her needs. And the warehouses of Karystos had surplus grain that could be bought cheaply, then resold at a substantial profit in Tarsus.

"Whom do you represent?"

"I am authorized to negotiate on behalf of Flordelis and the house of Searcy, both of whom have agents in Karystos who will witness any contract."

"An interesting offer," he said. "Most traders have already committed to their first runs of the spring, but there might be a few who would be willing to chance a new venture."

"Perhaps even your own house might be interested in participating, in the interests of improving trade relations between our two countries. I am empowered to offer a bonus to the first house that signs . . ."

She let her voice trail off, not needing to press her point. Septimus had proven himself an intelligent man. He would know that any contract she offered him would be on terms more favorable than she offered to his competitors. It was not a bribe but merely good business sense.

"I am new to my position, but I don't recall your predecessor Sir Aleron being quite so vigorous in his duties."

"May I speak frankly?"

"Of course."

"The unpleasantness several years ago caused many to question the wisdom of close ties with Ikaria. Sentiment against foreigners ran high at that time, as you may recall, and Sir Aleron was merely being cautious. But now that Empress Nerissa has secured the peace and the affections of her subjects, the climate is once again suitable for the mutual pursuit of profit."

"I see," he said. And he might even have believed her.

What Septimus did not realize was that in this venture Ysobel held all the advantages. If Empress Nerissa remained in firm control of Ikaria, then it was in Seddon's best interests to be perceived as a staunch friend. Building alliances through the mutual pursuit of profit would help tie the interests of Ikaria's leading families to those of the federation.

And if Nerissa proved unable to keep her grasp on her throne . . . Well, then, Seddon would be poised to take advantage of whatever chaos ensued, and there would be those on all sides who had cause to think of the federation as their friend. Either way, Seddon would emerge the victor, and Ysobel would secure her place within the ranks of the great council. Ikaria, after all, was merely the test. It was not the true field where power lay. Ysobel would wring every drop of advantage out of this situation, and upon her return to Seddon there would be none within her family or without who could deny her her rightful place.

Chapter 6

Two days after their meeting, Septimus sent word that he would accept her offer of a joint trading venture. Accompanied by their respective agents, they met in her newly rented house to finalize the details and sign the contracts. The terms that that they settled on favored Septimus slightly, as she had intended, but both sides would make a profit. Septimus complimented her on her choice of residence, noting that it was close enough to the port to provide easy access to the countinghouses and docks, but far enough away that she would not be disturbed by the frenzied activity when the shipping season resumed.

The very next day he sent over three dozen bottles of red wine, marked with the seal of the imperial vineyards. A gift for her new residence and a sign that he was pleased with their bargain.

Perhaps inspired by Septimus's example, her next caller was the merchant Jhrve. Descended from one of the captains whose ships had brought the newcomers from Anamur to their exile in Ikaria, Jhrve's house had prospered little during the intervening years. To his credit, Jhrve had tried to improve the fortunes of his house by diversifying their trading routes and partnering with other merchants. But his choices had proven unfortunate, first losing cargoes to pirates, then having one of his partners go bankrupt, leaving Jhrve liable for their shared debts.

Jhrve agreed to supply four ships, at terms that were fair if not as generous as the ones that Septimus had been offered for his six ships. Ysobel had hoped for a dozen ships, but no other potential partners came forward, and it was better to send ten ships now than to wait and risk others reaching port first. And with a partner from each side of the Ikarian factions, she maintained the public appearance of neutrality.

Working through the federation guildhouse, her agents purchased grain for the cargo, and Ysobel personally selected the pilots who would guide the ships. The skills of federation navigators were second to none, and she knew that at least one reason why Septimus and Jhrve had agreed to the venture was that they hoped their captains would learn the secret routes that enabled federation ships to outsail their competitors. To avoid this, the pilots were instructed to take the ships by a fast route, but not by the route they would have chosen if the ships had been crewed by Seddonian sailors.

A true trader was always careful never to show his full strength, and even if the Ikarians managed to memorize this one route, without the secret teachings of the navigators guild they had no chance of equaling the skill of federation sailors. There was a reason why they were nicknamed the People of the Sea, and they had no intention of giving up their hard-won advantage.

With her public role firmly established, Ysobel turned to her covert assignment. Her predecessor had left her a rudimentary spy network, suitable for knowing which warehouse held illicit goods or learning of a court scandal before the whispers became open gossip. Useful, but she needed better information to discover who was actively disloyal and who could be persuaded to consider treachery. Most of her former Ikarian contacts had been killed, or had accepted banishment to remote country estates. She was careful to avoid the few who still remained in Karystos, unsure of their current loyalties and whether or not they were still under observation by the empress's spies.

Instead she set about cultivating new contacts. Septimus introduced her to many of the leading merchants, some of whom had acquired sufficient wealth that they left the trading to the junior members of their house while they turned their own attention to politics. The winter court was dull, by Ikarian standards, but she and Ambassador Hardouin were invited to a series of entertainments that enabled her to meet the leading figures of the court. She did not confine her attentions merely to the wealthy and powerful, but also sought out clerks and trusted servants, who often knew more than their masters. She had not forgotten the functionary Greeter, though she had yet to discover anything that would be sufficient temptation for such a man.

Ysobel had let it be known that she would receive callers at her residence every third day, during the afternoon hours. Some aristocrats came out of mere curiosity, the novelty of a female minister having the entertainment value of a new creature in the imperial menagerie. A few brought their wives, as excuse for their visits, but most often they came alone. Poets and playwrights came as well, both male and female, in hopes of securing a new patron, or at the very least, of taking advantage of her hospitality for the space of an afternoon.

The high taxes imposed by Empress Nerissa on foreign goods had made luxuries out of ordinary delicacies, including imported wines and foodstuffs. As both a diplomat and a merchant with access to her own warehouses, Ysobel was exempt from most taxes, and thus could afford to entertain on a scale that would have bankrupted a minor noble. Small wonder that so many came to drink her wine, then to grumble quietly that Proconsul Zuberi's policies would prove the ruin of the empire.

She noticed that none blamed Nerissa aloud, but instead chose to focus their dissatisfaction on her chief minister. Zuberi was resented for his influence over the empress—for he alone seemed immune to her habit of changing favorites each season—as well as his penchant for elevating members of his own family to important posts. As her guests gossiped, Ysobel smiled and listened, and ensured that their wineglasses were always full.

Her duties as trade liaison occupied her mornings, and she met with merchants during those hours. Only the most idle members of that class came to her afternoon entertainments, and her salon became a place for seemingly impromptu encounters between those who could not afford to be seen together elsewhere.

She made good use of the bathing chamber, having engaged the services of a green-eyed acrobat who demonstrated both remarkable flexibility and the stamina of youth. He accepted both her summons and her ultimate dismissal with good humor. His replacement was even younger, a minor poet well-known in certain circles for his erotic verse. Alas his verses were far more inspiring than his touch. Ysobel expanded his repertoire, then, he, too, was dismissed with a purse of gold coins for his trouble.

The two had served their purpose, establishing her reputation, but from then on the pretty boys who discreetly entered through the garden gate were selected for their ability to run confidential errands and gather intelligence. From time to time she invited one to share her bathing chamber, but contrary to her growing reputation for licentiousness, these boys merely bathed with her. She had charms against both pregnancy and disease, but it was wise not to trust in their potency. And she could not afford any emotional entanglements.

She divided her time between her new household and her chambers at the embassy. Most of her time at the embassy was spent in her office, answering official correspondence with the help of her clerk, Perrin. There were trade agreements to be certified, bills of lading to be inspected, and the newest shipping regulations to be studied, then forwarded to the ministry in Seddon along with her comments. The registry of Ikarian merchants and ships had to be updated and certified, and a secret list of those merchants suspected of false dealings or imminent bankruptcy furnished to federation agents in all major ports.

For the time being, with only a handful of sturdy ships plying the unpredictable winter seas, her duties were light, and she had plenty of time to ingratiate herself with Ikarian society. Her way was smoothed by the open purse supplied by the embassy and the sheer novelty of her position.

Ysobel leaned back in her bath and took a sip of chilled wine, before returning her glass to the special holder that contained crushed ice, ensuring the beverage remained cool despite the heat of the baths. Her left hand trailed idly in the water, creating new currents that disturbed the gentle flow. The blue mosaic tiles and leaping fish along the edges of the pool reinforced the illusion of the ocean, and for a moment she fancied herself a goddess, raising a tempest to vex the impertinent sailors who had intruded upon her sanctuary.

She laughed and took another sip of wine, as the heat of the soaking pool relaxed her muscles and drew the poisons of fatigue from her system. Last night, she and fifty others had been Septimus's guests at dinner, then the company had proceeded to the lesser imperial theater to see the premiere of a new play celebrating Emperor Aitor the Great's victory over Vidrun. The dinner guests had been interesting, as much for their selection as for their wit. Septimus's guests were no higher than the second rank of the aristocracy, equally mixed between the newcomers and the old Ikarian blood. His guests reflected both his ambitions and how far he had to travel to reach the top ranks of Ikarian society.

Sadly the play was less entertaining than the dinner party. The playwright had taken substantial liberties with history yet still managed to produce a dull offering, bereft of both drama and spectacle. More than one audience member fell asleep during the first act, and it was only the booming drums meant to simulate the army's climactic attack that had interrupted their slumber. The empress had not been in attendance; instead her youngest son Anthor had sat in the imperial box and struggled mightily not to show his boredom.

It would have been a different matter if the playwright had incorporated more of the truth in his tale. Then all eyes would have been riveted on the stage as the story of a man who had used his position of imperial consort to usurp the Ikarian throne, murdering his firstborn son to seal his power, unfolded. Even Princess Callista, the rightful heir to the throne, had yielded, grateful for mere survival in the land that her father and sister had ruled before her. Aitor had claimed power not just for himself—during his reign, the newcomers had transformed themselves from wealthy outsiders into the supreme rulers of Ikaria. The Aitor of history was a commanding figure, but his most daring deeds were not spoken aloud, and instead it was his minor triumphs that Khepri had chosen to celebrate.

Still, she suspected the play would do well enough, if only because no one wished to appear to slight the empress by failing to pay due reverence to her legendary grandfather. Those who had not been able to gain admittance tonight would see the play later in the week, before it finished its run.

After the play Ysobel had invited those whom she wished to know better to return to her residence for refreshments. Servants circulated, bearing trays of delicacies, and cupbearers hired for their beauty ensured that the cups of the lounging guests were never empty.

Ysobel herself had drunk only in moderation, switching to unfermented grape juice while her guests continued to drink wine and brandies. Laughing at their witticisms, she noted who could be trusted and whose tongues loosened with wine until they babbled their secrets to any who would listen. As dawn approached, the litter bearers had collected the last of her guests, and Ysobel had gratefully sought her bed.

Rising a few hours later, she had broken her fast, then retired to the bathing chamber, a luxury that she made use of at every opportunity. The Ikarians might be backward in many ways. They were uninspired shipbuilders, and their so-called navigators were barely more than charlatans. But they were positively inspired in their reverence for bathing and in the skills used to create the lavish chamber that she so enjoyed. Baths in Seddon were simple, utilitarian, only large enough to ensure cleanliness. Whereas her cleansing pool was big enough for a couple to share, and the soaking pool was large enough that she could invite a half dozen friends, or host a small orgy.

When she returned to Seddon and set up her own household she would import masons from Ikaria to construct a bathing chamber of her own. Thus resolved, she turned her thoughts back to the previous evening. She'd had hopes of using Horacio, who had the passion of youth, but his behavior had shown that he could not be trusted. On the other hand, his older brother Idaeus was still a possibility. He was more cautious than his brother and considered himself something of a scholar. She would begin by appealing to his intellect.

She was beginning to doubt, however, that her mission to sow discord would succeed. The mood of Karystos had changed since her last visit. While some grumbled, there was no sign that they were willing to do anything more than trade scurrilous gossip. She had no doubt that there were still a few who wished to see Nerissa humbled, but such dissent had gone far underground.

Given the example of those who had gone before them and been punished for their treason, it would be difficult to find new recruits willing to risk their lives to challenge the empress. There might be more to gain from cooperation after all. She felt relieved—but as soon as she recognized her feelings, she felt ashamed of her weakness. She could not let personal feelings influence her mission.

The Seddon Federation was built on trade. Unlike Ikaria, they had no great armies or conquered lands to fall back upon. The rocky islands of Seddon could never support all of her people. For the federation to survive, her trading ships must be the preeminent merchant power on the sea. Ikaria represented a threat to that power and thus to Seddon's very existence. Ikaria had long been distracted by internal politics and its interminable conflict with Vidrun. But if the empire was united, and once again turned its attention to conquest, the federation could find itself barred from key ports and cut off from access to vital commodities.

Her ruminations were disturbed by the arrival of her maid, Anna, carrying a soft cotton towel and a linen robe. "Lady Ysobel, I beg your pardon for disturbing you, but you have a caller."

"At this hour?" It was barely noon.

"Brother Nikos, the head of the Learned Brethren," Anna said. "He apologized for inconveniencing you, but I assured him you would want to see him."

"Of course. You did well to summon me," Ysobel said. She rose to her feet and stepped out of the pool. Accepting the cotton towel, she patted herself dry.

With her maid's help she swiftly dressed, donning a light tunic and an overrobe of blue. Her long hair was twisted into a simple chignon, and she gave thanks that her youthful skin needed no cosmetics. Then she made her way downstairs to the small parlor she used for receiving guests.

Her staff was well used to visitors, and she was pleased to see a tray of delicate pastries on the table, along with a tea service. She offered him wine but was not surprised when he refused. Her informants had told her that Brother Nikos seldom drank wine in public, and never during the daytime. It was part of the image of an ascetic scholar that he so carefully cultivated. However, a keen observer would see beyond the image to notice that his robes, while in the simple style of the monks, were nonetheless made of a rare wool that cost more per yard than silk. And, while he seldom drank wine in public, when he did indulge himself, he was reported to drink only the finest of vintages.

They exchanged pleasantries as she waited for him to reveal the purpose of his visit. In general her callers fell into two categories—those seeking a business alliance and those who came because she was a curiosity. At first glance Brother Nikos fell into neither of those groups. The Learned Brethren had no need for her help in arranging cargoes or negotiating contracts. And Brother Nikos had traveled widely in his youth, so this was not the first time he had encountered a woman who held power in her own right. Though, in general, it was best never to underestimate the curiosity of one of the Learned Brethren, for they had been known to travel to the ends of civilization and beyond in search of knowledge, Brother Nikos was hardly a typical member of his order. If he wished merely to learn about her, he could have dispatched one of his subordinates.

His presence meant that he wanted something from her. Perhaps it was as simple as wanting to judge her for himself rather than rely upon the reports of others. She wondered if he was here on his own behalf or on behalf of the empress.

They exchanged pleasantries for half an hour, but as Brother Nikos set down his teacup she was no closer to understanding the purpose of his visit than she had been when he was announced.

"Ikarian politics can be difficult for an outsider to navigate, as I am sure you must know. I hope you will feel free to call upon me should you require advice from an impartial observer."

"Of course," she replied. And, indeed, in any other country she might well have sought out one of the Learned Brethren if she wished an outsider's view of local politics. But here they were tied so closely to the fortunes of the ruling family that speaking with Brother Nikos was akin to speaking with the empress herself.

Which he knew as well as she, and was most likely the point of his offer. As trade liaison she could not directly approach the empress on minor matters of trade, but that did not mean that the empress was indifferent to her efforts. Nikos was offering himself as an intermediary, so Lady Ysobel could ensure that she did not inadvertently offend the empress by entering into an arrangement with those who were out of favor.

"Your journey may have been inauspicious, but I am confident that you will succeed in your endeavors to bring our two countries closer together," he said, as he rose to take his leave.

Ysobel repressed a frown. Brother Nikos was not the first to mention her being stranded, though he had phrased it more delicately than most. Many in Karystos enjoyed the irony that one of the so-called People of the Sea had been shipwrecked on a remote island. A part of her wanted to point out that the federation had never claimed that their ships were unsinkable, nor their captains infallible. And that the stranding might have been a deliberate act of treachery rather than mere bad luck. But such information would hardly inspire confidence in those she dealt with.

"I was fortunate. And indeed I must praise one of your own. The natives who found my party spoke only their own barbarous tongue, but luckily there was one of your brethren who came to my rescue and interpreted for me."

"One of my monks?"

"Yes, a lighthouse keeper. Brother Josan, I believe he called himself. He was most courteous and helpful, though I was surprised to find a scholar in such a remote place."

She caught a flash of dismay before Brother Nikos's face stilled, then assumed the studied blankness of a man used to hiding his thoughts.

"I am pleased that he was able to be of service to you," he said.

"It was lucky for me that he was there. Though it seems to me that his education and talents are wasted in such a desolate place."

She was hoping for a hint as to what had disturbed him, but he was too polished a courtier to be so easily led.

"The brethren believe that knowledge is to be found

everywhere. And duty often takes one far from one's birth-place, as your own presence here attests."

She could not challenge the truth of his words, but Ysobel was convinced that he was hiding something. Some-how, her encounter with the lighthouse keeper concerned Brother Nikos. Perhaps it had something to do with the reason a scholar was assigned a task better suited to a me-nial laborer. Or perhaps Nikos knew something about Lady Ysobel's voyage and the events that had led to the shipwreck. She had suspected enemies back in Seddon of arranging her accident, but could it have been an Ikarian plot all along? Was Nikos's reaction a sign that he knew she wasn't supposed to have survived and that one of his own had been her inadvertent savior?

It was another layer of complication in a web that was already tangled beyond recognition. Lady Ysobel resigned herself to never cutting to the heart of it, until another caller provided the answer to this latest riddle.

Dama Akantha had waited a full two months after Lady Ysobel's arrival before calling upon her. Their reunion was conducted in the most public of settings, as Dama Akantha arrived during one of Ysobel's afternoon receptions es-corted by the playwright Khepri, who had so recently in-flicted his talents upon the Ikarian court with his account of the life of Emperor Aitor. Khepri had been Ysobel's guest before, and she had been fortunate to have a supply of pale yellow wine on hand since he drank nothing else. He had declared himself instantly enchanted and vowed to com-pose a poem in her honor.

So far he had not made good on his threat, for which she was grateful. But he had returned on other afternoons, bringing with him members of the court. And now he had done a truly great service. Out of all those she had known five years before, Dama Akantha was the only one whose counsel she trusted and whose discretion matched her own.

"Esteemed Khepri, how good of you to join us this afternoon," Lady Ysobel said, allowing him to take both her hands in his own. His hands were soft and rather damp, but she smiled brightly. "And may I be introduced to your companion?"

"Dama Akantha, may I present Lady Ysobel, the liaison for trade from Seddon? Lady Ysobel this is Dama Akantha of Neirene."

It was hardly the graceful introduction that protocol required, but Khepri, for all his aspirations, was not one of the court. Nor was this a formal occasion. Still, he had best look to his manners if he hoped to advance his career.

Dama Akantha gave a thin-lipped smile. "Your pardon for intruding, but Khepri has told me so much about you that I had to meet you for myself."

"Of course, and you are most welcome."

Lady Ysobel signaled, and the serving girl approached, offering Khepri a glass of his favorite wine. A second glass was offered to Dama Akantha, who demurred.

"It is fortunate that you came, Khepri, for we were lamenting your absence earlier. Marcus and Larissa have each brought poems to read, but none here felt worthy of judging their creations. Perhaps we could persuade you to lend your expertise?"

Khepri beamed, drawing himself up to his full height, which was not much more than Ysobel laid claim to. She tugged Khepri's elbow till he was facing in the right direction and gave him a small push. He wandered off without a word to his companion.

"A charming boy. His talents are indescribable," Dama Akantha said.

The boy was nearly forty, though his round face and awkward manners gave the impression of a younger man. And as for his talents... "I believe you mean unspeakable," Lady Ysobel said softly.

This time Dama Akantha's smile reached her eyes. "I know most of your guests, but would you be so kind as to introduce me to the rest?"

They made their way through the two rooms given over to her afternoon receptions, pausing to exchange greetings but moving on before they could be drawn into conversation. This afternoon there were over two dozen guests, all but three of them men. Servant girls and boys circulated with trays of drinks and delicacies, ensuring that the guests did not lack for anything. Indeed, as long as the wine was flowing, few would notice her absence.

"Dama Akantha, I wonder if I might beg a private moment? I find I do not always comprehend the household customs in Ikaria and would appreciate the advice of a woman of your breeding," Lady Ysobel said, pitching her voice so her request could be overheard.

"Of course. Shall we take a turn in the courtyard? The day is quite fine, after all."

A few glanced their way as servants brought their cloaks, but then returned to their own conversations when the women stepped through the door that led to the enclosed courtyard. Spring was still a few weeks off, but the sun had warmed the stones of the courtyard, and the protection from the damp winter wind made the courtyard almost pleasant.

It fell to Lady Ysobel to begin the conversation. "I am pleased to see you well. I trust you suffered no consequences from the unfortunate events?"

"I am as I always was. And you, I see you have done well for yourself."

"I have had some small success in my ventures." There was no reason to elaborate. Dama Akantha was not interested in matters of trade or the accumulation of wealth.

Dama Akantha gestured toward the fire pits, then turned in a half circle, pointing out the garden paths. Lady Ysobel followed her gaze, nodding, as if the two women were discussing how to best utilize the space for a feast. The odds that they were being observed were small, but they both owed their survival to caution and the avoidance of unnecessary risks.

On the surface they were an unlikely pair. Dama Akantha was of an age to be Ysobel's mother. A noblewoman who traced her lineage to the newcomers, she had ties of both blood and marriage to the imperial family. Widowed at an early age, she had used her caustic tongue and her husband's fortune to secure her place as one of the unofficial arbiters of Ikarian society.

"And Lady Ysobel, what brings you back to my country? Is this strictly a mission of trade, or do you have unfinished business to attend to?" Dama Akantha's voice was sharp, and it was easy to understand why she terrified the young ladies making their debut at the court.

"I had hoped to settle old debts, but I find that there is little interest these days."

"Cowards. Cowards and sheep," Dama Akantha muttered. "Nerissa betrayed us all, but they refuse to see it. They sit at her table, begging for scraps and thanking her for the privilege. Eunuchs all. There's not a man among the lot of them."

"If you were a man—"

"If I were a man, they would not follow me. I have the blood but not the right blood. My people have put their trust in Nerissa, more fools they. And the old line will only follow one of Constantin's get."

Dama Akantha seemed the most unlikely of revolutionaries. With her close ties to the imperial family, none would suspect that she had been part of the inner circle that had plotted to overthrow Empress Nerissa and replace her with Prince Lucius. That she, alone of Ysobel's former contacts, had survived was a testament to her cunning.

What few realized was that the failed uprising had not been a simple matter of the old Ikarians versus the new blood. There were many newcomers who felt they had a score to settle with the empress—some scheming for power, while others were zealots such as Dama Akantha, who believed that the empress had betrayed their people when she made peace with Vidrun. The cost of that peace had been acknowledging Vidrun's right to rule over Anamur, and there were many who saw this as a betrayal.

It did not matter that the newcomers had fled Anamur over three centuries before. To men and women like Dame Akantha Anamur was their homeland, and the descendants of those left behind were their family. It meant nothing that the people of Anamur had long since reached their own accommodation with their rulers. Nor had any of these self-professed patriots undertaken the long voyage to visit Anamur, to see for themselves how much the city had changed in their absence. Facts did not matter, it was the idea of Anamur as their sacred homeland that drove them. By their reasoning Nerissa had betrayed them, and thus she deserved to die.

Or at least so they claimed. Ysobel suspected that not all shared Akantha's patriotic fervor—that many found it easier to cloak their actions under the banners of honor and duty rather than admitting their own lust for power. After all, Aitor had been only a minor noble before he made himself emperor, and if he could do it, why not another?

Ysobel had known only a handful of the conspirators, but Dama Akantha had known them all. If there was even the slightest chance to stir up the rebellion again, Dama Akantha would know of it. Her pessimism did not bode well for Ysobel's covert mission.

"The prince's fate was never confirmed. His body was not publicly displayed..." She let her voice trail off.

Dama Akantha shook her head. "Not in public, but all know that his body was removed from the torture chamber and buried outside the city walls. There was even an attempt to dig him up, but the guards caught wind of it and moved the body before we could reclaim him."

Ysobel's eyes widened. She did not want to know what they had planned to do with the prince's body.

"We could find someone to play his part. . . ."

"Where will you find such a man? Only a fool would agree, and such a lackwit could never hope to carry off the deception. And Lucius had the look of the old imperial line; there are precious few purebloods left."

Ysobel cast her mind back. Lucius's face had still had the roundness of youth, but had been showing signs of the sharply chiseled features that graced so many of the now forbidden old-style coins. Hair could be dyed to match that shade of dark blond, but blue eyes would be harder to find.

And it was not simply physical features that they needed to match. Any impostor would have to be a man of education, intelligent enough to learn the courtly manners that had been drilled into Lucius from birth. Nothing less would serve their purpose.

She pictured the prince as he would be now, five years older. Then the picture in her mind's eye shifted, the purple tunic changing into a coarse robe, and his sharp features offset by his shaven skull.

No wonder Brother Nikos had been so troubled by her mention of the lighthouse keeper. Even back then she had thought his features familiar, but only now did she see the resemblance.

"There is at least one bastard of Constantin's line left in Ikaria," Lady Ysobel said.

"Nonsense. I would have heard of it." Despite her words, Dama Akantha appeared intrigued.

"A monk of the Learned Brethren," Lady Ysobel explained. "I had the good fortune to encounter him when I was stranded on the northern isles. Put him in a silk robe, let his hair grow, and most would swear he was Constantin come to life. Or Lucius, for that matter."

No doubt he had been sent from Karystos to keep him safe, in those troubled days when no one was above suspicion. She wondered if he knew of his lineage. Did he honestly believe himself a nameless bastard? How many generations back did the indiscretion go? Aitor and his descendants had ruled for the last hundred years. If there had been a male heir to Constantin, even a bastard, surely someone would have already exploited the connection.

Constantin's only legitimate children had been the ill-fated Empress Constanza and her sister, Princess Callista. Still, it was possible that he or one of his forefathers had sired a bastard line—from which the monk had inherited his damning features.

"If only . . ." Dama Akantha lapsed into silence as she thought through the ramifications of Ysobel's discovery. Then she shook her head. "No, the Learned Brethren are Nerissa's lapdogs. We dare not approach him."

Ysobel agreed. Brother Josan was a danger to himself and to any who dared approach him. No wonder he had been exiled so far from the capital. "We had best return before our absence arouses suspicion. For now all we can do is watch and wait. Gather information on who may be sympathetic and wait for the right opportunity."

"I have been patient for twice your lifetime. I can be patient a little longer," Dame Akantha said.

Chapter 7

Spring wore on but the mornings were still cool. Often the approach of dawn brought with it a misty fog that blanketed the island, obscuring both sea and sky. On those days, Josan would wind the clockwork mechanism that operated the brass warning bell, whose toll would warn ships until the morning sun burned off the fog. The bell was an ingenious device, but it required constant tending, needing to be wound every hour.

Brother Nikos had sent along a slender volume of travelers' tales, including the earliest known description of the island chain. Josan had forced himself to read the book slowly, no more than three pages a day, in order to make this treasure last. Josan had read it twice, and had begun to read it a third time, this time trying to sketch each of the various sights the travelers described, using the few details they had provided. But this pursuit had to be set aside as the fog once more took hold of the island. For over a week, Josan had spent each night at his duties, then several hours each morning tending the bell. Some days the fog did not lift until noon, and yesterday the fog had lingered until the dark afternoon had slipped into night. Josan's body craved sleep even as he prepared for another long night in the tower. But he reminded himself that this weather would not last forever. Summer would soon be here, and with it long, peaceful days in which he could get the rest he craved.

And once summer came he would no longer be alone on the island. In the spring, every hand was turned to the task of planting the fields, but once the crops were sown there were other tasks for the villagers. Some would turn fishermen, casting their nets in the sheltered waters of the sound. Others would come to the island, setting traps for the giant crabs or combing the beaches for the great spiral shells that could be found only along the seaward side of the islands. The deep blue lining of the shells would be ground into a coarse powder and traded to the southerners, who used it to make richly hued dyes.

In past years Josan, too, had wandered the beaches collecting shells, finding beauty not just in their shapes but in their diversity. His idle hours had given him time to discover a new talent, one for drawing, and he had put that to good use in his studies. From tiny shells smaller than his fingertip to great whelks as large as a man's head, each unique specimen was carefully sketched next to a description of its coloration and where it had been found. He had collected over one hundred different shell specimens before the great storm had washed them all out to sea. But the knowledge he had gained still survived on the scrolls he had sent back to the order.

He had thought about starting his collection anew, but the fickle weather had kept him far too busy for leisurely strolls along the shoreline. Perhaps once the spring had passed he would find time, although it was disheartening to think that he would have to start all over, for he dare not trust that he would remember each of the shells he had already found.

Or perhaps he could begin a new study. A previous keeper had spent his years describing the birds that came to the island each spring and fall, but that was nearly a century ago, and it would be interesting to note if any changes had occurred in that time.

As the morning wore on and the chill fog lingered, coating everything with a sheen of water, Josan turned over the possibilities in his mind. Anything to keep his mind focused and awake until the next time to wind the key, even as his body longed for sleep. He had come to no conclusions by the time the sun broke through the clouds, but that was of no matter. Time was the one thing he did not lack.

The bell continued its measured peal as Josan climbed down the ladder that led from the platform to the topmost course. In days past he had used this course to store firkins of cabbage-seed oil, but since returning to the tower he had cleared enough space for a pallet, for those times when the weather was foul, or he was too weary to make the long climb down to the base of the tower and hike over the dunes to his new cabin.

He walked round the half-circle course to the top of the ladder that led to the levels below, yet even as his hand touched the topmost rung he hesitated.

In his cabin there was a mattress stuffed with the soft grasses of springtime, but this luxury seemed impossibly far away as he gazed down the shaft. His head swam and his legs shook with weariness as the lack of rest finally caught up with him, and with a sigh he turned away. Wrapping himself in his cloak, he lay down on the course, his back pressed against the curved stone wall. He would rest for a while, and when he felt stronger he would make his descent.

He awoke suddenly, jerked into wakefulness though his body did not move. It, at least, remembered where he was and the dangers of his perch. He knew he had not been sleeping long, for his wits were still dull. He glimpsed blue sky through the narrow windows, and the sharply angled shadows indicated that it was not yet noon.

He had slept for barely an hour, which explained his tiredness—though not what had awoken him. Listening carefully, he heard nothing except the distant cries of shorebirds and the sound of waves gently lapping at the rocks. Even the clockwork bell had fallen silent, as it had reached the end of its cycle. Perhaps it was not a noise but rather the sudden silence that had awoken him, he reasoned.

He settled his head back down on his cloak and closed his eyes again. He would rest for a few moments longer, then it would be time to see about filling his empty stomach.

But just as he made that resolve, he heard the unmistakable creak of a ladder rung. This time when he opened his eyes, he saw a man's head rising above the wooden course.

Josan blinked. The stranger's face was level with his own. He knew at once that the man was not one of the villagers, for his dark brown hair showed the influence of the newcomers in his breeding.

"Who are you?" Josan asked.

The stranger did not answer.

Josan flushed, realizing the folly of trying to hold a conversation while still lying down, and rolled so his hands were under him, preparing to rise.

The movement saved his life as a silver object flew through the air, clattering off the stone wall behind him.

A part of Josan was frozen in shock, convinced this was an absurd dream. There could be no other explanation. Why else would a stranger invade the tower and try to murder him? There was nothing for a thief to steal, for only another lighthouse could use the precious objects contained above. And Josan himself was a mere monk, who had lived a blameless life of scholarship.

Yet even as his mind was paralyzed by the strangeness of his situation, there was another part of him that responded immediately to the threat the stranger presented. This part drove Josan to continue his roll until he reached the far end of the course, and with a flip that would have done any acrobat proud, Josan was on his feet.

It was as if another fought in his place, relegating Josan to the status of a mere observer in his own body. But there was no time to wonder at the strangeness of it all, for the assassin had completed his climb and now stood on the opposite end of the half-circle course, facing Josan. There was nothing to be read in his face except calm concentration as he reached his right hand into a hidden pocket and with a flick of his wrist sent another silver object spinning through the air. Josan dodged it, and the others that followed.

"Why are you doing this? I am no threat to you," Josan said. He kept his eyes fixed on his opponent, trying to read any clue that would give away his intentions.

He did not need to look away from the attacker to know that he was in mortal danger. This high in the tower, the wooden course was extremely narrow, barely two yards across. There was nothing to hide behind, and the stranger was between Josan and the ladder, which was his only route to escape.

Josan threw himself to one side as several silver objects flew by. One of them grazed his right shoulder as it passed, before bouncing off the wall and falling down into the shaft.

A triskel, his mind supplied, dredging out the name from the dim recesses of his damaged memories. A weapon of choice among assassins, who spent long hours mastering the techniques required to throw the spinning blade with lethal accuracy.

Perhaps this was not a trained assassin after all. Contempt arose within him for one who would blunder so badly, and his right hand curled on itself as if he were the one holding a triskel. In that moment, he knew he could show this man how such a weapon should be used, and his gaze raked the platform to see if any had landed nearby. But the wooden floor was bare, save for one blade near the assassin's feet, where Josan had been sleeping only moments before.

As the assassin's right hand dropped down to the long dagger tucked into his belt, Josan knew that he had to act.

"Please, I beg of you, this must be some mistake," he said, allowing his voice to quaver as if he were terrified.

The assassin smiled scornfully, and as he withdrew his dagger, Josan did the one thing he did not expect. He charged.

It took only three quick steps to cross the distance that separated them, and at the end Josan lashed out with a swift kick that knocked the dagger loose. He lunged for it, his fingertips brushing against the blade, but he was not quick enough to catch it, and he cursed as he watched it vanish into the darkness below.

He turned, rolling his head as a fist clipped him across the chin. Josan repaid the favor with a flurry of open-palmed strikes that forced his startled opponent to retreat a few paces. The assassin turned his head for a moment to gauge the space behind him, and Josan struck, his blow catching his opponent solidly in the ribs.

He should be frightened. He should be terrified. He was a member of the Learned Brethren, one who had dedicated his life to scholarship, not to the arts of war. And surely there could be no worse place for a deadly fight than this tiny half circle, where any misstep meant a lethal fall.

Yet Josan felt neither fear nor terror. Instead he was calm, his breath steady, his body poised as he stood lightly on the balls of his feet before advancing to trade another series of blows. Neither was able to completely block the other's blows, and this time Josan was the one forced to retreat. Yet his new bruises were worth the pain, for he had confirmed his earlier suspicions. His attacker might carry the triskels of a mercenary, but his fighting style suggested military training. When Josan had essayed the middle portion of the tiger attack, the assassin had responded with the traditional blocks as if they were at drill rather than fighting for their lives.

The intruder was used to fighting in the high style, and to watching an opponent's hands. A kick had caught the assassin off guard once. It was time to try it again.

Josan knew he had been lucky so far. But his luck would not hold forever, and all it would take was one careless step, one moment of being off-balance, and his opponent would need to do no more than give him a gentle push to his death.

Josan clenched his hands into fists and raised them in front of him, as if preparing to attack. As the assassin drew back his right hand for a blow, Josan whirled suddenly on his right foot, his robes flying around him as he extended his left leg upward. It caught the assassin just under the chin and there was a sickening crack as his neck broke.

As Josan completed his turn, he watched the assassin's suddenly limp body fall backward over the edge of the wooden course, disappearing down the shaft. After a long moment there was a dull thud as the body struck the floor at the base of the tower.

A wave of dizziness swept over him. Josan stepped back from the edge, his hands stretched behind him until he felt the safety of the stone wall. Back pressed against the wall, he slowly slid down until he was seated, his eyes still fixed on the ladder and the emptiness beyond.

The encounter had lasted only a few moments, yet he gasped for breath, his blood pounding in his ears as if he had just run a great race. Only now that the danger was past did panic threaten to overwhelm him.

I could have been killed, Josan thought. *He came here to murder me.*

It was a fantastic thought. What could have brought an assassin to this desolate spot, in the farthest reaches of the empire? And why would such a man wish to kill a peaceful monk? Josan was no one of importance. He had no enemies, and if the killer had borne a grudge against the brethren or the servants of the empire, surely there were far more accessible targets. People whose deaths would mean something.

Was it possible that he had been a thief after all? Yet that made no sense either. True the lenses and magically crafted mirrors were objects of value, but they could only be used in another lighthouse.

Or perhaps it was sabotage that the intruder had planned. To destroy the instruments that made the lighthouse function and thus imperil the ships that counted on the lighthouse to warn them of danger.

Each supposition was more fantastic than the last, but the mystery of why he was attacked paled beside the far greater mystery of his improbable survival.

Josan knew he should have died. There had been nothing in his training to prepare him for a life-and-death struggle against a skilled foe. From his earliest childhood he had devoted himself to the pursuit of knowledge for the enrichment of the order. He had learned to speak seven different languages, to read ancient scripts whose speakers had long since died out, and to use secret mathematical formulas to calculate the positions of the stars.

There were gaps in his memories from his illness, but nothing had ever led him to suspect that those gaps contained anything other than a life of peaceful study. He remembered nothing that would explain how he had recognized a weapon used by assassins. Nor where his body had learned to strike and defend itself from attack at a level that was purely instinctive.

He had fought as a man possessed by a warrior spirit. Courage and luck had played their part in his survival, but he knew that in the end he had prevailed because he was the more skilled of the two.

He shivered, the drying sweat suddenly chill on his flesh as he wondered what other hidden skills this body might have. He pulled his knees to his chest, wrapping his arms around them. A part of him desperately hoped that this was all some fantastic dream and that at any moment he would awaken. But deep inside he knew better. This was no dream, and he was not the man he had thought himself to be.

It was a long time before he could persuade himself to move. It was fear that kept him still. Fear of the new truths he might discover about himself. As long as he stayed still he could maintain the illusion that he was a simple monk with a blameless past. But once he climbed down from his refuge he would have to face the tangible evidence that he was more than that. He was a man who knew how to kill and a man that others sought to kill in turn.

At last, his thirst forced him to move. Carefully he descended the ladder that linked the three courses until he reached the stone staircase that wound down to the base of the tower. His right hand trailed against the wall, taking comfort from the smoothly dressed stones, as if it were his first descent. At last he reached the base where the assassin lay crumpled on the floor, his left leg resting on the bottom step.

Josan stepped over the body and went to the storeroom. Uncovering the wooden cask, he drank two ladles of water, then filled the small bowl he used for washing. Carefully he scrubbed his hands, driven by a compulsion that he did not understand. There was no visible stain on them; indeed, no blood had been shed. Yet as he washed his hands, he studied them as if they belonged to a stranger. There on the base of his left hand was the round white burn scar from his first days at the lighthouse, when he had carelessly touched one of the globes before it had cooled. His right hand had the calluses of a laborer on his palm and those of a scribe on his forefinger and thumb.

He had thought that he had known all that these hands could do. But he had never imagined that they knew how to hold weapons, or how to strike a blow that would kill a man. This was more than an unexpected talent for drawing. And while the order valued all learning, try as he may he could think of no reason why one of the brethren should have mastered such skills. His blood chilled as he realized that perhaps this was the true reason for his exile. Perhaps the fever had robbed him not just of his intellect but had also stolen the memories of the crimes he had committed.

It was an impossible puzzle, and the only ones who could answer his questions were far from here. The answers he sought lay with the members of his order and with whatever had brought this man to kill him.

Had it been a personal grudge? Or had he come to the lighthouse to do another's bidding?

Wiping his hands dry on a scrap of linen, Josan left the storeroom. He crouched beside the corpse, studying the man's face, but the features revealed no more in death than they had in life. The man was clearly of mixed blood, so he could have come from anywhere in the southern part of the empire. If he had spoken, Josan might have been able to place him by his accent, but the stranger had died without uttering a word.

Pushing aside his distaste, Josan straightened the man's limbs and began searching for a clue as to where he had come from. It took some time for him to find the hidden pockets in the man's tunic, but all were empty. There was no belt pouch, but around his waist was fastened a linen belt that was divided into individual pockets. Each pocket held two coins, one of round gold with the seal of the empire, the other the hexagonal silver currency of Seddon.

This told him nothing, and he dropped the belt on the ground with disgust.

Why had this man tried to kill him? Had he journeyed alone or were there others waiting for him? Had he sailed up the coast on a ship that even now lay anchored in some quiet cove? Or had he taken the overland route, convincing one of the villagers to ferry him across the sound? Surely there must be some trace of his passing, some sign of whence he had come.

The sandals on his feet were but lightly worn, a sign that he had neither ridden nor walked here along the road. Unless, of course, he had left his boots behind with his pack, hidden somewhere in the dunes. For all Josan knew the man had been watching him for hours or even days, waiting for the right moment to make his attack.

He might even have cohorts still out there, perhaps hidden somewhere in the dune thicket, watching. Waiting.

At that moment Josan heard a voice call out. He leapt to his feet, his right hand instinctively grasping at his waist as if in search of a weapon. But of course there was no weapon. Nor was there any means to bar the door from the inside. His gaze darted around, and he caught sight of the long dagger, which the assassin had dropped during their struggle. He picked it up, the cold hilt giving him a comfortable feeling of reassurance in his palm. Carefully he stepped around the body, taking a position slightly to the right of the door, where he would not be immediately visible. Anyone coming in from the bright sun to the dimness of the tower would be dazzled for a moment, and he could use that time to strike.

"Hello," a man called out, from just outside the tower. Josan's muscles sagged with relief as he recognized Marco's voice.

The door swung outward, and Marco stepped inside, blinking a bit as his eyes adjusted. Renzo followed behind him.

Josan stepped forward.

"Greetings to you both, and glad I am to see you," he said.

Even in the dim light he could see the blood run from Renzo's face as he saw the lifeless corpse on the floor. He paused, frozen, his eyes glancing back between Josan and the body, as if he could not quite believe what he was seeing. The canvas sack he was carrying slipped through his fingers to land on the floor with a dull thud.

Marco was quicker to react. "What have you done?" he demanded.

"This is not how it seems," Josan said.

"You murdered this man? And now you threaten us?" Marco's voice rose in disbelief.

Only then did Josan realize that he still held the dagger in his hand. Quickly he set it down.

"I did not know who approached, and thought only to defend myself," Josan said. "The dagger is his."

"What happened here?" Renzo asked.

Josan hesitated, wondering how he could explain something that even he did not understand.

"I was asleep on the topmost course when suddenly I awoke to see this man. I asked him what he wanted, but he did not answer. Instead he attacked, and we struggled. In the end he fell down the shaft. I had only just come down when I heard your hail."

"A thief then, come to rob you?" Renzo's tone was neutral but his face was troubled. Violence had no place in the lives of these villagers, nor did thievery. These evils were confined to traveler's tales of life in distant cities and towns. If Renzo had seen violence done during his youthful years as a sailor, such was long forgotten.

"A thief, yes," Josan said. "What else could he be?"

Even to his own ears his words sounded hollow. The lighthouse's artifacts would be poor compensation for the long journey, and the villagers had nothing to tempt even the meanest of thieves.

Marco rolled the body over with his foot, as if looking for signs of a stab wound. But in this he was bound to be disappointed, for there had been very little blood. Kneeling next to the corpse, he searched the body like Josan before him, looking for a sign that would reveal his identity.

"This was no petty thief." Marco pushed up the left sleeve of the dead man to reveal a fading tattoo on the inside of his left forearm. A stylized lizard encircled by a double ring, it was the symbol of the former rulers of Ikaria. It had been outlawed for generations, ever since Emperor Aitor had assumed the throne. Displaying the symbol was enough to earn one a lengthy stay in the catacombs, or enslavement.

No mere thief would endanger himself by having such a damning mark. Nor would an ordinary assassin so foolishly flaunt his loyalties.

"Why would a traitor seek you out? Who are you and what is your true name?" Marco's voice was cold, and he stared at Josan as if he were a stranger.

"You know me. I am Josan of the Learned Brethren from the collegium in Karystos. A scholar once, and now a lighthouse keeper."

"You are a murderer," Marco said.

"He is our friend," Renzo argued. "This was an accident, it must have been. Swear to us that you did not intend to kill this man and we will believe you."

It was a simple request. All knew that the Learned Brethren were men of peace, who eschewed violence. A monk could not be guilty of murder.

"I did not intend to kill him," Josan said. Which was true, in its way. He still did not understand the instincts that had governed his actions, but he knew that his goal had been survival, not murder.

Renzo's gaze searched his features. Whatever he saw there must have reassured him, for he gave a short nod.

But Marco was not so easily swayed.

"You lie. You killed this man, then you stood here dagger in hand, ready to kill again," Marco declared.

"No," Josan said, but even he did not know what he was denying. For he had indeed killed the intruder, and when he had picked up the dagger he had been prepared to use that as well. He had reacted as a warrior, not as a scholar.

"The proof lies here at our feet," Marco declared. "No doubt you killed him because he threatened to reveal your secret. And who knows how many others you have killed? What happened to the monk that the brethren sent to tend this tower? Does he lie somewhere in an unmarked grave?"

"How can you accuse me of such things? Have I not tended the lighthouse faithfully? Did I not warn your people when the great storm approached? Only last winter you asked me to bless your marriage, and now you are condemning me as a murderer."

He realized he had made a mistake, for rather than softening, Marco's face hardened. Mentioning the marriage had only served to remind Marco of his long struggle to win Terza's affections.

"I never trusted you. I always knew your soft words hid a false heart."

Josan wondered grimly what would have happened if the fates had been different. If Josan had not been able to tap into his hidden fighting skills, they might have arrived in time to discover his body lying lifeless on the floor with the assassin standing over him. Would his death have convinced Marco that Josan was innocent? Or would he have still found a way to blame Josan for inviting his attack and bringing violence to this place?

"This man is a stranger to us," Renzo said. "We know that the dagger is his, and a sign of ill intent. We will send word to Skalla, and no doubt the magistrates there will already know of his crimes."

"And what of this one? Your friend who claims to be a monk?"

"He is a friend to all of us."

"He is a killer, but your taste in bed-warmers has made you blind. Lucky for the rest of us that I can see clearly."

Renzo gave Marco a venomous glare. "Your mind is as tangled and filthy as your nets," he said.

"And you are a foolish old man. Others will listen to me."

"Will you believe him if he swears an oath?" Renzo asked. He turned to Josan. "Tell us that you have never killed before. Swear to us by the power of the tides and the salt blood that runs in your veins that you are innocent, and we will protect you."

Josan drew in a deep breath. He wanted to swear, wanted to protest his innocence. If Renzo had asked him this question only a few hours ago, he could have proclaimed his innocence with all of his heart. But that was before he had discovered that within him lay buried the skills of a warrior. Who knew what other secrets lay hidden in a past that he could not quite recall?

The Learned Brethren cherished truth above all things,

and despite what had happened, Josan could not imagine betraying their teachings. But the same beliefs damned him, for he could not swear an oath, not when he knew it might be proven false.

When Josan let his breath out without speaking, Marco smiled at him scornfully. "I thought as much. It will be a pleasure to see you brought to justice."

For the first time Josan realized that he had more to fear than their scorn. Before he quite knew what was happening, he had taken two steps back and seized the long dagger.

"You will not need that," Renzo said. "We will let you leave."

"But—" Marco protested.

Renzo put his hand on Marco's shoulder, preventing him from lunging forward. "One man has died here already today. Do you want to be the next?"

Marco glared but subsided. The odds were two against one, but Josan had a dagger and clearly Marco believed that he had both the willingness and the skill to use it.

It was ironic. He had committed no crime, had only fought back to save his life. But continuing to protest his innocence would win him nothing. Renzo might be prepared to give Josan the benefit of the doubt, to trust that in time a suitable explanation would be found.

But Marco believed Josan to be a murderer, and his voice would sway others. Josan could not afford to stay. Imperial law stated that only a magistrate could condemn a murderer to death, but the villagers paid little heed to written laws. They might well decide to hang him without ever giving him a trial or a chance to defend himself.

He had to leave. And he had to do so without harming anyone else. Marco was taller and stronger than Josan, but Josan was armed and had already demonstrated an uncanny skill for fighting. If they came to blows, Josan would prevail, but any such victory would be costly. Marco was too stubborn to surrender—he would not give up until he was gravely injured or dead.

Marco was a fool, but he did not deserve to die. In his own way he was acting honorably, to protect his people from someone he saw as a threat.

"I would go, but I cannot leave the lighthouse untended," he said.

"I will keep watch, and Marco can fetch Terza to help. We kept the light burning in all those weeks before you arrived, and we will keep it bright until the brethren send another to replace you," Renzo replied.

It was a sensible answer, but a part of him wished that Renzo had urged him to stay.

"You may run now, but I will see that word of your deception is sent to the city. One day soon your luck will run out, and you will face justice for what you have done," Marco added.

Josan swallowed heavily. He would be leaving behind not just the lighthouse, but also the certainty of knowing himself a member of the Learned Brethren. Who knew if the monks would welcome him back once Marco's account reached them? Even before today's events he had been warned not to return to Karystos.

Yet neither could he stay on the island, even if he could somehow convince the villagers that he meant them no harm. A killer had found him here once. Another could do so again.

It was of no consequence that he did not know why the assassin had tried to kill him, nor what he had done to earn the wrath of those who followed the old ways. Whatever the cause, he knew he must flee. Alive he could hope to learn the truth. Dead the secrets of his past died with him.

"The two of you must climb to the top platform," he said.

"Why?" Marco asked.

"Shall I turn my back only to have you attack when I try to fill a waterskin? You do not trust me, so why should I trust you?"

He had the satisfaction of seeing Marco's face darken with rage.

He was disturbed by how easily he had assumed the mask of cold calculation. Such behavior was foreign to his nature, or at least it had been before the attack. But calculation had already saved his life once and so he held his ground, his features bland, giving no hint of his unease.

Renzo turned and began to climb the stone steps. After a few muttered curses Marco followed. Josan watched them until they reached the bottom course.

"The sparker is in the tin box on the middle shelf. And you must strain the oil before filling the lamps," he called up.

Renzo nodded but did not glance downward. Instead he set his foot on the bottom rung of the ladder and began the slow climb. Marco followed.

Josan fought the urge to call up to Renzo, to try one last time to explain what had happened. It felt wrong to leave like this. A betrayal of the friendship that had sustained him for the last five years. Surely there ought to be something that he could say? But how could he explain what he himself did not understand? Only the truth would satisfy Renzo, but Josan had no truths to offer, only questions.

Instead he watched, craning his head as the two figures continued their climb until they were barely distinguishable. At last he saw a small square of daylight appear as Renzo opened the wooden hatch, and first he, then Marco climbed onto the platform. Turning away, Josan entered the storeroom, knowing he had little time. He trusted that Renzo would wait patiently on the platform until he observed the monk's departure, but Marco would no doubt try to make his way back down as soon as Josan was no longer watching.

The iron bar still stood in the far corner, and it was the work of a moment to retrieve it. He stepped back into the base of the tower, pausing for one final look at the dead assassin. Then he pushed open the door of the lighthouse. Shutting it firmly behind him, he threaded the iron bar through the metal slots that held the door shut when the lighthouse was closed for the winter. Now it could only be unlocked from the outside.

Marco would have no cause to remember the bar, since it was never used when the villagers were on the island, but Renzo knew it was there. Perhaps he had kept silent out of the remnants of their friendship, wanting to give Josan time to make his escape.

More likely Renzo had simply forgotten about it, distracted by the discovery of the stranger's corpse and the realization that his friend was not the man he had thought him to be.

Strangely, Josan felt far worse about the loss of Renzo's friendship than he did about having killed a man. He comforted himself with the knowledge that Renzo was in no danger. The storeroom held both food and water, and in a day or two at the most the villagers would send someone looking for the missing men.

He climbed the dune and followed the path through the bracken to his cottage. He kept a firm hold on the dagger but no one challenged him, and he was relieved to find the cabin appeared undisturbed.

Taking down his leather pack from its peg, he placed it on his bed. Wasting no time, he gathered food for a fortnight's journey—dried fish, a sack of beans, and another of ground millet, which he used for porridge. He hesitated over a small jar of honey, then ruthlessly discarded it as being too heavy. His two tunics and spare leggings went in next, followed by his writing case.

Josan hesitated as he eyed the logbooks that held the place of honor on the crude shelves, each wrapped in leather to preserve them from water and insects. Copies, for the originals were preserved in the collegium, the logs contained the record of his five years as lighthouse keeper, and the accounts of those who had come before him. It seemed a crime to leave them behind, in the care of the villagers, who could neither read nor write in the Ikarian dialect reserved for scholars.

Yet he could not take them with him. He was not certain that he even had a right to them. Better that they stay behind. Renzo would see that no harm came to them, as he would watch over the lighthouse until a new keeper arrived.

Someone who carried the confidence of the brethren. A man of scholarship and of peace. A man who could remember his past and for whom the future held no fears.

Josan shook his head to clear his thoughts. Turning away from the logbooks, he picked up two waterskins and filled them at the well. Then he returned to the cabin. Shouldering his pack, he rolled the blanket from his bed into a thin bundle and tucked it between the straps.

Leaving the cabin behind, he climbed to the top of the dune, pausing for one last look toward where the lighthouse stood, the dark gray stones standing resolute against the forces of time and nature.

He had spent five years on the island. It was the only home he could remember, for his years at the collegium were misty, as was so much of his life before the fever. He remembered what it had felt like to awaken, his body wracked with pain, not knowing where he was nor even his name. Slowly his memories had come back to him, but they were only bits and pieces, like an ancient mosaic that was missing most of its tiles.

He had listened when the monks had told him he should be grateful to be alive. That he should not trouble himself over his missing memories, but rather give thanks that there was still some small way in which he could serve the brethren. He had accepted their judgment, and while his exile had chafed, until today he had had no reason to question their motives.

He did not know when he had learned the ways of a fighter, nor why someone would seek his death. But the answers he sought were out there. Somewhere. It was up to him to have the courage to face his past, whatever he might discover.

Better to know himself a murderer than to live a life of lies.

Chapter 8

The Learned Brethren prided themselves on living lives of simplicity, disdaining anything that might distract them from their pursuit of knowledge. It was said that a monk would go without food for a week in exchange for a mere glimpse of a rare manuscript. From his birth, Josan had lived according to the brethren's ways, taking his turn at performing the most menial of tasks. And the last five years his existence had been even more spartan. If asked, he would have said that he lived a life of privation, though by his own choice.

Now he realized how foolish he had been. As his stomach ached with hunger, he grimly reconsidered the tale of the fasting monk. Starvation was a virtue only when it was a choice. Given the choice between a bowl of soup and a chance to be the first man in two hundred years to read the scrolls of Alexander, Josan would choose the soup.

His life as lighthouse keeper had been full of luxuries, though he had been too foolish to see it at the time. The food might have been plain but it was ample, there was a roof over his head to keep off the weather, and he had been able to sleep soundly at night, unconcerned over who might disturb him. All of this had been ripped from him when he had been forced to flee.

The stranger had not killed Josan, but in a real sense he had taken his life. Josan had lost more than mere comforts. He had lost the certainty that came from knowing who he was. While he had chafed at his exile, there had been security in knowing himself a monk, part of a chain of scholarship that stretched back through the centuries.

It had taken a stranger to show him that he was more than a scholar. That he was capable of killing when provoked. Once revealed, such truths could not be forgotten.

Even if Marco's accusations had not forced him to flee, Josan knew that he would eventually have left the island on his own. To stay there would have been to deny the uncomfortable truths about himself. And while he feared the answers he might find, he could not live in ignorance.

He had fled to the mainland bent on solving the riddles that the stranger represented. Who had sent the assassin? Why would anyone want to harm Josan? Why had the Learned Brethren sent him to the island, and why were they so insistent that he not return to Karystos? What crimes lay hidden in the parts of his memory that were still fogged by his illness?

Fine questions, and answering them was a worthy goal. But it was quickly supplanted by an even more important goal, that of simple survival. News of Josan's supposed crimes had swiftly reached the mainland, and he found himself being hunted. His shaven head made it impossible for him to hide from those who had heard of the renegade monk.

More than once he was forced to flee from those who sought to capture him. He grew lean as he relied upon his indifferent skills at foraging, supplemented by the occasional theft. Each time he stole it shamed him, and he swore that he would not do so again. But the next time hunger caused his limbs to tremble and his head to swim, he would once again forget his scruples.

As the months passed, his growing hair and tattered rags made it less and less likely that he would be recognized. Still, in isolated villages any stranger was viewed with suspicion, and he dared not stay longer than it took to beg or steal a meal. Gradually he began to make his way south, toward the more populated areas of the province. If he found a large enough town, he might be able to lose himself among the crowd, if only for long enough to earn a few hot meals and perhaps a coin or two to put in his pocket.

He still needed answers, but he had realized that he needed to stay alive long enough to find them.

Survival was a matter of living day to day, but he could not ignore the signs around him, as summer gave way to autumn. The orchards and fields would soon be barren, with nothing left for him to scavenge. The creatures with whom he shared the pine forests grew plump in preparation for the long winter, while he himself grew leaner and more discouraged.

Then disaster struck, when a party of hunters discovered his campsite. Josan had grabbed what he could and fled deeper into the woods, pursued by angry shouts.

He did not know what had led the men to his camp. Had they been hunters who simply stumbled across him? Or had they sought him on purpose? He knew he had stayed in that place for too long, but the village had been large enough that he thought no one would notice the disappearance of an occasional chicken, and the common granary had neither lock nor guard dog.

Still he had not been completely lost to caution. He had thought his campsite far enough away in the woods that no one would find him. He had been wrong.

And now he was worse off than ever. He had lost not

just his campsite, but also his blanket and food. Even his
tinder and flint had been left behind. In his haste he had
grabbed the sack that contained his spare clothes, and his
writing case. He could not have chosen more poorly if he
had deliberated for hours.

He was a monk. A scholar. He could speak seven languages flawlessly and make himself understood in a dozen
more. The ancient picture writings of the first Ikarians
were as clear to him as plain script, and he comprehended
the mathematical mysteries that underpinned the work
of the great builders and governed the movements of the
stars. He could plot a course across the great sea, and recite the epic tale of Zakar and Ata without a single prompt.

What he could not do was light a fire. He brought his
hands to his mouth, blowing on them softly to warm them
up, as he stared balefully at the contraption he had crafted.
It was not elaborate, merely two pieces of wood. In the
longer piece of wood, he had used a sharp stone to scrape
a furrow, exposing the soft inner wood. Along this furrow
he had placed shredded strips of bark. The second piece
was a sharpened stick, wrapped with string fashioned
from the torn hem of his cloak.

According to the writings of Brother Telamon, the
primitive natives of Abydos routinely used such a device to
start a fire. The sharpened stick was placed point first into
the trench, then rapidly spun until the heat from the rub-
bing created a spark. The monk had described the process
in great detail, but he must have left something out. Perhaps the trees in Abydos were harder than the soft pine he
had to work with. Or perhaps there was a secret step that
the natives had not shared with their visitor.

His failure was not from lack of trying. Indeed, his hands
were rubbed raw and cramping, with nothing to show for
his efforts. Beside him lay the trout he had caught earlier,
its glassy eye seeming to mock him. Josan's belly grumbled

with hunger, but he was not yet willing to concede defeat. He would try once more, then he would eat the fish raw. At least he still had the dagger, so he could clean the fish. Though that was a task that required daylight or firelight, and he was rapidly running out of the first.

Flexing his fingers one last time, Josan knelt on one end of the length of wood, to hold it in place. Grasping the sharpened stick with both hands, he began turning it back and forth, as fast he could make his hands move. "Come now," he told himself. "This time it will work."

But no faint wisp of smoke appeared. He concentrated even harder, putting all of his energy into twirling the stick, but it jumped out of his hands, skittering along the base until he jabbed himself in the thigh.

He cursed, giving vent to the anger and frustration of these weeks. The pain in his leg was just the latest indignity. Angrily he jerked the stick free, ignoring the blood that welled up from the puncture. With his right hand he felt the grooved trench. It was warm, but it would need to be many times hotter to start a fire.

"All I want is a hot meal. Is that too much to ask?"

Josan picked up the wood and threw it. It tumbled through the air into the growing darkness.

When it struck the ground, it burst into flame.

Later that night, his belly full of hot food for the first time in a fortnight, Josan allowed himself to ponder the events of that afternoon. Was it possible that the barbarian technique had succeeded in creating a faint spark, which was then fanned to life when he flung the wood across the clearing? But he had examined the wood and knew there was neither heat nor smoldering spark. Thus his first hypothesis had to be discarded.

Which brought him to the next question. How could

someone spontaneously create fire? Magicians regularly impressed the naïve with their ability to call fire at their command, but Josan knew their tricks were based upon a mixture of antagonist elements, which when combined in their powdered forms produced sudden intense flames. Any street magician could have produced a similar effect, but only if he possessed the ingredients of his trade, which Josan clearly did not.

Which left him with a third alternative. That somehow he possessed the talent for fire-starting—one of the hallmarks of the Old Magic, possessed by the ancient rulers of Ikaria. Legends said that the gift had been passed down to their descendants, but it had been two hundred years since a ruler of Ikaria had publicly demonstrated such talents. And their line had died out with the ill-fated Prince Lucius.

Plus, even considering the possibility that he had somehow performed magic offended his logical mind. If he had such a talent, shouldn't there have been signs before? Josan was nearly thirty; surely there would have been some sign if he possessed this latent power. He had made no study of magic, nor of the sorcerous arts, and knew nothing about how to invoke such power. And if it had been need that unlocked his talent, why now? He had been cold and hungry before.

Though he had never been as angry as he had been when he threw the stick. Such rage was foreign to his nature, and yet in that moment he had been filled with all-consuming anger, ready to lash out at anyone and anything. It was as if a stranger had taken control of him, and he was uncomfortably reminded of how he had felt during his fight with the assassin.

A stranger who possessed talents Josan might well need to stay alive. He could bank the fire to keep it burning as long as he stayed here. And when he was ready to leave, he could bring a hot coal, carefully wrapped so he could use its embers to start a new fire. But in time such a trick would fail him, and once again he would be faced with the challenge of trying to start a fire.

And then what would he do? He did not know how he had performed the trick once, so how could he hope to repeat it? What if rage was the only way to unlock this power? Did he truly want to drive himself into such a state of passion? What kind of man would deliberately give himself over to mindless anger?

He was already greatly changed since his days of scholarship at the collegium. How much more could he change before he no longer recognized himself? If he was not a scholar, then what was he? A criminal, as so many believed? A fugitive, with no ties to any person or any place?

Despite the warmth of the fire he shivered, drawing his cloak tightly around himself. His thoughts chased themselves in endless circles. He had too many hypotheses, but no facts to test them against. All of his life he had been taught that fear was no match for the power of reason. But the precepts that had seemed so clear in the marble learning halls of the collegium now seemed mere platitudes, suitable for a sheltered monk but not for a friendless man far from civilization—a man who feared the secrets that lay within him and had no one to give him counsel.

It took him a long time to fall asleep that night, and when he did his dreams were filled with violence, and the jumbled images of a city burning around him.

Josan stayed at his new campsite for two days, carefully tending the fire. Foraging yielded handfuls of wizened berries that the birds had somehow overlooked, and an afternoon's patience earned him another trout. But he could not stay indefinitely. Even if he fashioned himself a shelter out of pine boughs, he lacked both the tools and the

knowledge to hunt for game, and the late season's glean-
ings would only sustain him so long.

Carefully he considered his options. Fear of discovery
had driven him deep within the pine woods, where the only
tracks to be found were game trails. But survival meant
food and shelter, and to find both he would have to return
to the places where people dwelled. Carefully he ran one
hand through his hair. It was still short, but in another
month, or two at the most, it would reach a length not un-
common for that of southern laborers, who kept their hair
cropped because of the summer's heat.

As he packed his few remaining possessions, he considered the question of why a southern laborer would be
found in the northernmost fringes of the empire. Perhaps
he had left for the south in his youth and now returned to
claim his inheritance?

He gave a grim laugh. In a twisted way he had come
into his inheritance, though it was certainly one he had
never thought to claim. For the first time in years, he wondered about the person who had left a screaming baby on
the steps of the collegium, with no clue to his birth other
than the customary sack of golden coins. Had his father
been a nobleman whose revered ancestors once shared a
tie with the former rulers of Ikaria? Or was he descended
of a bastard line, kept hidden for fear of attracting Emperor
Aitor's wrath?

He had not forgotten the lizard tattoo that the assassin
had borne. It might have been the seal of the former imperial house, or it could be the sign of a secret society.
Lizards—with their talent for changing their appearance
and regrowing lost limbs—had long been associated with
magic. Had the assassin known of Josan's hidden talents?
And if so, why had he tried to kill Josan rather than recruit
him to his cause?

Unless, of course, Josan was already known to him, his fate sealed by deeds that he could not remember.

Whatever secrets the assassin had known, was it possible that Brother Nikos knew them as well? Was this the reason that he had refused to let Josan return to Karystos? Were his old teachers in league with his enemies, consciously keeping him in ignorance? Or was his long isolation playing tricks with his mind, making him see conspiracies and plots where there were none?

If answers there were, they would not be found among the whispering trees. Carefully he scooped up a coal from the embers and packed it in his clay cup. He had already prepared a handful of wood chips to use to feed the fire during the day's journey.

With a glance at the sun to mark his position, he began making his way south. His wanderings had taken him far from the main imperial road, but within two days he came across a narrow mud track where boot prints mingled with the occasional hoofprint. He followed that track to a small village, barely more than a cluster of a dozen houses. He was greeted with suspicion, as befit an unkempt stranger who had emerged from the woods. But rumors of a murderer posing as a monk had not reached these people, and for that he gave thanks.

The chill air proved his salvation, for fearing a frost that night the villagers were harvesting the last of the yellow gourds, making haste to bring them in from the fields before frost could kill them. Grudgingly they allowed Josan to help, in return for a hot meal of barley soup and the opportunity to sleep in a byre surrounded by a half dozen fragrant goats. The widow who offered him this hospitality seemed to expect him to refuse, but exhaustion won out over pride. And indeed the goats proved fine companions; for the first time in weeks his sleep was not troubled by nightmares.

He woke the next morning to aching arms and back, and a rime of white frost on the ground. The frost disappeared with the first rays of the sun, but it was an ominous reminder that winter was growing closer.

The widow gave him a bowl of groats, standing over him as he ate lest he abscond with her precious bowl. Then, firmly, he was advised to leave and not return.

Following her directions, he continued along the track that led from the village, taking the easterly fork when the road branched. He spent a night in the woods, then the next day he reached another village. The folk there were even more suspicious, and he was not permitted to drink at the common well. Still, they raised no hand to him and were content to let him pass through.

After he left the village it began to rain, a cold and miserable torrent that soon soaked through his cloak. At first, the wet leather of his sandals chafed his feet, then his feet became numb from the cold. Even the trees provided no shelter from the rain-driven wind and so with his head bent, he kept walking, even as the track under his feet disintegrated into a muddy swamp.

At last, when the clinging mud threatened to tear the sandals off his feet, he was forced to concede defeat. He found a pine tree larger than the rest and sat down with his back against its trunk, the hood of his cloak drawn over his head to shelter his face from the rain. A check of his clay cup revealed that water had seeped through the holes in the makeshift lid, extinguishing the embers within.

He felt oddly calm at this discovery. It had been bound to happen sooner or later. As sunset approached, the wind died down, and the rain lessened in intensity. Josan rose and foraged for the driest branches he could find, though there was no truly dry wood, merely a choice between damp wood and waterlogged branches.

He stacked the small branches in a neat pyramid, with

the dry kindling from his pack in the center. It was time to find out if the events of that night had been a fluke or if he really did possess the old power. He stretched both hands out over the wood, as if he were a street conjurer. With all the mental discipline at his command he focused his will.

"Light, I command you."

Nothing happened.

He tried again. "Fire, I summon you forth," he said, feeling foolish.

This, too, did not work. He banished from his mind the absurdity of what he was doing and tried to focus his thoughts on the belief that he would succeed. He had done this before; he could do it again. But even bending all his will to the belief that he could call fire from within the depths of the wood brought no results.

At last, reaching deep inside himself, he summoned anger.

Dancing flames filled his vision and his thoughts. His gaze locked on the fire before him, there was no room in his mind for anything else. Lost in admiration of its beauty, uncounted time passed, until the crackling of a resin-filled branch startled him out of his reverie.

The scene that met his eyes was so strange, he was convinced that he must still be dreaming. Frantically, he shook his head, then rubbed his eyes with the palms of his hands. But when he opened his eyes again, there was no change. He was still in this wooded place, with only trees for company and a dying fire to protect against the night's chill.

This was not the first dream that he had had. There had been others, filled with jumbled images of foreign places and the faces of strangers. But this dream seemed more real than the ones before. He could feel the warmth of the fire on his feet and the damp ground underneath him. He was cold, and his belly ached with hunger. He could smell the stench of the rags that he wore and feel the soreness of his legs. Even his skin itched, as if he had gone days without bathing.

What had happened to him? His last clear memories were of being in the collegium with Brother Nikos.

Was this some strange form of the afterlife? He had been prepared for death, after all. What if these dreams were a test? A series of challenges that he must pass through, in order to prove himself worthy of returning to his rightful station? It made sense, in a way. He could hardly imagine sinking any lower than he was already. But why would the gods do this? Surely they knew him well enough to judge him. And there was nothing of value that he would learn from living as a peasant.

Or perhaps this was a drug-hazed dream. Was his body still safely in Karystos even as his mind wandered in this wilderness? Or was this his first true awakening, his past dreams not mere dreams, but rather memories of the life he now led?

He shivered as he remembered his nurse's tales of the demon-haunted—men whose souls were possessed by great evil. It had been easy to scorn such tales in familiar surroundings, when abundant lamplight banished all specters. Now he wondered if there had been some truth in her stories.

Did it matter? Whether waking dream or hellish test, he would prevail. If this was a dream, he would force himself to stay in control until he truly awoke. He would not let himself be sucked back down into unknowingness. Even now he felt the echo of terror within him, and he imagined it was the demon fighting to break free.

If it was a test, then he would prove himself worthy of returning to the world he had left behind. It would be a simple enough thing to do, as long as he did not succumb to the madness within him.

And if this by some chance was part of some bizarre plot to destroy him, then he would find those who had betrayed him and see that they paid for their sins.

But if he was to stay awake, he needed food. He searched the leather sack that lay beside him, finding only a well-wrapped dagger and a handful of dirt. He nearly threw the dirt away, but on impulse brought his hand to his face as he caught the faint scent of dried oats. Any horse would have curled his lip at such fodder, but he forced himself to chew the mouthful, then washed it down with the last of the water from the skin tied to his belt.

Carefully he looked around, but clouds shrouded the moon, so he could see no farther than his small campsite. There must be a road nearby, but he would have to wait until morning to find it.

A road would lead to people, and where there were people there would be food. He had no coins, but he had a weapon of sorts, and he could take what he needed. And then he would set about finding his answers. For the moment he gathered tree branches for the fire. Tending it would keep him warm and his mind focused. He knew that he could not afford to fall asleep. This might be his only chance to free himself, and he would not waste it.

Josan started as sizzling fat dripped from the roasting chicken into the fire, then blinked in confusion. It was possible that he had summoned fire, but there was no magic that could create a roasting chicken out of empty air.

His unease grew as he realized that there were no trees nearby. Instead he was in a grassy meadow, a ring of beaten earth showing that other travelers had used the spot. But how had he gotten there? The last thing he remembered was a wretched day spent traveling through the rain and mud. He remembered making camp for the night, when he could no longer go on.

And he remembered trying to summon the old magic. Failing again and again, then at last reluctantly trying to summon anger. After that, there was nothing.

It was as if he had been asleep, but clearly he had not been. He had journeyed, and by the feel of his hands he had spent a day or more laboring. Was the chicken burning on the spit the fruits of his labors or of his newfound skill at thievery?

His belly knotted with sickness as he wondered how long he had journeyed unaware. Had it been one day? Or two? Or even longer? Where was he? What had he done? What strange spirit had possessed his body?

The chicken blackened and scorched unheeded as horror washed through him. What madness was this that had taken possession of his soul? He had blamed the breakbone fever for his shattered memories, but what if his illness was not the cause? What if this was not the first time that madness had seized him in his grip?

Everything that he knew to be true about himself was being stripped from him, one piece at a time.

He had started this journey seeking answers, believing that it was better to know the truth regardless of the cost. Now he was no longer certain that he wanted to find answers to his questions. Perhaps the monks were wrong. Perhaps there were things that were best left unknown.

And there was another grim possibility. What if he already knew the truth, and it had broken his mind? The part of him that commanded fire, and had ruled his body for the past days, perhaps that was his true self. Crushed by the weight of some terrible knowledge, he had taken refuge in unknowing. These hours were the illusion, this self the delusion, while his true self slept, protected from the consequences of his deeds.

If that was true, then finding the answers would surely destroy him.

Chapter 9

Holding her headstall with his left hand, Myles risked stroking the mare's nose with his right. "Easy girl," he said.

The mare flared her nostrils and danced a few steps sideways, making it plain she was in no mood for his clumsy reassurances. Cart horses he could handle, and a stout stick was all it took to make a balky mule see sense. But this mare was no ordinary horse. Bred to carry imperial messengers, her bloodline was far more distinguished than his own, and she demanded the respect due to her breeding, just as if she were a noble lady.

Myles tugged the headstall again, trying to get her to walk. Her flanks were dappled with drying sweat, and she needed to be walked to cool off, then carefully rubbed down. Not that her rider had shown any interest in her condition. He had simply dismounted and tossed her reins in Myles's direction, confident that they would be caught. His imperial tabard meant that the rider was above such petty concerns as the care of his horse, and indeed once he had dined he would expect to find a new mount saddled, waiting to take him on the next leg of his journey.

"Excuse me," a voice interrupted his thoughts.

Myles looked up and saw a man standing at the entrance to the stableyard. He was tall and whipcord-thin, a tattered cloak hung loosely on his frame, and his unkempt beard spoke of weeks of rough living.

"Excuse me," the man repeated. "Do you have any chores I can do in return for a meal? I am willing to do anything."

Myles was not used to such politeness in a beggar. And indeed he could use help. The previous stable owner had employed two stable hands, but both had refused to work for Myles, and as of yet he had found no replacements. Most days he was able to do the work himself, but at times like this he felt the lack. One man could not take care of a hard-driven mount and simultaneously saddle another so that the messenger could leave without delay.

But unskilled help was worse than none at all, and he allowed his frustration to color his voice as he replied. "I have no time for idlers. Come back tomorrow, and I'll see."

He tugged the headstall sharply, which was a mistake as it twisted out of his grasp, and the mare sidled away.

The stranger approached. "Here, girl, he's only trying to help," he said.

The mare watched, her ears pricked forward, as the stranger walked toward her. He kept talking softly, a constant stream of reassurances, until he reached her and caught her headstall. "There, now, you've done well. You know you need to walk first, then we'll feed you and let you rest."

Myles watched with amazement and a trace of envy, for when the stranger tugged her headstall, the mare began to walk.

"She needs to be walked, yes?"

"Yes," he replied. "A half hour, then bring her to me to be unsaddled, and I'll show you which stall to put her in."

Myles kept one eye on the stranger as he went into the stables. There were two post-horses stabled within, as specified in his contract. The roan gelding had not been used in a fortnight, so he let the gelding out of his stall and tied him to the fence rail as he began the elaborate process of tacking him up.

Each post-horse had its own saddle, custom-fitted to the contours of the horse's back. Unlike an ordinary saddle with its single girth, a post rider's saddle had three girths, plus a breastplate. In many ways it was similar to a war saddle, although much lighter in weight, for it did not need to serve as armor.

Before the half hour was up, the post rider had returned. He checked the roan's tack himself, grunting in approval when it proved to his satisfaction. Then he vaulted into the saddle and rode off without offering thanks or even a backward glance.

When the stranger judged the mare had cooled off, he tied her to the same post that Myles had used. Then, without a word, he began to unsaddle her. Myles watched, eyebrows raised, but there was no fumbling, and not a single wasted motion. He shrugged his shoulders, then went into the stable and emerged with cloth rags and a brush. He handed those to his newfound helper and accepted the tack in return. After she had been wiped down, and the grime of the road brushed off her, the mare was led into an empty stall, where water and grain were waiting.

"If you like, I could clean the tack," the stranger offered.

He turned to face him, and for the first time Myles had a good view of his face.

Myles drew in a sharp breath. Prolonged hunger had pared the man down till his features were mere skin stretched across bone, but he knew that no peasant had sired those sharp cheekbones, nor the piercing blue of his gaze. Even if his accent had not given him away as a stranger, his face surely would have.

He had never expected to see one of the old blood again—far less to find one standing as beggar in his yard.

"What did you say your name was?"

"Josan."

He waited, but no more details were forthcoming.

"I am Myles, a former soldier lately turned stable owner," he said. "You know your way around horses."

Josan, as he called himself, merely shrugged. "So it seems."

Despite his obvious need there was still some pride left in him, for Josan did not beg. He merely waited, motionless, while Myles made his decision.

"You'll find what you need to clean the tack by the racks at the far end," he said, indicating the direction with a jerk of his chin. "Then shovel out the first stall and get it ready for the next horse. Do that, then come find me, and we'll see about getting you a meal and a place to sleep for the night. Agreed?"

Josan nodded. "Yes. Thank you."

"Don't thank me until you've seen what you earned. You may not like the bargain you've made," Myles said, in a rare moment of honesty. Josan might not know what he was worth, but Myles did, and he had every intention of getting full value out of the prize that had just fallen into his lap.

Myles retired to the small room at the front of the stables that served as his office. He took down the logbook and added two entries, one to show the newly arrived mare and another to record the number of the imperial messenger who had taken the roan gelding and the direction in which he traveled. Stabling the post-horses provided a generous monthly stipend, but he would lose that stipend if his records could not withstand the scrutiny of an imperial auditor. Then, listening to the unfamiliar sounds of another at work in his stable, he laboriously began to pore over his accounts. Reckoning numbers did not come naturally to him, so he added each sum twice as he calculated the amount of grain he had used thus far, and determined that he had just enough to last the winter if he was careful.

When Josan announced that he was finished, Myles inspected his work. The mare's tack gleamed, the leather carefully oiled and the metal polished until it could have passed inspection by the strictest sergeant in the imperial guard.

"The edges of the saddle blanket are beginning to fray, see?" Josan said, indicating where several stitches in a row had come loose. A half dozen stitches in a row of two hundred, only the most eagle-eyed would have noticed the flaw.

Myles stared at him, wondering if Josan was somehow mocking him, or if he was indeed so desperate for work that he would do anything to impress a potential master. But he stood his scrutiny without comment, neither unnerved nor defensive.

"You sew?" he asked.

"No."

"Neither do I." Myles could stitch up a wound, but his rough technique would hardly serve here. Perhaps Carmela would be able to help. A servingwoman at the inn across the road, she could sometimes be persuaded to lend a hand, eager to earn a few coppers that her master knew nothing about.

With one last check on the mare, who was resting quietly in her stall, Myles barred the stable doors, then led the way down the street to the tavern where he took his meals. He paused for a moment on the threshold, eyes blinking as they accustomed themselves to the dark interior. A dozen tables were crowded into the small room, and a long counter served to separate the diners from the cooking area. Smoke hung in the air, and he sniffed appreciatively.

As it was just before sunset, there were only two other diners present. Myles nodded cordially to them, knowing better than to expect a response as he led the way to a table in the rear corner. Tucked up near the fire bed, it was the warmest spot in the tavern, except for that of the cook laboring over the grill.

The owner's son Guilio came over, bearing a dish of black olives and a plate of bread. "It's fish tonight," he said, in a tone of supreme disinterest.

The menu at the tavern varied by what was cheap in the marketplace and the mood of the cook. When Guiliano had been fighting with his wife, his customers had eaten savory barley for a week. Tonight it appeared that domestic tranquility once more reigned.

"Fish for two. And wine, with two cups."

"Yellow or the red?"

"Yellow," Myles decided. "And a pitcher of water to mix it with."

That got Guilio's attention, and his eyes flicked to Josan, then back again before nodding.

In a few moments the boy returned, with two wine cups, and two pitchers, one of yellow wine and one of water. Mindful of his guest's privation, Myles liberally mixed the water into the wine before serving them both.

They ate the olives and the bread, Myles being careful to eat enough so it was not obvious that he was giving his guest the larger share. By the time these were done, Guilio returned and set in front of each of them a wooden platter containing smoked fish wrapped in vine leaves, accompanied by seasoned broad beans.

Josan's manners were impeccable, cutting the fish into neat bites rather than devouring the meal with a few gulps as a beggar might. Still he cleared his platter before Myles had barely begun.

"More?"

Josan shook his head regretfully. "No, but thank you." Only then did he begin to drink his wine, toying idly with the cup as Myles ate his dinner in a far more leisurely fashion than his guest.

Guilio gave every appearance of disdaining his father's customers, but as soon as Myles set down his fork, he reappeared, taking away their platters and replacing them with two small bowls of honeyed quinces. Guiliano must be feeling very good indeed, since normally his guests made do with mere figs or sweetened cakes if the cook was in a generous mood.

Despite his earlier protests, Josan managed to eat his share of the treat. Around them the tables had filled with other bachelors like Myles, and servants enjoying a rare evening off. He wondered if Josan noticed that no one greeted him, nor indeed approached their table.

He waited to see if the wine would loosen Josan's tongue, but his guest seemed content to eat in silence.

"You did a good job today," Myles said, at last, when it became clear that Josan would not speak on his own.

"I know a bit about horses," Josan said.

"I could use a man who knows a bit about horses," he said.

Josan leaned back in his chair. "Why? What happened to your last helper?"

There spoke the confidence that came from having a full belly. This afternoon Josan had begged to be allowed to perform any task. Now he was asking questions, as if he could truly afford to turn down this opportunity. It showed a resilience of spirit and a sharp mind—both qualities Myles admired.

"I haven't been able to hire help. You may have seen that I am not the most popular of men in this town."

"I had noticed."

"It is none of my doing," he hastened to explain. "When the former owner died, his nephew Florek expected to inherit the business. He was furious when he realized that his uncle had sold the business to me just a few weeks before his death. My ownership is unquestionable, but Florek is a popular man in this town, and a powerful one. The former stable hands refused to work for me, and I have had no luck in finding replacements."

"Wouldn't Florek have inherited the money from the sale of the stable? Surely that would have appeased his temper."

"It would have, if he had found it. But his uncle had a comely young servingwoman ... who left town the day he died."

No doubt if the servant woman was ever found, she would claim that the money had been a gift to her, and indeed it might well have been. Not that she had any hope of convincing the aggrieved nephew or his friend the magistrate of her tale. She had shown uncommonly good sense in taking to the road so swiftly.

"What would you have me do?" Josan asked.

"Tend the horses, shovel the stalls, ensure that the post riders' mounts are taken care of. Can you ride?"

Josan hesitated a moment, then nodded.

"I'll have to see you up on a horse, but if you're any good, you can exercise the post-horses. I take my noon and evening meals here, and you will do so as well. There's a partitioned corner of the hayloft where the last hands slept, and you can have that. I'll pay your meals here, and"—he hesitated, not wanting to give away too much, but knowing that he could not afford to let Josan walk away—"I'll give you a week's trial. If you work out, it will be five coppers a week for you."

Josan drank down the last of his wine. Myles wondered if he should raise his offer to six coppers, or if that would tip his hand.

"A week's trial," Josan said. "And if we both agree, I'll stay till spring. I cannot promise any more."

"Agreed," Myles said.

Josan's shoulder muscles ached as he pushed the muck-laden barrow to the alley behind the stables. When he reached his destination, a fragrant barrel surrounded by buzzing flies, he stopped. Picking up the shovel that rested on the top of the barrow, he unloaded the manure into the barrel, doing his best to breathe shallowly to avoid the stench. Fortunately, it was not allowed to rot for long, for every third day the dung collector came by to collect the full barrel and replace it with an empty one.

Such an arrangement would not have been necessary in a village or even a small town, where a stable would have land enough for a dung heap. But Utika was large enough that space was at a premium. There was barely room for the stable and the small exercise paddock. Dung heaps were the domain of the farmers who lived on the outskirts of the town.

Given a choice, he would not have ventured into Utika. Not only was it a large town, nearly the size of a city, but it was also on the main imperial road that connected this province with its neighbors. Official messengers passed through with regularity, and if there were news of a renegade monk being sought for murder, then surely the inhabitants of Utika would know of it.

But hunger was a far crueler master than mere logic, and it had been hunger that had driven him to venture into the place. He had not planned on staying longer than the time it took to earn a meal, but fate had intervened. And so far it seemed that his fears had been groundless. Many looked on him with suspicion, but it was his association with the outsider Myles that drew their ire rather than any rumored misdeeds of his own.

When the barrow was empty he placed the shovel inside it and wheeled it back to the front of the barn, putting it in its accustomed spot under the overhanging roof, where it was protected from the rain. Returning the shovel to its hook beside the door, he turned as he heard footsteps.

For the past six days Myles had watched him like a hawk, as befit a man who had entrusted valuable horses to a stranger. Today was the first time that Myles had left Josan alone with his charges, and he wondered if this was an omen for good or for ill.

He held himself still, his features deliberately calm. No matter what happened, he was far stronger than he had been a mere week ago. Regular meals had filled his belly, and uninterrupted sleep had banished the dull exhaustion that had haunted him for so long.

He would leave if he must, but he wanted to stay. True, there were no answers to be found here, but there was food, shelter, and the opportunity to earn honest coin. He was still not certain if he dared return to Karystos, but there were other cities, and other libraries that might hold the answers that he sought. They would not open their doors to a beggar, but a wandering scholar with coins in his purse was another matter.

"It's been seven days," Myles said.

He nodded.

Myles waited, apparently waiting for him to speak, but there was nothing for Josan to say. He knew enough to know that Myles had already made up his mind, and whatever his decision, Josan would not demean himself by begging.

One corner of Myles's mouth twisted in what might have been a smile. Reaching his right hand into the pocket of his cloak, he pulled out a small leather sack and tossed it toward Josan, who plucked it out of the air.

"Five coppers, as I promised," he said. "You'll stay then?"

"Until spring," Josan replied, only then aware that he had been holding his breath.

Myles's gaze swept over him, lingering for a moment on the borrowed boots that Josan wore to keep his feet clean from the filth that inevitably accompanied a stable.

"The bootmaker Salvo has his shop at the corner of the third alley, just past the green fountain. When you're done here, go see him. He's expecting you."

"But—" Josan began. Five coppers would not cover the cost of new boots, or even remade ones. Ten coppers would not be enough.

"You can barely walk in those," Myles pointed out.

Josan's boots had belonged to the former owner of the stables. Made for a man with feet both longer and far broader than his own, he had stuffed them with rags to keep his feet from sliding around. Still, even as ill fitting as they were, they served him better than his tattered sandals.

"I will deduct the cost from your future wages," Myles said.

"Agreed."

Though Josan wondered if Myles would indeed remember to deduct the cost of the boots from his wages, or if this was simply a ruse to cover his charity.

He had known Myles for a week, but for all Myles's seeming openness, he could still not puzzle him out. Indeed, within the first day of their acquaintance, Myles had told Josan the story of his life. The youngest of six sons, he had chafed at the lot of a farmer's son, and when barely more than a boy had run away, eventually winding up in Karystos, the imperial capital.

There his choices had been simple. A boy with neither trade nor family could choose between a life of petty crime or prostitution, or he could enlist in the imperial army, which in those days had been hungry for recruits to fight in the endless campaigns against Vidrun. Myles had chosen the army, rising through the ranks to sergeant. After twenty years he had taken his pension and retired, using his carefully hoarded wages to buy the stable, sight unseen.

It was not done for a master to confide in a servant in this way. Nor was it seemly that the two should eat their meals together, as if they were equals. Josan had never played the part of servant before, but he knew the protocols as well as any. You did not try to make a friend out of one who was scarcely better than a slave.

But it was hard not to feel a bit sorry for Myles, who clearly had no one else to turn to. Florek, the late stable owner's nephew, not only owned the large inn that stood immediately across the street from the stableyard, he also owned a smaller inn on the opposite side of town, and three taverns. By the standards of Utika he was a wealthy man indeed, and he was not used to having his will crossed. Especially not by a foreigner, one who had neither ties of blood nor birth to this province.

Without Florek to stir their anger, the others in Utika might well have come to accept the newcomer in their midst, for Myles was a likable enough man, and from what Josan had seen so far, he was scrupulously honest in his dealings with others.

But until Myles found a way to win Florek over, or his enemy found a new target for his wrath, it was unlikely that any would choose to befriend Myles and thus risk inciting the anger of one who held the ear of the local magistrate.

Not for the first time, he wondered why Myles did not simply sell the stable to his rival and settle somewhere else. Perhaps one day he would ask. But for now Josan was careful to ask no questions of Myles, so that he would not be obliged to answer any of Myles's questions in return.

The small pouch containing the five coppers was fastened to the inside of his tunic, ensuring that if he had to flee he would not do so penniless. He took himself off to the bootmaker, who traced his feet, then bade him come back in three days. He did so, and found himself the owner of a pair of plain but serviceable boots, and he gladly set aside the ill-fitting pair he had borrowed.

On the day he took possession of his new boots, Myles instructed him to saddle the post rider's mare and bring her to the paddock. The intricacies of the tack posed no challenge to him, and he hoped that this boded well for the other skill he had claimed. In his travels, Josan had ridden on horseback on a few occasions, but always in the company of a guide who had ensured that the monk was given a placid beast well used to the antics of a novice rider.

When Myles had asked him if he rode, it had been on the tip of his tongue to say no. But some strange instinct had prompted him to say yes. The same instinct, he supposed, that had told him he could handle a highbred horse. Where he had gained these skills was a question he did not wish to examine too closely. Like his unexpected talent for combat, it was something he could not remember learning. And yet, this skill too, had saved his life. Myles would never have offered employment to a scholar who did not know one end of a horse from another.

He was aware that such deliberate blindness was a form of cowardice, but he brushed aside that thought as he had done many times before. The precepts that had governed

THE FIRST BETRAYAL 137

his life as a scholar had taken on less and less meaning as he was forced to battle for survival.

Josan led the mare to the paddock and at Myles's command swung himself up into the saddle with ease. Banishing from his mind the memory of his last jouncing, awkward ride, he guided the mare around the paddock at a slow walk, then at a trot, using only the pressure of his knees as he guided her in a circle, first one way, then the other. The mare was restless, having spent the last three days in the stable because of the autumn rains. He could feel her impatience to run, but he controlled her with ease.

After several circuits, Myles called a halt.

"You'll do. Take her out through the south gate, and you can give her a run in the campground. The dirt there is hard-packed, but keep an eye out for holes left by tent pegs and the like. An hour, no more, then cool her down before bringing her back, understood?"

"Understood," Josan said, offering a half salute, as if he were a novice soldier.

For the convenience of travelers arriving from the southern province, the stables were located close to the gate, as was Florek's inn. Once the two had been owned by the same man, since most travelers at the inn arrived by horseback or in carriages. Those who arrived on foot stayed at the cheaper lodgings outside the town proper. When the owner had died he had split his properties between his two sons, but at least they were still owned by the same family. Now Florek was reminded of his lost inheritance every day as the guests at his inn were forced to patronize his enemy across the street in order to provide stabling for their horses and shelter for their carriages. Florek had been heard to speak of building his own stables, but that would require buying and demolishing one of his neighbor's properties, and so far he had found no takers.

If Josan were in his place, he would have tried to win

over his rival and convert Myles from rival into business partner. Florek had a daughter, after all, of the right age and as yet unmarried. She could do worse for herself than a man of property who had no other claims on his purse. And, if in a few years Myles were to fall victim to a mysterious ailment, few would question his death. Nor would they question the right of his widow to manage her children's inheritance. With the help of her father, of course.

Perhaps it was best for Myles that Florek lacked the cunning to implement such a plan. Or perhaps he had already tried and failed before Josan had arrived.

Such thoughts provided a diversion as he guided the mare through her paces. He exercised her lightly, enough to work up a sweat but not enough to hinder her if she should be needed within the day. There was a fresher mount back at the stables who would be the next to be taken, but Myles had warned him that sometimes two imperial riders passed through on the same day. It was rare, but not unheard of.

It crossed his mind that Myles had shown great faith in entrusting the horse to him. The mare was worth more than he could hope to earn in years of labor as a stable hand. But she was imperial property, and stealing her would set a price on his head—if there wasn't one already.

Besides, he was not a thief by nature. He had stolen only when he had to, when stealing meant the difference between life and death by starvation. He could not claim such necessity now.

Josan returned the mare to the stables when she was thoroughly cooled down, and groomed her carefully before returning her to her stall. If Myles was relieved by their return, he gave no sign, merely grunting when he caught sight of Josan refilling the hay bags in each stall.

His days fell into a rhythm. Up at dawn to exercise the post-horses if they had not been ridden in the last three days. Then the horses were fed and turned loose in the paddock if the weather was fine, while he mucked out their stalls. If guests had stabled their horses or carriage overnight, Myles would be there to ensure that all was ready when they wished to depart and that the guests paid their fees without quibbling.

Afternoons were for cleaning tack, restacking hay, shifting grain from the barrels in the storeroom into the bin in the stables, and whatever other task Myles could think up for him. Then at the end of the day the horses had to be fed and watered again before he joined Myles for dinner at the tavern. The city gates closed at dusk, but such rules did not apply to nobles or imperial messengers, and so Josan learned to sleep with one ear listening for the ringing of the bell that announced a late arrival.

Myles was a generous master, allowing Josan a free hour each afternoon if there was no pressing business at the stable. With his second week's wages Josan took himself to the market. There he bought tinder and flint to replace those he had lost. With his last coin he paid a barber to shave him and trim his hair.

His hair had grown long enough that it fell into his eyes and brushed the top of his shoulders. Strange sensations for a man who had shaved his skull since he was a boy; they had made him feel like a stranger in his own body. Now he felt more himself, as the barber held up a polished tin mirror so Josan could admire his work. His hair was shorter than most men wore it, but the even crop made it clear that this was a choice. But what startled him most about his reflection was not his hair, but rather his face. It was far more angular than he remembered, with grim lines around his mouth. Even his eyes had changed. They were a stranger's eyes—the eyes of a man who had killed an assassin and tamed a fractious horse with the touch of his hand.

"I only did as you asked," the barber said, apparently unnerved by Josan's long silence. No doubt he was expecting a complaint.

"You did fine," Josan assured him. Hastily, he handed over the copper and took his leave.

He shivered, but not from the cold. It was nothing, he assured himself. It had been years since he had seen his reflection in anything other than a pool of water, or the curved distortion of the lighthouse mirrors. It was no wonder that he did not recognize himself, after all he had been through in the last months.

Chapter 10

Empress Nerissa, Most Gracious Sovereign, Heir to the Wisdom of Aitor the Great, Defender of Ikaria, and Blessed Mother of Her People, stifled a yawn as the actor advanced to the front of the stage and began proclaiming Aitor's heroic virtues in flowery couplets. The rest of the cast picked up the mock weapons they had previously cast off and gathered around the actor in a half circle, once more standing at attention as their leader rallied them to their duty.

She eyed the actor critically. Couldn't they have found a taller man to play the role of her grandfather? As it was, the stilted boots that the actor wore frequently made him wobble as he walked, which was hardly in keeping with the dignity of her noble ancestor.

Nor had Aitor been given to poetry, or indeed to speech-making of any kind. The plot of this play, if indeed there were anything resembling a coherent plot, had long ago diverged from the events that she knew to be true. Still, if this scene was meant to portray the night before the battle at the Denavian Fords, then the playwright had taken substantial liberties with history. When faced with doubting commanders, her grandfather had told them, "Stand and fight, or I'll kill you myself for your cowardice."

There had been no poetry, no impassioned speechmaking. But in the end, there had been a hard-won victory, so at least Khepri had gotten that part of his wretched play right.

Her son Anthor had sworn that this play was tolerable. She would have to find a particularly creative way to punish him for his impertinence.

She signaled to the attendant, who drew the heavy drapes on either side of the imperial booth closed. Her view of the stage remained unobstructed, but the audience members could no longer see inside. If the performance had been on any other subject, she would have simply left the theater or sent a messenger to the theater manager to bring the performance to a hasty close. But she had come to show respect to her grandfather's memory, and for the sake of her lineage she would endure till the end.

"How much longer does this go on?"

"We are approaching the end of the first act," Brother Nikos said, with a glance at the stage. "There will be a brief period for refreshments, and for the slaves to change the stage decorations from battlefield to the imperial palace. Another hour, I would guess."

Brother Nikos had already seen the play at least once, but she had not thought to ask him his opinion on the work. Now she regretted the omission—though from the monk's face, it was impossible to tell if he were enjoying himself or not.

Not that he had come to see the play. He had come for the prospect of two hours alone in her company, with none to distract her save the ever-present servants and her personal bodyguards. As an advisor, his voice was generally one of many, so this was a rare sign of favor. He would have been equally pleased to watch stonemasons erecting a wall, or wheat growing in the fields, as long as it meant that he had her sole attention.

But she had not invited him because he was a skilled conversationalist, which he was. Nor because he was one of the few that she trusted to give unbiased advice, although that was also true. She had invited him because she had questions to ask, ones she did not want to raise in a more public setting.

Nerissa selected a sliver of orange fruit from the tray beside her couch and chewed it slowly, savoring the sweet taste with just a hint of bitterness underneath.

She reached for another slice of fruit, which allowed her to keep one eye on Nikos's face as she said, "I have heard the strangest tale from the north. Something about a monk run mad?"

Nikos gave up all pretense to indolence, sitting up straight on his couch. "I hope that you were not distressed by what you heard?"

"I was distressed that I had to hear this from others rather than from you."

He spread his hands wide in the gesture of contrition. "I wanted to confirm the facts for myself rather than bringing you mere rumors."

"Tell me what you know of this."

"You know that the patronage of our order requires us to send one of the brethren to tend the lighthouse on Txomin's island?"

She nodded, for that much she did indeed know.

"Five years ago, when the last keeper died, we sent a young monk to replace him. His wits had been damaged by the breakbone fever, but he still wanted to serve, and that simple task was well within his capabilities. Or so we thought."

"And now?"

Nikos shrugged. "And now he has vanished. One account says that thieves killed him when they broke into the lighthouse to steal the enchanted silver mirrors. Another story says that he grew mad in his isolation and murdered the laborer who brought his provisions, then fled when his crime was discovered."

So far, both tales agreed that murder had been done. The story her spies had brought said that the monk had been an impostor, a criminal who had taken the place of the true monk, then killed the man who had threatened to expose his deception. Which still begged the question of what had happened to the young monk that Nikos had sent to the remote outpost. And why would a criminal choose to hide there, of all places?

"What do you think happened?"

"I do not know. I sent two of the brethren to investigate. They wrote back that they could find no sign of Brother Josan, though the lighthouse was intact. The native villagers offered conflicting tales regarding what may have happened. The provincial magistrate had issued orders that all should be on watch for a man matching the description of the missing keeper, but so far there has been no sign of him."

She noted that he did not refer to the keeper as one of his monks. Perhaps because Nikos thought the man an impostor, or perhaps because he wanted to distance his order from the crimes of a killer.

"I want to be informed at once if you receive any news. Even if mere rumors, I need to know."

"Of course."

This was not about the fate of the missing monk, nor the likelihood that a murderer was loose in the northernmost province of her domain. As empress, she had far more important matters to worry about than a single criminal. This was about the Learned Brethren overstepping their authority. The lighthouse was an imperial post, and if its keeper had been murdered or turned rogue, she should have been informed at once.

Nikos had provided wise counsel in the past, but she needed to keep his ambitions in check, and the missing monk provided her the perfect excuse to remind him that he served at her pleasure. She did not want to find another to replace him, but she would do so if she could not bring him to heel.

"This monk, would he be the same one that Lady Ysobel of Alcina encountered when she was shipwrecked?"

"I believe so."

"Strange that she did not mention any signs of madness. She called him courteous, as I recall. You may wish to question her."

"I have already spoken to her. She was unable to shed any light on his behavior, though naturally I did not reveal to her the true reason for my concern."

"She might have been more helpful if you had told her the truth."

"I do not trust her, and I advise you to be wary in your dealings with her as well," Nikos said.

It was an old complaint. Ever since Lady Ysobel's arrival at court, Brother Nikos had been hinting that her post as trade liaison was a mere mask to cover treachery. Naturally Nerissa had assigned spies to keep watch upon her, as they watched all foreign officials. But so far Lady Ysobel had done nothing remarkable save indulge in a taste for the company of young men. And even in that, she was discreet in her indiscretions, keeping her liaisons to the privacy of a rented house rather than inviting them into her official residence in the embassy.

It was not surprising that Lady Ysobel made Brother Nikos uneasy. The brethren were a strictly male order, and they were never comfortable around women, particularly not one as young and beautiful as Lady Ysobel. Nor was any man raised in Ikaria accustomed to the idea of a woman who wielded power in her own right.

Nerissa knew this from her own experience, and the long years it had taken her to consolidate her power, turning herself from empress in name to empress in fact. Even then, she knew that she would never have been named empress if it had not been for the two sons she had borne, which meant that the next ruler would be a male descendant of Aitor the Great.

"It is no coincidence that Lady Ysobel was last here six years ago, at the time of the troubles," Nikos said.

"Hundreds of other foreigners were in Karystos at that time, and I do not hear you naming them as conspirators." Empress Nerissa took a sip of her wine as she considered the matter. "I am convinced that Lady Ysobel was sent here to thwart her own ambitions. She had risen too far, too quickly, and earned herself powerful enemies. Here she can do little but bide her time and hope that her faithful service is rewarded with a swift recall to the federation."

It was hard not to feel a little envious of Lady Ysobel, who enjoyed freedoms that Nerissa had never been allowed to experience. What little she knew of Ysobel she liked, seeing a distant reflection of her own intelligence and ambition. It was rare that she met another woman who did not feel the need to hide her intelligence behind the mask of a dutiful matron, and she made a mental note to invite Lady Ysobel to the palace. She would enjoy the opportunity for pleasant conversation, and the invitation would show Brother Nikos that she would not be swayed by his prejudices.

Ysobel was surprised when an imperial messenger brought an invitation for her to join the empress for an informal dinner. Informal did not mean that she could eschew her court garb, nor that the meal would be anything less than stately, with at least ten courses. Informal, in the parlance of the imperial court, meant that there would be no more than two dozen guests, and thus it was a rare mark of favor, especially for a foreigner.

She had seen the empress several times since her official presentation and had spoken with her twice. But this was the first time that Ysobel had been invited on her own, rather than in the company of Ambassador Hardouin. She wondered at the reasons behind the invitation. Was Empress Nerissa truly interested in conversing with a woman half her age, to learn the perspectives of a foreign land where the aspirations of women were held equal to those of men? Or was Ysobel's invitation merely the next move in the intricate games of the court? Perhaps it was not Ysobel being honored, but another being taught a lesson by her inclusion.

Or perhaps both were true, for there was no reason the empress could not satisfy her own curiosity even as she played the games of power, granting and withholding her favors at will.

Ysobel was confident in her ability to dissemble, but she was also pragmatic enough to be grateful that she did not need to put her skills to the test—there were no dark deeds that she needed to conceal while sharing bread and oil with a woman she planned to overthrow. After several months in Ikaria, she saw no reason to change her initial assessment. Resentment there was aplenty, but there was no one capable of harnessing that anger and leading a true revolt. Even Dama Akantha, for all her carefully hoarded rage, counseled patience.

Especially now. Only a fortnight past, a gang of youths had been caught painting the stylized lizard sigil of the former rulers of Ikaria on the walls of the imperial playhouse.

If they had intended to remind people that the spirit of the rebellion still lived, it would have been a well-chosen target, since the playhouse was hosting Khepri's fulsome epic. But she was convinced that the boys had intended no such thing. It was likely that they did not truly know the meaning of the symbol, only that it was forbidden. Defacing the playhouse was merely the antics of spoiled children who saw no further than their own petty rebellions against the strictures of their parents.

But neither their youth nor their heedless folly had been enough to protect them from the full weight of imperial justice. Empress Nerissa had swiftly condemned them to death. The executions had been set for a week hence, which had allowed Nerissa to appear to be merciful, for after the parents of the boys had abased themselves, she had commuted all but one of the sentences to exile. At fourteen, Kauldi had the misfortune of being the eldest of the gang, and his relatives were neither rich enough nor sufficiently well connected at the court to win him a reprieve. Though the empress had shown him a share of her mercy as well, ordering a swift and private execution rather than the prolonged agonies spelled out as the punishment for treason.

Ysobel had needed no reminder of the stakes she played for; nonetheless, she took Kauldi's death as a warning. The empress was taking no chances, and neither should she. In time, Kauldi's grieving family might well be approached and sounded out to see if they were still loyal to their empress. But for the moment, Ysobel would be seen hard at work in her duties as trade liaison, ensuring that her time in Karystos was not wasted. Profit would always find favor, even when scheming had failed.

Hard on the heels of the empress's invitation was a far more pleasant summons, as a young sailor brought word that a federation ship was newly arrived in port, and her captain wished to speak with the trade liaison at her earliest convenience. The boy had already crossed the city twice, having traveled first to the embassy before being directed to Ysobel's private residence, and so she took pity on him and sent him off to the kitchen for refreshments while she went upstairs to change from the silk robe suitable for receiving callers into a linen blouse, short-cropped trousers, and rope sandals that were suited to a shipboard visit.

Such casual attire would scandalize an Ikarian captain, but to one of the federation it was a sign of respect, showing that she, too, had spent her share of hours on the deck of a trading ship.

The boy, who had appeared somewhat startled when he saw her dressed in the Ikarian style, was visibly relieved when he caught sight of her transformed appearance. Hastily cramming a final piece of bread into his mouth, he leapt to his feet.

"If you please," he said. "Captain will blame me if he's kept waiting."

"And his name is?"

The boy shook his head. "He asked me not to say."

Curious, but she could think of several reasons why a captain might not want his name mentioned where others could hear. And the boy had been prompt enough with his own name, and that of his ship, the *Swift Gull*—though since she had never heard of the ship, the mere name told her nothing about its master's probable loyalties. Ysobel had not reached her position by taking foolish chances, so as they left her town house they were trailed by a pair of bodyguards. Just in case this was a clumsy trap.

A point in his favor was that the guards did not unnerve the boy, and despite his unfamiliarity with the city, he led her by a direct route to the central wharves, where a gig was waiting for them, tied up to the pier.

"That's the *Gull*, just past the scow with the orange sail."

He pointed toward the eastern mole, and there, just where the mole curved in to protect the merchant harbor, she saw an old-style galley whose lateen sail had faded over the years from the bright red of luck to a dull orange that spoke of long service with little reward. Just beyond the galley, she saw the bulk of a much larger ship, its four masts reaching to the sky.

One of the new ship designs, and even without an invitation she would not have been able to resist seeing it for herself. Swiftly she climbed down the ladder into the gig, and the others followed.

In the height of the trading season, far more ships came to Karystos than could be accommodated at her docks, and so the harbor was crowded with ships, of all sizes and nations, which had dropped anchor, awaiting their turn to off-load their cargo and take on new goods. Lighters took water and provisions to these waiting ships, and off-loaded cargo for those who could not afford to wait for their turn at one of the precious berths. Her respect for the mysterious captain grew as she observed how skillfully the gig's crew maneuvered around these obstacles, with only a few soft-spoken commands from the boy, who had taken the tiller.

In barely a quarter hour they had reached the *Swift Gull,* whose dark timbers, gleaming brasswork, and blindingly crisp white sails proclaimed that she was indeed newly from the shipyard. In time, weather, harsh seas, and the wear and tear that came from loading and unloading cargo in dozens of ports each year would take their toll on the ship, but for now she was perfection. Ysobel wanted this ship, craved her in the way that an Ikarian woman might crave a ruby necklace or a rope of rare black pearls.

As they pulled along the port side of the ship, a knotted

climbing line was thrown down to them. She recognized this at once as a test, for if she had been wearing a robe, she could not have climbed it and maintained her dignity.

Ysobel rose to her feet, careful to keep her balance as the gig swayed gently from side to side.

She turned to her escort. "Will you steady the rope, please?"

The boy caught and held the end of the rope, which was knotted at regular intervals. Reaching up with her right hand, she grasped the rope just above one of the knots, and as the boy pulled the rope taut, she put her left foot on the rope. Swiftly she scrambled up, clasping the rope between her feet to steady her. She grinned as she wondered what Empress Nerissa would make of the sight.

As she reached the top, a sun-browned hand reached over the railing, grasped her hand, and smoothly hauled her up and over the rail in a single motion.

She smiled as she saw her helper.

"Captain Zorion, this is an unexpected pleasure."

"Lady Ysobel."

He started to salute, as befit a ship's captain reporting to his employer, but Ysobel would have none of this, and she embraced him instead. For a moment it was as if she was a child, for he still towered over her as he had before, and he smelled of salt water, pine tar, and the faint scent of tea, which was most likely his cargo.

They waited as her bodyguards scrambled up the rope, far less gracefully than she had, then the cabin boy. Zorion dismissed the boy, and she bade her guards go with him so she could speak with her captain in private.

"What are you doing here? And where did you get this ship?"

"The ship is yours," he said, answering the most important question first.

"Mine?"

There had been plans for a fourth ship, and the shipbuilders had promised that they would lay the keel this fall and construction would be finished by the spring. But this did not explain how Zorion came into possession of a ship that was both larger than the one she had commissioned and ready nearly six months sooner.

"This ship was commissioned for Charlot, but when they could no longer pay for it, the shipbuilders stopped work with the ship half-built. No others wanted a ship of this size, but I knew you could turn a profit on it. I allowed the builders to persuade me to purchase the ship, and they finished it to my specifications."

It was big. She had commissioned another three-master, but this was a four-masted giant, at least a third longer in the keel than her others.

"You got a good bargain for us?"

"The best. Less than we had planned to spend, on account of our having to adapt Charlot's clearly inferior design."

"And does she live up to her name?"

"She's fast." Zorion grinned, the flash of bright white teeth startling against his dark skin. "Very fast."

"I want to see her. All of her."

"As you command," Zorion said. He bowed, with an extravagant flourish, inviting her to take the lead.

She spent two hours inspecting the ship, from the very top of her masts to the bottom of her holds, which were indeed tight-packed with bundles of tea leaves. The holds were large, in keeping with the size of the ship, with cunningly fashioned wooden barriers that could be taken down as needed to accommodate bulky cargoes. The rounded stern lent an odd shape to the aft compartments, but other than that she found little that she could quibble over.

Many of the crew were familiar to her, having served with Zorion on his last ship, and she greeted them with absent pleasure, though it was clear to all that her focus was on her ship, which was as it should be. At last she forced herself to stop. She could have spent days learning every inch of the *Gull,* but she did not have time to indulge herself. Nor would seeing it in port show her what she truly wished to know. She itched to experience the ship under sail and see for herself how she handled when the canvas was set. How long did it take to set all the sail she could carry, and how quickly could it be reefed in when the weather turned foul?

But these pleasures would have to wait for another day. She was no longer an apprentice sailor under Zorion's crew, nor even an owner out on a trading voyage. She had responsibilities of her own, and delightful as the ship was, she knew there was more to Zorion's presence than allowing a master trader to inspect her newest ship.

Reluctantly she ended her inspection and followed Zorion back to his quarters. There he poured out two cups of pale wine.

"To the *Swift Gull,* may she have fair seas, a loyal crew, and luck in every harbor," she said, raising her cup in salute.

"To the *Swift Gull,*" he echoed, raising his own cup.

They each drank, then poured a few drops of wine on the deck of the ship, as was proper when toasting her fortune.

Zorion's quarters were spare, an outer room with a table and a half dozen chairs where he conducted business and dined with guests. A half-closed door led to his sleeping room, which was barely large enough for a bed, and a chest of drawers built into the wall.

She sat down on one of the chairs, and Zorion followed suit, his long legs stretched out before him. His wine cup was set aside, and she knew that he would not drink another drop until he turned the watch over to his junior.

"So tell me, why are you really here?"

"To show you the ship, and to gain your approval for what I have done in your name."

"A letter would have sufficed," she said dryly. Though no mere letter nor sketches could have conveyed the size and the beauty of the *Swift Gull,* Zorion knew better than to indulge in foolish whims. She had placed great power in him, allowing him to act as her agent in all things while her duties in Ikaria kept her from her proper place. He would not have abandoned those duties lightly.

"I came to report that I have nothing to report," Zorion said.

"No news of Captain Tollen? No news of *Seddon's Pride*?"

They had exchanged a handful of carefully ciphered letters since her arrival in Karystos, but Zorion had had nothing to report save the ordinary matters of trade and commerce.

"Tollen's family received a death bounty, given into their hands by Lord Quesnel himself. It was generous, but not so large as to raise suspicions."

This she already knew for herself, so she waited for Zorion to elaborate.

"After I received your letter, I sent word to our agents in ports large and small, but no one has reported seeing the *Pride*."

"So everything is as it should be."

"By all appearances the *Pride* was the victim of ill luck, caught by one of the vicious storms that are the bane of late season sailings."

"But you do not believe this." His presence told her as much. For the past months she had pushed her own worries to the back of her mind, focusing instead on her mission, and the very real dangers that it presented. But in the face of Zorion's suspicions, her own doubts came to the fore.

"The storm was fierce, and I witnessed the damage to the ship with my own eyes. The foremast was jury-rigged, but it seemed doubtful that it would hold, which is why Captain Tollen ordered me set ashore," she mused.

It had not all been an illusion. The damage had been considerable, even though they'd only been brushed by the edges of the storm. It had been all they could do to turn aside and make for the nearest landfall. Tollen had not reckoned that the storm would turn as well, and by the time he had realized his mistake, it had been too late for him to do anything but set his passenger ashore and hope he could ride out the storm.

"Fine logic, but what were you doing up by The Hook? That is where he left you, is it not?"

"Here they call it Txomin's Island. There's a lighthouse on the far end from where we landed. I don't think Tollen knew which of the islands it was, or that the lighthouse was there."

The Hook was a string of tiny islands that extended in a gentle curve northward, marking the limits of the Ikarian Empire. Most of the islands were uninhabited, and a few were so flat that in a large storm the waves simply washed over them. As shelter, the islands had little to recommend them.

"It would take the storm of a lifetime to blow the ship so far off course that you found yourself near the shoals of The Hook," he said.

"The course did seem strange, but Captain Tollen said he was following a circuitous route to avoid the deeper waters where the most treacherous storms breed."

"I don't like it," Zorion said. "Too many strange events for my taste. One is ill luck, two is a coincidence, but three—"

"Three is a conspiracy," she said, finishing the old saying for him.

"You should not have let matters get so far," he said.

"It was not my ship."

"It was your life. Your mission."

She nodded, acknowledging his rebuke.

"And what would you do, faced with the same situation again?"

"I would not hesitate. I would take command, even if the only crew I could trust was myself and my serving-woman."

"Good girl," he said, as if she was once again an apprentice who had just demonstrated her mastery of a particularly tricky bit of seamanship. "Tilda would have my head if anything happened to you."

"My aunt has been dead these five years."

"And how would that stop her? She had her ways . . ."

Zorion tried for a laugh, but it rang oddly hollow. Despite the years, his grief, like her own, was still sharp and fresh. Tilda had been barely fifty when she died, her immense vitality no match for the fever that had killed her and half her crew in a matter of days.

She knew that Zorion held himself responsible for Tilda's death, even though it had been Tilda's wish that Zorion leave her employ and take charge of the ship she had given to her favorite niece. Zorion's experience had provided a perfect balance for Ysobel's lack, and with his having left her direct employ, Tilda felt free to take him as a lover.

Always one to wring every advantage from a situation, that had been Tilda's way. And Zorion had fallen in enthusiastically with her plans, content to let others serve Tilda, as long as he was the one that she turned to for pleasure when luck brought both of them into the same port.

But there was a part of him that believed that if he had stayed on as her senior captain, there would have been something he could have done to keep Tilda from dying. If he had been her captain, he would have found profit enough that there was no need to try the new route. Or, if fate had indeed brought them to that cursed place, that he would have been more vigilant. He would have recognized the signs of the sickness in time to escape before the port was sealed off.

No logic would dispel his feelings of guilt, and Ysobel knew better than to try.

"It's a dangerous game you play," he said.

"We knew that when I left. Tell me something I do not already know." Reawakened grief made her words sharper than she intended.

"Charlot is not the only house that finds its fortunes in disarray. Deep dealings on the merchants' council, but none can tell which of the factions will emerge triumphant, nor indeed who is setting one against another."

Their public façade was one of unity, but among themselves the merchant houses bickered and fought for every advantage, even as their fortunes declined. In the east, the armies of Vidrun threatened the free ports that had always welcomed federation traders, while in the west the Ikarian Empire once more looked to expand its realm of influence. And where the Ikarians held sway, their ships would have the advantage, and the federation traders would have to fight for the scraps left behind.

The situation was not dire; indeed, there were still fortunes to be made by the bold, as Ysobel herself had proven with her rapid rise. But it was true that there was less wealth to go around than before, and the merchant houses seemed far more interested in fighting with each other than they were in developing new sources of revenue.

While the majority of the merchants' council had sanctioned her secret mission in Ikaria, there were those who had objected to the tactics proposed. And even among those who had voted in favor of sending her . . . Many of them no doubt were hoping for her failure, rather than her success.

And she had a growing certainty that at least one person was not content to wait for her failure, but instead had bribed Captain Tollen to arrange a suitably tragic fate for the newly named liaison for trade with Ikaria.

The irony was that Tollen might well have been caught in his own trap, for she had survived, and by all evidence he had not.

"Flordelis will distance itself from you. You can expect your father or his agent to send word."

She swallowed to relieve the tightness of her throat.

"Things are that bad?"

"They aren't good. You had best be wary."

"I will take due care," she said. "But a ship that never leaves harbor is no more than a pile of rotting timbers. Nothing ventured, nothing gained."

"Safe harbors are the dullest, that's what Tilda would say."

She took it as the tacit blessing he had intended. Zorion did not like politics, and he strongly disapproved of Ysobel's involvement in them. He would rather sail unknown waters in a leaking ship with a mutinous crew than navigate the treacherous shoals of the interhouse rivalries.

He had come to give her a warning, and that he had done. And perhaps news of his journey would give her rivals pause, reminding them that she had her own resources to draw on and those who would be loyal to her until death.

"So tell me," she said, steering the conversation to safer waters. "Why tea?"

She listened as Zorion explained the importance of not overloading a ship on her first voyage and the bargain that he had struck on the bales of tea. It had been a well-chosen cargo, and when he asked she was able to reel off a list of a half dozen merchants, any of whom would be willing to pay a good price for it.

But even as she listened, she could not help wondering what to do about the information that Zorion had brought her. All signs seemed to urge her to caution, but perhaps that was just what her unknown enemies were hoping. Inaction could be just as deadly as action.

This was a problem for another day. Much as she trusted Zorion's advice in all things regarding trade, he could not help her with her current dilemma. She would have to rely on her own wits, which had served her well enough in the past. For now she had a new ship and an old friend, and she meant to enjoy them both to the fullest.

Chapter 11

Myles did not consider himself a religious man. Religion was the province of barren women praying for healthy children and young recruits pissing themselves before their first battle. He had sworn allegiance to the triune gods, but this had been a matter of political expediency rather than true faith. Experience had taught him that the gods cared little for the affairs of men, and even the most fervent prayer was no match for a strong sword arm.

Yet for all his vocal disbelief over the years, it seemed the gods had not been ignoring him after all. Surely it was no mere coincidence that had led the man who called himself Josan into this very stableyard, to the one man in the town who would recognize him for what he was. The gods, or fates, or whatever name they went by, had decided to test Myles, and now he had to decide what to do with the perilous gift they had dropped in his lap.

He had come to Utika because it was a quiet town, far enough from the imperial capital to be removed from its troubles but still within the civilized provinces of the empire. The town was small to one who had lived in Karystos, but it was large enough to boast the decencies of civilization. Myles had planned on spending the rest of his life here, using his carefully hoarded savings to purchase a business that would provide him a steady stream of income.

His vision had even stretched to the idea of a companion with whom to share the years while he was still strong and vital. Children he did not want, but a bedmate who could be trusted not to knife him or rob him in his sleep would be a pleasant change.

His plans had not included a vengeful innkeeper, who was doing his best to drive Myles out.

Nor had his plans included the man who even now slept in the hayloft while Myles paced in his quarters, unable to sleep because of his churning thoughts.

It was ironic. Before Josan's arrival, he had been giving serious thought to selling the livery stable to Florek and starting over elsewhere. It had been too much for one man to run on his own, and there had seemed no sign that any would dare cross Florek's ban and hire on to help him. But now, with two men to share the work, he could stay as long as he wanted. All he had to do was pretend that Josan was no more than he claimed, a wanderer of no particular lineage who was content with the most menial of employment.

If all he had wanted was a helper, he could have found none better. Josan did the dirtiest and heaviest jobs in the stable without complaint. The horses liked him, and he rode with the grace of one born to the saddle. If he made himself scarce when an imperial courier passed through, he still performed his duties, even as he kept the hood of his cloak raised to obscure his features.

And he had other talents, ones that only a keen observer would pay heed to. If Josan set the horses out in the paddock, the day was bound to be dry, no matter how gray and threatening the skies appeared. If on a clear day he began bringing loose gear into the storerooms and fastening the shutters, then you could be sure that a storm was coming. Josan never spoke of his weather sense, but the evidence was there all the same.

Just as he never claimed to be a linguist, and yet when Myles had tested him, calling out a greeting in rusty Decanese, Josan had replied flawlessly in the same tongue. His years in the army had given Myles a smattering of a half dozen languages, and as he tried these, one after another, Josan had easily followed, seeming not to realize what he was doing.

When Myles spoke of his talent, Josan grew angry, giving the first hint that there was a fierce temper under his calm exterior. He had refused to speak to Myles for the rest of that day, nor did he join him for dinner. The next day Josan behaved strangely, seeming bewildered by his surroundings and having to be told each task twice. Yet after a night's rest he was fine, and acted as if they had never quarreled.

But Myles had learned that he could not push Josan too far. Instead he had given Josan ample opportunity to confide in him, but Josan still held tightly on to his secrets. And he dared not speak his suspicions aloud and risk driving Josan away. Not until he knew the truth.

On the surface his suspicions were ludicrous. Everyone else in Utika treated Josan as a common laborer. A man of no distinction, unworthy of their interest. Were they correct? Why was he the only one who saw the truth—the noble bloodline that had been hidden under rags and grime?

Perhaps it was because the uprising had never touched this sleepy provincial town that they could not see the truths so evident to Myles.

Josan was his friend, and he did not wish to cause him harm. But Myles also had a duty to those friends he'd left behind in Karystos—both living and dead. Six years before he had pledged his life to their cause, and mere distance did not mean he could ignore his oaths.

Regardless of his wishes, Josan had a part to play, and Myles did as well. It did not matter whether Josan was truly ignorant of his past or merely feigning blindness; it was a luxury that they could not afford. Myles would have to find some way to force Josan to face the truth.

His decision was made, but it left a sour taste in his mouth. He knew that sooner or later someone was bound to recognize Josan for who he was, but that thought brought him no comfort. Josan had found sanctuary, and he would not thank Myles for thrusting him back into danger.

Josan knew that he could not stay in Utika forever. He had promised Myles that he would stay until spring, but it seemed increasingly likely he would have to break his vow. He knew enough to hide himself from curious travelers and the imperial messengers who regularly rode through, but he had a new worry.

From the first, Myles had treated him as a friend rather than a servant. He had thought this the result of Myles's loneliness, but lately he suspected another motive. Often he would turn and catch a glimpse of hunger in Myles's gaze, though his expression was always carefully neutral whenever Myles knew he was being observed.

He supposed it was flattering, in a way, to be the object of such longing. He had not shared his bed since before the fever had broken him, and his memories had no faces, merely the vague impression of slender sun-kissed limbs and bright laughter. Having broken so many vows already, the restriction on lying with one not of the brethren no longer held any weight. And certainly there was a part of him that would enjoy losing himself in the pleasure of another's touch, even if only for a few hours.

But he could not risk such closeness. Myles had already witnessed Josan's madness, though he had not seemed to realize the significance of Josan's strange behavior. But the intimacies between lovers were far greater than those between master and man. He could not risk Myles falling asleep next to Josan, and waking up beside the Other.

That was how Josan thought of him, as the Other. The self that ruled his body during those days and hours he could not recall. Even to think of the Other was to risk inviting him in, so Josan seldom allowed himself to ponder the strangeness that had entered his life.

Josan was living a life of lies. He had turned his back on every precept of his order, abandoning his lifelong search for truth. He had become a hare, frozen motionless in the high grass, hoping inaction would keep him safe from the hawk circling above.

He carefully did not question his knowledge of horses, nor his talent for knowing what weather the day would bring before he had even caught a glimpse of the sky. If he needed to light a fire he used his newly purchased tinder and flint. He had thought his skill at languages was his own, but something about the game that Myles had played had awakened the Other, and when Josan had returned to awareness he had been terrified to learn that nearly two full days had passed.

He knew Myles had sensed something amiss, for his master had watched him even more closely in the days that followed. But whatever Myles thought of his servant's odd behavior he did not speak, and for that Josan was grateful. There was no reasonable explanation he could give, and he would hate having to lie yet again to a man who had offered him only kindness.

Nor could he afford to share his fears. If he was indeed suffering from soul madness, as he suspected, then his fate was already sealed. The law required that such tormented souls be turned over to the magistrate, locked up so they could not harm others. Whether they harmed themselves was of no concern to their jailers, and such unfortunates seldom lived long once they were apprehended.

Of course, most often the soul-mad were only discovered after their madness had driven them to commit the most horrific of crimes. Monsters clothed in human flesh, their ordinary appearances masks for deeds of unspeakable foulness. Mothers who drowned their children; kindly men who lured innocents to their rooms and dismembered their bodies; bright-eyed children who slew their siblings over the theft of a toy.

He had never given them much thought, other than the reflexive horror that all felt whenever news of such a one reached the capital. Now he wished he had paid more heed to the tales. Had their madness come on them suddenly? Or had they experienced the slow descent into unreason, feeling their wits slipping away but unable to do anything to avoid their fate?

Not all the mad turned violent, but that was scant comfort, since there seemed to be no way to know if his Other carried the taint of evil.

There were those in the Learned Brethren who studied soul magic. A handful of the most senior scholars were entrusted with the rarest of knowledge that the brethren had acquired over the centuries. Such knowledge was deemed dangerous, and those who studied the ancient scrolls were aged men who never left the walls of the collegium. Few outsiders had any idea that the monks held such knowledge, and even fewer suspected that the monks not only studied soul magic but also practiced it when the occasion warranted.

It was another example of the irony that ruled his life. The one place where he could seek to understand what was happening to him, and whether it was possible to banish the Other, was also the one place where he dared not go.

The brethren's insistence that he remain on Txomin's Island had taken on ominous significance. Had they known of his soul madness, and was that the reason they had sent him so far from civilization? If so, then to venture into Karystos would be proof that he was no longer obedient to their will, and they would have no choice but to turn him over to the magistrates, who would condemn him to the catacombs.

Yet staying at the stable held its own risks. Each day he lingered, he knew himself for a coward. A selfless man would leave immediately and seek out an isolated wood or distant mountain, where his eventual madness would bring harm to no one but himself. A good man would not risk staying here, endangering a man who could have been his friend if they had met as equals and not as master and servant.

Josan told himself that madness was not inevitable. That he would leave this place of refuge the next time the Other returned. And yet even as he made the vow, he tasted the bitterness on his tongue and knew it for the hollow promise it was. Despite all his care to avoid strong emotions and to center himself through meditation, he knew that one day his defenses would crack, and the Other would return. And then the Other might seize his body forever, leaving Josan's soul trapped in the unknowing grayness, as his body committed acts of unspeakable horror.

In the days that followed his vow, the Other remained mercifully absent. Winter was full upon them, but that did not mean there was any less work to occupy his hours. True, there were fewer travelers on the roads, but those that did travel arrived with mud-caked horses that required extensive grooming, and hard-pressed carriages that inevitably needed some type of repair. And on those days where there were neither travelers nor imperial messengers, there were still the dozen residents of the stables to be seen to, who had grown increasingly fractious as days of hard-driving rain kept them indoors.

Josan was grateful for the work and found that by concentrating on each individual task he could, at least briefly, forget about the dilemma that he faced. He took more and more upon himself, occupying even his so-called free hours by mending perfectly serviceable harness and carefully arranging and rearranging the storeroom until Myles lost all patience with him and ordered him to leave well enough alone.

Banished from the stableyard with instructions that for once he was to enjoy his half day and spend some of his hard-earned coins, at first Josan wandered the streets of Utika aimlessly. He knew the town fairly well, although he could not say the same for the townspeople. There were many he recognized by sight, and a number who knew him as Myles's servant. But none were particularly friendly, and he could not imagine conversing with any of them. His employment barred him from associating with those who would normally have been his equals, and even other servants avoided him for fear of being tainted by association.

Which was as well, he supposed. He had too many secrets to guard to risk friendship. Even if it meant that on an afternoon such as this, he had no one to turn to, to help him pass the empty hours.

Strange how he had never felt this loneliness when he was on the island. There weeks had passed without his seeing another soul, and nonetheless Josan had been content.

Of course, back then he had had a purpose, a duty, and

a firm sense of who he was. Now he had none of these things. Instead there was a vast emptiness inside him, an aching hollowness that could be filled neither by his assumed role nor by the company of others. He was a fraud, a shell of a man, and it was a wonder that others had not seen through him.

These bitter reflections were precisely what he had been trying to avoid with his frantic labors, but even that respite had been denied him. Josan's steps slowed, and as the rain began once more to fall in earnest, he ducked inside a nearby wine shop.

Inside the taverna it was so dim he could hardly see, the low ceilings and tiny windows reinforcing the impression of a small cave. The stone floor was slick with mud tracked in by the patrons, and the air was filled with the stench of smoke, wet wool, and the faint scent of blood. The last puzzled him, until he remembered that the taverna was adjacent to the butchers' district, and the patrons must have brought the scent of their own labors with them.

He wondered if his own clothes and boots carried the smell of horseshit, then shrugged. If they did, this was hardly a place where anyone would complain. Picking his way carefully across the floor, he made his way to an unoccupied bench. A flash of bright copper brought him a jug of red wine, along with a wine cup and a pitcher of water.

There was a ritual to wine pouring, a style that hovered at the edge of his memory and called for his attention. He ignored the thought, and instead poured the wine into the cup carelessly, letting it slop against the sides. Eschewing the water—for no doubt the shop had already watered it heavily—he took a deep gulp.

The wine was bitter, the taste so dark as to be nearly gritty. He could almost taste the crushed grape skins on his tongue and wondered what people were so barbarous that they did not think to strain the wine before storing.

The same people that sold a jug of wine for an imperial copper, to men whose taste buds could barely determine the difference between old wine and new. It was not that the wine was primitive, but rather that Josan was remembering a time when he had drunk perfectly aged wine out of crystal goblets, when each sip had been a new revelation of taste and refinement.

But even that memory rang false as he considered it. True the brethren did not drink swill, but neither were they known to indulge in worldly luxuries such as rare wines or crystal goblets. This memory, too, was not his own.

He emptied his cup and filled it again. This time he forced his mind clear of all other thoughts, almost as if he was meditating, concentrating on this cup of wine as if he had never before drunk the red wine of the northern provinces. Slowly he drank, but when his cup was empty, he conceded defeat. He could still feel the Other, roused to awareness, hovering at the edge of his thoughts.

It had been a mistake to come in here and let strong wine dull his wits. Josan stood, tossing a copper to the servingwoman, who would no doubt sell his unfinished jug of wine to the next patron. With his hood tugged over his head to protect him from the chill rain, his steps turned inevitably toward the stable. Myles had ordered him to stay away for a full afternoon, but it was better to face Myles's wrath than to risk having the Other surface in a public setting.

When he returned he saw two men leaving the stable-yard. Their high boots and long cloaks proclaimed them to be travelers, and as he drew near, he saw the vague outlines of short swords under their much-patched cloaks. He felt a faint prickle of unease, wondering what business such men could have with Myles. Their boots were made for walking, not riding, and by their appearance they could not afford to hire a horse. When he drew abreast with them, their eyes widened.

Both men were of mixed blood, with dark brown stubble on their faces from days without shaving. They were young, barely out of boyhood, but that did not make them any less dangerous.

"Greetings of the day to you," he said.

He was not surprised when they did not respond, studiously ignoring him after that first glance. He should have felt comforted by their disregard, for clearly they had recognized him as a servant. One with nothing to steal, a man not even worth a polite greeting.

And yet his unease deepened as he paused at the paddock gate, watching as the two men continued down the street until they turned off into an alley. Only then did he turn his back on them and make his way into the stables.

Myles was standing next to his office at the front of the stables.

"I told you to stay away for the afternoon," Myles growled. His cheeks were flushed with anger, either from this morning's quarrel or Josan's early return, or perhaps both. "It is still light, or had you not noticed?"

Josan shrugged. "It is dark enough, with all these clouds."

It was a poor excuse, but he could hardly tell the truth. Perhaps if he made himself scarce, it would give Myles's temper a chance to cool.

Removing his cloak, he ran his fingers through his short hair, flicking off the raindrops that had gathered. "What did those men want? The two who just left here?"

Myles frowned, and for a long moment Josan thought that his master was too angry to answer.

"Nothing."

"Nothing?"

"Nothing. They wanted work, but I had none to give them."

"But—"

They had looked hungry, yes, but not the type to stoop to common labor. They had seemed more like those who turned to robbery when all else failed.

"Don't worry, your job is safe enough for now," Myles said, misinterpreting the source of Josan's unease. "Though if you plague me again, I may reconsider."

Josan drew a breath, then let it out slowly. He could not afford to quarrel with Myles, not when all he had was a vague feeling that the two men intended harm.

"If you do not need me, I will take myself off to rest. I drank more than I intended, and the wine has gone to my head."

"Go," Myles said, and he retreated to his office.

Thus dismissed, Josan made his way to the rear of the stables and climbed the ladder that led to his hayloft. He had not lied to Myles. In a way the wine had gone to his head, though mercifully he no longer felt the Other stirring. A few hours of sleep that afternoon would help him stay awake later. If the strangers intended mischief, they would return after dark. And Josan would be ready for them.

"Wake up, damn you, wake up," a voice growled in his ear.

" 'm wake," Josan muttered.

His eyes firmly shut, he tried to roll over to grasp a few more moments of sleep, but the voice was having none of it. Strong hands grabbed his shoulders and shook him.

"Wake up," the voice ordered.

Josan opened his eyes and sat up. He shook his head to clear it, but this proved a mistake, for a wave of nausea swept over him. The same hands that had so rudely disturbed his sleep held him steady as he squeezed his eyes shut once more against the sickness in his gut and the pounding ache of his head.

"Stay with me," the voice ordered, and, as his wits returned to him, he recognized the speaker as Myles.

Once more he opened his eyes, blinking as he tried to make sense of what he was seeing. He was on the floor of the stables, just inside the double doors. The scene was dim, illuminated only by the customary lantern that burned at night, but he could see the concern in Myles's face and hear the horses moving restlessly in their stalls, complaining over whatever had disturbed their rest.

The bitter taste of nausea mixed with fear as he realized that his last memories were of climbing the ladder to his loft. He had intended a short rest, so he could stay on guard during the night. After that there was nothing.

If the Other had surfaced, as Josan dreaded, then there was no telling what the demon might have done while in control of Josan's body.

"What happened?"

Seemingly convinced that Josan was not about to pass out, Myles relinquished his hold. He did not answer at once, but instead his gaze traveled to where two dim shapes lay on the floor not far away.

His legs would not support him, but Josan managed to crawl the short distance. Even before he reached them, he knew what he would find. As he approached, the unrecognizable shapes resolved themselves into the figures of two men. The strangers from earlier that day, now lying dead on the stable floor. Now the ache in his head made sense, as did the tightness in his chest that told of one or more broken ribs. His hands were sticky, and he knew if he looked at them closely, he would see blood. Blood that was not his own.

"Robbers," Myles said, coming to stand beside him. "You must have surprised them."

A comforting tale, but the evidence did not fit. Josan summoned his strength and climbed to his feet. Ignoring Myles, he crossed back to the front of the stable and lit the spare lantern. Holding the lantern before him, he looked around. The office door was closed, the bar on the granary door still lowered, and the stall doors firmly locked.

Returning to the two bodies, he knelt beside them. From the scuff marks on the floor he could see that they had been dragged there after they had fallen, their short swords placed neatly at their feet. Heedless of his aching ribs, he knelt once more. So close, the signs of death were hard to ignore—the stench of blood and shit and the open eyes staring at him in endless surprise.

Placing the lantern on the floor beside him, he grasped the left forearm of the first man and pushed up his sleeve. Carefully he inspected it, but there was no telltale tattoo. He repeated the procedure with the man's right arm, then with the second man.

Neither bore the rebel's tattoo, but that did not mean that he could accept Myles's explanation. Robbers would have come prepared to steal one or more of the valuable horses, but there was no sign of halter or tack.

Nor did it explain their deaths. Josan had never intended to face them alone. Two armed men against an unarmed man was suicide, no matter what strange skills lay in Josan's past. Josan had thought no further than to alert Myles to the danger and let him summon the watch.

But instead two men had died, and apparently at his hand.

"Robbers," Josan repeated.

"So it seems. You must have annoyed them, for I heard the racket and decided to investigate. When I saw them they were dragging you out of the barn. Lucky for both of us that they had no idea how to use those swords they wore, for I was able to put them down with barely a scratch."

"You? You killed them?"

Myles puffed out his chest. "I was a soldier, you remember?"

"Of course."

He had not meant to offend; rather, he had been so convinced of his own guilt that he had not considered any other possibilities.

But while Myles's explanation offered the comfort of knowing that he had not killed them, it was troubling in another way. The men who had died had not been trying to steal horses or coin. They had seized Josan. If he had interrupted their robbery, then they would have simply killed him. Instead they had knocked him unconscious, then tried to kidnap him.

Were they opportunists, seeking the bounty that must now be on the head of the so-called killer monk? Or were they somehow connected to the assassin who had tried to kill him so many long months ago? In either case, he had Myles to thank for his life.

"I am in your debt," he said.

Myles shifted his weight on his feet, seemingly discomfited by the simple statement of truth.

"Are you strong enough to lend a hand?" Myles asked.

Josan nodded.

"Good, then go and get the manure cart from the back."

"What?"

"The manure cart." Myles blew out a breath. "We have to get rid of these two before the sun rises."

"But the magistrate—"

"The magistrate is Florek's cousin. He has been scrupulous in his observance of the law so far, but I do not want to give him an excuse to throw me in jail." Myles looked over at him. "And I assume that you cannot afford to speak with him either. So we'll take care of this ourselves, agreed?"

Myles knew that Josan was not who he said he was. He felt dizzy, as this latest shock piled on top of the others he had experienced this night. It was too much to take in, so Josan simply said, "I'll get the cart."

As he stepped outside, he saw the clear stars above him. The rain had stopped, and he knew the coming day would be fine. The horses would enjoy the chance to spend time in the paddock, and he could give their stalls the thorough cleaning they deserved.

Then he laughed as he realized the absurdity of his thoughts. Two men had been killed, and whether their deaths were justified or not, his life was once again about to change. He would not be here to clean the stalls. He had been a fool to let himself grow comfortable, for it had taken only moments for his refuge to be destroyed. Once more his life had been in danger, and he was no closer to finding out why.

He could not wait to find his answers. Caution had availed him nothing. He would have to risk Brother Nikos's wrath and return to Karystos.

But first he had to help Myles erase the evidence of what had been done here. In helping Josan, Myles had risked far more than he knew. Myles's hand had wielded the sword, but it seemed clear that it had been Josan's presence that drew the men, and thus Josan bore the responsibility for their deaths.

Returning with the manure cart, he saw that Myles had already stripped the bodies. The wounds, which had looked bad enough when hidden by clothing, gaped obscenely. One man had been skewered through from front to back, apparently taken by surprise. The second had had time to fight. He had bled from cuts on his arms, and a nasty wound to his thigh, before a final stab through the belly.

Even as Josan watched, the body of the second man gave a faint twitch.

He was not dead. Despite everything, the man was not dead. What would they do? What would he say if he lived long enough to talk to the magistrate?

Josan stood there, frozen in horror, but Myles had no such compunctions. He placed his large hand over the man's mouth and nose, pressing down until the body gave one last spasm, then lay still.

This had been murder. Death done not in the heat of combat, but a cold-blooded killing. It could be argued that Myles had acted out of mercy, for the man's wounds ensured that his future held nothing but a long, lingering death. But he knew Myles had not killed him out of mercy. Myles had killed him because he needed silence.

It seemed Myles had secrets of his own, and Josan did not know whether to be grateful or to curse the fates that had brought them together.

At Myles's direction, he lined the cart with two old horse blankets. Then he took the arms of the victim whose body was still warm, and Myles took his legs. They loaded him in the cart, folding his body in half to make it fit. Josan steeled himself to the gruesome task, even as the nausea once more welled up inside him.

Who are you? a voice in his head demanded. *Can you still maintain the pretense that you are a monk if you do these things?* He ignored the voice and returned to help Myles pick up the second body. This one, too, was folded, crammed in next to his comrade. A final blanket was spread over them both to disguise their gruesome load.

It took both of them, one on each handle, to move the cart out into the alley that ran behind the stables and down its length. The creak of the wheels on the hard-packed gravel seemed impossibly loud to his ears, and with every step he waited for the inevitable discovery. But they reached

their destination unmolested: a narrow track behind a taverna that was known to cater to the lowest of the low. Rats
scurried away as they unloaded the two bodies facedown
into the mud.

Josan wanted to argue against the disrespect, but it
seemed foolish to protest. Silently they made the trip back
to the stables. Only when they were once more inside, with
the door barred behind them, did Myles give a sigh of relief.

"The watch will find them, or the taverna owner, and
assume they were victims of a robbery or a brawl," he said.
"There will be nothing to connect them to us."

"The blankets? Their clothes?"

"We'll burn the lot tomorrow, along with a pile of straw
that has gone moldy."

"What straw?" He knew he had not neglected any of
his tasks.

"The straw that you were too lazy to turn, and has now
gone moldy from all this rain," Myles said. "I'll complain
loudly of course, but that will be the end of it."

Clearly Myles had given this careful thought, even as
Josan's own wits went begging. He wondered if this was
the first time Myles had had to dispose of an inconvenient
body but could think of no polite way to ask. You did not
accuse the man who had just saved your life of being a
killer.

Even if it was true.

Myles looked around. "Come. Tomorrow will be soon
enough to scrub the floors."

Josan did not move.

"Come." There was steel in Myles's voice, so Josan
roused himself to follow. Myles led him across the stableyard to the adjacent stone house where he lived. The house
was close enough so that the owner could keep an eye on
the stables, but if the commotion had been loud enough to

wake Myles, it was a wonder that their neighbors had not come running as well.

Once they were inside, Myles stirred up the fire. Josan had not realized he was cold, but even the rebuilt fire was not enough to warm him. He shivered, standing as close to the fire as he dared. Myles disappeared, and a moment later a blanket was dropped over his shoulders and a cup pressed into his hand.

Josan clutched the blanket around himself and raised the cup to his lips. It was wine, as he had expected, but mixed with fruit juice, which he had not. The sweet taste nearly gagged him, but he forced himself to swallow several mouthfuls, recognizing the mixture as a treatment for shock.

Myles returned with his own cup. "Sit," he ordered.

Josan perched on the bench nearest the fire. "I have to leave. I will stay and burn the straw, or mayhaps it is better if I leave first. You can tell the others that you fired me because I was so lazy, and the straw will be seen as evidence."

"Tell me what you were looking for on their arms," Myles said, ignoring Josan's words.

"Nothing."

"Hardly nothing. You searched them both."

Josan took refuge in another sip of the sweetened wine. The taste was foul, but it calmed his stomach.

"It would be better for us both if you did not ask these questions. Just let me leave, and I will trouble you no longer."

"These were not robbers, were they?"

"No."

Perhaps it was the wine, or the lateness of the hour, or the shocks he had endured. Whatever the reason, he confessed, "They were looking for me."

"And this is not the first time, is it? You were looking for a sign, a symbol that marked them."

Myles was too canny for his own good.

"I do not know."

It was the truth. He did not know for certain. But he had his suspicions. Myles had been a soldier and fought against the uprising. If Josan were somehow involved with Prince Lucius's followers, it was unlikely Myles would be willing to help him flee imperial justice.

"Who are you, that two mercenaries would try to steal you away?"

"That I do not know either." He gave a bitter laugh.

Myles leaned forward intently, his wine cup dangling forgotten from one hand. "You do not know? You do not know who you are?"

His intellect screamed at him for silence. Myles may had saved his life, but he had no reason to trust him. Not with a secret that might cost both their lives.

But his tongue continued on its own, seemingly impervious to his commands. "I know who I am. Or rather who I thought I was. But the man I was would not be the target of assassins and kidnappers. So either they are mistaken, or I am."

"Surely your own memories can be trusted."

"For an ordinary man, yes. But the man in my memories never learned the intricacies of an imperial war saddle, nor how to tell a saber thrust from the cut made by a short sword. So it seems my memories are no more trustworthy than those mercenaries."

It was a relief to share even that much of his burden with another. If Myles was silent, at least he was not questioning Josan's story, nor calling him mad.

He wondered what Myles would say if he revealed the existence of the Other to him, but he dared not. It was enough that he had given Myles reason to suspect that

Josan was demon-haunted. It would not do to provide confirmation of his fears.

"When did the false memories start?"

"In Karystos." He had given the matter much thought, and the strangeness that had come upon him had appeared after the breakbone fever that had nearly killed him. Afterward he had journeyed to Txomin's Island and lived the quiet life of a lighthouse keeper. There was nothing in that life to inspire an assassin to seek him out. If anything had happened, it had happened to him before he left Karystos.

"Then you must return there and seek out those you once knew. Surely they can help you unravel this mystery."

"It is not so simple. There may well be a price on my head. This is not the first time that I have had to defend myself. And if I have enemies, then they will be in Karystos."

"And if you have enemies, they will believe you far too wise to risk journeying to the center of their power. You can slip into the city, unnoticed, and find what you need. If there is an answer to these riddles, it will be there."

"I will think on your counsel," Josan said. Brother Nikos had forbidden him to return to the collegium, but he had not known the extent of Josan's peril. Surely the monks would agree to help him. And if he could not be helped, if he was indeed demon-bound, then they could be trusted to ensure that he could not harm another innocent.

"You will do more than think on it. You will go. With me."

"You cannot."

"I can and I will. Before your arrival I had made my mind up to sell the stables to Florek. Now I can get a good price from him before he realizes that you are to leave. A journey shared is a journey halved, and I have friends in Karystos who will shelter us both while you seek your answers."

The offer was beyond the simple kindness of master to man. Myles had already broken several laws this night, killing the second mercenary before he could be questioned and covering up all evidence of the attack. If he were discovered traveling with Josan, he would be treated as an accomplice.

His actions went beyond mere friendship, and Josan uneasily recalled his earlier suspicion that Myles lusted after him. Still, even that did not explain the risks he had taken by killing the two strangers. For all Myles knew, Josan was a criminal and a traitor. Or worse.

And yet he needed Myles's help, now more than ever. One man traveling on his own was far more vulnerable than two.

"Once again I am in your debt," he said.

Myles's mouth twisted in a wry grin. "Be wary what you promise. When you have your answers, I may decide to hold you to your words."

"Whatever you ask it is yours."

"I will remember that, my lord," he said, as if he were the servant and Josan the master. Then his face grew solemn. "Finish the wine and get some sleep. We have much to do tomorrow."

Indeed the dawn was only a few hours away. Josan knew he should be worried over what was to come, but instead he felt comforted by the knowledge that whatever happened, he would not face his demons alone.

Chapter 12

It took three days to make their preparations for the journey, and Josan spent most of that time fearing arrest and discovery. If not for his promise to Myles, Josan would have fled. That his flight would no doubt have raised the finger of suspicion that they had so far avoided was a truth he acknowledged, but better to be followed by mere suspicion than arrested and executed for murder.

But so far, luck had been with them. The bodies had not been discovered until late on the afternoon of the next day, when a servant at the taverna opened the back door to throw out slops. By that time the bodies had been heavily gnawed by rats, disguising the precision of Myles's sword work. Josan heard of the gruesome discovery from the laundrywoman as she dropped off Myles's freshly cleaned linens. She seemed convinced that the men had brought their fates on themselves, as foolish strangers who did not know better than to venture into the rough quarters at night.

If they had been residents of Utika, it might have been different, but there was no pity to be spared for two humble travelers, nor were there any signs that the magistrate was investigating their deaths.

The bloodstained clothes and blankets had been hidden deep in the pile of straw that Josan had carted out to the side yard and burned. The tunic he had worn that night had been burned as well, for the lump on the side of his head had bled freely. If any asked, he planned to explain the bruise as the result of a blow Myles had given him when he had discovered the moldy straw. But none questioned his injury, as the signs of a master beating his servant were too ordinary to be worthy of comment.

Displaying a shrewd grasp of tactics, Myles went about his normal routine, settling his monthly accounts in person with the grain merchant, the farrier, and the victualer. At each, almost idly, he remarked upon his growing boredom with life in Utika, though naturally since the livery stable was making a fine profit, he could not contemplate leaving. His musings reached the ears of Florek, as he had intended they would, and the next day Florek sent an intermediary to make an offer for the business.

This was not the first offer that Florek had made, nor even the twelfth. It was, however, the first time that Florek had offered to pay Myles more than he had paid for the business, so that he could turn a small profit on the deal. Having failed at his attempts to drive Myles out of business, or to ensure that he lacked the help needed to service the imperial contracts, it seemed Florek had grown tired of their endless battles. Or perhaps Florek feared that Myles's vocal dissatisfaction was merely the voice of melancholy that came with the winter rains, and if he waited till spring, he would lose this opportunity.

Myles allowed himself to be persuaded, and after some haggling struck a deal with his former nemesis. He took his payment in coins, then converted half of them into imperial scrip, which was easier to carry and could be exchanged for coins in any provincial capital.

While Myles made his preparations, Josan was busy as well. He had always known that he might have to flee at an instant, and thus his pack already held spare clothes, a flask for water, and his knife. His carefully hoarded wages were enough to purchase sandals, a cloak that was nearly new, and three pairs of thick socks to cushion his feet.

It would take at least a fortnight to cross the border into the heart of the empire, the province of Karystos, which took its name from the imperial capital. And then it would be another three weeks—four if the weather was unkind—before they could hope to reach the city of Karystos. They would have to carry what provisions they could with them, though as they approached the capital there would be few chances for camping alongside the road, and hunting or foraging for food would result in swift arrest. Instead they would have to beg hospitality from farmers or stay in the hostels that catered to poorer travelers.

Myles, however, had other ideas.

"Bring Ugly and Crop Ear to the farrier, and have him put heavy shoes on both," he ordered.

Ugly was a rawboned gelding with a particularly unfortunately shaped head that belied his supposedly noble bloodline. Myles claimed his former owner had gelded the beast in sheer horror at the prospect that one such as he should spawn foals in his likeness. Crop Ear was a mild-mannered mare who had been savaged by a stable mate. Of the half dozen horses that he rented out to any who could muster enough coins, these two were the most reliable, willing to work hard with little fuss.

"Why pay for shoeing them if Florek is going to get the benefit?" Josan asked.

"He's not. These two weren't part of the sale. I had enough walking in my days in the empress's service, and

I've no mind to wear my feet down to bones and blisters again."

Josan paused. It had never occurred to him that they would ride, which seemed foolish when he considered that his master owned a livery stable. Horses were Myles's world. Of course he would not want to plod along like a common peasant.

On his own, Josan could not have afforded to buy a horse. It would have taken all his remaining coin to rent one for even a few days' journey. A part of him wanted to protest this generosity, but then was it fair that Myles be forced to walk simply because Josan could not afford to ride?

"I'll see to it at once," he said.

It was another evidence of Myles's kindness, though by then Josan knew better than to thank him. Being reminded of his generosity merely made his master angry. And indeed, compared to what Myles had already done for him, the loan of a horse to ride was a small thing.

Josan did not understand Myles. He knew that the man had his own secrets, and indeed the cold-blooded way in which he had dealt with the kidnappers spoke of a dark side. For all the weeks that he had spent with Myles, Josan knew little more than that he was a fair master and was skilled with both horses and a sword. Beyond that, Myles could have been anything. An assassin, a murderer, a mercenary who had improbably survived long enough to retire with his booty. Or he could indeed be the former soldier that he claimed to be. And the alacrity with which Myles offered to accompany Josan on his journey would have raised suspicions in a far less wary man.

But his instincts were telling him that he could trust Myles. The same instincts that had warned him that the two strangers intended harm told him that Myles genuinely wanted to help.

Once again there was someone who called him friend, and Josan could not help thinking of Renzo. Would this newfound friendship with Myles be strong enough to bear the weight of Josan's secrets? Or would Myles one day turn on him and call him a madman and a murderer?

Only time would tell.

They left Utika at dawn, on a morning so cold that the guards at the gates merely waved them through, loath to leave the warmth of the gatehouse. Josan felt neither triumph nor relief as the town slowly dwindled behind them. He had slept little since the attack, for each time he had closed his eyes he had jerked back to wakefulness, remembering how he had been taken unawares. Exhaustion had dulled his wits and blunted his emotions until he felt only a strange fatalism. If he were to be arrested, so be it.

As the morning wore on, the sun slowly broke through the clouds, warming his numb hands and face. There were no signs of pursuit by irate guards, nor did assassins spring out from behind the tidy villas and surrounding orchards.

If Myles shared Josan's fear of pursuit he gave no sign, though the fact that he had chosen openly to wear his sword belt and leather armor showed that he was mindful of the dangers they might face. Still, as each mile disappeared under the steady gait of their horses, it seemed more and more likely that they were not being pursued.

Which meant nothing, a cynical voice in his head reminded him. His enemies had no need to pursue Josan, for Josan was delivering himself to them. Willingly entering the place where they held power, in search of truths that could only be found in Karystos. His only hope was that he would find the answers he sought before his enemies discovered him.

And what if the truth was something he could not face?

What if he was indeed a madman, a killer, exiled from Karystos so that he could not inflict his madness upon others? What would he do then? What would the brethren do when they discovered that their wayward brother had returned?

Josan pushed such thoughts from his mind. It did no good to dwell on disquieting speculations. And until he had facts, that was all they were. The fears of a restless mind, making him no better than an ignorant peasant jumping at every shadow. A disgrace to his training, which had taught him to value cool reason and logical arguments built upon verifiable truths.

He turned his mind outward, but the passing countryside held little of interest. Carefully spaced villas, their white plaster gleaming in the dull sun, lined either side of the road, each with its own orchards or vineyards. Few workers were to be seen, for there was little to be done in the winter, and there were even fewer travelers on the road. His horse, Crop Ear, required little guidance, having settled into a steady pace that matched that of her stable mate.

At midday they paused to unwrap the bread and cheese they had packed that morning, washing it down with chill water. By late afternoon his thighs and backside were complaining over the hours spent in the saddle, and from the way that Myles shifted back and forth, it seemed he, too, was feeling the pain of one unaccustomed to riding all day. By unspoken consent, they turned their horses into the yard of a hostel, even though there were still at least two hours of daylight left.

Myles's coins bought them space in the stables for their horses and a room they had to share with only two others— a father taking his young son to be apprenticed to a cousin in Utika. Dinner was a quiet affair, with six sharing a single long table in a room that could easily hold three dozen.

There was no chance to talk privately, and for that Josan was grateful, though he knew he was only delaying the inevitable.

He passed a restless night, unused to hearing the sounds of others as he slept. Long ago he had shared a dormitory with the other novice monks, but like much of his past, this was a skill that he had forgotten. Rising the next morning, every muscle in his body protested as he swung himself into the saddle. But he ignored his body's complaints, and after a while the sharp pains had settled down into a dull ache.

Once they had left the hostel behind them, Myles put an end to his reprieve.

"Is Josan your true name? Or is there something else I should call you?"

"Josan it is," he said. "Of the collegium of the Learned Brethren in Karystos."

Myles frowned, as if he had been expecting a different answer. Perhaps he had assumed that anyone pursued by assassins would have had the wit to change his name, to avoid detection. Or perhaps Josan was misreading him. It was difficult to hold a conversation on horseback, when he could only see Myles's expression through sideways glances.

"And what do you remember of the time before?" Myles prompted him.

"I am told that I was left on the steps of the collegium as a newborn babe for the brethren to raise as one of their own. I remember my childhood among them and studying with the other boys in their care. After I made my final vows I traveled the great sea, studying with the brethren in Xandropol, then later traveling to Anamur and Seddon."

Strangely enough, his earliest memories were the clearest. He remembered the faces of his tutors, the long vigil on the night before his final vows. The wonder of his first journey outside of Karystos, and even how the great library of Xandropol smelled, the unique combination of musty parchments underlain with a faint sweetness from the beeswax tablets.

Once past his youth, his memories were fragmented. His mind held knowledge presumably gained from his studies, but he did not remember the books he had read, nor where he had found them. And as for his own history, he did not know whether these were true memories or merely what he had been told by the brethren as he was recovering from the fever.

If indeed a fever it had been. Even this he now doubted, though he was not ready to share those doubts with Myles.

"The ship that brought me back to Karystos was stricken with the breakbone fever, and all aboard fell ill. The brethren nursed me back to health, and when I recovered they sent me to Txomin's Island to tend the lighthouse. There I lived a quiet life, until the day a stranger tried to kill me. The rest you know."

Myles growled. "The brethren are Nerissa's lapdogs. If they are involved in your troubles, it means no good."

"But I am one of them," Josan insisted.

"Are you? And did the brethren teach you how to ride? Or how to handle a sword?"

He had asked himself the same questions a dozen times before, but it cut him to the quick to hear his doubts voiced by another.

"I know I am of the brethren," he insisted. "They would not harm me."

"When we get to Karystos you will find out who your true friends are."

If his words were meant to be comforting, they fell far short of the mark. There was more than one way to define friendship. After all, it was possible that the brethren had acted as true friends while Josan was the one who had betrayed them.

But regardless of what he might find, he knew he had to press onward. Even the possibility of learning that his worst fears were true was better than living in the veil of ignorance. Truth, no matter how harsh, was valued above all else. That was the sacred principle of the brethren who had guided his days. And if the truths he sought meant the end of his life, well so be it. At least he would die with integrity.

Josan wondered if he should tell Myles about the Other, but the moment when such a confession could have been made passed in silence. He was conscious of the Other, in a way he had not been before. His attempts to meditate during the journey were often interrupted by a mocking inner voice that derided him as a coward clinging to archaic rituals best suited to beardless boys and shriveled-up men. And at night, his dreams were filled with strange images of people and places that he had never known.

But for all his unease, he was able to maintain his control. Perhaps it was the strength of his will or the focus of the hours of meditation. Or maybe it was as simple as the company of Myles, whose mere presence kept Josan focused on the here and now. Whatever the reason, while the Other hovered on the fringes of his mind, he had yet to seize control, and for that Josan was grateful.

He knew better than to hope that the Other would sleep forever, but for however long it lasted, he would be grateful for the respite.

The first days of their journey were hard, as Myles was no longer used to spending days on the road in good weather and bad. Riding horseback was a mixed blessing, for while it spared feet that had lost the toughness of his infantry days, he more than paid the price with aching backside and chafed thighs. Yet these were petty annoyances, and as the first days passed, his body adapted and Myles settled into the routine of travel.

It should have been harder to leave Utika. To abandon the dream that had kept him from despair during his long years in the army. He had grown from boy to man, enduring Empress Nerissa's wars and the tedium of garrison duty, all with one thought in mind: to carve a new life for himself as a man of property. Not a mere farmer, pensioned off onto state-owned land, but a man of substance, with his own business and the respect of his peers.

Utika had been the place where his dreams would come true. His store of coins, carefully hoarded over the years of soldiering, had been enough to buy a prospering business, with some left over to see him through lean times.

He had not counted on Florek's enmity, which had ensured that the townspeople firmly closed ranks against him. But even this he could have overcome, given enough time. Florek was stubborn but no fool. In time he would have seen the virtue of partnering with Myles rather than making an enemy out of him.

Yet from the moment that the man who called himself Josan had come into his life, Myles had known that the future he had sought for himself was not to be. Myles had done his best to put the past behind him, but old loyalties could not be so easily forgotten. Still, he had been cautious. He had worked to gain Josan's trust and waited patiently for him to confide in him.

But weeks had passed, and Josan remained an enigma despite all Myles's attempts to draw him out. It had taken the failed kidnapping to convince Josan that he could not hide from his past, and the perceived life debt that lay between them for Josan to trust Myles enough to let him help.

And even there he had taken a huge gamble. He had arrived at the stable in time to witness Josan defeating the last of his attackers, then collapsing to the ground. For one horrifying moment Myles had thought him dead, but he was only unconscious. When Josan had woken with no memory of what had happened, Myles had instinctively protected him by claiming the killings as his own.

Their relationship had changed on that night, as the roles of master and man were left behind, and they became coconspirators instead. Now they traveled as equals. The coins might be Myles's, but he did not fool himself into thinking that his purse gave him any authority over Josan. All he had on his side were the bonds of friendship and the simple logic that a solitary traveler was more vulnerable than two. Slim threads indeed, but so far Josan had shown himself willing to follow his lead.

It was strange that Josan trusted him with his life but did not trust him enough to share his true name or lineage. Myles had been angered when Josan clung to his lies in spite of the evidence that proved he was not who he claimed to be.

But as the days wore on, Myles came to realize that Josan might be telling the truth. Or at least the truth as he knew it. If the Learned Brethren were responsible for his exile, as Josan claimed, then who knew what they had done to him before setting him loose in the world? His head might have been filled with poisonous half-truths, designed to conceal Josan's identity from himself as well as from strangers.

Josan might not be able to tell his friends from his enemies, in which case it would do more harm than good for Myles to challenge his carefully held delusions. Instead it was up to Myles to protect him until they reached Karystos and the members of the alliance. The brethren might be powerful, but the alliance had its own strengths, and surely they knew of someone who would be able to heal Josan.

Myles had sent word ahead, informing those few he still trusted that he was returning to Karystos and would need their aid. But he had dared not reveal too much in his letters, lest they fall into unfriendly hands. And there was no guarantee that the letters would arrive in Karystos before he did, or that those who received the letters would take action. For now he was on his own.

"I believe we are near Sarna, is that not so?" Josan asked, breaking into Myles's musings.

Myles looked to the west, where the orderly farms on the flat plains gave way to rolling hills. He searched his mind for a moment, remembering the map that they had viewed at the hostel the night before.

"Yes, though we will not pass that way. There is an imperial crossroads up ahead, where you would turn east for Sarna, while we will go west, on the main road to Karystos."

Josan nodded. "I thought as much. I recognized these hills, and I see the provincials still follow their quaint custom of using orange tiles for their roofs."

He fell silent for several moments.

"I spent summers here as a boy. The villa wasn't large or fashionable, but there were horses and a lake that was bone-chilling cold even in the height of summer. It was a good place, though when I grew older I hated every moment spent away from the city and my friends there."

Even his accent was different, the consonants sharper as he spoke of his youth.

Myles made a noncommittal noise that could be taken for interest, but Josan once more fell silent. Still it had been a telling lapse. Myles knew full well that the brethren did not send their young novices off to summer in the hills, safely away from the fevers that swept through Karystos during the hottest part of the year.

It was the confirmation he had long sought, but he did not rejoice. Gratitude would come later, when they were safe. For the time being Myles had to remain vigilant. They were still days away from Karystos, and until then Josan was his sole charge. He had to be protected, from both his enemies and himself. Myles had been given a second chance, and this time he did not intend to fail.

Chapter 13

Lady Ysobel's rented town house was proving everything that she had hoped it would be. The large gracefully appointed rooms on the first floor hosted informal gatherings at least twice a week, while the classically designed dining chamber was well suited to intimate dinners with up to a dozen of her new friends. For her official role, she continued to divide her time between the embassy and her small office here, having observed that the more conservative Ikarians preferred to visit her at the embassy, where the uniformed clerks and trappings of authority helped overcome their reluctance to deal with a woman.

The enclosed courtyard had proven its worth, providing a pleasant sanctuary to enjoy the fair weather. During her evening entertainments it was a favorite among her guests who wished for quiet conversation, away from curious listeners. And, of course, the gate that led into the garden from the alleyway was always left unlocked, to accommodate those who could not be seen entering the front door. The visitors who came through that gate were generally young, male, and heavily cloaked. They tended to glide through the gate in the early hours of the morning or late at night, slipping in as quietly as fog risen from the harbor.

At first the imperial spies had stationed themselves in the back alleyway to take note of her visitors, writing down the descriptions and presumed identities of each. But the alleyway was cramped, and gradually the watchers removed themselves to a nearby tavern, contenting themselves with paying bribes to Ysobel's footman to determine the identity of her secret guests.

No fool, the footman had accepted the coin, then promptly reported the bribe to his mistress. Ysobel ensured that he was well rewarded for his loyalty and given a complete description of her so-called guests to pass along to the watchers. Having gained their confidence, he was then instructed which guests to see and report and which rare few he was to overlook.

The lissome young men that Dama Akantha preferred as messengers served to reinforce Ysobel's reputation with the Ikarian spymasters, and thus were allowed to be seen and reported. But tonight's second caller was a far different matter.

For several weeks, Ysobel had allowed him to make use of her town house for his own liaisons. She had been careful not to be present when he arrived, allowing him to grow accustomed to the luxury of uninterrupted time with the object of his desires, in a place where no one would disturb him, save for servants bringing chilled wine or freshly warmed towels for the bathing chamber.

Now she had broken that routine, positioning herself in a comfortable chair in the parlor, with a brazier to ward off the chill of the hour and a book of poetry to keep her company. As the door from the patio swung open, she looked up and carefully set the book aside.

"Good evening," she said.

The figure paused on the threshold for a moment, his

hand still on the door. Then his hesitation passed and he came into the room, shutting the door softly behind him. His gaze swept the shadows of the room, confirming that there were no others present. Only then did he throw back his cowl and unfasten the ties of his cloak.

"Greetings of the evening to you, Lady Ysobel Flordelis," replied the functionary whom she thought of as Greeter, in remembrance of their first meeting.

There were only a few lamps lit, as befit the late hour, but even in the shadows Greeter's tattoos stood out, the dark swirling designs a shocking contrast to the fair skin underneath. He was dressed modestly, but the maid assigned to the bathing chamber had reported that the tattoos did indeed cover the whole of his body, from his head down to his feet.

The very tattoos that marked him as the empress's own within the palace walls, anonymous among his peers, served to brand him in the city. He could not go anywhere outside the imperial compound without being noticed.

"Is something wrong? Was my friend delayed?" he asked.

"Nothing is amiss. Your friend is waiting for you upstairs. But I thought we might try her patience a moment or two longer if you would consent to drink with me."

"Of course," Greeter said.

There were two carved-crystal glasses on the table next to her, along with a pitcher of a red wine so dark as to appear nearly black. She poured two glasses, then handed one to Greeter and took the second for herself.

He took the glass and sipped politely, though he refused her invitation to sit.

"I heard there was another disturbance in the old city today," she began. "Some said it was a riot, while others claimed it was nothing more than a few mischievous boys throwing rocks at a passing patrol."

"If it had been serious, I would have heard about it," Greeter said.

Which was true, since the functionaries were the eyes and ears of the imperial household. But she noticed that he did not say whether or not he had heard of a riot, merely that if there had been a riot, he would have been informed.

"I trust that the empress is not distressed by the recent unrest," she said.

"The empress is naturally concerned with maintaining order," Greeter replied.

"As am I," Lady Ysobel replied, though her concern was the exact opposite of the empress's. Where Nerissa sought order and harmony, Ysobel sought to sow unrest and discontent.

"You will understand my concern, of course," she added. "Six years ago the unrest spilled from the walls of the palace down to the very ships in harbor. Many traders lost everything, and I do not want to repeat their mistakes. If unrest comes, I wish to be prepared."

Greeter inclined his head. "I understand your concern, but the troubles of the past will not repeat themselves."

Unfortunately for Ysobel's covert mission, it appeared that Greeter was correct in his assessment. Nerissa had made many enemies, but none were powerful enough to take her on. Even Dama Akantha agreed that without a charismatic leader to unite them, there was little chance of the rebellious factions accomplishing anything more than the occasional act of vandalism or petty violence.

Still, she had accomplished what she had set out to do. She had reminded Greeter that there was a price to be paid for his indulgences but ensured that the cost was not so high that he would balk and suddenly recall his loyalties. It had been a marvel that she had discovered his weakness in the first place—a forbidden liaison with a young matron from a noble family. Unable to be seen together publicly, even the private places used by other couples who required discretion were too dangerous for one marked with the tattoos of an imperial functionary.

"Forgive me, I have kept you waiting too long while I indulged my curiosity. Accept my apologies and do not keep your friend waiting any longer."

He did not demur or reply that he was in her debt. Both were true, but the rules of the game demanded that they pretend that she was simply a friend offering her hospitality to another friend so he could conduct his affair in private.

Instead, Greeter set down his nearly full wineglass and gave a half bow of respect. Then he departed, walking so quietly that he made no sound as he left the parlor and climbed the stairs to the second floor, where his lover was no doubt eagerly awaiting his presence.

At least they could be happy for one night, though both must know that the relationship was doomed. They could never be together publicly, and even with the help of Lady Ysobel, every secret meeting increased the chance that they would eventually be discovered. If the fates were merciful, they would burn their passion out and go their separate ways before that time came. But, of course, regardless of whether the affair flourished or withered, Ysobel intended to extract full value for her services.

The difficulty with conspiracies was in knowing whom one could trust. After all, once a man had decided to commit treason, what was there to stop him from committing a second betrayal? More than one disenchanted young man or disaffected noble had dabbled in the talk of treason, only to draw back at the first hint of danger, buying the empress's forgiveness by betraying his erstwhile comrades.

No sworn vow could hold a man who had already betrayed his oaths by joining the rebellion, nor sense of honor silence the tongue of a man who had already committed dishonor. And even the strongest ties of friendship were not proof against the rumored torments of the empress's torture chambers.

Ysobel was wary of self-proclaimed patriots and passionate ideologues. She preferred those with simpler motives. Greedy men could be bought and merely needed to be watched to ensure they understood the consequences of trying to sell their services to two masters. Vengeance, too, was a motive that she could understand and use. As with Nikki, the elder brother of the boy Kauldi, who had been executed for treason. His parents had retired to the countryside to nurse their grief out of view of the empress, but Nikki had refused to accompany them. Instead he had remained in Karystos, frequenting taverns where he poured out his rage to any who had the price of a second jug of wine. Subtle Nikki was not, but he could be used, provided he did not know who was using him.

Men like Greeter and Nikki were commodities, tools used for a purpose, then discarded when they no longer had value. It was the others, those whose hatred for the empress was based on political ideals or out of a lust for power, who could prove the most dangerous. And yet meet with them she must.

Six years ago such meetings had been the task of her senior, while Ysobel merely ran errands for the conspirators, her contacts with them limited to a trusted few such as Dama Akantha. Now Ysobel was the public face of federation support for the rebels' aspirations, and the risk of exposure was tenfold what it had been before.

Which was one reason why each day she memorized the names and berths of every federation-crewed ship in harbor, and which ones could be made ready to sail at a moment's notice. Her frequent visits to the harbor for her official duties had also allowed her to plot out four different ways of entering the dockyards unobserved and the fastest routes from the center of Karystos to the harbor.

Though she sincerely hoped that she did not need to put her knowledge to the test. Fleeing Ikaria would not only put an abrupt end to her hopes of a diplomatic career, it would also damage the standing of her trading house, perhaps irreparably. As Captain Zorion had predicted, the house of Flordelis had taken public steps to separate itself from Ysobel, though in private letters she was assured that she could still draw upon the credit of the house if all other resources failed. Opinion in the Seddonian court, which had been divided over Ysobel's covert mission, had swung firmly against the minister of trade, Lord Quesnel, and by extension Ysobel was tainted with that displeasure. Flordelis would survive, but Ysobel's own fledgling trading house would be crushed.

Never mind that she was only doing her best to fulfill the orders that she had been given. Anything less than complete success would be seen as a failure.

Ironically she was proving a success in her public role. The grain shipments she had negotiated on behalf of Seddon with Jhrve and the house of Septimus the Younger had been profitable for all involved, and led to a number of other ventures. In turn the harbormaster had persuaded Empress Nerissa to grant federation ships a partial dispensation from the taxes levied on foreign vessels, which meant that they could sell their goods at lower prices and still turn a fine profit.

Ysobel's own ships had taken to stopping at Karystos during their trading runs, where her influence meant they could secure profitable cargoes that more than compensated for the extra distance traveled. She knew that Captain Zorion had motives other than mere profit when he had issued his instructions to her captains, but as long as she made a tidy profit, she would not deny herself the pleasure she felt whenever one of her own sailed into the harbor.

The Ikarian Empire still posed a very real threat to Seddon, but she was no longer convinced that promoting internal strife within Ikaria was in the federation's best interests. Yet neither could she abandon her duty, not until new orders arrived from Seddon or Lord Quesnel was replaced.

Her carefully encrypted reports back to Seddon had contained her assessment that there was little hope of promoting a successful rebellion at this time, though naturally she continued to seek out new allies. Such temporizations were unlikely to win her any friends among the ministers, but if she continued to advance Seddon's commercial interests, in time her other failures might be overlooked.

Unless, of course, the situation had changed. She could not imagine any other reason why Dama Akantha had summoned her, using the cover of a masked fete to shield the gathering of those who could not afford to be seen together in public. Over two hundred guests filled the rooms of Dama Akantha's gracious mansion, representing the very cream of Ikarian society. A few of the elders wore simple domino masks that covered their eyes, along with formal attire, but the younger and more daring wore elaborate headdresses and masks that covered their features. The more elaborate the mask, the more revealing the costume, and as the hour grew late, guests slipped away from the dancing into the formal gardens, seeking out darkened corners to exchange embraces.

Ysobel wore a colorful gown made out of brightly colored silk ribbons that had been slashed in strategic places over an underdress of flesh-colored silk. As she spun in the steps of the dance the ribbons flared out, giving the illusion of naked flesh underneath. On her face she wore a half mask of stiffened silk, painted with colorful swirls that matched the streamers on her gown. It was not much of a disguise, but then she did not intend to conceal her identity.

She accepted offers to dance from several of the men present, amusing herself by trying to identify the man behind each mask. Septimus the Younger had made little attempt to hide his appearance, wearing the simple domino affected by those of his father's generation. He proved an able dancer, and she idly wondered if he was equally athletic climbing the rigging of a ship—or between the silken sheets of a soft bed, though from his formal courtesy she doubted she was ever likely to discover the answer to either question.

Two of her partners had to be put in their places for having made the mistake of assuming that the illusion offered by her costume was a sign that she would welcome liberties taken with her person. Neither man was of particular importance, so a crushing grip on the offending hand and a sharp rebuke were enough to send them away chastened.

Ysobel danced, conversed, and took a stroll through the formal dining chamber, which had been cleared of its couches so that tables offering delicacies to tempt even the most refined palate could be erected. She accepted a glass of wine but did not drink, preferring instead to observe those around her. When a servant approached, she slipped away from the crowd, leaving her wineglass behind.

The servant led her through the portico, as if to a tryst in the gardens, but then, after pausing to make certain that no one was watching, opened a hidden door that led down to the wine cellar. Ysobel slipped through the door and, as she began climbing down the stone steps, heard the door close behind her. Carefully she held up her long skirts so that she would not trip, though a moment's observation showed that the stairs were freshly swept, as was the floor of the wine cellar. Details were everything in a conspiracy, and after all the trouble of assembling in secret, it would be folly to have those preparations undone by having the conspirators return to the party covered in dust and cobwebs.

As she turned at the foot of the stairs, she saw six figures gathered around three sides of the wooden table the steward used to decant wines before serving. There were open bottles of wine on the table, and several glasses with splashes of wine in front of each place, as if Dama Akantha were conducting an impromptu wine tasting for a few friends.

And if the imperial guard followed them, they might well accept her excuse, though six years ago such a gathering of seeming political enemies would have been automatically ruled as treason.

Alone among her guests Dama Akantha wore no mask, having declared that her guests were free to amuse themselves but she had no need for such deceits. Lady Ysobel's own half mask did little to conceal her identity, but the others gathered wore fantastic masks of metal and leather that completely obscured their features. Only Dama Akantha would know their identities, but all would know hers.

"Your summons said this was urgent," Ysobel said, taking her place on the fourth side of the table, which had been left open.

Silently the man next to her slid two wineglasses into place in front of her. He wore the head of a badger and a bulky fur costume that must be incredibly warm even on a cool night.

"There was some discussion on the wisdom of involving you at this time," Dama Akantha said, her gaze sweeping the table to single out those of their number who had apparently incurred her displeasure. "But I persuaded them that you had proven yourself a friend capable of holding confidences, and if our hopes are indeed true, then your help may be needed at a moment's notice."

Curious. So they had been assembled for some time, arguing. She noticed that some of the wineglasses were nearly empty, and wondered if there were any dissenters who had been asked to leave before Ysobel was brought down to join them.

"If I am to help, you must explain what you require of me. Seddon is sympathetic to your aspirations, but we will not blindly commit ourselves to folly."

All eyes shifted toward the man who wore the beaten-silver mask and white-hooded cloak of Death. An ominous choice in this place of shadows and secrets, but well chosen for purposes of disguise. At least a half dozen young men had also chosen to dress as Death, in an attempt to appear shocking or mysterious. Once he ascended to the public rooms, it would be difficult to single this one out from his fellow poseurs.

"I received news this week from a friend of ours and sought Dama Akantha's counsel," Death said, using the phrase that connoted a member of the rebellion. He spoke in a raspy whisper, but there was something familiar about how he held himself, the slight stoop of his shoulders, and in the cadence of his words.

"And what news was this?" Ysobel prompted. She had no patience for those who loved drama and the sound of their own voices.

"He has found one of the true blood. The letter was brief, but indicated that they had been pursued and would require a place to hide once they reached Karystos."

The true blood. Had they really found an heir to Constantin's line? Or merely one who looked the part?

"This is wonderful news indeed," she said, forcing a smile to her lips. She should be rejoicing.

Dama Akantha returned her smile with one filled with equal parts malice and unholy glee.

"How well do you trust our friend? Are you certain that this is not a trap?" Ysobel asked.

"He has proven trustworthy in the past. I can vouch for his honor and his dedication to our cause. He would not have sent word unless he was certain," Death answered.

In that moment Ysobel knew his identity. Magistrate Renato, one of the seven judges who presided over the imperial courts. Dama Akantha had played this one very close, for there had not been even a whisper of his involvement in the events six years before.

"If he is of Constantin's line—" Ysobel began.

"The natives will rise up and drag Nerissa from her throne," Dama Akantha proclaimed. "She will pay the price for turning her back on her own people, for they will not lift their hands to save her."

Dama Akantha's hatred allowed her to believe what she wanted to believe. Ysobel could not afford such blindness. Six years ago the rebellion had been utterly crushed—despite having had Prince Lucius, a legitimate heir to Emperor Constantin, as their figurehead. Now they were at a disadvantage in two ways. First there were the memories of Nerissa's ruthlessness in putting down the last rebellion. There would be many who would sympathize with their goals but would not risk their lives out of fear of the empress's wrath.

And second they did not have a legitimate heir, merely one who had convinced this mysterious informant that he could play the part. He could be an unlettered bastard with all the charisma of a lump of stale cheese.

Or he could be exactly what they had been hoping for. A presentable fool who could be carefully managed to act as figurehead but would allow others to rule from the shadows of the throne.

Not that the rebellion had any hope of succeeding. But a prolonged rebellion would weaken Ikaria and allow Seddon to expand its trading empire unchallenged. That was what she had been sent to accomplish. It was the very goal that she had thought out of reach and had worried that her failure would mean the end of her career in politics.

It was a moment for celebration. Ysobel picked up the nearest wineglass. "A toast to the new emperor. May the triune gods watch over his journey and deliver him safely to his people."

They raised their glasses, and said, "To our next emperor."

The others sipped decorously, but Ysobel tossed the contents back in three quick swallows. It had been a long night already, and her adventures were far from over.

"When do you expect him to arrive?"

"Within the fortnight," Death said.

"Dama Akantha, what do you require of me?"

"A safe hiding place if he is followed. As for the rest, I will call upon you in two days' time, and we can discuss how you can best aid us."

"Of course," she said. In her head she began making lists. They would need weapons, of course. She had already amassed a small stockpile to replace those that had been lost when the *Pride* sank. She should assemble small sacks of coins to use for bribes, old coins of mixed lineages so they could not be traced back to their source. And any new trading ventures would need to be put on hold, at least temporarily.

She would return to the embassy to sleep so she could catch Ambassador Hardouin before he began his day's duties. He should be informed of the new development, though as of yet they had nothing more than hopes and unfounded rumor. Still, her danger sense was tingling— the sense that warned of hidden sandbars under placid seas or that a crowded marketplace was about to turn violent. Perhaps it was Dama Akantha's excitement, so different from the reserved pessimism she had displayed in the past months. Or perhaps it was merely the uncanny effect of discussing rebellion and treason with a man wearing the mask of Death.

A storm was coming, and Ysobel had best prepare. This was the test that she had wanted, and for good or ill she would make her mark on the place.

She smiled again, wondering if the others could sense the falseness of her emotions as she pretended to an enthusiasm she did not feel. And she wondered again if one of the masks concealed the face of one who would betray them.

She shivered and blamed it on the chill of the wine cellar, whose cool dampness was more suited to the comfort of grapes than people.

"I will take my leave. Dama Akantha will pass messages to me. I ask that you not contact me directly unless there is no choice."

There was a vague murmur of agreement.

As she climbed the stairs the others stayed behind, no doubt to talk more among themselves. Carefully she eased the door open a fraction, waiting until the corridor was empty before she slipped out. She continued down to the garden, making certain that she "accidentally" stumbled across two lovers locked in an indecorous embrace. The young woman shrieked, then hid her face behind her partner, as Ysobel stammered apologies while fighting off a grin.

Thus having established her presence in the garden, she returned indoors. The playwright Khepri called out when he saw her, and she joined the circle of his admirers for a short time. Then, judging that she had stayed long enough, she summoned her litter bearers to take her to the embassy.

It had been a long night, but she doubted that she would sleep. She realized that, until now she had been certain that there would be no rebellion. That any attempted uprising would be doomed to failure. She had made endless preparations, but had been confident that they would never be used. Ironically she was made uneasy by the prospect of success.

"May the gods give you what you wish for" the ancient curse ran, and Ysobel felt herself the recipient of such largesse.

Still, a good trader could turn even the most dire situation to his advantage. She should not let herself be dismayed by the coming events. Instead she should keep her eyes firmly fixed on her goals and seize any opportunities that arose. She had asked for a chance to prove herself, and at last she had it.

The federation councilors who had opposed Lord Quesnel's plan had done so because they feared the consequences of failure. In their view, the uneasy truce between Ikaria and Seddon was preferable to the open warfare that would ensue if the empress ever discovered proof that agents of Seddon had been behind the rebellion. But success was the universal coin, accepted in any market. If she succeeded in miring Ikaria in internal strife without revealing her hand in the matter, then the council would be quick to claim her success for its own and to reward her for her efforts.

She could achieve in her lifetime what it had taken Flordelis generations to accomplish. She would be head of a trading house of the first rank, with a fleet of the finest ships and the capital boldly to explore the most distant markets in search of the rarest treasures. And she would be able to put politics firmly behind her.

But first she had to survive, and hope that Dame Akantha and her allies remained cautious. Otherwise, she risked falling into the empress's hands, and if Nerissa suspected her of inciting treason, there was not enough gold in all of Seddon to save Ysobel from a slow and painful death.

"Please, no more, no more," the prisoner gasped between shuddering breaths.

He had stopped screaming sometime ago, after Nizam had cut off the last of his fingers. Not because the agonies he had endured since then had been any less painful, but by then his broken body no longer had the strength to scream, or indeed to resist in any way as Nizam demonstrated the skills that had made him a master at extracting information from even the most reluctant of subjects.

Not that Paolo had been reluctant to tell everything he knew or suspected. Indeed, after five days of Nizam's personal attention, Paolo had eagerly shared every thought he had ever had in his miserably short life. Once satisfied that he had broken the prisoner, Nizam had sent word to the empress.

Upon receiving the missive, Nerissa dressed in a simple linen gown and made her way to the cells that lay beneath the imperial garrison, through the door that was not spoken of, and down the corridor that led to the rooms of pain that all knew existed but few had ever seen.

Patiently she had waited as Paolo—a onetime sneak thief and petty criminal—was led from his cell. She knew the moment that he recognized her, for he began to struggle in earnest, and it took the efforts of four guards to strap him into the wooden interrogation frame. Like most prisoners, until that moment he had nursed the hope that his secrets might win him his freedom, or at least spare his life, but even the dullest of minds knew that her presence in the chamber meant that they could not be allowed to live.

Still, the days of agony had given him strong incentive to cooperate. Nizam and his assistants had stood carefully back as the thief poured out his confession to her. Sweating, his eyes darting round the chamber, unable to stay focused on her face, Paolo told what little he knew.

Some months ago he had happened to overhear a conversation between a pair he judged to be a noble and a mercenary. The mercenary had been hired to find a man and bring him back to Karystos in secret, but the noble was offering to treble his payment if he killed the man instead. A strange, twisted plot, which would ordinarily have been of little interest to Nizam, were it not that the intended victim was described as bearing an uncanny resemblance to the late Prince Lucius. Like enough to be his cousin, or even his brother, was how he had been described.

Paolo, who had been caught with a sackful of gold and silver objects belonging to a minor noblewoman, had thought to bargain with this knowledge to gain forgiveness for his thefts. It had been a poor choice. At most the thefts would have cost him his right hand. But the knowledge he held ensured that he would never face a magistrate.

Once Paolo had finished his tale, he begged for her mercy.

"Have you told me everything? Absolutely everything?" she asked.

He swore he had.

Nerissa had nodded, then had turned to Nizam and given him the instruction to begin.

Now, hours later, Nizam's strongest persuasion had proven that there was nothing more Paolo could tell them. He had given them a description of the mercenary and the name by which the mercenary allowed himself to be called, but it was doubtful that the mercenary had returned to Karystos.

Of the noble, Paolo could tell them nothing. He had not seen the man, nor heard him called by name. He might not be a noble at all, merely one who spoke with the accent of an educated man, which was how Paolo had identified him.

Nerissa studied Paolo, who hung limply in the torture frame, each breath a rasping effort that brought bubbling blood to his lips. Despite Nizam's care not to inflict lethal damage, it seemed one or more of the prisoner's ribs was broken. Blood, vomit, and piss stained the floor beneath him and filled the air with their stench. Her sandals would have to be burned, as would her cloak.

"There's nothing more he can tell us, your majesty," Nizam observed. His tone was flat, as if remarking on the weather. Nizam achieved no pleasure from inflicting pain, but neither did he shirk his duties. He could be trusted to do whatever it took to secure the information needed, but when a prisoner had told them all that he knew, Nizam had no interest in prolonging his agonies.

"I agree," she said.

Nizam stepped behind the prisoner and with a swift motion looped a length of wire around his neck. As he pulled the wire taut, Paolo's eyes bulged, and his limbs jerked within their restraints. She forced herself to watch until he ceased twitching and his body finally sagged.

She'd asked Nizam once why he used a garrote, rather than a more traditional knife or sword. "Less mess," he'd explained.

The chamber would still have to be scrubbed down, a job reserved for the prisoners in the outer cells who were awaiting their own executions, though they, at least, could be grateful that they had been spared Nizam's attentions.

"Send the description of this mercenary to the captain of the watch," she ordered.

"Yes, your majesty."

A glance at her cloak showed it was spotted with blood. Reaching up, she unfastened the clasp, and let the garment fall to the floor.

"You have done well, and I thank you for your service," she said. Then, with one final glance at the prisoner, she turned and left.

Her escort was waiting for her at the entrance to the outer cellblock. Their faces were impassive, but she was certain they all understood how she had spent the past hours, and the reason she no longer wore a cloak.

This was not the first time she had observed Nizam at his labors, nor would it be the last. Her advisors had been shocked when she had first insisted on visiting the torture chambers, but Nerissa had held firm. She would not pretend that the torture chambers did not exist. If torture was done in her name, then she was strong enough to bear witness.

Not that such scenes were a daily event. Indeed, it had been over a year since Nizam had last sent word of a prisoner that would be of interest to her. Rumor painted the torture chambers as pits of hell, where screams echoed day and night. That was true, when the secret cells were in use. But prisoners requiring Nizam's special talents were rarer than most thought, and those that would be of personal interest to the empress even rarer still.

Six years ago it had been a different matter. Then the secret cells had been filled with the supporters of Prince Lucius. The information extracted by Nizam had been instrumental in identifying the ringleaders and ultimately suppressing the rebellion.

She had thought those days behind her, but the recent unrest in Karystos troubled her, as it did her advisors. Brother Nikos was quick to cast the blame upon the Federation of Seddon, and in particular on Lady Ysobel, accusing her of stirring up old resentments and secretly working with those who opposed Nerissa's rule.

Which would be a shame if it were true. She liked Lady Ysobel, or at least she liked what she knew of the woman's character, having invited her to the palace on several occasions. Nikos had urged her to expel the new trade liaison, but none of her other councilors saw Ysobel as a threat. Most dismissed her as inconsequential because of her sex, not seeming to realize the folly of arguing such a position in front of their ruler, who was also a woman.

There were a few who praised Lady Ysobel and pointed out the advantages to be realized through cooperation with the federation. The harbormaster Septimus could be excused his partiality, for his dealings with Lady Ysobel had already fattened his purse. But Nerissa had her own reasons for wanting to expand the partnerships between Seddon and Ikaria. The captains of federation ships were without peer, masters of sailing routes that were closely guarded secrets. Past attempts to discover those secrets had failed, but each time a federation ship allowed Ikarian merchants or Ikarian sailors aboard, it was another opportunity for knowledge. She would not destroy such chances lightly. Only when she had proof of Lady Ysobel's deception would she act.

But if Seddon was not behind the unrest in Karystos, then who was? How many enemies had escaped detection those long years ago? What had stirred them into action again? Had they truly found a pretender to the throne? Was this the price of Aitor's mercy? Allowing Princess Callista and her daughters to live had been a magnanimous act of charity and proof that Aitor had nothing to fear from the former rulers of Ikaria.

Aitor II had followed his father's example, and when Nerissa ascended the throne, she had seen no reason to change the status quo. Lucius might have been the great-grandson of Callista, but it had been a hundred years since one of his blood had sat on the throne, and there had seemed little to fear from the squalling child. Nerissa had shown her mercy in allowing a male heir of Constantin to live and demonstrated her prudence by insisting that he be raised under the watchful supervision of the court.

Tragically, Lucius had confused mercy with weakness. Rather than being thankful for her generosity, he had allowed himself to be swayed by those who sought only to use him. And for his folly he had paid the ultimate price. Most believed that he had screamed his life away in the very chambers she had just left, and she had done nothing to discourage that belief.

The truth, that Lucius had escaped her justice, was known only to her, Brother Nikos, and a few of her most closely trusted allies. Six years ago, as the rebellion was collapsing, Lucius's own followers had turned on him, hoping to buy their own forgiveness with the prince's corpse. Mortally wounded, Lucius had escaped their clutches, only to be discovered by a member of the Learned Brethren. Taking his own revenge, Lucius had revealed the names of his former allies before he died, and she had then used that information to good advantage.

She would send for the records of those long-ago interrogations to see what they might have overlooked. There had been more than one who had fallen under suspicion, but there had not been enough evidence to bring them in for questioning. They would have to be reinvestigated and watched carefully until she could be certain where their loyalties lay. Last time she had been taken unawares; this time she would be ready. And she would do whatever it took to secure her throne, even if it meant she had to wield the lash herself.

There was a time for mercy and kindness. And there was a time for strict discipline and punishing wayward children to teach them their places. The native Ikarians would come to heel, and in time they would learn to thank her for her care.

Chapter 14

Home. Josan could feel the pull of the city, calling to him. The weight of his years of exile on Txomin's Island and the longing to be once more among his own kind rose within him, pulling him inexorably toward the one place he associated with safety—the high stone walls and quiet courtyards of the collegium. The closer they came to Karystos, the more impatient he became.

The night before, he had been unable to sleep, knowing that the coming day would bring them within the walls of his native city. His restless pacing around their rented room had brought grumbles from Myles, who slept lightly in recent nights, as if fearing an attack. So Josan had settled himself as if to meditate, but such mental discipline was no longer within his grasp. Perhaps it was simply the anticipation of his long awaited homecoming. Or perhaps it was the pressure of the Other, who stirred restlessly, an unwelcome presence beneath the surface of Josan's thoughts. Whatever the reason, he could no longer summon the calm reflection that had been as natural to him as breathing by the time he was a novice.

Instead he had let his mind drift to recollections of his

days in Karystos, calling to mind the perfect order of the central library of the collegium, the low hum of the brethren chanting the praises of the twin gods, the feel of cool marble beneath his feet. His mind stretched outward from the buildings of the collegium, traversing the great square, then following the Road of Triumph that led from the great square of the people up the central hill to the imperial compound, where the palace was surrounded by buildings of state.

In his imagination he stood on a balcony at the topmost floor of the palace, gazing over the city spread below him as it sloped down to the central harbor. The sun glinted off the white-stone buildings as if the city was new-built, or a noble's toy laid out for his pleasure. For a brief moment he allowed himself to wonder if this was what the empress saw when she gazed out the windows of her apartments. Did she see the city and think of the lives contained within it? Or did she see merely the wealth and power at her command?

The question occupied his mind for some time till he realized how foolish his speculations were. How could he expect to know the mind of an empress? He was a monk, accustomed to obedience, not leadership, and his studies had focused on science, not politics.

Though his arrival in Karystos would be seen as a sign that he had not learned the lessons of obedience. Brother Nikos had strictly forbidden his return, but surely once he understood Josan's circumstances, he would also understand the reasons that had compelled him to return. And if all Josan had to fear was punishment for disobeying that order, he would be a fortunate man indeed. More and more, he had become convinced that the gaps in his memories hid the knowledge of some unspeakable crime.

Which, paradoxically, only increased his eagerness to return to the brethren. He was tired of being protected from himself, treated as one not capable of making his own decisions. The brethren might have been trying to protect him, and indeed the confused man who had left their care six years before had been much in need of guidance. But Josan was no longer that man. He did not need protection; he needed the truth. Regardless of how ugly it was. He could not move forward until he had faced his past.

Such thoughts had occupied his mind throughout the long night. An hour before dawn the shreds of his patience had snapped, and he had risen from his cot and awakened Myles. With only a few words they dressed in the darkness, then went down to the common room of the hostel, where a few coppers convinced the yawning attendant to stir the kitchen fire so they could have hot tea and barley soup before they set off.

The road leading to Karystos was wide and level, with a raised berm on either side to channel rainfall away from its surface. At first traffic was sparse, but soon after sunrise the road became packed with travelers on foot, drovers taking beasts to market, wagonloads of goods to feed the ever-hungry city, plus the occasional rider or carriage. If the road had been clear, they could have reached the city in just a few hours, but as it was it took them most of the day to make their way through the press of humanity.

On either side of the road, villas whose modest size belied their expense alternated with orchards that bore exotic fruits to cater to the wealthiest residents of Karystos. Gradually these open spaces disappeared, until either side of the road was lined with buildings—merchants' and artisans' shops mixed in with apartments for those who made their living serving the great capital but could not afford to live within. This was the outer city that had sprung up beyond the city walls, and as the buildings enclosed Josan and Myles on both sides, it felt increasingly like a trap.

It was barely spring, but Josan felt the sweat running

down his back as if it were high summer. He fought the urge to draw the cowl over his head, knowing that hiding his face would only serve to draw attention to him. Myles, too, was doing his best to appear an ordinary traveler, having decided not to wear his leather armor.

As they approached the gate that led into the city proper, Josan tensed. He knew at least one magistrate had issued a warrant for his arrest in connection with the death of the assassin at the lighthouse. It was unlikely that they would expect him to return to Karystos, but if they did, then the guards at the gates might well have been alerted to look for him. It was small comfort that he bore no resemblance to the shaven-headed monk of the island. He no longer recognized his own face in the mirror, but his enemies were not as easily confused. They had had no trouble finding him in Utika, after all.

"Easy," Myles murmured, as it came their turn to pass through the gates.

Josan noticed that Myles had loosened his sword in his scabbard, though if it came to blows, a single mounted soldier could not expect to prevail against a half dozen guards, even if they were on foot. Crop Ear, who had shown a remarkably placid disposition for the entire journey, chose that moment to take offense as a kid goat ran bleating between her hooves. She reared back just as a young boy dived in pursuit of the goat.

Josan jerked hard on the reins to keep Crop Ear's hooves from dashing the boy's skull. After a few dancing steps, and much head tossing, she settled down.

The two nearest guards had seized both goat and boy, and were impugning their probable joint ancestry with rough eloquence. With a mere glance they waved Josan and Myles through, still caught up in berating the boy for his carelessness.

It was only when the angry shouts of the guards had

faded behind them that Josan allowed himself to relax. Luck had favored them this time, but he knew better than to assume it would last. As they reached the first of the ring streets that encircled the city, Josan guided his horse toward the right, only to have Myles seize his reins.

"Hold," Myles said. "Where are you going?"

Josan glanced around, but none of the passersby seemed interested in them. Still he lowered his voice to a whisper as he replied, "The collegium, where else?"

Myles shook his head. "And how do you know it is safe?"

How could he not trust the brethren? This was the whole point of his journey, was it not?

"But—"

Myles pulled the rein, guiding their horses to the left. "We will stay this night with a friend of mine. Find out what is happening in the city and whether there are watchers at the collegium, hoping for you to fall into their hands."

Josan hesitated, then gave in. "For tonight, only," he said.

On the journey it had been easy for him to let Myles make the decisions. Simpler to play at master and man rather than to risk their friendship becoming something else. He knew Myles wanted more than mere friendship from him, but Josan had nothing to offer. He could not trust himself, not while madness threatened, and not while so much of his past was still veiled in darkness.

Fortunately, Myles was not put off by Josan's diffidence, seemingly content for the moment with friendship. And he had once again proven his worth with his clear thinking. The collegium had fewer entrances than the city and was far easier to watch. If his enemies had set a trap, it would most likely be there.

He had been so focused on the collegium as a place of refuge that it had not occurred to him that, the closer he came to that refuge, the greater danger he would be in.

Fortunately, Myles was able to reason logically while Josan had been blinded by his emotions.

Still he would only be guided by Myles for so long. If Myles reported that it was unsafe to approach the collegium, then Josan would send word to Brother Nikos to arrange a meeting in a safe location. Either way, he would have his answers.

The city streets were too steep and crowded to navigate on horseback, so they left their mounts at a livery stable, where the price of a month's stabling in Utika bought them a week of care and a promise that the horses would be cooled off before they were put in their stalls. With their saddlebags slung over their shoulders, Myles led them unerringly through the streets, giving a wide berth to the imperial compound before turning down the wide avenue that separated the second ring from the third. A respectable neighborhood inhabited by government ministers and minor courtiers, it seemed an unlikely place for a friend of a former mercenary. In the late afternoon the streets were quiet as the inhabitants dozed in their chambers or went about their business elsewhere in the city. Still, there were a few people about—mostly servants hurrying by on errands, who eyed the travelers askance, as if suspecting they were criminals bent on mischief.

Myles turned into a narrow alleyway between two of the great houses. He paused as soon as they were out of view. "Your cowl, raise it."

"Why?"

"Because."

Josan shrugged, then tugged his cowl so that it hid his face, wondering why Myles had not done the same. To his surprise Myles continued down the alleyway, which led to a narrow lane behind the great houses, used for access by servants and delivery carts. Now their route made more sense. Undoubtedly Myles's friend was a servant in one of these great houses.

To Josan's eyes, each iron gate set in the low stone wall appeared identical to its neighbors, but Myles must have been here frequently since he stopped at the sixth gate and lifted the bar. No one challenged them as they made their way along the stone path to a plain wooden door.

Myles tugged on the rope that hung from a hole next to the door, and they heard the faint sound of a ringing bell. After a moment the top half of the door swung open, revealing a youth dressed in the sleeveless tunic of a common servant.

"I have business with the steward," Myles said.

The boy looked at them dubiously.

"Go. Fetch him," Myles barked.

The boy jumped and hastily swung the top half of the door shut.

This time the wait was longer, and Josan wondered what they would do if Myles's friend was no longer a servant there. He had enough coins left for lodgings down by the wharf if it came to that, and Myles still had coins in his purse, along with the imperial scrip.

This time the entire door swung open. The man who stood there was middle-aged, his spotless livery girded with the belt of his office, his round cheeks and pale skin giving evidence of a comfortable life. He did not seem the type who would call Myles friend, and Josan braced himself to be turned away.

"I am the Sergeant and this is a friend of ours," Myles said. As he spoke, his right hand flashed a series of complicated gestures.

The steward's eye flickered once to Josan, then returned to Myles. "Of course. If you would follow me," he said, with a subtle inclination of his head.

These were not the mannerisms of two old friends

greeting one another. On the contrary, coded phrases and recognition signals were the hallmarks of criminals or conspirators.

Myles started through the door, but Josan caught his arm. "What is going on?" he hissed.

"You have trusted me this far," Myles replied. "Trust me a little longer, and I will explain everything."

Josan's gaze searched his face, but found nothing in it except concern, and he realized that he was acting foolishly. He would stake his life that Myles did not intend to harm him. Myles was entitled to a few secrets of his own, and if he trusted these people, then Josan would give them the benefit of the doubt. For the time being.

The steward led them up through the kitchens, then up the stairs that led from the servants quarters into the public spaces of the mansion. Pausing outside a paneled door, he knocked once, then opened the door.

"Magistrate Renato, your guests have arrived," he announced. He bowed, then gestured for the two men to precede him into the room.

Josan started as the doors swung shut behind them.

Magistrate Renato rose from his seat behind his desk and advanced to greet them. A tall man, whose shoulders were stooped from age, his face broke into a broad smile.

"Sergeant, I remember you. You had no trouble getting here?"

"We were not followed," Myles said.

Josan tugged back the cowl of his cloak, revealing his features, watching closely as Magistrate Renato's eyes widened in shock.

"And this is—" the magistrate began.

"This is a friend of ours, who calls himself Josan," Myles interrupted.

"This is a great honor for me," Renato continued smoothly, though Josan had no doubt that he had originally intended to say something else. "You are both welcome in my home."

"How do you know each other?" Josan asked.

"We met in difficult times, when the sergeant was kind enough to do me a favor. I promised I was at his service if ever he had need of a favor in return," Renato said.

It was an explanation of sorts. Difficult times could refer to anything from a petty brawl in the marketplace to the bloody uprising six years past. Whatever service Myles had done for Renato, it had obviously impressed the magistrate enough that he remembered him.

Renato's initial shock had given way to satisfaction. He rubbed his hands together and licked his lips as his gaze flickered from Josan to Myles and back again. There was something in the way that Renato's eyes swept over every detail of their appearance that made Josan feel as if he were on display. Renato did not have the air of a man repaying a favor, but rather the air of a man whose long hunger was about to be satisfied.

Perhaps the relationship between Myles and Renato had been one of an intimate nature, and what he was seeing was simple lust. That could also explain why Renato was so interested in him, seeing Josan as a potential rival for Myles's affections.

Though a mere physical relationship would not explain why Myles had been given code words that gained him entry to this house, long after he had left Karystos. Josan's unease grew as he remembered his suspicions that Myles had been more than the mere soldier he claimed to be.

"You must be tired from your long journey. Let me summon servants to take you to rooms where you may refresh yourselves. You will join me for the evening meal, and we can talk about how I may best help you."

Renato looked at Josan as he spoke, so after a long moment he replied, "Thank you."

A bell instantly summoned the steward, who must have been waiting outside in the corridor while they talked. He led them to a large room that adjoined an ample bathing chamber. After so many weeks of travel, when bathing had been a rag dampened in a basin, Josan and Myles took turns scraping the dust of the road from their bodies, then soaking in the warm bath.

When Josan returned to the sleep chamber, he found a linen tunic and cotton trousers laid out for him. From the fineness of the silk bands that adorned the tunic he guessed the clothing had once been part of Renato's own wardrobe. The tunic fit well enough, for Renato was his equal in height, though the drawstring of the trousers was the only thing that kept them from slipping off his hips.

Clothing was laid out for Myles as well, plainer than what was offered to Josan, no doubt because of the differences in their sizes. Still, freshly bathed, with their itching beards trimmed off, and in clothing that was not held together by dust and sweat, the two of them appeared entirely respectable. They would be fit dining companions for the magistrate and whoever else of his household would be in attendance.

Myles had just finished retying his sandal straps when the boy who had greeted them earlier returned to conduct them to the dining chamber. Magistrate Renato was apparently a bachelor, for there were only three couches set out around the dining platform.

Perhaps it was the fatigue of the journey finally catching up with him. Or perhaps it was merely the strangeness of a day that began with the fear of capture and ended as an honored guest. Whatever the reason, Josan felt a strange sense of unreality as he sipped a glass of pale yellow wine while Magistrate Renato inquired as to his comfort. He assured the magistrate that their rooms were to their satisfaction, noting yet again that while it was Myles who held the claim of friendship, it was Josan's approval their host sought.

The wine tasted sweet on his tongue, and he could feel fatigue creeping up on him. As he held the wine cup in his hand, he found himself wishing that the magistrate's palate was less refined. For a moment it seemed that the cup grew warm in his hand, but then realized it was merely because the cup was half-empty. After Renato refilled it, Josan took another sip. The wine wasn't as sweet as he had first thought, and indeed it went well with the bread and olives that had been set out as the first course.

They conversed as if they were old friends recently returned to the city, as Magistrate Renato shared tidbits of recent events. The olives were followed by salads of fresh greens drizzled with vinegar, then the main course, pork cooked in wine, garnished with both red and green grapes. By the time the savory was set out, slices of apples topped with melted cheese, Josan could eat no more.

Renato had kept everyone's wine cups filled, and though the wine served with the main course had been generously watered Josan had taken care to drink sparingly. Despite his caution, Josan felt his head drooping with exhaustion.

"I can see you are both fatigued," Renato said. "We should wait until you have rested to discuss serious matters."

"But—" Josan began.

"I agree with the magistrate," Myles said. "We will have clearer heads in the morning."

Something was wrong. Myles had not mentioned the Learned Brethren once, and following his lead Josan had kept his own tongue silent as well. Still, they had come to the magistrate for his help, had they not? Or was it that Myles trusted Renato with their persons but not with their secrets?

After thanking Renato for the excellent dinner, Josan and

Myles made their way back to the chamber that had been assigned to them. The hour was early, but his sleepless night had caught up with Josan, and as he sat down on his bed he felt the urge simply to lie down and wrap himself in the blankets.

"Who is Renato to you?" Josan asked. "And why did you not speak to him about the brethren?"

Myles sat down on the opposite bed. "I met Renato a few years ago when I did him a favor. Something that could have caused him much embarrassment if it had been improperly handled, but I was able to help him, and in turn he has been a friend to me."

Myles reached down and began unfastening his sandals. "I want us both clearheaded when we talk to Renato and ask his advice. And your story is too long to do it justice in a few sentences, which is all we have left before you fall asleep."

Josan opened his mouth to protest, but instead he yawned, thus proving Myles's point. It was true, he could hardly think. His head was swimming with weariness, and it was all he could do to strip off his tunic and untie his sandals. Gratefully, he stretched out on the soft mattress, leaving it to Myles to blow out the lamps.

Dimly he heard Myles moving around the room. Josan rolled over onto his side, savoring the feeling of a mattress that held neither lumps nor unwelcome critters. The soft blanket caressed his skin, a far cry from the coarse wool he was accustomed to. Such luxury was to be his only for a night, so he would make the most of it.

Yet even as a part of him welcomed sleep, there was another part that cried out for wakefulness. That something was wrong, and he dare not rest. *You have been tricked*, the Other told him. *This is a trap.*

Cold fear replaced his earlier lethargy as he realized that the Other was in ascendance. Josan could not afford to lose control. Not now, not when he was so close to the ones who could help him. He sought to center himself, inhaling and exhaling in carefully measured breaths, focusing his mind on the underlying order of the universe and his place within it. But the disciplines of meditation were no match for the Other, who continued to whisper of danger and betrayal.

Abandoning meditation, his mind raced for alternatives. Chants, meditation, even asserting his identity had not proven enough to silence the Other in the past. He needed to focus his mind on a single thought. He cast his mind back to the years spent living with the brethren, wondering what secrets of soul magic they would be able to offer him. His thoughts turned to Brother Thanatos, which was odd since to his knowledge Thanatos had never studied soul magic. Numbers were his life, and he had shared that passion with all of his pupils.

Slowly, Josan began mentally ticking off the sacred numbers. One. Three. Five. Seven. Eleven. As he counted, the strange whispers of the Other grew quieter. He was congratulating himself on his success when he heard the door to the chamber open.

Opening his eyes, he saw Myles's figure silhouetted against the light coming in through the partially opened door.

"Is he asleep?" he heard Renato ask.

"He'll sleep till morning. I assume there was something in his wine?"

"Of course."

Myles slipped through the door and as he closed it behind him, the room plunged into darkness.

Betrayal the Other chortled, and this time Josan agreed. It would have hurt less if Myles had merely stabbed him. He had trusted Myles, at a time when he could trust no one else, not even himself. And now Myles had turned on him.

Josan sat up, his earlier exhaustion forgotten. He located his sandals and tunic by touch and quickly dressed. By then his eyes were accustomed to the darkness, and he made his way unerringly to the door. Cracking it open, he glanced down the corridor, which was empty.

Instinct told him that Renato would feel safest speaking to Myles in his study, and memory guided him back along the route he had taken earlier that day. The Other whispered for Josan to flee, but Josan needed to know the extent of Myles's treachery. It would not do to escape this trap only to fall into another.

When he reached the lower level he passed a servant who was just leaving the study. The servant kept his eyes firmly fixed on the floor, not acknowledging Josan's presence except by the way he was careful not to block his path. The sign of a well-trained retainer, one accustomed to serving in a house of secrets.

It was a bitter reminder of how blind he had been. From the moment they had approached this place the signs of conspiracy had been all around him, but he had willfully closed his eyes. He had put his faith in Myles's friendship rather than demanding to know the truth.

That was about to change.

The door to the study had been left slightly ajar, and through it he heard voices. He waited till the servant was out of sight, then moved closer, wondering what to do next. Should he attempt to spy on them? Confront them with their trickery?

But what he heard made his blood run cold and froze him in place.

"And he has no idea who he is?"

"None whatsoever." He recognized Myles's voice, and

knew from the tone that his erstwhile friend was frustrated. "The brethren have filled his head with lies."

"A glance in the mirror ought to be enough to prove his lineage."

Myles gave a grim laugh. "He is stubborn, and disinclined to take anyone's counsel except his own."

"Well, he has Constantin's arrogance."

"And that will not be enough. I'd hoped one of the alliance would know a magician who could break whatever spell the brethren have put him under."

Myles must have seen more of the Other than Josan had realized and apparently decided that his madness was the result of an evil spell. But if Myles did not believe that he was the monk Josan, then who did he think he was? Why had he kept his knowledge to himself? Had he done so out of a sense of misguided friendship? Or were there darker motives at work?

And why would Magistrate Renato help him? What had he to gain?

"I thought such magics the province of legends and children's tales. It is unlikely that there is anything that can be done."

"But you will try?" Myles sounded genuinely concerned, which made his apparent betrayal even more puzzling.

"I will try," Renato said. "And perhaps our friends from the Seddon Federation have resources that we do not."

"We cannot afford to wait for one to journey from Seddon. I could barely convince him to spend the night here. If we do not do something, he will be off to seek the brethren tomorrow, and our hopes will be dashed."

"I agree, we have no time to wait. Healed or no, we can still use him. We must use him," Renato said. "If your path had taken you through the old city, you would have seen the signs. The killings have started, and already we are on the verge of losing control. We need him, as much as he needs us."

"And what if we cannot persuade him to join us? What then?"

"We will give him no choice."

Josan had heard enough. He moved forward to confront them, ready to demand an explanation. But as he reached to push open the door, his hand froze.

The killings have started, the Other whispered.

He tried to move forward, but his mind was filled with strange images. Buildings burning, the flames turning the dark of night into day. Corpses filling the streets, blood running through the gutters. He scrubbed his eyes with the heels of his hands, trying to force out the visions, but they persisted.

A woman's body, naked, her bowels gaping obscenely through her slashed belly. The torso of a man, his limbs hacked off in evidence of the savage violence of his death. Two maniacally grinning skulls, posted on stakes outside the imperial palace.

These were more than mere nightmares. To his horror he realized that these were images of his past. A past that was threatening to repeat itself—if Renato had his way.

Josan was paralyzed with fear, overwhelmed by images of sickening violence. He could not move, but the Other— perhaps immune to the horrors that lurked within—did not share his weakness. Josan's terror rose as he felt his body move without conscious volition. Turning on his heel, he lurched down the corridor. He struggled to regain control of his body, but succeeded only in waving one arm, and knocking a figurine off a table. The crash as it hit the tile floor seemed loud enough to wake the dead, and he knew that Myles would waste no time in coming to investigate.

He had no choice. He needed to flee, and he could not do it alone. Reluctantly, he stopped fighting the Other.

As his body fled, with a speed that he had not known he possessed, he could not help wondering if in fleeing one evil, he had made the mistake of embracing another.

Chapter 15

Sandals slapped against tiled floors as the sound of running footsteps disturbed the ordered tranquility of the collegium. Brother Nikos looked up from his journal as he heard the footfalls approaching. It was far too late an hour for the noises to be the sounds of a heedless novice at play, and he wondered what crisis had provoked such haste.

He rose to his feet as there was a sharp knock, then the door to his private rooms was flung open.

"Brother Nikos, beg your pardon, but we need you," Jeno gasped out, in between panting breaths. A young novice in his first year of service, he had never before shown signs of an excitable disposition. "There is a madman at the postern gate who demands to speak with you."

Nikos stilled. The room was colder than it had been moments ago, and the shadows seemed even darker, as if reminding him of the lateness of the hour. "A madman, you say?"

Jeno nodded vigorously. "And a noble. He claimed to be one of us and insisted on being admitted. I summoned Brother Basil, but when Brother Basil did not recognize him either, the man grew upset and began insisting on seeing you. I thought to summon the watch, but Brother Basil said I should consult you first."

"No," Nikos said swiftly. The time he had long feared had finally come; his renegade monk had returned. Inviting Josan in was dangerous, but involving the watch would expose too many of Nikos's own secrets. It was unlikely that Empress Nerissa would believe that his actions six years ago had been driven by a desire to preserve order and ensure peace. And far better that the danger Josan represented be contained within the walls of the collegium rather than wandering the streets of Karystos, ready to tell his tale to whoever would listen.

"Run back, as quick as you can, and have Brother Basil bring the man to me."

"But—" Jeno protested, his confusion evident.

Nikos laid his hand on the novice's arm to reassure him. "I cannot turn away a troubled soul. It is our duty to help him, or to see that he is brought to those who can. Now go, swiftly, before the watch finds him on their own."

Nikos watched him disappear. Jeno posed a problem, but he could be dealt with later. The novice on postern duty served at his post until dawn, so there were several hours during which he would have no chance to tell his tale to another. By the time dawn came, Nikos would know what was to be done with him.

But first he had an old student to confront.

He carefully marshaled his arguments, hoping that they would be more persuasive in person, since clearly his letters had been ignored. Josan had always followed the path of intellect, of cool reason over emotion. If Nikos was lucky, some trace of that logic would still remain.

The sight of his visitor destroyed his carefully ordered arguments. Curtly he dismissed Brother Basil, knowing the elderly monk would know better than to speculate on the identity of Nikos's late-night visitor. As the door swung shut behind Basil, he gave voice to his anger.

"Prince of Fools, what have you done now? Are you trying to destroy us all?" He told himself it was anger that lent the sharp edge to his words, but in his belly he felt the cold knot of fear. His visitor's eyes were wild, and his face flushed from anger or perhaps the force of his argument with the hapless Jeno. In a monk's robes he might have gone unnoticed, but the silk-banded tunic he wore was nearly as obvious as if he had waved a flag proclaiming his lineage.

"The time has come for you to tell me what you have done." Josan's voice was calm, in eerie contrast to the emotions that flashed across his face.

"I told you not to return. You bring danger to us all by being here. And if the empress discovers you—"

"If I have to turn to her for answers, so be it. But I would rather hear them from you."

Nikos searched his visitor's face. Six years ago, when he had left the collegium, he had been a shell of a man, barely capable of following the simplest of instructions. From his frequent letters Nikos knew he had changed but assumed that his memories remained lost beyond recall. Now he wondered if that were true, or if the lighthouse keeper had been playing a game with him, pretending obedience and ignorance while secretly plotting his return.

"Who am I speaking to? Josan? Or Lucius?" Was this body ruled by Josan, one of the finest minds of his generation? Or by the spoiled princeling who saw no further than his own petty desires?

His visitor's face stilled with the careful blankness of one practiced in meditation, or in the art of courtly deception. "Both. Neither. Does it matter?"

It mattered. It might well prove the difference between life and death.

Turning away, his visitor made his way to Nikos's desk, sitting down in his chair as if these were his quarters and Nikos a mere supplicant. Such arrogance was well within Lucius's character, but the words that came out of his mouth had the cool reason that Josan had once possessed.

"Tell me how it is that two souls came to share this body," he commanded.

Nikos hesitated, then took a seat on the bench that was used by the rare visitors to his private room.

"What do you remember?" he began. It seemed wise to treat his visitor as if he were indeed Lucius, but his questions indicated that there were still gaps in his memory. It might be possible to minimize the role Nikos had played in the events past. And the less Lucius learned, the better, for anything he knew he would confess once Nerissa's torturers got their hands on him.

That is, if Nikos let Lucius leave the collegium alive. There was still time to undo the choices he had made six years before.

"Assume that I know everything, but that I want to hear it from your lips."

Nikos hesitated.

"You owe me the truth."

"I owe you nothing. I gave you life. Both of you would have died were it not for me."

Lucius nodded. "The breakbone fever," he said, showing that he did indeed remember something of the past.

"And your reckless folly." Nikos rose to his feet and, crossing to the shelves on the far wall, poured out a cup of wine. While ordinarily he despised those who turned to wine to steady their nerves, surely he could be forgiven for making an exception on this night. After a moment of hesitation he poured a second cup and offered it to Lucius.

Lucius waved it away. "I know better than to take a drink

from someone who calls himself my friend as he hands me the poisoned cup." There was a bitter edge to his voice.

Nikos flushed, remembering that it had been his hand that had held the cup six years before, promising Lucius that the drugged wine would provide a painless passing.

"It was your choice," he reminded him. "You chose to die, knowing that Nerissa would be far less merciful once she got her hands on you."

"But you had something else in mind. Lucius was an embarrassment to you. A former pupil who learned so little from your lessons that he fell into the hands of those who used him for their own ends. When the scales fell from his eyes he turned to you for help, only you betrayed him."

"I did not betray you."

"You did not turn me over to Nerissa, true. But you had plans of your own. Who was it that thought of using soul magic?"

"Brother Giles."

"So you decided that all his years of studying ought to be put to use, and who better to practice on than a man you despised?"

"We did what we thought best. It was not just a matter of hiding from the empress. You swore that you could not live with yourself, nor with the blood that had been shed in your name."

"And then there was Josan. Your perfect student. Yet even his obedience would surely have been strained had he known what you were going to do. Did he ask to be saved?"

"He was too ill to make a choice, so I made it for him. Letting both of you die seemed a senseless waste."

His words painted a picture of altruism, but Nikos's motives had been far less pure. Saving Josan's knowledge was a worthy goal, but if the supplicant had been anyone other than Prince Lucius, then both men would have been allowed to die. The risks of practicing the forbidden soul magic would have far outweighed any possible gain. But the chance to put his own man on the throne, even if it was only a slim one, had been too great an opportunity for Nikos to ignore.

There had been great dissatisfaction with Empress Nerissa, but Prince Lucius had lacked both the charisma and wisdom to unite the disparate factions into a cohesive whole. Lucius's own character had doomed the rebellion, but if he had been a different man, it might have succeeded.

Nikos had the power to make him a different man, and the temptation to reshape history had proven irresistible. He had gambled, but Brother Giles's efforts had produced only a gibbering half-wit, unfit for any purpose.

"Pity for you that your efforts yielded a drooling simpleton who could not further your plans. No wonder you sent me away, so you would not have to look at your failure," Lucius said, showing far more insight than he had in his youth.

"I sent you away so you would be safe. And now you have ruined that by returning."

"Safe? Then it was not you who sent an assassin to kill me?"

The thought had crossed Nikos's mind, but he had believed himself safe as long as the man in the lighthouse still obeyed his orders and continued to sign his missives as "Your Obedient Servant, Josan." And there was still a chance that circumstances would change, and Nikos would have a use for him.

"It was not I," he said. But clearly someone else had seen through Lucius's disguise and tried to kill the exiled prince, thus prompting his flight. He had known all along that the body found at Txomin's Lighthouse was no mere thief, but the question of who had sent the assassin still lingered.

"My enemies continue to hunt me, but I have also found friends who wish to help. They brought me here to finish what I started six years ago."

"The empress will crush you."

"I know. But I was not consulted as to my wishes."

Perhaps it was Josan's knowledge tempering Lucius's arrogance, for he seemed genuinely distressed at the prospect of another uprising.

It seemed that Nikos's scheme to create a worthy prince had indeed worked, but the opportunity for him to be of use had passed. The empress had used the past six years to tighten her grasp on power. Any rebellion would be swiftly put down, and there would be no mercy for those involved.

Nikos could not afford to have Lucius fall into the empress's hands. He was no match for him physically, so he would have to persuade Lucius that he would be safe in the collegium. Then, surely the brethren's stock of herbs and potions would contain one that would destroy Lucius's mind, so they could deliver a witless, gibbering husk to the empress's dungeons. Killing him outright was too much of a risk since it would imply that Nikos had something to fear from what Lucius might say. But if Lucius's arrival at the postern gate had been observed, the witnesses would confirm that he had behaved as an incoherent madman, thus avoiding any need to explain where Lucius had been for six years, or why he had chosen to come to the collegium of all places for sanctuary.

Brother Basil could be trusted, but Jeno would have to be dealt with. Novices were often sent to other countries to study, and he would accept such a posting without question. But if he were to return one day, it might be awkward. Instead, Jeno would have to be sacrificed, a tragic victim of the mad prince. And his death would explain the violence of Lucius's capture and any damage the prince might suffer as a result of his apprehension. A skull fracture would be more convenient than relying on herb lore.

"You cannot keep me here," Lucius said, as if he had read Nikos's thoughts.

"But we can protect you. If you venture out into the city, you will be recognized and arrested."

"I have already been recognized," Lucius said. "My friends know that I have come here. If I do not return, they will begin asking questions that you cannot afford to answer."

"What do you propose?"

"Let me return to them and persuade them that the time is not ripe for rebellion. Convince them to disband, then disappear once I am certain they will not commit further folly."

And if Prince Lucius were indeed the leader of the rebels, his plan might work. But six years ago he had been a mere figurehead with no true authority. It was unlikely that anything had changed in the intervening years.

"At least stay long enough that we may consult with my advisors. They may see a different path." If he summoned reinforcements, among them they could overpower Lucius.

Lucius shook his head. "No. It is too dangerous for me to stay here."

Despite the peril that he faced, a part of Nikos was fascinated. More and more he was convinced that though Lucius's mouth gave voice to the words, it was Josan's intellect that shaped them. He had thought the soul transfer spell an utter failure, but it seemed he had been wrong.

If only he could be certain how much of the man before him was ruled by Josan and how much was the remaining traces of the foolish and impetuous prince. If Josan were in control, then Nikos might well gamble on letting him leave alive, but if it were Lucius's personality in ascendance . . .

"You will give me a robe to hide this tunic and let me

leave," Lucius said. "The rebels are more highly placed than anyone dreams, and they have Nerissa's ear. You will not survive if she turns her gaze upon your activities."

Lucius had been a fool, but he had been an honest one. He had never lied to Nikos, not even when a lie would have served his purposes far better than the truth. And Josan had been a scholar who valued truth above all. If this man said that the rebels knew enough to endanger Nikos, then he would have to assume that was indeed the case.

He considered calling out, summoning monks to restrain Lucius to prevent his leaving, but concluded that he could not afford the spectacle that would result. Such an uproar would be witnessed by dozens of monks, and it was too much to hope that they would all remain silent at his command. A few words whispered to one of the imperial guard, and Nikos would find himself on trial for his life.

Instead he heaved a sigh, giving the air of a man persuaded against his will. Let Lucius think himself victor, and perhaps he would not think too closely about Nikos's own plans.

"You may go, but first you will swear to me that you have no intention of trying to take the throne and that you will do everything in your power to disband the rebellion," he said.

"This I swear. I have no interest in power and no taste for killings."

It was little enough, but it would have to do. Nikos rose and retreated to his sleeping chamber, where he pulled out a dark wool robe from his wardrobe. It was plain, in keeping with his position, but unlike the light-colored robes that the brethren wore as their uniform. There would be nothing to tie its wearer to the collegium.

Lucius accepted the robe and donned it in silence.

"Should I summon an escort?"

"I know my way out," Lucius said. "And I know what I have to do."

"As do I," Nikos said.

He waited until Lucius had left before summoning the boy assigned to tend his quarters. "Fetch me Brother Gregor, and Brother Thanatos. Wake them if they are sleeping," he said.

Lucius might believe that he could stop the rebellion, but Nikos was not as sanguine. He had his own plans to put in place. By the time Lucius was captured, Nikos would ensure that there was nothing to link him to the prince. And if he handled the situation just right, he might even be able to turn Lucius's appearance to his advantage. A few words here and there would point the finger of suspicion firmly away from Nikos and the collegium. Anything Lucius might say would be seen as desperately lashing out against one who had helped to bring him to justice.

Nikos would do whatever it took to survive.

As soon as the walls of the collegium were out of sight, Josan fell to his knees and vomited. He and the Other had managed to cooperate long enough to fool Nikos into giving them the answers they both sought, but now his head pounded with the strain caused by his warring selves, even as his stomach churned. A pack of youths returning home from their revels mocked his seeming inability to hold his drink, but they contented themselves with mere jeers. The dark robe hid both his features and the damning tunic with its bands of crimson silk, the color of royalty.

Fool that he was, it had taken Nikos's sharp tongue to reveal the obvious. On another man, such a tunic would be a sign of his close connection to the imperial household, and it would be fitting for a magistrate to wear such to an official function of the court. But worn by one who styled himself a prince...

Yet was that who he was? he wondered, even as a voice inside of him whispered *Yes*. The Other was growing stronger, refusing to be silent now that he had been given a name. Prince Lucius, whose great-grandmother had been Princess Callista, full sister to Empress Constanza, the last of the old blood to sit on the imperial throne. Constanza had married the newcomer Aitor, elevating him to the rank of Prince Consort, then Aitor had needed only his own ambition to win the title of emperor for himself.

Lucius, who owed his very existence to Aitor's seeming charity in sparing the lives of Princess Callista and her daughter, and to his heirs who had allowed Callista's descendants to live quiet lives of obscurity until a vain and reckless youth let himself be used in an attempt to topple the empire.

It was beyond comprehension. He was Josan, a dedicated scholar who knew the secret harmonies of numbers and the histories of the civilized peoples. He was a man of peace. Violence was no part of him.

And yet it was. From his blood-soaked dreams to the arcane skills that he had used against his attacker, it seemed violence was very much a part of this Other. The rebellion of six years ago had not been an orderly affair of two armies meeting upon a field of battle. It had been a time of assassinations, of rape and pillage done in the name of ancient hatreds. Entire families had been executed from the oldest down to the babes in arms, as each side seemed determined to outdo the other in sheer horror. Prince Lucius might not have wielded the sword personally, but that did not make him any less responsible for the atrocities that had been done in his name.

I agree.

He shivered, as he realized that the prince was able to

speak directly with him. If this had been happening to anyone else, he would have been fascinated. But faced with the twisted horror that he had become, he felt not curiosity but revulsion. His greatest fear had been that he was afflicted with madness, but now such fear seemed laughable. Josan had been made party to an abomination—and he was not alone in his torment.

It was strange to conduct a conversation in his own head, and he wondered if his lips were moving, even as his voice remained silent. *So what do we do now? Do we run?*

All of his possessions had been left behind in his hasty flight from the magistrate's. Still, he could survive without them if he had to. Fleeing would mean breaking his promise to Brother Nikos, but that did not trouble him. Nikos had been the first one to break faith, when he had allowed Brother Giles to perform the obscene magics that had chained two men's souls within a single body.

We can't leave. Remember what Renato said? He said "The killings have already started."

Josan swallowed hard, tasting the bile from his earlier sickness.

Renato had known that they were coming, and it was unlikely that he had kept the news of Prince Lucius's return to himself. At the very least, he would have informed the most trusted members of the alliance, to prepare them for whatever scheme they had in mind. And it seemed that at least some of them had not waited for their prince to return before acting.

He did not know if they would heed his words, but he had no other choice. He owed it to his people to try and put right what his unheeding return had provoked.

If only he had obeyed Brother Nikos and remained in the distant north, the rebels would never have known of his existence. Not that this made him inclined to follow

Brother Nikos's advice. Josan had once trusted him utterly, but the blended man he had become did not. His instincts told him that Nikos was willing to murder to gain his own ends. The wonder was that he had not seen this before.

What would you do? he asked, but there was only silence. He could feel the Other's impatience as if it were his own. It seemed he had no use for careful deliberations, nor the weighing of potential courses of actions. The pressure in his skull grew, and he stumbled as spots appeared in front of his eyes. He could not think, he could not reason; there was room for nothing except the overwhelming sense of pain, until even that was taken from him and he vanished.

At last, Lucius thought. Finally, after endless torment, he was aware of who he was, and in control of his own body. A body that felt strangely uncomfortable, like an old tunic that no longer quite fit. He ran one hand over his face and longed for a mirror.

Are you there? he asked, and was pleased when he heard no response.

So the demon was gone. At least for the moment.

He had been too busy struggling for ascendancy to pay attention to where the demon had taken them, but as he glanced around he realized that he had traveled only a short distance from the collegium and was far too close to the imperial grounds for comfort. He set off downhill, toward the sector that served as the unofficial pleasure district, where taverns and brothels stayed open until the dawn's light. There he could lose himself in the crowds as he pondered a course of action. He patted his robe and the tunic beneath it, but it seemed that the demon had been so foolish that he had fled the magistrate's house without bringing with him a single coin.

Pity. He could have used a glass of wine. Or a bottle for that matter.

Even as he walked, his eyes cataloged the changes in the city that he had once known well—a new fountain at the entrance to the fourth tier and the iron grilles that protected even smaller shops. The cobblestones along the streets of the pleasure district were no longer merely uneven, now numerous cracked stones posed a threat to unwary pedestrians.

His fists clenched in rage at this further proof of the years that had been stolen from him. He wondered how much time had passed since he had trusted Brother Nikos to give him a painless death. He thought as hard as he could, searching his memories, but the answer would not come to him.

He snorted in disgust as he realized that the demon's knowledge was beyond his reach. The interloper had no such restrictions. Not only had he stolen Josan's body, but he had made free with his skills—rummaging through the storerooms of mind and looting the riches that he found within.

Years must have gone by, while he slept, a prisoner in his own flesh. He could remember dreamlike fragments— walking on a muddy road, a tiny cabin, laughing as a grizzled peasant refilled his wine cup from a chipped jug. The weight of a sword in his hand as he stood over a fallen enemy.

A painted whore smiled and beckoned, until he drew near enough so she could see the expression on his face. Abruptly her smile fell as she turned aside to seek easier custom. He brushed by a group of drinkers who had overflowed from a wine shop, wincing at their raucous laughter. His belly rumbled as he passed a vendor selling skewers of grilled meat wrapped in bread, but he had far weightier concerns on his mind than mere hunger.

He must have woken before, but it had not been true consciousness. He had been a shadow of himself—nameless and unable to remain in control. At last he knew who he was, and what had happened to him. Brother Nikos had thought to use him, to replace Lucius with a demon puppet obedient to his control. But something must have gone wrong with his plan, for, rather than using him, he had exiled the one who wore Lucius's body.

Years might have passed for his body, but Lucius's clearest memories were of the last days when his soul had been his own. When he had attempted to pay for his mistakes with his life. The blood-soaked horrors were as fresh to him as if they had occurred only yesterday.

Though apparently time had blunted the memories of others, for the magistrate had spoken of a new uprising and a new cycle of violence. Lucius had meant what he said when he told the demon that they could not flee. He had to stay and find some way to convince the rebels to disarm before any more murders were done in his name.

It would not be easy. He did not know how much longer he could stay in control of his body before the demon pushed him aside. It was no comfort to know that the demon shared his goal of confounding the rebels. Lucius was a royal prince, while the demon was a mere peasant. Leadership was his by birthright, to accept or reject as he chose. But how could he command the rebellion when he could not command his own body to obey him? Even now he felt the demon's presence, as he sought once more to take control.

Lucius knew this was a fight he would lose. The demon was stronger than he was, at least thus far. And he needed his cooperation in order to put down the rebellion.

But he also knew that he had been growing stronger in the past months, awakening more and more often. The day would come when he was strong enough to take control permanently, and when that happened he would see that the demon was banished forever. Then he would set about punishing those who had betrayed him.

As Josan came to himself, he realized that he was standing in the alleyway that ran behind Magistrate Renato's residence. He was drained, his mind sluggish as if he had spent all day and night trying to unlock the mysteries of an ancient manuscript.

He wasn't sure what had happened. Had he somehow wrested control of this body away from Lucius? Had Lucius surrendered to the darkness voluntarily, or had his spirit been too weak to remain awake?

He called, but there was no answer. Still, his being there meant that he and Lucius shared the same goal, and both agreed that Renato was the key to their plans. When Josan saw the magistrate again, it must be in the guise of Prince Lucius. He would start with the magistrate, then bend the rest of the rebels to his will.

There would be danger for him in this, and if he were captured by the empress, he could not expect any mercy. Prince Lucius's body bore the guilt for his crimes, no matter that another man now inhabited it.

Though for how much longer that would be true was a question he did not want to face. Lucius's spirit must have been dormant for years, existing only in the strange dreams that haunted Josan from time to time. But gradually Lucius had grown in power. Lucius had taken control of this body before, banishing Josan to a strange unknowingness. Now he could even speak directly with Lucius, two spirits in an uneasy cohabitation. Josan sensed that the revelations of this night had shocked Lucius as much as they had himself, but that did not mean that the prince would be content to remain a mere ghost inside his own flesh.

Lucius would rise again, and Josan would once more

disappear into oblivion. And perhaps, if the prince grew strong enough, eventually that oblivion would be permanent. He wondered when that day came if he would see it as a blessing or a curse.

He pushed such thoughts aside and focused himself on the immediate task at hand. Renato must have left instructions for his servants to be on the lookout for his wandering guest, for the boy on watch at the rear door admitted Josan at once. This time he was led to a morning room, where the newly risen sun revealed two anxious men, empty crystal glasses of tea showing signs of a sleepless night.

"Where have you been? Are you well?" Myles asked. He made as if to embrace Josan, but the expression on Josan's face must have warned him off, for he merely squeezed Josan's forearm as if to ensure that he was indeed real and not a phantom.

"Were you followed?" Magistrate Renato asked, showing a commendable concern for what truly mattered.

"I was not followed," Josan said. It was easier to answer Renato's question. Myles's betrayal still cut like a knife. He had trusted Myles as a friend, but all these weeks Myles must have known his true identity and not said a word. He had not consulted with Josan to ask his wishes, but instead had decided for himself how best to help the lost prince.

"I don't know what you heard, or what you think you heard," Myles began. His features were as easy to read as ever. He was worried, anxious, as any man might be who had quarreled with a friend.

Josan's instincts still told him that Myles intended him no harm. But his instincts could not be trusted. Myles intended Prince Lucius no harm, and that distinction made all the difference.

"It does not matter," Josan said, cutting off whatever

explanation Myles had been about to make. There was nothing that Myles could say that would change what had passed between them, and no explanations that would change what Josan must do.

"You took a great risk leaving here," Renato said.

"I had my reasons."

"And did you find what you were looking for?"

"Yes. I know who my friends are. But I do not recall your being one of their number six years ago," Josan said, prompted with the sure knowledge of the Other. Lucius's spirit might be resting, but it seemed his memories were still there for Josan to draw upon. "Prince Lucius finds it strange that you would have chosen his cause."

Myles drew in a quick breath as the forbidden name was uttered.

"Does he?" Renato asked.

"Yes, I do."

Renato considered Josan as if he were on trial in his court. Then, after a long moment, he bent down on one knee, in the genuflection owed to the heir to the throne.

Myles, trained as soldier, not courtier, dropped to both his knees and bowed his head.

Such seeming devotion sickened him, for he knew how little Lucius deserved it. And while Myles might be sincere in his faith, he doubted that Renato cared for anyone's interests except his own.

"Rise, and be done with such displays unless you are anxious to see our heads decorating the walls of Nerissa's great palace."

"How did your memory come back to you? Or did you have it all along?" Myles asked.

"I had my secrets, as you clearly had yours." It was all the explanation he was willing to give. "For now, call me Josan, since that name has served me well enough in my exile."

"Six years ago, I was among those selected as spies in Nerissa's court. We met only with the inner circle of your supporters, lest a traitor reveal our names. I was fortunate enough to escape arrest, but many of the others were not. I never wavered in my contempt for the empress, but I had given up all hope of defeating her until Myles's letter reached me," Renato explained.

"And naturally you have told others of my pending return."

Renato looked away. "A few, perhaps."

"I want to meet them. As soon as possible."

"I am not sure that is wise—"

"I am," Josan interrupted, trying for an imperious tone. "They will want to see me, to know for themselves that I am not some impostor."

"It is not safe," Myles said.

"I must agree with the sergeant. We dare not risk you. Let me meet with the others to lay our plans, then you can meet with a chosen few, who can bring word to the others."

Leaving Renato as the de facto leader of the rebellion, since he would control all communication between the prince and his so-called followers. He wondered what Renato expected in return for his service. Would he be satisfied as magistrate or was the title of proconsul more to his liking?

"The time for caution is over. We must act swiftly, while surprise is still on our side. You will arrange for me to meet with those who have remained faithful, or I will leave here and meet with them on my own. Is that understood?"

"Yes, my prince," Renato said.

"I will give you three days to prove your worth."

"And what can I do to serve?" Myles asked.

Go and never speak to me again, Josan thought, but he did not say the words aloud. Josan might have lost a friend, but a prince would always have a use for a man who was quick with a sword and not afraid to use it.

"Leave me in peace," Josan said.

Myles appeared shocked, so he clarified. "It has been a long night for all of us. Leave me in peace while I take my rest, and we will talk again after I have slept."

"Of course," Myles said. But the hurt look did not leave his face, and his eyes followed Josan as he left the morning room.

He would have to be careful. Myles had apparently accepted his apparent transformation from diffident monk to commanding prince, but such a role was hard to sustain. Others would see what they wanted to see, but Myles knew him well enough to see the cracks that would inevitably appear in his mask. It would be hard enough to take control of the rebellion as Prince Lucius, but if Myles were to hint that the prince was not in full command of his faculties, then his task would be nigh unto impossible.

He could not predict what Myles would do in such a case. He had already misjudged him badly, mistaking loyalty for friendship and worship for affection. Myles had not offered him the devotion of a lover but rather that of a follower. Renato was predictable in his greed, but Myles was not. By all appearances Myles truly wished to serve his prince and was willing to take any risk to place the man he had called a friend upon the imperial throne.

Such devotion was frightening in its mindless intensity. Yet he could not afford to push Myles away. He needed Myles's loyalty, and thus he needed to maintain the pretense of friendship, which was the only lever he had to control Myles.

It was madness, but he could see no other course. His only hope was that he could end this new rebellion swiftly, before madness engulfed them all.

Chapter 16

Tell me, Lady Ysobel, what manner of fish these are? Flavian here thinks them painted carp but I say the fins are all wrong," Octavio declared.

Lady Ysobel paused beside the rock pool where two of her guests were admiring the brightly colored fish that swam within. Formal gardens in Ikaria often included small ponds filled with tame carp. Gold was the most common variety and sometimes served at table by serious gourmands, while carp mottled in shades of red, white, and the rare green were prized strictly for their decorative qualities.

Ysobel had kept the usual fishpond in her walled garden, but twisted the custom to make it uniquely her own.

"You are correct. These are not carp but rather a breed called winged darters, which inhabit coral reefs. One of my captains brought them as a gift, and so far they seem to be thriving."

"Are they difficult to keep? I might want to try some for myself," asked Flavian.

"Not that difficult. A boy keeps the seawater fresh and feeds them every second day with live minnows bought at market. If you are still interested, when these breed I will make you a gift of a pair."

"You are graciousness," Flavian said. Then, in a hissing whisper that served only to draw attention to his question, he asked, "Is he here yet?"

Lady Ysobel simply shook her head. "If you will excuse me, I must see to my other guests."

"Of course," he answered, not bothering to conceal his disappointment. She wondered yet again at Dama Akantha's decision to invite Flavian to join this select gathering. Not only was he the youngest by far, but he had no talent for dissembling. It was fortunate that he had his family's wealth to fall back upon, for he would never be able to make a living as an actor or a trader.

The heat of the warm spring afternoon filled the walled garden, and the harbor breezes that normally rose each afternoon were unaccountably still on that day. She had ordered canopies erected over the mosaic patio so her guests would be shielded from the sun, but at present they chose to wander the paths, as she did. A young lizard darted across the path ahead of her and she grimaced at the sign that her gardens were once again home to the troublesome pests. Though she supposed that there were some who might be foolish enough to take their presence as a good omen.

By all appearances it was one of her typical entertainments, a dozen guests gathered to sip chilled wines and discuss the latest in literature and politics. Couches had been arranged in a semicircle on the patio, around tables where suitable delicacies had been set out. Raw fish pickled in vinegar, baked dough balls filled with sweetmeats, and sliced fruits arranged in colorful patterns were just a few of her cook's creations. Yet for once the offerings were untouched, the guests preferring to wander as they spoke with one another rather than sitting and taking their ease.

Such nervousness was understandable, considering their identities. In the far corner by the roses, Dama Akantha spoke to Septimus the Elder, while Magistrate Renato looked on. She wondered if Septimus the Younger knew that his father dabbled in treason. Shaded by the blossoming fruit trees, young Flavian, heir to his ducal father, was speaking intently with Benedict, who had overcome his common birth to become second-in-command of the city watch. Octavio, a wealthy trader with aspirations to a noble title was listening intently to the elderly Salvador, formerly minister in charge of the imperial treasury and still a force to be reckoned with.

Such an eclectic gathering might well be deemed suspicious were it held in the dead of night, behind closed doors. Instead, in response to Dama Akantha's urgent message, Lady Ysobel had chosen to hold their meeting in daylight, in the seeming openness of her garden, where the high walls prevented any from getting close enough to overhear their conversations.

Still, despite the warmth of the day, she shivered as she recalled the danger. This time there were no masks to hide behind. Those present had come so openly, as commanded by Dama Akantha.

Dama Akantha had been tight-lipped about whom she had invited, but Ysobel had carefully compared each guest to the costumed figures she had met in the wine cellar. At least two were missing, whether because they had other obligations or because they refused to reveal their true faces she did not know. And it was not them that she had to fear. Those who stayed away showed a commendable prudence. No, if Nerissa had a spy among their number, he was present, confidently barefaced among them, taking note of each name so he could inform the empress.

Even as she circulated, exchanging tepid pleasantries with her guests, her eyes kept darting to the gate in the garden wall. At last her patience was rewarded, as the gate swung open, and a figure stepped within. She was close enough to see that he was stocky, with the light brown hair and the ruddy skin of the native Ikarians, but he looked more peasant than noble. Fury welled up inside her as she realized that no one would believe this one an heir to Constantin, and thus they had taken the risk of meeting openly for naught.

The newcomer looked carefully around the garden, catching the eye of Magistrate Renato, who nodded to him. Then he stepped aside and a second man stepped within.

This man wore the hooded robe of a penitent or leper. As the gate swung shut behind him, he pulled off his robe and revealed his features.

"By the gods it is him," Dama Akantha muttered.

Ysobel swiftly closed her mouth, which had fallen open with amazement. The man did not merely having the look of the old blood, she would swear that he *was* the old blood. It was as if Emperor Constantin had sprung to life from one of the forbidden coins that bore his visage.

Swiftly she crossed the distance that separated them. As she drew near she hesitated, wondering how she should greet him. She had been prepared to meet a pretender to the throne, one who would know he was a tool and not expect the royal courtesies. But this man, who had the look of the late prince, might well be offended if he was not greeted properly. Yet she could not risk a formal obeisance, lest she be observed by one of her servants. She had no wish to test the depths of their loyalty to her.

The man made the choice for her, extending his hand toward in the manner of old acquaintances.

"Lady Ysobel, I had not realized that you were a friend of ours. Had I done so, our last meeting might have gone differently," he said.

As she took his hand in hers, she recognized his voice.

"Shall I call you Lucius? Or do you still claim to be the monk Josan?"

"Josan will serve well enough, for now," he said.

It was true that clothes made the man. Dressed in rags, with shaven head and downcast eyes, he had seemed a mere monk, a bastard connection of the old imperial blood. But with his blond hair grown out to a fashionable length and his blue eyes gazing directly at hers, there was no mistaking him for anyone other than the royal prince.

"You should introduce me to your guests," he prompted. "Some I know of old, but other faces are new to me."

"Of course."

As they toured the garden, she was comforted by the reactions of her guests to the newcomer. Even Dama Akantha had expected a bastard or impostor, not the return of Prince Lucius in the flesh—though six years had changed him. Gone was the soft roundness of his face and the impatient petulance that had made the prince as much a danger to his supporters as to his enemies. His face bore lines of maturity and determination, and his careful exchanges with the guests gave away nothing of his true feelings. He was as calm as if this were an ordinary garden party and not a meeting of treasonous conspirators.

By unspoken consent, after Prince Lucius had greeted each person, they wandered over to the couches. Lucius took the place of honor, at Ysobel's right side, as servants moved among the guests, refilling their wineglasses and placing chilled decanters within easy reach. Then the servants were dismissed, as was customary when Ysobel's guests wished to discuss discreetly the indiscretions of those not present. Months had been spent establishing a routine just for this very purpose, so that the gathering would seem no different than any others. It was time for all her careful preparations to be put to the test.

"Three nights past, the watch heard rumors that the ghost of Prince Lucius had been sighted in the old quarter, running through the streets in search of his faithful followers. I dismissed it as a drunkard's fantasy," Benedict said, as if recounting an idle bit of market gossip.

"I cannot explain what drunkards see," Lucius replied.

"But you do claim to be Prince Lucius, do you not?" Benedict pressed.

"I am he."

She swept her eyes over her guests to gauge their mood. Renato appeared triumphant, as well he might, since he was the one to whom Prince Lucius had turned. Dama Akantha's face was still, but her eyes shone with a zealot's fire. She would press for sudden, decisive action. Benedict, despite Lucius's avowal, looked doubtful, and as for Salvador, perhaps his ancient eyes failed him, for his face was drawn in harsh lines, as if displeased to see his prince. The rest of the conspirators appeared cautious, wavering between the hope of Lucius's return and their own private doubts.

"If you are indeed the prince, then why should we listen to you? Why, after you ran off to save your skin and abandoned your supporters to the racks and the pyre?" Salvador demanded. His raised voice caused his neighbors on both sides to hiss at him in warning.

"It was not my choice to leave. Those who called themselves my friends spirited me out of the city to a place far away. By the time I came to myself it was too late to return. There was nothing that I could have done."

"Then why have you returned now?" she asked.

Lucius shrugged. "I could not forget the past, nor could my faithful friends, it seems. I came to see for myself the state of Karystos and to judge whether the time was ripe to unseat Nerissa."

He was lying. She knew that, with the same certainty

that told her when a merchant was trying to pass rotten goods off as fresh. It was not mere curiosity that had brought him to the capital after all these years. Someone or something had summoned him back, by telling him that the time was once more ripe for rebellion.

She wondered if it was her presence that was the cause for his return, and if the federation's secret support had been the key to stirring the rebels to action after their long years of dormancy. She was well aware that it was her sacks of coins that paid for the seemingly spontaneous riots that targeted businesses owned by the newcomers and encouraged cutpurses and gutter thieves to spare their fair-headed victims while dealing harshly with anyone with dark hair and porcelain skin.

So far, such deeds had done nothing but encourage the watch to come down even more harshly on the native Ikarians, guided by Benedict's sure hand behind the scenes. In time, such punishments would breed resentment and encourage the native Ikarians to rise up against their masters. But it was a chancy proposition at best. She'd had no real hope that their efforts would do anything more than inconvenience Nerissa, but Prince Lucius's return changed everything.

If it were indeed Lucius—which Salvador apparently doubted. His whispered mutterings grew louder as Prince Lucius patiently asked each person in the circle what he or she could bring to the rebellion and where they judged Nerissa to be weakest. Lucius's face was still giving nothing of his own thoughts away as he gave each speaker the benefit of his full attention. It was a masterful performance. Even Dama Akantha, who had spoken derisively of the boy prince in the past, now nodded approvingly as he spoke, while Flavian was nearly vibrating with excitement.

Salvador scowled, his grim expression in stark contrast to the enthusiasm of the others. Perhaps sensing his resistance, Lucius had saved the old man for last, and when his turn came Salvador was defiant.

"I have nothing to say and nothing to offer you. I have seen no proof that you are anything but a pretty face, a bastard whoreson whose resemblance to Lucius has these lapdogs panting for another chance to get us killed. Even if you were Lucius, I would not trust you. Our best and most loyal were killed six years ago for his miserable hide, and no explanation can put that right."

Salvador started to rise, but Lucius was quicker.

"Hold," he said, as he rose to his feet. Now those reclined on the couches had to twist their necks to look up at him. Salvador, half-propped on his elbow, subsided with a grumble.

"Constantin gave me more than this jawline. The old blood flows in my veins, as does the power of my forefathers."

Lucius extended his right arm, palm upward. He closed his eyes for a moment and his lips moved silently. Then, as he opened his eyes, golden flames sprang to life on his palm. Ysobel sat bolt upright, propriety forgotten. The flames danced for several moments, but just as she reached to touch them, Lucius closed his palm.

"The Old Magic, the gift of the true blood," Septimus the Elder proclaimed.

"A conjurer's trick," Salvador countered.

It had been generations since the former royal line had publicly demonstrated a talent for the old magics. Ysobel herself had believed them mere children's tales, a bit of conjury meant to impress gullible fools.

It seemed wisdom was not the only thing that Lucius had gained during his exile. She wondered what else he had learned, and resolved to meet with him privately as soon as possible. She had thought the rebellion doomed to failure, but for the first time wondered if he might actually succeed in overthrowing Nerissa.

"My friends, I urge you pay no heed to his words or to his tricks. We have seen better on any market day," Salvador said.

Prince Lucius pinned Salvador with his gaze. "When lightning strikes the roof of the imperial palace this night, you will remember your disbelief with shame."

He spoke with surety, as if he were accustomed to calling lightning at his command. She swallowed hard, wondering if he were indeed gifted, or mad, or perhaps both.

"Only those present today are to know of my return. You will think on what we have discussed but take no action until I have had time to lay my plans. You will wait for my word, is that understood?"

"We hear you," Dama Akantha replied, and the others murmured in agreement.

"It will be as you say," Septimus said. "Only do not wait too long. For years your followers have lived in despair and they deserve to know the joy of your return."

"Do not worry. I know what I owe to them," Lucius said. He smiled, but to Ysobel's eyes it was a false smile. If Lucius were half as intelligent as he seemed, he would realize that this group would not be able to keep their tongues silent for long. Each would tell a trusted confidant, or two, swearing them to secrecy. And then those would tell others, until the news had spread throughout the city.

Which might well be what Dama Akantha had intended, by ensuring that young Flavian was present in place of his father the duke. Even if all others held their tongues, it was doubtful that Flavian would be able to resist the temptation to impress others with the secret. And the more people who knew of the prince's return, the more pressure there would be for Lucius to act.

With a final nod, Lucius made his way to the garden gate, accompanied by the man who had identified himself only by his rank of sergeant. Lucius once more donned the all-encompassing robe that allowed him to pass unchallenged through the streets, and then the two disappeared.

Salvador was the next to leave, his curt farewell showing that he was not ready to support a new rebellion.

Ysobel fought to retain her patience as the rest of her guests continued to murmur quietly among themselves, making their own plans on how to take advantage of Prince Lucius's return. Gradually, in ones and twos they left, just as the sun was setting.

Finally, only Dama Akantha remained.

"I see your worry, but we should celebrate. The time will come when we show Nerissa for the liar and craven coward that she is," Dama Akantha proclaimed. "All those years Nerissa led us to believe that the prince had died in her torture chambers, and now he has returned to confront her lies."

"We have not won yet," Ysobel cautioned.

"But we will. Victory will be ours. Can you not taste it?"

Dama Akantha was intoxicated, not by wine, but by the prospect of seeing Nerissa brought low, forced to pay for the crime of abandoning her countrymen in Anamur to their fates. Akantha's eyes glittered and her cheeks were flushed, as if years had melted away. Such excitement was dangerous if it meant she forgot the caution that had kept her alive all these years.

"The race is not won until we have crossed the line and taken the laurels for our own. He who celebrates before the end will find his victory stolen by another," Ysobel said, quoting the ancient proverb.

"And he who will not throw the die wins nothing," Dama Akantha countered, dredging up a proverb of her own.

Ysobel smiled but did not speak. There was nothing more she could say that would be in keeping with her role as a friend to the rebellion. Instead she would have to remain vigilant, to ensure that she did not become swept up in the madness around her.

As Josan left the walled garden, Myles fell into step behind him. They walked in silence, exchanging not a single word as they made their way from the southwestern district, where Lady Ysobel had her house, to the second tier on the north, where Magistrate Renato lived. The last rays of the setting sun painted the white buildings in fantastic colors, but Josan had no heart for the spectacle. To him the rosy hues were an ominous omen, foretelling that once more blood would run in the city streets.

His thoughts were uneasy as his two selves struggled to interpret what he had seen and heard. Lucius had been touched by the devotion of his followers, inspired by their loyalty despite the years of danger and hardship, whereas Josan had seen only self-interest and heedless folly. It was as if he were viewing the same scene through two different lenses. Each distorted the image, and the truth of the matter lay somewhere in between.

Josan had seen Salvador's doubts as the voice of reason among a crowd too eager to see what they wanted to see, but Lucius had been cut to the quick by his doubts. It had been Lucius who called upon the Old Magic to impress his followers, and who had made the prediction that lightning would strike the high towers of the palace. Left to his own inclinations, Josan would have done neither. Not that he doubted Lucius's powers; indeed, he could feel the impending storm in the prickle of the dampness upon his skin and the faint taste of copper in the air. But it would not have occurred to Josan to use such tricks to sway his followers. In matters so grave men should be ruled by reason and logic.

What did it matter if he could summon a flame in his palm? Empress Nerissa could extend her hand and summon a thousand troops to do her bidding. And that was just the garrison within the city walls. His powers were nothing compared to hers.

When he returned to Renato's residence he shut himself up in his quarters. A private room, now that Myles was no longer pretending to be his equal. Myles had taken the next chamber over, the one closest to the stairs, and he slept with his door open so he could hear any possible threat to his prince. Or his prince making another escape, the more cynical part of Josan observed. He did not know how Renato explained matters to his servants, nor did he care. Not as long as they allowed him his solitude, and were content merely to call him "sir" when he had cause to summon them.

As midnight drew near, Josan threw open the shutters and stood watching as the storm finally broke. Thunder rolled and flashes of lightning lit up sky as if it were day. He could not see the palace from the window, but he did not need to. He watched as a jagged bolt cut across the sky, and knew that it had been struck. Then, the clouds opened, and rain began to fall in torrents, so heavy that he could barely see. Still he stood there, as the wind drove the rain through the open window, soaking him and his borrowed finery, as he savored his bitter triumph.

The next morning, Magistrate Renato greeted him at breakfast with the news that the palace had been struck by lightning, just as Josan had predicted. It was unclear whether this display would convince the reluctant Salvador, but Renato appeared awed. A royal prince who needed his help to regain his throne was one thing, but a man who could call lightning at his command was clearly marked by the gods, and Renato showed the deference due Lucius's newly revealed gifts.

Myles was even more awkward around Josan. He supposed it would be difficult to reconcile the tattered beggar who had shoveled manure for you with the man Josan was now pretending to be. Once Josan had called Myles "Master." Now Myles called him "my lord," in lieu of more damning titles. Josan needed him, but he could not pretend to the easy friendship that they had once shared. Myles had even made a wry jest of it, saying that he had known that things had to change, but he would always treasure the memory of his future emperor having been tossed in the muck pile by a balky steed. Josan had joined in the laughter, but swiftly sobered as he remembered Myles's betrayal.

"When did you know who I was?" he asked. "Was it from that first day?"

Myles shook his head and, strangely, Josan was comforted. He had not wanted his memories of Myles's first kindnesses to him to be tainted with the knowledge that it had been not kindness but rather cool calculation that had driven Myles to offer his friendship.

But Myles's next words dashed even that hope.

"I guessed who you might be kin to from the first," Myles said. "I thought you a bastard of the old blood, fleeing the empress's persecution."

It was foolish. Myles had betrayed him and yet he could still be hurt by the knowledge that it had been his stolen face that had convinced Myles to offer him aid. If Josan had arrived in that stableyard with his green eyes and light brown hair, he would have been turned aside.

"It was clear that you feared pursuit, but you would not confide in me," Myles added.

"But all that changed when I was attacked," Josan said.

Myles flushed and Josan felt an ugly suspicion grow within him.

"It was fortunate for me that you were there. Or was it more than just luck?"

Myles took a deep breath and drew himself to attention. "They weren't supposed to harm you," he said.

They must not have expected Josan to resist. But Josan, or rather Lucius, had fought back. Myles had claimed the kills as his own, but deep inside him Lucius demurred.

"You were my friend, but I'd sworn an oath to see the old blood restored to the throne," Myles explained. "And I thought even a bastard would be better than the bitch empress. Then, once we left Skalla, you told me of your damaged memories. I knew you must be the true prince and that you belonged in Karystos with friends who could help you regain your true self."

He supposed it was all quite logical from Myles's point of view. Myles had not stopped to question whether Josan wished his memories to be restored. Even now he did not ask if his friend truly wanted to risk all in an almost certainly doomed attempt to seize the throne. Lucius was a prince of the old blood, and his wishes did not matter. It was no comfort that Myles had chosen to gamble his own life in Josan's service.

Myles met his gaze calmly, fully prepared to face the consequences of what he had done. Lucius might well have ordered Renato to have Myles executed for his scheme, but Josan had no taste for revenge.

"Is there anything else you wish to confess, while I am in a mind to grant pardon?" he asked.

Myles shook his head. "No, my lord prince. I have done nothing else of which I am ashamed."

Josan sighed. "What was in the past is in the past, and

there it will lie. But if you keep secrets from me again, you will face my wrath. Understood?"

"Understood."

Fortunately, he was too busy to brood on Myles's betrayal and the strange workings of fate that had entwined their paths. The members of the inner circle who had met him at Lady Ysobel's now sought him out in ones and twos for counsel. Sometimes they met at Renato's. Other times he traveled in a closed litter, heavily swathed as if he were an elderly man whose bones could not be warmed by the fiercest sun. He lived in constant fear of arrest, for Nerissa's spies were everywhere.

Rumors that Prince Lucius had returned continued to sweep the city, and Benedict brought word of patrols randomly bringing in fair-haired strangers for questioning. Although Josan's disguise often included the face mask of a leper, which ensured that people did not get too close, it would be difficult to explain why a leper would be frequenting a noble house; so the most dangerous time for him was when he had to walk without his mask when he left Renato's residence or was making his way back.

Salvador refused to see him, pleading ill health, but others were swift to pledge their loyalty and make great promises. But when it came to things of substance, they had little to offer. He divided them into two camps. The fanatics, led by Dama Akantha, burned with zeal to see Nerissa destroyed and to pay back the newcomers for every ill—both real and imagined. No act was too heinous in pursuit of their goals, no risk too grave. If he called for an uprising, they would follow. He suspected a tragic martyr would please them as well as a triumphant emperor, just as long as they had their fill of violence and retribution.

The rest of his so-called followers were opportunists. Those who had fallen afoul of Nerissa or one of her supporters, or who, like Benedict, knew that they could rise no further while Nerissa sat on the throne. These would carefully calculate the risks and potential rewards before deciding to follow him. Some even tried to bargain with him, pledging gold and fighters in return for courtly honors or control of certain ministries. To each he promised that he would consider their requests carefully. These, at least, he did not have to fear acting on their own. They would wait carefully, until victory was assured, before risking their hides.

And victory was far from reach, despite Renato's and Akantha's enthusiasm, Myles's blind faith, and Lady Ysobel's generous supply of federation gold.

In the poorer quarters, where the native Ikarians lived, hatred for Nerissa and for the hardships her high taxes imposed ran deep. Given a charismatic figure to lead them, and a stockpile of weapons, they would rise up and riot, as they had six years before. This time, they might burn half the city before reinforcements arrived to mow them down.

But for all their high-flown rhetoric and enthusiasm, the conspiracy lacked trained soldiers. There were a few scattered units of the army that might defect, but the senior officers were firmly behind Nerissa. Aitor the Great had remade the army in his own image over a hundred years ago, and loyalty to his house was ingrained in the officers' corps.

Benedict, as second-in-command of the watch, could influence their orders and provide valuable intelligence to the rebels. But if he were to declare his loyalty to Lucius, it was doubtful that any would follow him. Indeed he would most likely be arrested by his own troops.

Unable to resist openly, assassination had become their weapon of choice. A merchant one day, a minor official the next. If their goal was to make the newcomers feel uneasy, and unsafe within their own homes, then it was an admirable one. But it was a cruel and cowardly way to fight a war, and no way to topple an empress.

Dama Akantha had hinted at striking the imperial family, perhaps even assassinating Nerissa, but Josan saw such talk as folly. Nerissa was too well guarded for such a tactic to succeed, and even if she were killed, it would not make him emperor. The army would swear its loyalty to Nestor, her elder son, then ruthlessly hunt down any suspected of being complicit in his mother's death.

As each day passed, Josan became more and more convinced that the rebellion was doomed. Fortunately, Lucius's spirit also agreed with his assessment, for Josan needed his help to maintain his role. Lucius remained content to whisper suggestions and to prompt him when encountering one of his former friends. He had not tried to regain control of his body—though perhaps matters would have been different had he thought that there was a chance that he could seize the throne. Then his ambitions might have come to the fore and undone all that Josan strove to accomplish.

Despite his orders to his followers to await his commands, the killings continued, and Josan felt responsible for each death. He knew his presence in the city, even if it were only rumors of ghostly sightings, had stirred up passions long forgotten.

Try as he could, he could not see a way to end the violence. If he could not convince Myles that he had no wish to be emperor, what hope did he have of convincing faceless rebels to lay down their arms and accept Nerissa's imperfect rule?

Like Myles, they saw no difference between the title and the man, but Josan saw far more clearly. For the first time he wondered if Nerissa had wanted to be named empress, or if she, too, had once engaged in dreams of a simpler life, with only the cares of an ordinary woman. And he knew that her blood would run just as red as his own if it were to be shed.

He would have to find a way to end the killings before it came to that. For all their sakes.

Chapter 17

Weeks passed, but despite his determination, Josan was still no closer to uniting the rebels under his leadership so he could convince them to disband. All he had accomplished so far was to discover that it was much easier to study history than it was to shape it. Numbers had been his passion, and the pursuit of logic, not the secrets of men's hearts. He could calculate the steadily diminishing odds of success, but he could not find within him the skills to bend men to his will.

Even Renato, who continued to proclaim his complete loyalty, had taken to leaving the house on secret errands that he would not reveal. He claimed that such secrecy was meant to protect the prince, but only a fool would believe such lies. Secrecy did not protect him; rather it protected those that Renato met with and whatever schemes they were hatching.

Ironically he would have respected Renato more if he thought that the magistrate was meeting with Nerissa's emissaries, preparing to betray him. But he judged it far more likely that Renato had grown impatient with a prince who counseled caution and had decided to take matters into his own hands. After all, the prince was hardly likely to disdain his followers once they had raised his banner in the streets.

Which left him with one more lever to try. He had sent Myles to arrange a meeting with Lady Ysobel. It was a test, for he knew Renato would certainly object if he knew that the prince was negotiating privately with Lady Ysobel. But Myles had apparently held his tongue, for Renato made no mention of the meeting, and at the appointed hour, Josan slipped out of the town house.

Heavily swathed despite the stifling heat of the afternoon, Josan was flushed and sweating by the time he reached the rear entrance to Lady Ysobel's garden.

A servingwoman was waiting on the other side. "You're late," she proclaimed. "Hurry now; her ladyship doesn't like to be kept waiting."

Apparently the sight of a man wrapped from head to foot in an all-encompassing robe, with the hood drawn down to cover his features was nothing new to this woman, as she tugged on his sleeve and began to lead him through the garden paths.

"Mind your manners and do as you're told," the woman advised. For all she was old enough to be his mother, he had to hasten his steps to keep up with her. Grumbling under her breath, she gave the distinct impression of a woman with better things to do with her time.

As he was hurried into the house and upstairs to the private living quarters, he wondered what story Ysobel had told her servants to explain his presence.

Halfway down the corridor, the woman paused in front of a paneled door and pushed it open, revealing an elaborate bathing chamber.

"If you're quick there's still time for a wash before she gets here," she said, punctuating her remark with a disdainful sniff.

He paused on the threshold, blinking. On his left, water cascaded from a fountain mounted on the wall down into a cleansing pool, where swirling currents would carry away dirt into the trough below. On his right, an elaborate soaking pool occupied the place of honor in front of the large windows that overlooked the city and the harbor below.

"In with you, and strip off," the woman ordered.

At that he knew why she thought he was there. He wondered if this was a test, or merely Lady Ysobel's unique sense of humor.

"I am here for your mistress's pleasure, not yours," he said. Stepping inside the room, he shut the door behind him.

He removed his outer robe and hung it on one of the hooks on the wall, then untied his sandals. He stripped off his tunic and pants, then sank gratefully into the cleansing pool.

Despite what the woman had implied, he didn't think he smelled that bad; nonetheless he used the pumice stone to scrape his body until his skin glowed bright red. Only then did he emerge from the cleansing pool. As he made his way over to the soaking pool, he noticed a table with a chilled pitcher of wine and a plate of fresh fruits. He poured himself a glass of wine, then stepped into the soaking pool. Ledges built into the sides of the tub allowed him to gradually immerse himself in the heat, until at last he sat on an underwater bench. He sipped the wine and looked out over the city as if he had not a care in the world.

Lady Ysobel had a taste for the finer things in life if this room was any indication. But he wondered if it reflected her true self, or if it was yet another self-serving mask, just as he suspected that she used her licentious reputation as a cover for conspiracy.

He heard the door open, then shut, but he did not turn

around. There was the barest whisper of silk, as it slid onto the tiled floor, then Lady Ysobel stepped into view.

She paused to pour herself a glass of wine, giving him ample time to admire her slender form. Her breasts were small but firm, the dusky rose of her nipples a perfect complement to her exotic golden skin. Ikarian women were praised for their soft curves, but Ysobel's body was firm, with muscles that rippled lightly under her skin. As she climbed into the soaking pool, she met his gaze frankly, then allowed her eyes to travel downward, inspecting him as if he were there solely for diversion.

Intellectually he knew she was beautiful, and her bold confidence would prove irresistible to many. But he admired her with the same spirit with which he admired the delicate mosaics that graced the walls. She was pleasing to look at, but he did not lust for her, and he would not allow her charms to tempt him from his path.

Josan wondered if his disinterest came from his lifelong adherence to his vows? Or did it come from the knowledge that the flesh she admired was not his own?

He raised his glass in salute. "Lady Ysobel."

"Prince Lucius," she replied, raising her own glass. Whatever her plans might have been, she apparently sensed that he had no interest in dalliance, and she adjusted her tactics accordingly.

"I do not know what to make of you," she said. "Your friends agree that you have changed much in your exile."

"All men change," he said.

"But few return from the dead, bringing with them the gifts of the gods."

"I was not dead."

"Of course," she said. Reaching over to the table next to her, she selected a quartered peach and devoured it in neat bites. "Tell me, how did you summon the lightning that struck the palace?"

"Lightning strikes the palace in nearly every storm," he said.

"But you knew that there would be a storm that night. Just as you warned the islanders that the great storm was coming," she said.

He shrugged. He had not come to discuss his feeble gifts.

"A useful talent for a sailor to have," she said.

"Since I am not likely to find myself on a ship, it makes no difference," he said. "Surely Seddon has more at stake here than a mere interest in predicting the weather."

"The weather is important to a sailor, as important as a sound ship or a good captain," she pointed out. "Misjudging the weather cost Captain Tollen his life, and his ship."

He could not fault her logic, but both knew that he was not here to discuss the weather, or the hazards of sailing. He held his silence, waiting to see what she would say next.

"Tell me what stake the Learned Brethren have in this? Was it their idea for you to hide on that island? What has Brother Nikos told you, and what is he prepared to do to help our cause?"

The less she knew of the brethren's involvement, the better for them both. "Our cause? Since when has the federation interested itself in who sits on the imperial throne? And do not try to tell me that you care about restoring the ancient bloodline. Dama Akantha may profess to believe that nonsense, but I do not."

A swift attack was the best form of defense.

"The federation seeks mutual cooperation against the common threat of Vidrun's unchecked expansion," Lady Ysobel explained. "In the decade since Empress Nerissa made peace with Vidrun, their empire has grown even stronger. Nerissa should be gathering allies of her own, but she has been unwilling to see the advantages of closer partnership between our two lands."

"So you want to replace her with someone who will be suitably grateful to the federation. An emperor who will be inclined to see matters as you do."

"Of course."

He shook his head. "If I had an army of ten thousand in the field, I might believe you. But there is no logic in your argument when success is so far from our grasp. Tell me, do you really think these rebels have any chance of overthrowing Nerissa?"

"Surely you cannot doubt the loyalty and devotion of your followers?"

It was not their loyalty he doubted, it was their intelligence. Though he could hardly say as much to Lady Ysobel—not if he were to keep the pretense that he was indeed Prince Lucius.

"Even with your help, my followers have accomplished nothing except petty crimes and meaningless deaths. I see no profit for any of us in this," he observed. "I came here to rule, not to hide in the shadows while murderers and arsonists tear apart the city in my name."

"You must be patient," Ysobel counseled. "With you to lead them, your people will accomplish great things. They will put you on the throne."

"But even if I seize the throne, can I keep it?" he mused aloud. "Nerissa's allies are too numerous to be ignored, and they will not sit there quietly as I strip them of their power."

A flash of impatience crossed her face, then her expression smoothed back into its placid lines. "Have faith, Prince Lucius, and trust in those who wish you well."

"Of course," he said. He had learned what he had come for, and there was no sense in further argument.

Ysobel had no grand plan to put him on the throne; indeed, the more she proclaimed her faith in his ultimate victory, the more certain he became that she was lying. She did not believe that he would be able to defeat Nerissa.

She had been honest about one thing. Vidrun was the key. Not because of the idea that Seddon and Ikaria would someday unite against Vidrun—for even the most foolish would realize that Ikaria, newly emerged from civil strife, would be unwilling to engage in another war. But Vidrun had steadily squeezed the federation out of the easternmost trading routes. With the east closing, that left the routes to the west. There Ikaria was making its own inroads, but if the empire were torn apart by civil war, then the federation would be free to expand.

Lady Ysobel and the federation that she represented did not care whether Prince Lucius was victorious or if he died a tragic martyr. An impostor would have served them as well. They needed only a figurehead to launch a rebellion, to ensure that Empress Nerissa's attention was firmly occupied within her own borders.

And if Nerissa were to react even more harshly than she had six years before, even those who had stayed neutral would be forced to choose sides. The resulting violence could well engulf the whole of the empire.

Lady Ysobel had to know this, just as she had to know he was almost certainly doomed. Yet she was able to smile casually as she refilled his wineglass and passed him a cluster of dark red grapes. It took a certain coolness to smile at a man while calculating the odds of his imminent demise. He admired her determination even as he deplored her goals.

Lady Ysobel was dangerous, not just for what she knew but for what she represented. He had hoped that her instincts as a trader would help him convince her that the rebellion was a losing proposition; but he saw that she had already made those calculations and was not interested in victory. She and her people were prepared to turn a profit regardless of the ultimate outcome—and regardless of how much suffering they caused.

Despite the heat of the water, he felt a chill come over him as he realized how firmly the trap had closed around him.

Lady Ysobel was furious. She paced the confines of her small office in the embassy, unable to sit still. Perrin, her clerk, had taken one look at his furious mistress and wisely discovered errands that took him elsewhere.

In her fury, she alternated between cursing herself for the ambition that had led her to accept this assignment and cursing Prince Lucius, who was proving to be the most uncooperative of conspirators.

From the very beginning, nothing had gone as planned. By all signs, Captain Tollen and *Seldon's Pride* had perished during the great storm, and she herself had been lucky to survive. But the council did not recognize any excuse for failure, and once she arrived in Karystos she had worked hard to prove herself, to overcome the stigma of having lost both the gold and weapons entrusted to her.

That she had done ably, establishing a network of spies who confirmed her assessment that the time was not ripe for fomenting rebellion. Instead, she strove to prove herself through her skills as a negotiator, using her public role to fatten the coffers of federation traders. In the year that she had served as trade liaison, she had brokered more deals than her predecessor had in his five years in the post.

Pursuing profit was in itself a worthy task, though it would be a slower means of achieving her goals. Bringing Ikaria to its knees was an accomplishment that would gain her entry into the very first rank of trading houses and a seat on the merchant's council. While a successful term as trade liaison would increase her stature and her personal wealth, it would serve merely as a stepping-stone on the path to power.

Failure, on the other hand, would destroy all that she had worked so hard to achieve. And ever since her meeting with Prince Lucius, she had seen failure as a distinct possibility.

Not merely that the rebellion would fail, for that was a certainty. But that she, along with the federation, would be implicated in the unrest. Painting Prince Lucius as the villain would tear Ikaria apart, as the uneasy truce between the native Ikarians and their newcomer rulers fell apart. But if Nerissa were able to portray the rebellion as the act of a foreign aggressor, putting the blame on agents of the federation, she could use this connection to her advantage, uniting her people in the face of a common foe. And Seddon would find itself embroiled in a costly war.

The odds were still in Ysobel's favor. True, events were spinning out of her control, as the various factions quarreled over how best to use Prince Lucius—even though the prince himself was showing a marked disinclination to be used. Although she could not see the ultimate outcome, she could still win this game if she prepared for every eventuality.

The most likely course was an ill-coordinated uprising, as the leaders lost control of their most volatile followers, who then took to the streets. And that day might come sooner than anyone thought. She had been troubled to learn that young Flavian had taken into his service Nikki, the elder brother of the boy who had been executed by Empress Nerissa. Flavian's recklessness coupled with Nikki's rage could well prove the spark that touched off the rebellion. It would be crushed by the empress's forces, of course, but the hunt to uncover the full extent of the conspiracy would occupy Nerissa's time and attention nicely.

If Prince Lucius were turned over to the empress for questioning, then Ysobel and the members of the inner circle of the rebellion would be at greatest risk. But in that case, perhaps, she could use Prince Lucius's sudden attack of conscience in her favor. Surely she was not the only one who was disturbed by his doubts. For all their professed devotion to the royal blood of Constantin, the conspirators saw themselves in control of the newly reformed Ikaria. They did not intend to raise up one who would truly rule over them—particularly one who showed signs of putting the interests of his people ahead of those of his supporters.

A few well-placed hints, and the rebels might come to share her view that a dead martyr was of far more use than a balky and uncooperative princeling.

Her furious pacing slowed, and her anger diminished as she crafted her plans. By the time Perrin returned to tell her that the ambassador was ready to see her, she had managed to convince herself that this was merely a setback and not the disaster it had first seemed.

Perrin led her to Ambassador Hardouin's private chamber, where an attendant was arranging the folds of his crimson silk overrobe, which meant that the ambassador was preparing to leave for an evening's entertainment.

They exchanged greetings, then Hardouin dismissed his attendant.

"What is so urgent that it cannot wait till the morning?" he asked.

"I met with the pretender this afternoon," she said. "Alone."

"Was that wise?"

Of course it was not wise. Wisdom would have been staying in the federation, choosing the deck of one of her ships over this quagmire of politics and intrigue. But having committed herself to her course, she was prepared to take the risks necessary to accomplish her task.

"He requested the meeting, and it seemed wise to find out what he wanted."

"Gold," Hardouin said, turning from her as he opened his jewel case. After a moment's study he selected a ring with a large square-cut ruby, and slipped it on his right hand in place of the signet ring he wore for official duties. "He wants money, and an assurance that we'll send soldiers when the time comes."

She shook her head. "He doesn't want gold. He may not even want our support. It seems he's grown a conscience in his years away and is rethinking whether or not he wants the throne."

Hardouin turned to her, giving her his full attention. "This is no time for jests."

"I am not joking. Nor do I think that his remarks to me were a test."

Not for the first time, she wondered what part the Learned Brethren were playing in this. Why had they sheltered Prince Lucius all these years? Had it been done with Brother Nikos's knowledge, and the full support of the brethren, even as they swore their public loyalty to Empress Nerissa? Or was his presence at the lighthouse mere serendipity? Perhaps a merciful act of compassion on the part of one of the monks, who had kept the secret from his superiors?

Whoever had sent him to that lighthouse, his years of exile had changed Prince Lucius—though it was a damned inconvenient time for him to discover that he had a conscience. She did not know if his doubts were honest caution or mere vacillation, but she would be prepared for either eventuality.

"The pretender's diffidence may alienate some of his

followers," she said. Even here, in the security of the embassy, prudence dictated that they not speak his name aloud. "It is possible that one of them will decide there is more to be gained by betraying him to the empress, along with any that are suspected of helping him."

"What would you have me do?" he asked. Doubtless he had his own ideas, but he was testing her, waiting to see what she would propose.

"It is possible that my name may come up. If so, it is vital that I be seen as acting on my own."

Hardouin nodded.

"Now would be a good time to drop a few hints. Say that you suspect me of diverting official monies into my own personal coffers. Mention that Lord Quesnel has sent word to you that he is displeased with my performance and thinking of replacing me. A few merchants already know that I no longer speak for Flordelis house, so it would be a good time to remind them that my own family no longer trusts me."

"I can do this, but once the rumors take hold it will be difficult for you to act as trade liaison."

She shrugged. She had already reckoned the cost. No reputable merchant would want to deal with one suspected of being dishonest and corrupt, but it was an acceptable sacrifice. Even with her precautions, suspicion would fall upon the embassy and upon Seddon. But as long as the empress had no proof of official involvement, it should stay her hand.

"If this all blows over, then it will be easy enough to correct the rumors. You will discover that the evidence against me was planted by a disgruntled clerk, and all will soon be forgotten."

"You must take care. If you are betrayed, you must not fall into Nerissa's hands," he said.

She knew it was not concern for her safety that prompted

his words. Ysobel knew too much, and she had no illusions
about her abilities to hold her tongue once handed over to
Nerissa's torturers. Given enough time, even the strongest
would break.

"I know my duty. I will not allow myself to be made
prisoner."

Neither did she intend a noble suicide, though she had
no intention of saying so to the ambassador. Hardouin
could be trusted only so far. He, too, had his ambitions,
and given a choice between her survival and his own interests, he would choose himself. Should it come to the
worst, he might well decide to purchase Nerissa's forgiveness with the presentation of Ysobel's corpse.

In theory, if she suspected that she was in imminent
danger, she was to return to the embassy, and Hardouin
would make arrangements to have her smuggled out of the
city. By treaty, the empress could not search inside the
grounds of an embassy, so Ysobel should be safe.

But she had not come this far by putting blind trust in
others. If it came time, she would flee the city on her own
and leave Ambassador Hardouin to make his own explanations.

"I trust that matters are not so grave as you fear, but I
will do as you ask. You will keep me informed of all devel-
opments?"

"Of course."

They exchanged polite farewells, then went their separate ways—Hardouin off to start spreading rumors, while
she would work to salvage what she could. She had done
her duty by warning the ambassador, but she did not truly
believe all was lost. If she kept her wits about her, she
could still turn events in her favor. The seat on the council
was not yet out of her grasp.

And if Lucius would not cooperate, it was time to find a
new scapegoat. Brother Nikos might play the role of learned

scholar and loyal advisor to the empress, but the fact remained that his order had sheltered the renegade prince. She remembered how anxious Nikos had been to question her when she first arrived in the city. She had thought his unease attributable to the same affliction that many Ikarian men felt when faced with a woman who held rank in her own right, but now she saw that conversation in a different light. Perhaps Nikos had been testing her, trying to find out if she had recognized the lighthouse keeper for who he truly was.

Still, the empress was hardly likely to take Ysobel's word over that of one of her most trusted advisors. She would have to find proof of her suspicions. If evidence could not be found, it would have to be manufactured. Just enough to bring the glare of suspicion upon Nikos and his monks. Once the empress started investigating, Nikos's treachery was bound to reveal itself.

In that Benedict would be helpful, for he could use his position in the city watch to arrange the fortuitous discovery of evidence that would link Nikos to the conspiracy. Bring Nerissa proof that there were traitors within her court, and she would tear her empire apart looking for the rest of the conspirators, while Lady Ysobel and Seddon emerged unscathed.

She would call upon Benedict tomorrow, she decided, ostensibly to complain about pilfering from the dockside warehouses and to ask that the night watch be strengthened. Once they were alone she would question him, to see what he knew of the brethren's secret activities. If she handled him deftly, Benedict might come to believe that discrediting Nikos was his own idea.

In the meantime, she returned to her chambers and summoned a maid to help her change into a fashionable gown and dress her hair. Empress Nerissa was hosting a concert in the evening, which would be held in the gardens of the imperial palace. Ysobel had been invited but had originally decided not to attend since it was unlikely that the empress would be in personal attendance. But she changed her mind, since Dama Akantha would almost certainly be there, in her role as a patroness of the arts. It would be a perfect chance for a seemingly casual encounter, and under the cover of the music Ysobel could share her doubts over the suitability of the pretender to the throne.

Dama Akantha was passionate in hatred of the empress, but her hatred was matched by her cunning. If the time came for Prince Lucius to be sacrificed, Ysobel could count on Akantha to see that the prince met a suitable end before his loose tongue brought them all to grief.

Chapter 18

Josan rose before dawn, dressing himself in a sleeveless tunic over loose cotton pants in expectation of another scorchingly hot day. A yawning servant fetched barley cakes and sweet tea, which he ate while standing at the bedroom window, watching the buildings change color as the sun's rays broke over the city.

Passing Myles's room, he glanced through the open door and saw that the room was empty. Josan was not the only one to have arisen early, and he wondered what had driven Myles from his bed at that hour.

As he reached the foot of the stairs, he encountered Myles, who was about to head up. One glimpse of Myles's face was enough to tell him that something was wrong.

"Good, you're awake," Myles said. "I was on my way up to wake you."

"What has happened?"

Myles glanced around the open hallway and shook his head. Renato was convinced of his servants' complete loyalty, but neither Myles nor Josan was inclined to take risks.

"Come," he said.

It was telling that he had fallen back into their old ways.

He had not called Josan "my lord," nor had he bothered disguising his order as a polite request. Whatever had driven Myles from his bed had disturbed him.

They went into Renato's study, and Myles barred the door behind them.

"There's a bundle by the gate in the back with your things. If trouble comes, if you hear any noise, don't wait to find what it is. Slip out the back and head for the docks. There's an inn at the southern end called The Sailor's Ease. Stay there, and if I do not come for you within a day, you are to take passage on any ship you can, understood?"

"What happened?"

"Lady Zenia was murdered last night."

The name meant nothing to Josan, but it meant something to the Other, who stirred within him. "The empress's cousin?" he heard himself ask.

"The very same." Myles sank down heavily on the nearest chair, and after a moment Josan followed suit.

He recalled the mischievous smile on the face of a young woman who had taken pity on a young boy bored by a formal court event. She had taken him aside and shown him where the guards hid their dice, teaching him how to cast them and reckon his score. Then they'd raided the elaborate refreshments table, snatching sugar cakes and devouring their stolen treasures while hiding behind the commoners' screen.

He remembered her laughter as if he could hear her still, and recalled the devotion of a young boy who had fallen in love with her. He had thrown a tantrum on the day that she was married, for all he knew himself a beardless boy still far too young for her. Though their paths had seldom crossed except on the most formal of court occasions when all would be invited, she had always held a special place in his heart.

In Lucius's heart. Josan had never met her, never known the woman, yet he felt Lucius's grief as if it was his own.

"Was she alone?" he forced himself to ask, though in his heart he already knew the answer. Myles's face was too grim. There was more bad news to come.

"No. The assassins killed Zenia, her three children, and her husband. Plus the servants in the house. They said there was blood everywhere. The screams alerted the neighbors, who summoned the watch."

"Whoever did this will pay for what he has done. I want him brought to me by sunset, or so help me——"

"You are too late. He is already dead."

"Who? How?" He felt robbed, thwarted of his chance to inflict pain upon the one who had caused him this grief.

"Flavian. The young fool was arrested by the watch, along with those he had paid to do his foul work." Myles's disgust was palpable, as he contemplated the folly of the youngest member of the inner circle of conspirators. Not only had Flavian been stupid enough to be caught, he had been caught in an act so horrific that it would alienate those who might have otherwise have been sympathetic to Lucius's cause. If Flavian had been intending to destroy the revolution, he could not have chosen a better way.

But Flavian, it seemed, was already beyond whatever retribution anyone could mete out.

"How did he die? Was it Benedict?"

"No, but Benedict sent a messenger to us with the word of what had happened. Flavian took poison and died before he reached the prison. Still, at least two of his thugs are still alive and in the empress's custody, and if he told them anything, then we are all at risk."

"Where is the magistrate?"

"Gone, to talk with the others. He suggested that we wait here for word."

Josan shook his head at such folly. "And if the empress's

spies are watching any one of the conspirators, they will be able to follow them right to the gathering and arrest them all."

Myles nodded in agreement, though still he forbore to criticize Renato aloud.

"What will you do?" he asked.

What would he do? Josan was disgusted by the slaughter of innocents, while Lucius grieved for the death of one he had counted a friend. But both souls were united in their understanding that events had passed beyond their control. He could no longer pretend that there was any chance of steering the revolution, nor of his convincing his followers to lay down their arms.

But there was still time to flee. To remain any longer was an act of utter folly, for surely it was only a matter of time before they would all be arrested. Already the conspirators had begun to panic, and such men would be swift to turn on each other. For all they knew, Renato's early-morning errand had taken him not to meet with the conspirators, but rather to the palace where he was making arrangements to trade Prince Lucius for his own safety.

"What should we do?" Myles asked, after the silence had stretched on.

Josan hesitated, and in that moment the prince struck. Propelled by the strength of his anger and grief he rose up within, seizing control of what was his by birthright. For a brief moment Josan felt the prince's rage, then he was bludgeoned into insensibility.

Lucius tasted the demon's terror, and it pleased him. Now the invader knew what it was like to be brushed aside, unable to control what would happen next. But there was no time to savor his victory, for his lackey was gazing at him expectantly.

"You will go to the collegium. Tell Brother Nikos that Magistrate Renato has urgent need of his counsel and fetch him here."

"The brethren?"

"Brother Nikos," he repeated. "If Renato's name does not move him to haste, then tell him that his old pupil Josan wishes to speak with him before he summons the imperial guard."

"But Nikos will tell the empress—"

"Brother Nikos will do as he is told. He knows I hold his life in my hands."

The soldier made no move to obey, and Lucius realized that he had been too abrupt. The monk, for all that he played at being a royal prince, was more used to reasoning than commanding. "Go, now, there is no time to be lost. I promise I will explain everything to you later," he said, imitating the monk's earnestness.

"As you command, my lord," Myles said. With one last searching look, he took his leave.

And now it was a race against time. The invader trusted Myles, but Lucius knew that the lackey's loyalties were divided between the man he called prince and Magistrate Renato. If Renato were to return too soon, he might convince Myles to disobey his orders. All in the name of protecting the prince, of course, but any delay would be fatal.

The invader was too weak to do what must be done. Caught between his guilt and urge to flee, knowing that the empress had the power to turn the city into a trap from which no escape would be possible. If he were to act, Lucius had to do so immediately, before his choices were taken away from him.

And before he lost control of this body. He did not fool himself into thinking that he had won anything but a mere skirmish. The invader was not vanquished; he was merely banished for a time. It was inevitable that he would surface again, once more reducing Lucius to the status of a prisoner within his own flesh.

The invader might be willing to live a half-life, but Lucius was not. He would end the killings—but not before he had made those responsible pay. The passage of years, or perhaps the dispassionate wisdom of the monk, had made him realize how much a fool he had been in his youth. He despised his youthful self and how he had gloried in the destruction wrought in his name. But he reserved his full hatred for those who had taken advantage of an arrogant youth, and who sought to use him again. He would see them punished for their crimes.

All of them bore the responsibility for Zenia's death, and for the other innocents who had been killed in the name of restoring the old blood to the throne. Their debt would not be repaid until their own blood had been shed in return.

He glanced down in disgust at his bare arms. If he was to meet his fate, he would not do so dressed like a clerk. Returning to his room, he shaved his face and anointed his hair. Then, searching through the wardrobe till he found a suitable silk robe, he dressed himself as befit a prince.

He had never been good at waiting, and fearing that the invader would use his distraction to attack, Lucius kept the image of Zenia in his mind, stoking the flames of his anger. When Myles returned with Brother Nikos, he was ready.

Brother Nikos froze on the threshold of the library as he caught sight of Lucius. It was only for a moment, but his cheeks were flushed with anger or perhaps fear as he came toward Lucius.

"You should not have summoned me. It is too dangerous for us both, especially after the savagery of last night," Brother Nikos said.

"Do you already feel the lash upon your back? Is that

why you came, so you would know where to send Nerissa's troops now that you have decided to betray me? How many followed you here?"

"No one followed us, this I swear," Myles said.

He would have to trust the ex-soldier's competence in this. But simply because they had not been followed did not mean that they were safe.

"Did you use the name Josan to fetch him?"

Myles shook his head. "No, he came when I told him that Magistrate Renato needed to speak with him about Lady Zenia's murder."

"Good," Lucius said. So he still had time. No doubt Nikos had come to find out how much Renato knew.

"I would not betray you," Brother Nikos said.

"You already have," Lucius replied. Then, with a glance at Myles, he switched to the scholar's tongue. "You betrayed us both when you cast this spell."

"Prince Lucius?"

"Yes," he answered, still keeping to the scholar's tongue. He wondered if it was his accent or perhaps his harsh condemnation that had given his identity away. Not that it mattered. Both monk and prince had their own reasons to distrust Nikos. And both shared the burning desire to stop the violence before it claimed another victim.

"I can help you," Nikos said. "There is a ship in the harbor that will leave for Xandropol tomorrow. One of the novices has already booked passage. You could take his place and none would be the wiser."

The scholar would like that. He would enjoy being confined amidst musty books and rotting scrolls, spending the rest of his life deciphering the writings of long-vanished civilizations. But the monk's pleasure would be Lucius's torment, and as long as their two souls were bound together, neither could truly be content.

"Xandropol," he repeated. From the corner of his eye

he saw Myles's sudden interest, as he recognized the name of the foreign city. Myles was shrewd enough to realize that Nikos must be offering safe passage, and no doubt he would urge his prince to accept.

But Myles did not know what he knew.

"Would they wait till I was at sea to dispose of my body? Or would you have me killed aboard ship, my body left in the harbor for the empress's men to discover?"

"Why did you summon me if you do not want my help?"

"But I do want your help. I want you to take me to the empress. Now."

"You are mad," Nikos said.

"If I am, we know who is to blame."

"The empress will kill you."

Quite probably. But even death was better than this twisted half-life. "The empress will hear what I have to say first."

"I will not help you," Nikos declared. He turned on his heel as if to leave.

Lucius caught Myles's eye, and Myles moved to block the door, his sword drawn. The ex-soldier might not understand what they were saying, but from the tones of their voices it was clear that they were arguing.

Nikos turned back. "You cannot force me to help you."

"You are mistaken."

As Lucius advanced, Nikos retreated. At last Nikos was forced to stop, lest he impale himself on Myles's sword. Lucius stepped in close enough that he could smell Nikos's fear, see the beads of sweat on his brow. He was a small man, really, for all his posturing, and Lucius wondered that he had ever been afraid of him.

"You have two choices. First, you take me to the palace and use your status as chief counselor to demand a private meeting with the empress. When she arrives you will tell her that you persuaded me to surrender and accept her gratitude."

"What is my second choice?"

"My friend summons the watch. They arrest us both, and I will tell anyone who will listen of your treason. They will not believe me, not at first. But they will be forced to investigate. I doubt Brother Giles will take much persuasion before he tells all, and soul magic is such an ugly thing, is it not? A man who would dabble in soul magic might well be guilty of any crime."

"Brother Giles is dead, and there are none who carry on his work," Nikos avowed.

"But surely his notes survive. The monk knows your ways—he knows you would never throw anything of value away. You kept me alive when you thought me a witless shell. The proof of your deeds is in the collegium and, once they know the stakes, the brethren will be all too eager to help Nerissa's men find it."

Nikos was trapped, and from the defeated look in his eye, he knew it.

"This is how you repay me for my help? For all I have done for you?"

"You, at least, may come out of this alive and relatively unscathed. Which is more than you would offer me," Lucius said. He held Nikos's gaze until the monk finally nodded.

Lucius stepped back. "Summon a litter for two," he told Myles. "Brother Nikos and I are going to call on an old friend."

The excitement of finally taking action, and of being in control of his own fate, carried him through the delay as they waited first for the litter, and on the long, jostling trip through the streets of Karystos. Myles had been ordered to stay behind, to wait for Magistrate Renato to return. But even if he had disobeyed his orders, it was unlikely that he would realize the litter's destination until it was too late.

As they reached the first gate into the palace, Lucius placed one hand on the dagger that he wore at his side, but Nikos needed no persuasion. No doubt he had spent the journey weaving an elaborate web of lies and truths that would cast his actions in the noblest of lights, and ensure that whatever Lucius said would be seen as an attempt to discredit one who had proven unshakably loyal to the imperial house.

Nikos's name and face were enough to gain them entrance onto the palace grounds. As they left the litter, several glanced at Lucius, who was once more wearing a hood to conceal his face, but no one questioned him.

The guards at the entrance to the palace were not as accepting. They refused to let Lucius pass unchallenged, until Nikos assured them that the stranger's presence was a matter of the utmost discretion, and that he would take full responsibility. Even with these assurances the guards still searched Lucius as if he were a commoner, finding and confiscating his dagger.

They were led to a small antechamber off the imperial receiving room. On his own, Brother Nikos could have been expected to be taken directly to the empress, but the presence of a second man meant that they would have to wait for the empress to deign to receive them.

Servants offered water and fruit juices, in deference to Brother Nikos's reputation for moderation. Nikos accepted a glass of melon fruit juice, but Lucius simply shook his head. He glared at Nikos, who sat lounging on a couch as if he were at ease in his own quarters. He could tell that the balance of power had shifted. In the magistrate's house it had been Nikos who was afraid, while Lucius held the power.

Now, having been given time to scheme, Nikos showed

every sign of being in control of the situation, while Lucius paced restlessly, trying to hide the trembling of his limbs. He knew that he had to see the empress. It must be done. And yet the anger that had sustained him earlier was no match for the knowledge that directly under his feet lay the infamous dungeons where the empress's torturers held sway.

He heard the clicking of bootheels in the corridor and knew that Empress Nerissa and her bodyguards approached. Fear welled up within him as he felt the faint stirrings of the invader. He struggled to remain in control, but the harder he exerted his will, the more he felt himself slipping away. To his horror he realized that he could no longer feel his own limbs.

There was no time. With his remaining strength he brought the details of his plan to the forefront of his thoughts, and then pushed them toward the invader, hoping against hope that it would be enough.

I'm sorry, he thought, and Lucius surrendered. He had one moment to feel the horrified shock of the invader as he realized where they were, then he let himself fall into the blackness of unknowing.

Empress Nerissa listened impassively as Benedict, second-in-command of the city watch, finished making his report.

"My men searched the traitor Flavian's residence, but have found no signs that he had any accomplices. His servants claim to know nothing, but of course they will be questioned under the severest forms to see if they are telling the truth."

The severest forms were a polite euphemism for torture. Given the magnitude of their master's crimes, it was likely that some of the servants would die before the imperial questioners were satisfied as to their veracity. Others would be crippled by the lash or hot irons. Still, their fates could have been worse. It was within Nerissa's rights to order the entire household put to death for what Flavian had done. For all that Lady Zenia had been related to her noble mother rather than her imperial father, Zenia was still kin to the empress, thus to shed her blood was an offense against the imperial house.

"You think this the act of a madman rather than a conspiracy?"

Benedict hesitated. His nervousness was understandable, for it was rare that he spoke directly with her. For ordinary matters she gave instructions to Proconsul Zuberi, who then passed on her orders to Petrelis, who commanded the city watch. But Petrelis was personally supervising the questioning of Flavian's household, and had thus delegated his subordinate to make the report.

"In these past weeks we have searched the city but found no signs of conspiracy; only a handful of malcontents. If I may offer my humble opinion, I believe that when Petrelis has finished his investigation he will find no signs that Flavian conspired with others in this deed."

She did not know if Benedict was allowing his hopes to overcome his good sense, or perhaps he merely feared being the bearer of bad news to his sovereign. It was more than mere unrest that had plagued the city in these past weeks. Just as a poisoned well revealed its presence through the dead animals that surrounded it, the conspiracy revealed itself through the ripples of violence that had spread out across the city, touching first commoners and now the noblest blood.

But there was nothing more to be gained from interrogating one who was himself no more than a lackey, so she dismissed Benedict with the instructions that he or Petrelis was to report to her the moment they had any information.

Even deep within the marble walls of the palace, the

heat of the city penetrated, and she felt the sweat beading on her brow. A terse order summoned slaves to tend the massive fans that blew fresh breezes through her living quarters, but even their efforts were barely able to make things tolerable.

Karystos in the summer was an uncivilized place, where the blazing sun drove the residents inside during the heat of the day, and periodic fevers swept through the poorer quarters. Anyone who could afford to do so retired to a country estate in the summer months, to avoid the heat and the disease. Nerissa herself possessed a half dozen estates, ranging from the imposing palace that Aitor had built on the island of Eluktiri to the modest estate near Sarna, which could house a mere fifty of her household. And their retainers, of course. But the unrest in the city had forced her to remain in Karystos—and when the empress stayed, her courtiers also remained behind.

She had urged Lady Zenia to leave, to travel to Sarna for the health of her children; but Zenia had chosen to stay, and that loyalty had cost her her life.

This time, her enemies had gone too far. So far Nerissa had held her hand, but from here on she would be merciless in her quest to hunt down those who opposed her. Benedict and his master Petrelis might hesitate to use the word *conspiracy*, knowing that it would reflect badly on them to discover that such had flourished under their very noses, but Nerissa would not hesitate. Nor would she wait for absolute proof.

Those who were currently under observation by the imperial spies would be brought in for questioning. The basic forms to start, though she would not hesitate to invoke the harsher disciplines. And Lady Ysobel would be brought in as well. There was no proof against her, but she had had one too many accidental encounters with those who were under suspicion. Lady Ysobel would have to be treated with caution, for she was still the official trade liaison. But she was also a pragmatic woman, used to reckoning the odds. A quick tour of the torture chambers ought to be enough to convince her of the wisdom of sharing whatever information she might have.

Nerissa's musings were interrupted by the news that Brother Nikos had arrived and requested an audience with her. Her interest was piqued when the messenger informed her that Nikos was not alone. She knew it was no coincidence that Nikos had arrived unbidden on this of all days, and as she made her way to the receiving room, she wondered what information he had brought her.

Opening the door to the antechamber, her bodyguards took up their positions on either side of the door.

As she entered the room, Nikos rose to his feet, then dropped to one knee.

"Most Gracious Imperial Majesty, forgive me for intruding on your grief," he said.

"Rise," she ordered. "I trust you would not do so lightly."

Her words were for Nikos, but her gaze was fixed on the second man in the room. In defiance of custom he made no obeisance. Instead he gave a slight bow, then lifted his hands and drew back his hood.

Her breath froze as his blue eyes stared directly into hers.

"Empress," he said.

"What is the meaning of this? You swore to me he was dead!"

Nikos dipped his head low, in a gesture of contrition. "It seems we were both deceived."

This was more than a simple mistake. Nikos had assured her that Prince Lucius was dead, that he had personally witnessed the prince's death and subsequent hasty burial.

She opened her mouth to summon the guards, but Lucius spoke swiftly, recognizing her intent.

"Don't you wish to hear what I have to say?"

"You will tell me all I wish to know, once Nizam is done with you."

He swallowed once, but that was the only outward sign of his fear. And indeed, he must be feeling terror, though his face was still, betraying no hint of his emotions. She studied him for a long moment, noting the changes the years had wrought. Memory recalled a man whose features still held the roundness of youth and who wore petulance as if it were a cloak, while this man held himself with dignity, his level gaze and sharp features conveying the impression of intelligence and resolution.

"How long has Nikos been your ally, conspiring behind my back?"

Prince Lucius shook his head. "The learned brother agreed to bring me here this morning, nothing more. I persuaded him that you and I needed to talk."

"And what do we have to discuss? All was said between us years ago, when you raised yourself in opposition to me."

"I have come to beg for your help."

"My help?" She laughed. So much for thinking that he had grown wits over the years. "The only help you may expect from me is a swift death."

And that would be more mercy than she was inclined to grant. Lucius had earned himself the slow death of a traitor for his actions years ago, and the latest violence had done nothing to soften her temper toward him.

"I come to you as one who loved Lady Zenia and is sickened by the violence being done in my name. I have come to ask for your help in ending this, before anyone else is killed."

She remembered the summer he had taken to following Zenia around the court and how Zenia had been endlessly patient with the youngest of her admirers. But that had been over fifteen years ago, and calf-love was hardly a motive for him to seek out the one person who had most cause to wish him dead.

Especially here, in the stronghold of her power. She had but to raise her voice and he would be captured, bound over for torture. It made no sense and she was not a woman who liked puzzles.

"Was Flavian one of yours?" she asked.

He grimaced. "Flavian was one of those who conspire against your rule, but he was not acting under my orders."

"I persuaded Prince Lucius to come here, to tell you the names of the conspirators in return for your mercy," Brother Nikos said.

Perhaps Lucius had been foolish enough to believe that she would be merciful though surely Nikos knew better. And by placing Lucius within her grasp, the monk had done much to redeem himself for his earlier mistake.

"I can tell you what I know freely, or you can summon Nizam and have him drag the information from me along with my lifeblood. But that alone will not break the conspiracy; nor will it end the violence."

"Maybe not. But seeing your body hanging from the palace walls will certainly dissuade your followers," she said, wanting to see his reaction.

To his credit Lucius did not flinch, and she felt a flicker of admiration for his poise. "Do not make the mistakes of six years ago, when your enemies were allowed to disappear back into the shadows, brooding and waiting until they could strike again."

"What do you suggest?"

"I can only tell you the names of those whom I have met, but there are others behind the scenes who guide their actions. I will summon them to a meeting, then your men will swoop down and arrest us. There will be no chance for any to escape."

"And you expect me to let you leave here? To walk free?" Such presumption was absurd, though the prospect of being able to crush the conspiracy with a single blow was indeed tempting.

"Send one of your own with me. A bodyguard, to ensure my behavior. The others can follow, discreetly, and await his signal."

"And what do you gain from this?"

"The rebellion is doomed to failure. The only question is how many people will die on both sides before you are triumphant. I choose to stop the killings now."

"A noble motive, but hardly in keeping with your character. You forget that I have known you since you were a babe at your mother's breast."

"Men change," he said.

He waited patiently as she pondered her course of action. He did not beg or plead, and she was struck by the truth of his words. Lucius had indeed changed. His mannerisms, even the cadence of his speech had altered, perhaps a sign that he had spent at least some of the past years among foreigners. If it were not for his features, she would not have recognized him.

The spoiled prince she had known would never have risked his own skin to save someone else, not even someone he loved. This man, if he was to be believed, was prepared to sacrifice himself to save his enemies. And, in so doing, he would condemn to their own deaths those friends who had supported him.

It was a noble sacrifice or an act of utter desperation, or possibly both. But in the end his motives did not matter. She would use him as she saw fit; and then, when he could be of no further use to her, she would mete out the justice that had been delayed for too long.

"You swear that you will do as you have said?"

"I swear that I will do my best to bring the conspirators

together, to face your justice. And as for myself, I will trust in your mercy."

The last was said with an ironic glance in the direction of Brother Nikos, and in that instant she knew that he clearly understood that the mercy the monk had promised him was a mere illusion. If he did indeed hand over the conspirators to her, then her mercy might stretch to a painless death versus the protracted agonies dictated by the law for traitors; but that was the most he could hope for, and it was clear that he knew it as well as she did.

She felt herself warming to him. She had detested the young man he had been, but under different circumstances she might have liked the man he had grown to become.

"Agreed," she said.

Lucius nodded. "I will give you this in token of my good faith. Benedict, of the city watch, is not to be trusted. He is one of the inner circle, so make certain that he knows nothing of your plans."

She hoped her face showed nothing of the shock that she felt. Could it be true that Benedict was a traitor? Was that why his investigations had yielded no proof of conspiracy, because he himself had destroyed any evidence before it could fall into her hands?

"Is there anyone else I should be wary of?"

"Trust no one. Remember, I do not know all their names, and some have hair as dark and skin as pale as your own. Select only those guards whose loyalty is absolutely certain for the arrests, and once you have them in hand you can question the traitors at your leisure."

"I do not need you to lecture me on how to run my empire," she snapped.

"Of course," Lucius said, and he bowed his head in a sign of respect.

It took some time, and a few suggestions from Brother

Nikos, to smooth the way, but at last they were agreed upon the arrangements. Prince Lucius had the span of the next day and night to complete his task—when dawn rose on the following morning her guards would arrest him, whether or not he had been able to keep his promise of handing over the rest of the rebels. The prospect of breaking the back of the rebellion with a single blow was tempting, but she would not let him slip through her fingers again. Prince Lucius had escaped justice once, but this time she would see that he paid for his crimes. His death would be a lesson to all who had flouted her authority.

When she was finished there would be no doubt who ruled in Ikaria—and none left alive who would dare challenge her in the future.

Chapter 19

Nerissa had assigned a single guard as his escort, though he did not doubt that others were following, preparing to keep the magistrate's residence under close watch until Lucius fulfilled his promises. Josan rode in a litter, alone with his thoughts, as the guard Farris walked alongside, his imposing presence ensuring that none drew too close. The fears that had plagued Josan during these past weeks were gone, because there was nothing left to fear. The time for anxiety had been when his fate was unknown. Now his path was laid out before him, and there was no turning back. He did not know whether to be angry or relieved that Prince Lucius had forced his hand in this way.

Left to his own inclinations, Josan would never have dared approach Nerissa directly. That had taken courage, and even if the prince's will had failed at the end, he had gone further than Josan would have dared on his own. With no choice, Josan had found the strength within himself to face Nerissa with seeming confidence and complete the bargain that Lucius had planned. On their own, neither he nor the prince were strong enough to end the madness, but by working together there was a chance.

The time for secrecy was past, so instead of leaving him in the nearby square, the litter bearers had been instructed to take him to Renato's residence. When the litter came to a halt, Farris drew back the curtains, and offered his hand to help Josan alight. Josan waited while Farris paid the litter bearers their fee and dismissed them. The sweat that prickled on his skin had less to do with the heat of the late afternoon sun than it did with what he must do next.

"Remember, you are to follow my lead. Do nothing to rouse their suspicions," Josan said.

"I will obey my mistress's orders," Farris replied. Tall and solidly built, his muscled bulk brought to mind one of the massive pillars of the imperial palace. Some might take his placid features as a sign of dullness, but Josan knew that was a false impression. Nerissa would not have chosen a stupid man for this assignment.

Farris's gaze swept the street. Josan looked as well, but did not see anything out of the ordinary. If Nerissa's men were already there, they were well hidden.

Inside he found both Magistrate Renato and Myles anxiously waiting for his return. When he entered the study they appeared relieved to see him, then shocked when Farris followed him, one step behind and to his right, as befit a personal guard.

"Where have you been? And who is this?". Renato asked.

Josan paused to strip off his cloak, tossing it on the floor in the manner of a man who has grown up surrounded by servants.

"This is Farris. Brother Nikos did not want me walking the streets unescorted, and Benedict agreed." This last was a gamble, though Nerissa had assured him that Benedict would have been too busy to meet with the other conspirators.

"Now you have returned, dismiss him. We have much

to talk about," Renato said. "You owe me an explanation of why you saw fit to involve the Learned Brethren."

"Farris stays."

"He's one of Nerissa's own guards. Do you truly want him to hear what we have to say?" Myles asked.

He knew he had but to say the word and Myles would attack Farris, giving his own life to buy his prince time to escape. But such a sacrifice would be pointless when Nerissa's men had no doubt already surrounded the house. So instead he gave what he hoped was a reassuring smile.

"We have allies in unexpected places," Josan said.

He sat down on one of the couches, and after a moment's indecision, Renato and Myles did the same. Farris moved to stand behind him, looming over the gathering in quiet menace.

"At first I thought Flavian's recklessness would destroy us all. But then I realized that the uproar has created a unique opportunity—one we must seize before it is too late," Josan explained.

"And what has Brother Nikos to do with this? The empress is his patron. He is not likely to betray her," said Renato.

"On the contrary; Nikos is the key to everything." Which was the truth, though not in the way that his listeners imagined.

It was difficult to force himself to exude confidence when he was all too conscious of the man standing directly behind him—a man who had orders to kill him the moment it seemed that the prince intended to betray his oath to Nerissa. He searched within himself for the remnants of Lucius's arrogance, reminding himself that the prince did not explain. He commanded, and he expected his followers to obey.

"What reason have you for trusting him? Or indeed any of the brethren?" Myles asked.

"Nikos is the reason I am alive today." Josan directed his next words to Renato. "Nikos has already proven his loyalty, but I have my doubts about the rest of my so-called followers."

"My prince, surely you do not doubt my faithfulness," Renato protested.

"You will prove your loyalty by summoning the others here, for a council tomorrow night. Nikos has given me the key to defeating Nerissa, and I will not wait any longer while my supporters temporize or run reckless in the streets."

"You cannot expect us—"

"I expect you to do as I command," Josan said. "Victory is within our grasp. Those who gather here will be remembered when I come to power. Those who are not here will be remembered as well."

"And what plan have you for destroying Nerissa? Assassination, perhaps?" Renato's gaze strayed to Farris, whose presence seemed to show that not all of Nerissa's guards were loyal.

"You will learn of it at the same time as the others," Josan said.

"But if you have already told Benedict and Nikos—"

"Enough. I owe you no explanations. Be grateful that I still have use for you, though if you continue to question me, I may reconsider your usefulness."

"Of course, my prince. It will be as you say." Renato bowed his head in a show of meekness, but Josan knew it was just that, a show.

Renato must realize that the prince was no longer solely dependent upon his good graces. Lucius could go to Benedict, or Dame Akantha, or any of the others that he had met, and ask for their help in arranging the meeting that he had requested. Renato would not want to lose his position of privilege to another, particularly if success was indeed within their grasp. He could count on Renato to do as he was told, in order to preserve his status as one of the inner circle of Lucius's advisors.

Josan had but to play the part of the soon-to-be-triumphant prince for a little longer.

After the meeting, Renato's ambitions would no longer matter.

Lady Ysobel had not reached her position by taking foolish chances. She knew when to take calculated risks and when to exercise restraint. Unfortunately, it seemed her instincts were not shared by the rebels. The murder of Lady Zenia and her family had inflamed tensions in Ikaria, bringing the city closer to open warfare in the streets. Now was the time for action, but instead Prince Lucius and his self-appointed advisors had decided it was a time for talking and had summoned the key members of the conspiracy to a meeting at Magistrate Renato's residence.

When the summons came, she gave serious consideration to refusing, as her earlier doubts about Prince Lucius rose to the fore. Bringing the leaders together in a single place was a tremendous risk, especially when it was likely that the prince would do no more than scold his followers for their wanton violence.

Unless, of course, recent events had forced his hand. If he were to declare himself openly and call for an uprising, then she needed to be there, to encourage him and his followers in their doomed endeavor. She had invested too much time in grooming these rebels to falter at the last moment. The larger the uprising, the more damage would be done to the empire, and the more damage done, the more praise Ysobel would receive when she finally returned to Seddon.

She took precautions, of course, reviewing the escape

routes from the district where Renato lived, ensuring that they were still viable. Then she sent a coded message to Ambassador Hardouin suggesting that he might wish to forgo his usual nightly entertainments and remain in the embassy. If there were trouble, the guards would think twice before venturing into the sovereign territory of the embassy to arrest Hardouin. Though it was unlikely that they would seek him out; he had done his best to put distance between them, spreading rumors about Ysobel that had caused some merchants to cancel their contracts with her. At social gatherings her presence now inspired malicious whispers—and only those who needed to take advantage of her bounty sent invitations or called at her town house.

She dressed with care, selecting a silk gown whose daringly split sides offered glimpses of her slender legs—and would enable her to move swiftly if the time came. A dagger was strapped to the inside of her right thigh, and the belt that encircled her waist was made out of gold disks that could be easily broken apart and used as currency. Her hair was piled on her head, the elaborate arrangement held together by two sticks of ivory that were tipped with sharpened steel. Over one arm she carried a light linen cloak, in case the evening grew chill.

The sun was setting as she emerged from her town house, and she wondered why they had chosen such an unfashionable hour. Only peasants and slaves ate with the sun. Even the rawest of newcomers to Ikaria knew that one did not dine before the third hour after sunset. If the magistrate's residence was being watched, such an untimely gathering was bound to raise suspicion.

Gino, the most senior of her male servants, was waiting outside beside the litter she had ordered. Normally unflappable, he had demonstrated remarkable poise in dealing with the occasional drunken noble or ejecting interlopers who arrived unannounced. But now he shifted his weight from one foot to another with uncharacteristic impatience, and as she approached he looked up at her once, then hastily dropped his eyes.

Something was wrong. She scanned the street, which was crowded with those returning to their homes after a day spent in the city. Among them she noticed a few standing idly, islands amidst the fast-moving stream of those who rushed by. These idlers wore servants' tunics, but their posture spoke of time spent at attention rather than menial labor.

She had expected that the watch upon her residence would be increased, but these men were more than casual spies hired to report on her comings and goings. They were soldiers, and their presence boded ill.

She bent, fiddling with her sandal strap to give herself time to think. If she went back inside the house, they would know that she had seen them. What they did next would depend on their orders. Were they here to follow her? Or to arrest her?

Fortunately, she had not confided her destination to Gino, merely ordered him to fetch a litter. She could direct the litter to the embassy and see if her new watchers chose to follow. If they did, then she would know it was time to flee. If they did not, then she could assume that their presence outside her house was mere coincidence, though she doubted this.

Thus decided, she rose and walked down the steps to the litter. Gino held open the curtains for her, though he kept his gaze firmly downcast, apparently fearing that she would be able to see his betrayal in his eyes.

As she prepared to step inside the litter, a young girl darted from the crowd. "Gracious lady, a posy to perfume your travels?" she asked, holding out a wreath of flowers that had been nearly crushed.

"Go now, we have no use for your kind," Gino said, pushing the girl away.

Ordinarily Ysobel would have ignored the girl, for to give money to one street beggar would only encourage the rest to flock around her. But Gino's actions sparked a contrary spirit within her.

"Wait," she said. Reaching into the small purse concealed within the folds of her cloak she withdrew two pennies and handed them to the girl.

"Thank you, noble lady," she said, pressing the flowers into Ysobel's palms as if they were the rarest of jewels. Then she darted away, scampering between the litter bearers and disappearing into the crowded street.

"Have them take me to the embassy, then wait for further orders," Ysobel instructed Gino.

He nodded, then helped her climb into the litter. The curtains were left open, tied back so she could take advantage of any breeze that might alleviate the oppressive heat. Bringing the posy up to her face, she sniffed the flowers, but any scent they had held was long gone, and she wondered at the impulse that had prompted her to buy it. The flowers were so old they were practically dried, as evidenced by how they crinkled in her hands.

She squeezed the flowers, and again heard that crinkling sound. Carefully she picked apart the posy until she found the message scroll buried within. In the fading twilight she could barely make out the words.

Nerissa knows all. Tonight is a trap. Flee now, before it is too late.

The message was signed with the stylized symbol of the imperial house. It took her a moment to recognize this was also one of the tattoos that masked the faces of the functionaries.

The message was from Greeter. And with that realization came another, as she glanced outside and saw that they were approaching the square of the seven fountains. A picturesque spot, but it was not along any route between her town house and the embassy. She was being taken to the palace.

Greeter's warning had come too late, or perhaps there had been a change in plan when it became clear that she was not going to lead them to the other conspirators.

She had one thing in her favor, and that was the Ikarians' habit of underestimating a woman's strength and cunning. They might expect her to protest once she realized that she was not being taken to the embassy. They would not expect her to act boldly.

She brought to mind the map of Karystos. Assuming that the palace and its dungeons were indeed her destination, once they left this square, they would enter the Road of Triumph. Hemmed in on both sides by official buildings, the road would be a trap. If she was to escape, she would have to do so immediately.

Carefully she unfolded her cloak and arranged it behind her, tying the clasp around her neck. Her gown alone would bring too much attention in the places she had to venture.

The litter paused to let a wagon pass. Ysobel gathered herself but waited until they were once more moving. Then she threw herself to her left. The cobblestones bit into her flesh as she hit the ground, but she rolled to absorb the impact and sprang to her feet. As she began to run, she risked a quick glance behind her. The litter hung askew, as two of its bearers joined the pursuit, accompanied by at least one of the soldiers she had observed earlier.

Holding her cloak around her with one hand she ran, her sandals slapping at the stones as she weaved among the startled crowds.

"Halt, in the name of Empress Nerissa. Halt!" The cry rose up from behind her. One man reached out to catch hold of her cloak, but an elbow to his face dissuaded him. She could still hear her pursuers, but they were far behind as she left the square. She ran a few hundred paces down the street, then ducked down the alley next to a merchant's shop, ignoring the noxious scents. The alley brought her to another street, which had fewer lamps to pierce the twilight, and she let her steps slow to give the impression of a woman with no reason for haste.

She walked for several moments, but just as she thought she had escaped, she heard the sound of pounding boots behind her.

Fools, she thought to herself, even as she cursed her overconfidence. If her pursuers had simply walked up to her, they could have taken her, but their haste had betrayed them.

She took flight once more. This time when she lost them, she did not let down her guard. The streets were filled with patrols, far more than on any ordinary night, and she realized that she was not the only prize being sought.

It took much backtracking and one mad scramble across a stone wall before she reached the warehouse district. There the dangers were different, as her now-tattered finery led some to believe that she was a whore seeking customers for the evening. Fortunately, the dagger that she held in her right hand was enough to dissuade them from approaching too closely.

Safety was at hand, but this was also the moment of greatest danger. Having lost her trail in the streets of Karystos, her pursuers would expect her either to seek out her allies or try to flee the city. Of the two, escape was most probable.

By this hour of the night there was little reason for water traffic. If she went down to the docks and tried to hire a lighter, it was likely that she would be spotted. The same was true if she simply tried to steal a boat and row herself across.

There were three federation vessels docked alongside the wharves, thanks to her negotiations with Septimus the Younger, which had opened these berths to foreign vessels for the first time. But they would be watched, and even if she could slip aboard one unnoticed, any ship would surely be searched before it was allowed to set sail.

As she hid next to a warehouse whose sickly sweet smell told her that it most often handled imported fruits, she noticed a group of men bearing torches advancing steadily across the docks from the west. Leaning farther out, she saw that another group was approaching from the east. If she did not act quickly, her hiding place would turn into a trap.

There was only one thing left to do. She took several deep breaths, calming herself. She forced herself to forget the fatigue from her earlier frantic escape across the breadth of the city and the dull aches of muscles grown soft with city living. There would be time later to curse Prince Lucius for his folly, and herself for the arrogance that had led her to this place. For now she would think of nothing except survival.

She untied her cloak so that it was held together only by a simple twist of the ribbons, and with her dagger slashed the neckline of her gown. Then she took one last breath and darted out from her hiding place. Running past the shuttered customs house, she leapt over a coil of rope carelessly left at the foot of the wharf and continued down its length. Behind her, she heard shouts of pursuit, but did not look back to see if these were sailors intent on sport or guards sent to arrest her. As she reached the end, she dived off.

It was a long way down to the water—a jump that no sane person would make. Her hands were extended before her to cut into the water, but still the impact shook her as she plunged downward into the murky depths. Finally, her descent slowed. Her cloak had already fallen off, so she unclasped her heavy belt, abandoning a month's wages to the harbor floor. The newly widened neckline of her gown allowed her to swim free of it.

Her lungs burned as she kicked her way back to the surface, but she forced herself to take a diagonal route, so she would not resurface at the same spot she had gone under.

Raising her head above the waves, she took in a lungful of precious air, then sank beneath the waves and swam several more strokes. She repeated this maneuver until she was several dozen yards from the shore. As she looked back, she saw several men with torches standing at the foot of the pier, but no one seemed inclined to follow her suicidal plunge. One man cried out as he spotted her cloak, and his voice carried across the water as he ordered a boat be summoned to fetch the body.

Ysobel turned away and began to swim toward the eastern side of the harbor. The waning moon illuminated the ships moored in the bay, and she was careful not to swim too close to any of them, lest she be spotted.

She swam for what seemed hours, or perhaps days, until at last she reached the great ship that was anchored at the far end of the eastern mole. It was the farthest spot a ship could be and still be within the harbor, and thus one of the least desirable since it made bringing cargo to and from the ship an onerous task. But for her purposes the ship was perfectly placed.

She clung to the anchor chain, blinking her eyes against the light of the lamp that swung from the prow. "Sanctuary," she called up, in her own tongue. "I claim sanctuary."

No one responded, and she forced her panting breaths

to slow. "Sanctuary," she cried again, and this time she was heard, as a sailor's head appeared above the railing.

"Who are you?" he asked.

"A countrywoman in need," she said. "Throw me a line, then fetch your captain."

A knotted rope was thrown over the side. As she pulled herself up, hand over hand, the gentle rocking of the ship caused the rope to sway, scraping her naked flesh against its wooden sides. At last she reached the top, and with a weary sigh she heaved herself over the top railing.

The sailor stood by, along with two of his fellows, gaping at the apparition before them. Only her breast band had survived the swim, and her naked flesh, shivering in the night air, told the story of her adventures. She was bruised and bleeding, but she was alive, and she refused to feel ashamed of her appearance.

"By the gods, girl, what happened to you?" Captain Zorion's voice boomed over the forecastle. His shirt hung loose outside his pantaloons, indicating that he had been roused from sleep.

"It's a long story," she said. "Nerissa's men are searching the harbor for my body, and they will think to look here next. We need to leave now."

Stripping off his own shirt, he handed it to her. "Put this on. Mayhew will take you below and see to your needs, while I get us under way."

In that moment she was reminded yet again of why her aunt had loved him so much. Zorion did not argue, nor did he waste time with questions. Once he decided to act, he was unstoppable.

"We need to move swiftly or we will lose the tide," she said. "How many are ashore?"

"Two dozen of the crew. We've a dozen on night watch, and the rest are in their bunks."

"You'll need every hand," she said. "Mayhew, rouse the crew, then fetch me a pair of pantaloons."

As Captain Zorion barked orders, the sailors on watch threw themselves against the bars of the capstan to lift the anchor. It began to turn, first slowly, then more swiftly as their fellows arrived to lend their muscles.

"We'll have to leave those sailors behind," she said.

Zorion nodded. "They'll be fine. I declared hostile port before they left, and they know the rules."

In a friendly port the majority of the crew would be on leave at night, returning during the day when required to assist with the loading or unloading of cargo. When a captain declared hostile port, only a small portion of the crew was allowed to leave the ship, and they were given instructions on what to do if the ship had to leave without them. Once they made their way back to Seddon, Ysobel would see that they were compensated for their trials.

Mayhew returned, holding out a pair of pantaloons and a blouse. She handed Zorion back his shirt, finding that both blouse and pantaloons were a perfect fit. He must have carried them on board for this very purpose.

She looked up as sailors were scrambling up the four masts, preparing to unfurl the sails.

"We're short two topmen, and a bosun to call their orders," he observed.

She'd noticed that as well.

"She's your ship. You take her out, while I go aloft and lend a hand," he said.

For a moment Ysobel was tempted. It had been too long since she conned a ship, and she had been itching to sail the *Swift Gull* since she first beheld it. But her desires would have to wait a little longer.

"You know this ship, and I don't have time to learn her ways," she said. "I'll go up."

She ripped a strip from the hem of her blouse and tied her hair back.

"Are you certain you can do this? You're still bleeding," he said.

"This is what I was born to do," she replied.

Chapter 20

Josan retired to his quarters, emerging the next morning only long enough to confirm that Renato had the preparations for the gathering well in hand. Then he retreated to his room, listening with faint amusement as Myles and Farris squabbled over who should be guarding him. Josan solved the dispute by sending Myles on a series of errands. Farris appeared suspicious, but he could hardly object while the others were listening.

When it came time for the afternoon meal, servants brought a tray to his room. He had no appetite, but forced himself to eat, knowing that he would need his strength later. Farris, still on his self-appointed watch, refused the offers of food, and Josan wondered idly if he had eaten anything since entering the magistrate's residence. A fast seemed pointless, but perhaps he took his rations when he made his periodic forays outside. Each time he returned from one of his tours of inspection, he loudly assured Josan that all was quiet, which no doubt meant that Nerissa's men were in place and poised to strike.

As sunset approached, Josan summoned Renato's valet and instructed him to prepare the silk robes from the back of his wardrobe. Renato had trained his servants well, for the valet showed no sign of surprise as he unwrapped the cotton coverings to reveal a dark purple robe embroidered with golden lizards—the seal of Constantin's house. Josan glanced over at Farris, whose face turned red with fury, then studiously blank under Josan's regard.

The mere existence of the robe was proof of Renato's treason. Having it made was a foolish risk, and for what? Yards of silk and golden thread did not make a man an emperor. If men were prepared to risk their lives for him, they should be willing to serve him regardless of whether he was wearing rags or silk.

Myles had seen the man underneath the dirt and beggar's rags he wore. Had recognized him and judged him worthy of his loyalty, though his prince had nothing to offer him but danger and hardship. But Myles was the exception, and those invited tonight would be expecting to see the symbol and not the man.

After the valet left, Farris let his disgust show. "Do not think of betraying your oath to Nerissa. I will not hesitate to kill you at the first sign of treachery."

"I understand."

The threat had been intimidating the first time he had heard it, but after dozens of repetitions, Farris had lost any power to terrify him. Josan had passed beyond fear, to the point of numbness. He just wanted the night to be over and to meet his fate.

He searched his thoughts for any trace of the spirit of Prince Lucius, but felt only a vague echo of his own feelings. It was the prince's plan, but it seemed it would be up to Josan to see it through to the bitter end.

At last, Renato came with the word that the guests had assembled.

"Is everyone present?" Josan asked.

"Lady Ysobel has not arrived. Salvador sent a servant

with word that his master has fallen ill," Renato explained. "And your man Myles is not back from his errands."

Josan frowned as if surprised by that last bit of news. He had taken advantage of one of Farris's patrols to give Myles a final set of instructions that would ensure he was far away when the arrests took place. Myles had argued, but Josan had not hesitated to invoke the debt of friendship to ensure that Myles did as he was bidden.

He could not protect Myles, but at least he could give him a chance to escape. Whatever debt lay between them, he had repaid it in full.

"Salvador's illness is mere cowardice," Josan declared, in keeping with his role of imperious prince. "And Lady Ysobel has been helpful, but she is not one of us. I will wait no longer."

Gathering his robes about him, he swept from the room, trailed by Renato and Farris. When they reached the foot of the stairs, Farris bowed and took up position by the front door.

Josan tasted bile as he realized that in moments that door would be opened and the empress's men would stream in to arrest them all. There was just one act left in the drama.

The drawing room had been cleared of its usual furnishings, with stools brought in to accommodate the three dozen guests Renato had invited. At the front of the room was the massive chair from Renato's study, now adorned with a purple cushion.

Josan repressed a snort as he regarded this monstrosity. Did Renato think him so simpleminded that he would be appeased with the trappings of power? Was this merely Renato's way of trying to cement his influence over his future emperor? If so, it was poorly chosen—though he suspected that the Prince Lucius of old would have very much enjoyed such a display.

As he entered the room, the conspirators turned to face

him, separating themselves into two lines in order of precedence. One by one they knelt, giving their obeisance.

"My lord prince," one murmured, while another addressed him as "Gracious Majesty," as if Lucius had already ascended the throne.

He was sickened by this farce, but forced himself to smile as he accepted their pledges of fealty. At last he reached the mock throne and took his seat. Only then did the conspirators rise and take their own places.

Josan's eyes swept the room. All those he had met at Lady Akantha's gathering were present, with the exception of Lady Ysobel and the elderly Salvador. And there were new faces as well, proving the wisdom of his plan to gather them all together to be unmasked.

He waited for a moment, wondering why Farris and his men had not yet burst in to arrest them. What was he waiting for?

"I summoned you here tonight so you could hear my will, and so I could find out who was truly loyal to me," he began. He had to stall for time. "Flavian paid for his crimes with his life. I had thought his fate might give some of you pause, but it seems your hatred for Nerissa and your greed outweigh your intelligence."

Renato frowned, while a few others chuckled nervously.

"My years in exile changed me," he said. "I learned many things, including what it meant to be worthy of respect. A prince must have more than mere lineage. He must have courage and honor if he is to lead his people."

Many heads nodded at this. Dama Akantha's gaze was fixed on him with seemingly rapt attention, but he knew this was a mask for boredom. She and many of the others did not care what he had to say, not as long as he was still willing to be used, a tool in their hands.

These people called themselves patriots, but they were merely zealots and lying opportunists who cared nothing for the people of Ikaria. At this moment he hated them all for bringing him to this point and took a perverse pleasure as he contemplated their fates.

He heard a faint sound, as if a voice was raised in alarm, then another. Those seated closest to the door began to turn their heads.

"I found my honor. Pity for you that you cannot say the same."

As he finished speaking the door flew open, and the steward staggered within. "Master, we have been betrayed," he gasped out, before falling to his knees and toppling over on his side. Even from here Josan could see the blood that spilled from underneath the hands that clutched his belly.

There were loud gasps as the conspirators scrambled to their feet. But it was too late, as Farris stepped over the servant's body, his bloody sword extended in front of him. Behind him were a troop of soldiers, who quickly fanned out among the guests.

"You betrayed us," Benedict said, pulling his dagger as he lunged toward Josan.

Josan sat, motionless, making no move to defend himself. But before Benedict could reach him, he was cut down from behind.

Pity. A swift death would have been a mercy.

He watched as the guards took the conspirators into custody, binding their hands behind them to prevent any from taking poison and thus evading the empress's justice. Two drew weapons and tried to resist, but they were clubbed into submission.

At last it was over. Farris approached the chair where Josan was seated and gave a brief bow. "Empress Nerissa thanks you for this gift," he declared loud enough to be heard over the grumbling of the prisoners.

"It is my privilege to serve her," Josan replied, making sure his voice carried as well.

The scene was staged not for his benefit, but to destroy any last flickering loyalty the conspirators might feel for him. Their hatred of him would loosen their tongues and might make them more willing to cooperate with Nerissa's questioners.

Farris remained at his side as the prisoners were led out to begin the last journey they would ever take. Finally, only Josan, Farris, and two guards remained.

"Prince Lucius, it is time. If you would rise," Farris said.

Josan rose, pleased to find that his legs did not tremble. He stood impassively as Farris stripped off the damning robe, leaving him shivering in his tunic. His hands were tied behind him, and a cloak was placed over him, the hood drawn down to obscure his features.

Farris's earlier words had been for show, but Josan had always known that it would come to this. A guard seized each of his arms and guided him to the carriage that waited outside. They had to help him in, for his bound arms made climbing awkward. At last he was seated, with the guards beside him and Farris on the seat opposite.

With his hands behind him, he was forced to lean awkwardly forward in his seat, but at least that gave him an excuse to keep his head lowered. He had no wish to meet Farris's eyes for fear of what he would read in his gaze. Bad enough that terror made his heart race and curdled his bowels. He would not shame himself, nor this body, by letting others see his distress.

He thought again of the swift death that Benedict had offered and how Farris had thwarted that release. Josan had fulfilled his part of the bargain, but Nerissa had promised him justice rather than mercy. There was still the price to be paid for the uprising six years before, and for all those who had been killed in the misguided effort to bring Prince Lucius to the throne.

Prince Lucius had thought this a fair trade—a chance

to punish those who had misled him and used him in their own murderous schemes. Lucius's life was already forfeit, but by bargaining with Nerissa, he had secured a measure of justice for Lady Zenia and all those other innocents who had perished.

But Josan had committed no wrongs. He was as much a victim in this as any. Just as Lucius's life had been twisted by the rebels, Josan had been betrayed by those he trusted. They had made him party to an unspeakable crime as they attempted to destroy one man's soul to make room for another.

Josan was guilty of nothing more than wanting to live and trusting his fate to those who had proved unworthy. He had had six years more than the fates intended for him, living in another man's body while his own rotted in an unmarked grave. Indeed, if it were not for the assassin, he might have lived the rest of his life tending the lighthouse, unaware that the body he inhabited was not his own.

And would that have been so bad a thing? Was he really better off knowing the truth? Once he would have said that it was always better to know the truth, regardless of the cost, but now he was not sure.

He could not help thinking about what had happened to Prince Lucius's spirit in those years when he had slumbered unaware. Had the Other journeyed to the spirit realm, only recalled to his flesh when deadly peril forced him to act? Or had he been trapped in an endless dream, a nightmare from which he awoke only briefly?

Two souls bound together, but sharing a single fate. Whatever happened would happen to both of them. At this, Josan felt the Other stir within him. *Not alone,* he heard a voice whisper. He waited, ready to relinquish the body to the prince's control, but Lucius's spirit seemed content to linger on the surface of his thoughts. Still, even the mere shadow of companionship was a comfort.

He smiled grimly, wondering how Nerissa would react if he explained to her that this body housed two different souls—though he knew that even if she believed him, it would not change his fate. Lucius would die for his treason, while Josan would be put to death as an abomination. Handily, a single thrust of a sword would serve for both.

He was still smiling as Farris grabbed his chin and jerked his head upward. He had one last glimpse of Farris's puzzlement, then a sack was pulled down over his head, blocking out all sight.

His breath quickened as the sack was drawn tight around his neck, but the pressure eased before it choked off his breathing. He heard the sound of the carriage wheels as they left the cobblestones and began to roll over smooth pavement, and he realized that they had reached the grounds of the palace. Moments later, the carriage drew to a halt.

Blind, his arms still bound, the guards had to practically lift him from the carriage. He was half-led, half-dragged across the pavement, up a short flight of stairs, then down a long hallway. For a moment they paused, then his guide pushed him forward. Josan's left foot fell on empty air, and only a swift grab of his shoulders kept him from pitching forward.

"She wants him alive," Farris growled. "Guido, you go first to guide him."

As he went down the stairs, the man behind him kept a firm grip on his shoulders. Another went before, presumably to keep him from falling. They descended until he lost count of the individual steps.

"That's the last of them," the man in front of him announced.

He heard the jangle of a key in a lock, then creaking hinges as an iron gate swung open. They walked a short distance and there was another delay as a second gate was opened.

He was pushed inside, then spun around. His hands, which had gone numb sometime ago, burned with pain as his arms were untied and the blood once more began to flow. His arms hung limply by his sides for a moment, then he was shoved against a wall and each arm fastened to a manacle high up in the wall.

Only when he was secured was the concealing sack stripped off his head.

"There's no need for this. I kept my oaths, and I'm not likely to try to escape."

Farris didn't bother to reply. He merely tugged each arm to make sure it was secure. Then he left, taking his men and the torchlight with him. Josan had only a moment to look around his cell before he was plunged back into darkness.

Even with the protection of the cloak, the stones were chill against his back. His shoulders ached from his earlier confinement, but he could not move his arms to ease them. The cell smelled of damp earth and other less wholesome scents. From far too close he heard a man scream once, and again.

These were the rooms of pain, that none dared speak of except in whispers. As a boy Prince Lucius had explored the palace looking to find this forbidden spot, but the guards had chased him away whenever he had ventured into their territory. Now his curiosity was satisfied, but this, too, was knowledge he could have lived without.

The elaborate steps to conceal his identity had been a surprise. He had expected that Nerissa would want to parade her newest captive, to show that she had nothing to fear. As it was, only Farris and the men who had arrested him knew that he was here.

If only he knew precisely where here was. There were

two sets of secret cells. Those in the outer cells were held pending execution. Those unfortunates in the inner cells could expect to be tortured before they would be allowed to die.

Judging by the sobbing screams that he heard, he would wager that he was in one of the inner cells. He strained his ears, but could not identify the man's voice, unable to discover whether he was one of the rebels or merely an unfortunate who had run afoul of Nerissa's justice.

He wondered what more secrets Nerissa expected to wring from him. He had already delivered the conspirators to her. Did she suspect that he was protecting the remnants of the conspiracy? Or would she torture him not for information but as punishment for his crimes? The ritual death prescribed for traitors was a horrific affair, involving seven separate steps, and could stretch out for days depending on the skill of the executioner. But even that might not be enough to satisfy her need for vengeance.

"You are wise to be afraid of Nerissa. Pity I learned fear too late."

This time Prince Lucius's words came to him as if Lucius had spoken aloud, and Josan answered in kind.

"What do you think she will do to us?" he asked.

If anyone were spying on him, they would think him mad for conversing with himself, but he had long since passed the point where anyone else's opinion mattered.

He felt himself shrug, a slight movement of shoulders constrained by his upraised arms.

"My mother drank hemlock rather than face these rooms," Prince Lucius observed. "She knew nothing of what I was planning, but that would not have saved her."

"I'm sorry," he said, feeling within himself an echo of the prince's grief.

"I knew I had killed her, and I could not face what was to come next. I fled to Brother Nikos, begging him for sanctuary. He offered a cup of poison, but his plans for me did not include a clean death."

"I did not know what he was planning. I swear it." It was suddenly important to him that Lucius realize this. That he had never wished for this fate.

"I know. You are too honest a man to have done such a thing." There was a long moment of silence. "Any other man would have fled Karystos rather than staying and trying to put right all that I had done wrong," Lucius added.

"No, I do not believe that. I did what any honorable man would do. What you yourself would have done if you had been given the chance."

"You flatter me," Lucius said. "But I have lost the taste for pretty lies."

There was nothing he could say that would not seem insincere or condescending. Ironically, though they shared the same body, he did not know Prince Lucius well enough to know what words might comfort him. He suspected the prince would face the same dilemma. The only comfort they could offer each other was the fact of their presence, and even that was tenuous at best.

When it came time for torture, Josan knew he would seek the release of oblivion if he was able, and he would not begrudge the prince if he chose the same. No reason for both of them to suffer.

"If by some miracle Nerissa decides to grant us our freedom, is there any hope for us? Any chance that our souls might be split apart?"

The question showed how much Lucius trusted his honesty. Josan had every reason to want to cling to the body he had stolen, for to leave it would be his death.

"There is no spell that I know of. Even the monk who performed the soul magic did not expect this," he said.

"Pity," Lucius said. "Then perhaps this is the best. Death for both of us before we drive each other mad."

"Be certain then that you thank Nerissa for her kindness," Josan said, and was rewarded with the sound of a chuckle.

The prince fell silent, and Josan was left to his own thoughts. He longed to sleep, but each time his body relaxed, it was jerked upright by the chains, and he was awoken once more. The ache in his bladder grew until he could no longer ignore it, and he fouled himself, pissing on the floor as countless others had before him. It was a deliberate humiliation, meant to remind him that he was less than an animal in the eyes of his captors. He could feel Lucius's shame, but for his part he felt only anger. Whatever Lucius had done, he deserved better than this.

Chapter 21

When Josan woke the next morning, he was alone. He had not been able to find true sleep, but just as his body had gone numb from discomfort, so, too, his mind had finally fallen into a trancelike state that was neither sleep nor true wakefulness. He searched within himself but found no trace of Prince Lucius. Despite the promises the prince had made, it seemed Josan would face whatever the day brought alone.

He did not blame the prince. If he had been able to, Josan's own spirit would have fled as well, leaving an insensate husk behind for whatever tortures Nerissa had planned.

He heard footsteps, and a faint glow revealed the direction of his cell door. Two guards stopped in front of the cell. One held a set of keys, which jangled as he unlocked the door, while his comrade held a torch. After hours of staring into the darkness, Josan's eyes could not bear the light, and as the two guards approached he turned his head, blinking his watering eyes.

"What—" he tried to say, but his voice was a mere rasp.

He coughed to clear his throat and tried again. "What has Nerissa planned for me?"

They gave no sign of having heard him. The torchbearer stood by, as the second guard reached for Josan's right hand. He braced himself for the pain that would come from being unshackled, but such was not their intent. Instead the guard merely checked both manacles to make certain that they were secure. Only then did the guard reach down to his belt and unfasten a waterskin. Bringing it to Josan's lips, he poured in a mouthful, then another. Josan swallowed eagerly, but all too soon it was withdrawn.

It took all his will not to beg for more.

Then, as silently as they had entered, they left, and he was once more alone in the darkness. It occurred to him that perhaps this was the punishment that the empress intended for him. Leaving him to starve to death in the darkness, giving him sips of water to prolong his suffering.

A cruel death, but he was confident that other prisoners had died far more agonizing ones at her command.

At some point she would surely want to witness his suffering, before his wits had gone begging and he was no longer able to recognize the author of his torments.

Hours passed. He heard screams from the rooms of pain, this time a woman's voice, and he wondered if it was Dama Akantha or Lady Ysobel. Twice the darkness was briefly illuminated as guards passed his cell door. The second time he heard the sound of something or someone being dragged, but he could not see into the corridor to confirm his suspicions.

His mouth was parched, and his belly ached with hunger, though it had been only a day, or perhaps two since he had last eaten. Time had no meaning for him. Finally, he heard steps and the welcome sound of a key being inserted into the lock of his cell. He raised his head and peered at the door. This time he would beg, if it would gain him even a single more mouthful of precious water.

Four guards entered his cell this time, followed by Empress Nerissa.

Josan opened his mouth, but all that came out was a harsh croak.

At the empress's gesture, one of the guards approached him, and offered a waterskin. He gulped eagerly, sputtering as he realized that the water was mixed with wine. The guard was patient, allowing Josan to drink his fill before he withdrew the skin. Two others approached, and as they unlocked the manacles that held him upright, it was only their grip on his arms that kept him from falling to the floor.

They dragged him to the center of the cell, where he stood swaying under Nerissa's cool gaze. He did not doubt that she saw everything—from his piss-stained tunic to the agony of limbs wrenched out of shape.

"Does this please you?" he asked.

He waited for a blow for his impertinence, but to his surprise it did not come.

"This was not my wish," she said.

"On the contrary, I think that nothing happens here that you do not command. Are you satisfied with my humiliation, or is this just a taste of what you have planned?"

"I did not intend to leave you here so long." It was not quite an apology.

He noticed that she showed no signs of distress at her surroundings. She might have been at a party in the imperial gardens, rather than in a dank cell that reeked of human suffering.

"I kept my oath," he reminded her.

"So you did." She walked around him, but he was too tired to crane his head to follow her movements. When she spoke next, her voice came from behind him. "In a way, your honor is to blame for your present trials. When I saw the list of those arrested, I was convinced that it was a trick on your part, implicating those I knew to be loyal."

He wondered that she spoke so freely in front of the guards, then realized that the men wore dark uniforms without insignia of any sort. They must be part of Nizam's interrogators, and as such had heard far more damning secrets.

"Surely Farris was able to convince you otherwise."

She circled around to face him again. "Farris had much to say. So, too, did Renato, Akantha, and even Salvador, who was dragged from his supposed sickbed to explain his role. I have no doubt the others will confirm their guilt, once we have had time to question them all."

"What of Lady Ysobel?"

Nerissa frowned. "She evaded those sent to arrest her and made her escape before we were able to close the harbor."

He wondered why he felt relieved. Perhaps it was simply that Lady Ysobel was both young and female, and thus he felt pity for her, even if she did not deserve it. After all, she was inadvertently responsible for his fate, for it had been their meeting that had revealed his presence on Txomin's Island, prompting the chain of events that had led him to this place. Federation gold had supported the rebels, while her counsel had inspired their acts of violence.

"Many of those questioned have also mentioned Brother Nikos, though he was not among their number," she said. "Would you care to explain his role?"

The wine he had drunk had gone straight to his head, as she must have intended. Fortunately, he had expected the question and already prepared his answer.

"I sought out Brother Nikos and convinced him to bring me to you, as you already know. Then I used his presumed aid to convince the conspirators to assemble, telling them that Nikos had revealed the key to your destruction," he said. "As for Nikos's true loyalties, I leave you to determine where they lie."

He made no mention of soul magic, nor of the role that Nikos had played in the events of the first uprising. It was not pity that stayed him, nor remnants of whatever loyalty Josan had once felt for the head of his order. Rather it was out of friendship for those members of the brethren who were true scholars and would inevitably be tainted by the actions of their leader. Nikos deserved whatever punishment the empress could devise, but the others did not.

"What do you intend for me?" he asked. He was tired of fencing words with her.

"I had intended death," she said. "A clean death by the sword, far better than a traitor deserves."

"And now?"

"Now I find myself in your debt."

His breath froze, as he felt the first stirrings of hope. "I will swear any oath you ask. If you spare me, I will leave Ikaria and never return. You will never hear of me again."

Josan would happily bury himself in the library of Xandropol for the rest of his life, safe in the anonymity of a scholar's life. Or, if she would not allow that, he could live quietly anywhere she named. His years in exile had taught him to be content with the most humble of circumstances. He did not need to live the life of either prince or scholar, just as long as he was allowed to live.

"I cannot allow you to go free." She sounded genuinely regretful as she dashed the hope that had sprung up within him.

"I understand," he said, then wondered at what had prompted him to offer her forgiveness for what she must do.

She tilted her head to one side. "Yes, I believe that you do. Wisdom has come late, but it becomes you, Prince Lucius."

He blinked at the unexpected praise.

"I still have a use for you, if you are minded to swear another oath. I cannot let you walk free, but a dead martyr serves me no purpose. Instead I have a mind to follow in the footsteps of Aitor the Great."

"And you have cast me in the part of Callista?"

She smiled in approval of his quick wits. "Yes. I will pardon you for your crimes, in return for your public pledge of fealty. You will stand at my side as your followers are executed, and you will praise me for my justice."

"And then what? After a few months I quietly disappear into an unmarked grave?"

"You will live here, in the palace, under constant supervision. Give me no reason to suspect you, and you will live to a ripe old age."

He hesitated. Moments ago he had been willing to beg for his life, but it was no easy bargain that she was offering. It was not just a life sentence of humiliation, a prisoner in all but name, as his every deed, every word was watched and weighed. He was also agreeing to a lifetime in the role of Prince Lucius. If he swore this oath, he would be forced to live his days as the prince.

And as the days turned into months, the pretense would become reality. Josan the scholar would be lost, subsumed by the part he was forced to play. It would not be a painful death, but it would be a death all the same.

It was a harder decision than even Nerissa knew, but in the end he did not have any choice. He could not condemn this body to death, not knowing that such an act would kill not one soul but two.

"I accept your mercy," he said. "My empress."

The guards were surprisingly gentle as they helped him kneel, and he began to recite the formal words of submission.

Epilogue

Summer wore on, and as autumn approached the executions continued. As each traitor was put to death, Josan stood at Empress Nerissa's right hand and uttered words of praise. Repetition had not numbed him. On the contrary each new killing only increased his sense of outrage and helplessness. If this is what it meant to rule, then Lucius was a fool ever to have wanted the throne.

Dama Akantha was the first. As a woman and a noble she was granted the courtesy of a swift, private death, witnessed only by Josan, the empress, and two dozen members of the court. Renato was next, and his death was a public affair, held in the great square outside the palace, attended by thousands of jeering spectators. Weeks went by as the fates of the conspirators and those they implicated were decided.

Most of those who had been arrested that night were executed. In some cases their family members were also executed, in others they were merely stripped of their titles and properties. Salvador, who had been a close confidant of both Nerissa and her father before her, was found dead in his cell. It was possible that his elderly body had been unable to stand the strain of his imprisonment, but more likely that he had been granted the mercy of poison.

Josan had dismissed Salvador as a querulous old man, but he later learned how badly he had misjudged him. It seemed that while Salvador had supported Prince Lucius's original bid for power, he had then blamed the prince for its failure, and for the deaths of so many whom Salvador had called friend. When Dama Akantha had shared the news that a potential pretender to the throne had been sighted at a remote lighthouse, Salvador had been the first to guess that the man might actually be Prince Lucius and sent an assassin to kill him.

Ironically it was this very assassination attempt that had brought Prince Lucius back to the capital, though it was doubtful Salvador realized what he had set in motion.

But if Salvador had not supported Lucius's attempt to raise a new rebellion, neither had he informed the empress of the threat against her. Thus it was only in the manner of his death that the empress showed the remnants of the affection she had once held for him.

To his knowledge Myles had not been captured, though since he was a commoner, it was uncertain if Josan would have been required to witness his execution. Lady Ysobel had escaped to freedom, as had Septimus the Younger, who had fled on one of his own ships when he learned of his father's treachery. Ambassador Hardouin had been expelled for failure to control his subordinate and a new ambassador appointed to fill his place. Along with the new ambassador, Seddon had sent profuse apologies for the actions of their rogue liaison, and for the moment Empress Nerissa seemed inclined to take their explanation at face value. She had enough enemies within her borders to occupy her attention.

Brother Nikos had called upon Josan once, at the empress's request. There had been nothing for them to say to one another. All meaningful topics were too perilous to be spoken aloud, for Josan's rooms were watched at all hours of the day and night. Still, the visit had been of some use, for he had persuaded Nikos to lend him scrolls from the library at the collegium.

Every week a slave brought new scrolls for him to read and took back the ones he had finished. They were the only means he had of alleviating his boredom. Most days he was confined to his room in the palace, allowed to leave only when it was time for his daily stroll or he was summoned by the empress.

There had been two attempts on his life. The first, by poison, had been insufficient to kill him, producing only a night and day of fevered sweats and agonizing cramps. The second attempt was less subtle; a servant stabbed him while he was walking in the gardens. If the gardener had known how to handle a dagger, he might have succeeded, but his first strike was a wild glancing blow that merely grazed Josan's skin. The guards that accompanied him everywhere ensured that the servant did not have a second chance to strike.

He had few visitors since none dared seek him out unless they were ordered to by the empress. Prince Anthor came by, but he merely inspected Josan and his quarters, then left without speaking. Others came, but no one he knew. They called him Lucius, and spoke to him of trivialities—plays that he would not see, people that he did not know. When other topics failed they turned to the weather and the prospects for the harvest. He would have preferred the solitude of his lighthouse to these false-faced strangers.

Everyone called him Lucius, although only the empress addressed him by the title of prince as well. There was no one to speak his true name, no one to remind him of who he had once been. All thought of him as Lucius, and he wondered how much longer it would be before he thought of that name as his own.

As for the prince's spirit, he had heard not a whisper since the night of his arrest. He wondered if it was possible for a soul to will itself out of existence, and if that was what Lucius had done.

Or was the prince's spirit still trapped somewhere within him? Was he slumbering now as he had been before? What would it take to recall him?

But even if he knew how to summon Lucius, he did not know if he would do so. It was not pure selfishness, though the prince might see it as an attempt for Josan to keep the body he had stolen as his own. But rather he did not know if it was fair to inflict his trials upon another. It was a mercy that Lucius had been spared witnessing the deaths of those who had supported him. The prince might well have been driven mad by this existence, but Josan was stronger. He was strong enough for both of them.

He knew better than to try and guess what the fates had in store for him. Two years ago he had been a lighthouse keeper, intent simply on surviving the great storm. Last year, he had been an outcast wanderer, fighting for survival as he battled what he thought was the onset of madness. Now he was living the life of a captive prince, and doing so might well prove his greatest test yet.

Still, he would survive. If he had learned anything in the past years, it was that he was a survivor. Every day he lived was a triumph over those who had sought to destroy him.

He refused to believe that this was the end. It was merely the newest beginning.

About the Author

Patricia Bray is descended from a long line of storytellers, all of whom understood that a good story was far more important than the literal truth. She uses her power only for good—to confound survey takers, telemarketers, and others of that ilk. A corporate I/T project manager by day, she wishes to note that any resemblance between her villains and former coworkers is entirely coincidental. When not at her home in upstate New York, she can be found on the SF convention circuit, or taking long bicycle trips to exotic locations destined to become settings for future novels. Fans can find out more about Patricia and her books by visiting her website at www.patriciabray.com.

Be sure not to miss Josan's further
adventures in

THE SEA CHANGE

the next exciting novel in
The Chronicles of Josan
by

Patricia Bray

Turn the page for a special preview...

THE SEA CHANGE

Patricia Bray

On sale Spring 2007

As chief advisor to Empress Nerissa, Brother Nikos was seldom called upon to act in a spiritual role. Head of the Collegium of the Learned Brethren, he had long ago delegated his religious duties to lesser monks, leaving them to offer prayers to the indifferent gods while Nikos reserved his energies for temporal matters. Some in the court had been known to mutter that Nikos wielded too much influence for one who called himself a monk, but these were the mere grumblings of those who had no power of their own. If the empress preferred to have him at her side dispensing advice rather than meditating in the collegium among musty scrolls and ancient tomes, who was he to question her judgment?

The last time he had served as priest was three years before, when he had officiated at Prince Nestor's wedding. Now he was called again once more to take up his role as priest—this time to lead the public mourning for Prince Nestor's bride, who had died yesterday, after giving birth to a stillborn son. The twin losses had shaken the imperial family, especially Prince Nestor, who had grown unaccountably fond of the bride that politics had chosen for him. Empress Nerissa, though normally free of the sentimental weaknesses that governed her sex, had chosen to delay the public announcement until today, to give the prince a chance to grieve in private. Once the announcement was made, the needs of the empire would take precedence over private mourning.

The death of the princess was a tragedy, to be certain, but Nikos was pragmatic enough to see it was also an opportunity. Ever since Prince Nestor had achieved his majority, there had been calls for Empress Nerissa to resign in favor of her son. She had only been intended as a placeholder, after all. There were many who had never been easy with a woman on the imperial throne, and they had found allies among those who had been unable to secure Nerissa's favor.

Nikos had tutored the imperial princes, but they had never warmed to him, and he knew that when Prince Nestor took the throne, his influence would be greatly diminished. Nestor would have his own advisors, and would undoubtedly overturn many of his mother's policies in his drive to set his own stamp upon the empire.

Fortunately for Nikos, the empress had shown no signs that she was eager to relinquish her throne. Though the pressure upon her would have undoubtedly grown even greater if Prince Nestor had produced an heir of his own, now that question was moot. The prince's supporters had been dealt a mighty blow, while the position of Nikos and Nerissa's other allies had been strengthened.

A new wife would have to be found for Nestor, as soon as the official period of mourning was over. And perhaps it was time for his younger brother, Prince Anthor, to wed as well. Lost in calculating the favors that could be extracted from those who had suitable daughters, it took Nikos a moment to realize that they had arrived at the entrance to the imperial palace, where a large crowded blocked their way. With harsh words and sharp elbows, his acolytes cleared a path to the iron gates, which were unaccountably closed.

A man tugged on his sleeve, and as he turned he recognized Priam, a minor noble with an insignificant estate in the southern lands.

"Brother Nikos, do you know what is happening? The empress summoned us to her morning audience, but the gates are barred and the guards will not let us in."

Nikos had no answers for him. Even in the recent civil unrest, the palace gates had never been closed during daylight hours. But he would not betray his ignorance, not even before one as inconsequential as Priam.

"All will be explained when the empress wills," he said.

Brother Basil had managed to attract the attention of one of the half-dozen guards who stood on the other side of the gate, apparently deaf to the strident pleas of those outside.

"This is Brother Nikos, summoned to counsel by the empress herself," Basil shouted.

It was undignified. Never before had he had to beg for admission.

But the guards did not seem impressed by Basil's shouts. Instead their eyes were hard, and their hands rested on their swords, as if they feared attack.

It did not take a scholar to know that something was gravely wrong.

He pushed Basil aside, and stood directly before the gate. "I am Brother Nikos, chief advisor to her imperial majesty Nerissa, and I demand to be taken to her," he said, in the booming voice best suited to leading the faithful in prayers.

He fixed his gaze on the sergeant, who nodded in apparent recognition. The sergeant gave orders to two of his men, who unbarred the gate. As it began to swing open, the crowd surged forward, but the remaining guards drew their swords.

"The priest only; no one else," the sergeant called out. And at the sight of naked steel, the crowd drew back.

Nikos slipped through the gate, not surprised to find that it swung shut before his acolytes could follow.

"Wait for me here," he instructed.

The sergeant turned to one of the guards. "The proconsul asked to see this one. Bring him to the proconsul's office, and see that he stays there."

"But the empress is expecting me—" Nikos began.

"The proconsul. Or I'll send you back through that gate."

Nikos nodded, accepting defeat for the moment, though he memorized every feature of the sergeant's face. When the time came, he would be punished for his disrespect. As the guard escorted him through the imperial compound, Nikos observed more signs of chaos. Armed men were everywhere, but few servants—and those that he did see rushed by with bent heads and ashen faces.

Was it possible that Princess Jacinta's death had not been a tragic accident? Had Empress Nerissa discovered that the princess had been poisoned, and the baby's death an act of deliberate malice? Surely the empress would want him by her side, but instead he was forced to cool his heels in Zuberi's outer office, under guard, as if he were a common criminal instead of a trusted imperial advisor. He waited with growing impatience until Zuberi finally returned.

With a curt order, Nikos's escort was dismissed, and Zuberi led him into the private office.

"Sorry to leave you waiting, but Anthor just died," Zuberi said.

It took a moment for his words to penetrate.

"I must go to the empress," Nikos said. "She will be devastated."

Zuberi stared at him in disbelief.

"By the twisted fates, I forgot. You don't know?"

"Know what? How did Anthor die?"

Zuberi sat down heavily, and after a moment, Nikos did as well.

"After you left yesterday, Nerissa, Nestor, and Anthor retired to the royal chapel to hold private vigil for the princess," Zuberi said. He took a deep breath, then continued. "Sometime during the night, an assassin entered. Nerissa and Nestor were slain. Against custom, Anthor was wearing a dagger, and he struggled with the assassin, killing him in turn, but he was gravely wounded. He must have bled for hours before they were found. The royal physicians did all they could, but he died moments ago."

Zuberi's words made no sense. This was not possible. Nerissa, dead? And both her sons? How could such a thing have happened?

"How? Who?"

"The assassin bore the tattoos of a palace functionary, and thus was allowed to pass unquestioned. As for who, we both know Prince Lucius is behind this, and I have already dealt with him."

"No," Nikos said, the word escaping his lips before he could call it back.

"No?" Zuberi echoed, his eyebrows raised in astonishment.

Nikos thought furiously. He knew without a doubt that Prince Lucius was not behind this assassination, but he could not share the reason for his conviction with Zuberi. Not without exposing his own damning secrets.

"I do not think Lucius is behind this. His penitence seemed sincere."

Zuberi snorted in disbelief. "You are too trusting."

"At the very least, he must have had help," Nikos said. "He was too closely watched to hatch this plot on his own."

He waited, wondering if Lucius was indeed alive, or if Zuberi had already killed him in revenge for Nerissa's death. In many ways, it would be better for Nikos if Lucius were indeed dead, and his secrets buried with him. But then they might never discover who was behind the assassinations.

"I will have Nizam drag the names of his accomplices from him," Zuberi said, confirming that Lucius was still alive. At least for now.

"How can I serve?" Nikos asked, content now that he had won this point.

"I will draft the announcement, and you have a funeral to plan," Zuberi said.

"Of course. And the next emperor..." Nikos let his voice trail off delicately. "Shall I consult him as to his wishes?"

Zuberi smiled grimly. "You will know his name as soon as I do," he said. "For now, we have an empress to bury."

Interesting. He had half-expected Zuberi to announce his own candidacy, to try and secure Nikos's support. Perhaps Zuberi felt that it was too soon to make his move, with the empress's body not yet cold. Or perhaps Zuberi was merely being prudent—biding his time to see who else would try to claim the throne, so he would know the faces of his enemies.

The difficulty was that there was no clear heir. Indeed, as a woman, Nerissa would never have been allowed to take the throne if there had been any legitimate male descendant of Aitor the First. But Nerissa had been the only child of Aitor the Second, and had two sturdy sons of her own at the time of his death. The young princes had ensured the continuation of Aitor's line, and their mother's seat on the imperial throne.

Now the field was wide open. With Nerissa's death, Nikos had lost a powerful patron, but if he maneuvered carefully, his own position might be strengthened. Whoever was chosen as emperor would need loyal advisors. And Nikos knew how to offer loyalty—in return for his own self-interest, of course.

What was good for the empire had proven to be good for Nikos as well, and he saw no reason why this should change. It was simply a matter of backing the right candidate for the throne, which made it all the more vital that those behind the assassinations be uncovered as soon as possible.

And if the emperor-to-be turned out to have blood on his hands, well then, there was always Prince Lucius. Nikos's first service to his new emperor would be to arrange evidence confirming Lucius's guilt . . . for a suitable reward. Prince Lucius was already doomed, from the moment the next emperor was named. At least this way his death would serve a dual purpose—to bring stability to the empire, and to ensure that Nikos remained in a position to guide the new emperor through the difficult days ahead.

Nizam shook his head in disgust as he examined his newest charge. Prince Lucius lay sprawled on the floor of his cell, his naked flesh patterned in dark hues, clear evidence of the savage beating he had endured. Nizam motioned for his assistant to bring the lantern closer as he knelt down next to the prince.

They had not cut him, but from the swelling of his belly, he suspected the prince was bleeding inside his gut. His jaw was broken, and his face was so swollen that he was incapable of opening his eyes. If the bleeding in his gut did not kill him, the broken jaw would.

There were lesser injuries as well—a broken arm, and knees swollen to twice their normal size. As Nizam turned the prince's body over to check for injuries to his back, the prince moaned.

It was the sound of an animal in pain. There was no thought, no reason behind it. Lucius was beyond awareness, incapable of recognizing who was hurting him, nor who had the power to end his suffering. It would be impossible to get any information from him in his current state.

Nizam understood that men could be driven by revenge, and many would say that Lucius had been treated as he deserved. But this was a pointless waste. It offended his sense of order, and he knew Empress Nerissa would never have permitted it.

The empress had understood his work as few others did. Even among his chosen assistants, most were merely competent rather than inspired. The empress had never personally wielded the lash or the irons, but he had no doubt that she would have done so with skill. If she had been present in this cell, Lucius would have spilled all of his secrets before begging for death.

"Shall I send for the healer?" his assistant asked.

Nizam shook his head. "No. The proconsul's men said that he should be left untouched. I merely wanted to see him for myself, before I made my report."

Rising to his feet, he gave the prince one last look before leaving the cell. He then made his way swiftly through the passages and stairs that led from his secret domain up through the public spaces and finally into the palace itself. He knew the way, though he had seldom traveled it. Nerissa had preferred to meet in his domain, and was often present for the interrogation of important prisoners, but her ministers lacked her spirit. Proconsul Zuberi had never set foot in the catacombs, preferring instead to summon Nizam to him on those rare occasions when he needed to speak with him.

Nizam smiled mirthlessly as servants blanched at the mere sight of him, then quickly scurried out of his path. They did well to fear him. The assassin must have had help in gaining access to the palace, and until his accomplices were caught, all lived under suspicion.

Nizam had no fear for his position. Whether Proconsul Zuberi was crowned emperor or another, there would still be a need for a man with his talents. Especially now, with the assassin dead and Prince Lucius unable to speak, Nizam's services would be in high demand as they sought to ferret out the rest of the conspirators.

A dozen courtiers paced in the corridor outside the proconsul's offices, while more crowded inside the anteroom, along with an officer from the guard, and one of Petrelis's lackeys from the city watch. Each was badgering the clerks in turn, demanding immediate admittance.

Nizam said nothing, knowing his reputation would serve him far better than any words could. True enough, the petitioners drew back as they recognized him, and with a hasty swallow, the senior of the two clerks motioned him forward.

"Please, he is waiting for you."

The proconsul was still wearing the formal court attire he must have worn when he announced the deaths of the imperial family. The only concession to the summer's heat had been to remove the black shawl of mourning, which was now draped carelessly over the back of his chair. The empress's death must have hit him hard. Though it had been only a few weeks since Nizam had last seen him, the proconsul seemed to have aged years.

"You are authorized to use all lawful measures to enforce the peace—" Proconsul Zuberi's voice broke off as he saw Nizam.

The scribe, who had been taking notes, looked up and then rose swiftly to his feet even before Zuberi waved him away.

"Wait outside. I will summon you when I am ready to finish this," Zuberi said.

The scribe bowed as he gathered up his writing things, then swiftly backed away.

"There is a curfew in the city tonight, for all the good that will do," Zuberi said, by way of greeting. "I expect that Commander Petrelis will have his hands full."

"Have him hang the first dozen violators that he finds, and leave their bodies dangling as a warning to the rest."

It was what Empress Nerissa would have done. It would be impossible to arrest all of the violators, but the deaths would discourage honest citizens from trying to test the limits of the curfew. Those still out on the streets could then safely be assumed to be lawbreakers and dealt with accordingly.

Zuberi shrugged. "And what of the hundreds of mourners out in the square? Now that sunset has fallen they are all in violation of the decree, but for each one that leaves, another two come to take their place."

Rumors had swept through the city far ahead of the official announcement, and the square had been packed for most of the day. Zuberi had ordered a curfew, to quell unrest, but privately Nizam doubted that there would be any riots tonight. The city of Karystos was in shock, the loss too enormous to comprehend. If trouble were to come, it would come tomorrow, once the shock had worn off and men began to reckon what they had gained and lost with Nerissa's death.

"Have the priests send them home. Or to the temples, where they may pray all night, and leave the streets free for patrols."

Zuberi nodded. He did not thank Nizam for his suggestion. It was not his way.

"What of Prince Lucius? My men said he told them nothing."

"Your men were ignorant brutes who smashed his jaw to stop his screams. Of course he told them nothing, since he is no longer capable of speech."

He had thought to shock Zuberi with his bluntness, but Zuberi appeared unmoved. Perhaps he was no longer capable of being shocked, after the tumultuous events of the past two days.

"He must have had accomplices, and I need you to discover who helped him."

"And how do you suggest I do that? The prince can not speak, and he is not fit to be questioned."

Zuberi shrugged and turned away slightly, his attention seemingly caught by the overflowing basket of scrolls on his desk. "Then we will question all those that Lucius has had contact with since he became the empress's guest. One of them must be guilty, and they will lead us to the others."

"And as for the prince?"

"He is to be burned alive at the foot of Nerissa's pyre, so the sound of his screams may ease her passage."

Zuberi had spent too long in the corridors of power,

far removed from the realities of life and death. He could have benefited from a few hours spent observing Nizam's apprentices at their craft.

"The prince will not live that long," Nizam said. "Your guards were undisciplined, and the damage they did too grave. The prince will die within days, either from the bleeding in his gut or from his broken jaw, if he is unable to swallow water."

"They were under orders to leave him alive."

"He is alive. But he will not stay that way."

Zuberi growled in frustration. "I will not let him slip away this easily. The funeral is nine days from today. Do what you must to keep him alive until then."

"I will do what I can, but I do not think it will be enough," Nizam said.

Zuberi nodded, apparently satisfied. "If he dies, notify me at once, and we will display his body in the courtyard. I will send you a list of all those who have been in contact with him, and you may start questioning them immediately."

"As you command, proconsul," Nizam said, recognizing the dismissal.

Returning to the secret catacombs that were never shown on the official maps of the palace compound, Nizam sent a runner to fetch Galen the healer. He doubted that there was anything a healer could do to prolong Lucius's life, but he had promised Zuberi that he would try.

A former slave himself, Galen normally tended the servants of the imperial household, but he had worked with Nizam before when his special skills were required. As he entered Lucius's cell, followed by a slave carrying the tools of his trade, Galen took in the situation with a single glance.

"This was not your work," he said.

"None of mine did this," Nizam agreed. "But now it falls upon me to keep him alive long enough that he may be properly executed."

Lucius had been moved to a low cot in preparation for Galen's visit, but other than that he was untouched. Unlike earlier, this time he did not make a sound as his abused body was turned one way then another. Galen's face darkened as he manipulated the rigid abdomen, then carefully felt the shattered jaw.

"No matter what I do, he will be dead before morning," Galen announced.

This matched Nizam's own conclusions.

"Proconsul Zuberi will be most displeased," Nizam said. It was both a statement of fact and a warning. Nizam, by his position, was immune to Zuberi's displeasure, but Galen was not.

"Why? Was this one of the assassin's helpers?"

"This is, or rather was, Prince Lucius."

Galen gave a low hiss of surprise, turning the prince's face toward the light. "So it is." Then he shrugged. "Prince or prisoner, it makes no difference. He will die nonetheless."

"Do what you would if you expected him to live," Nizam advised. Galen had been of use to him in the past, and there was no reason to sacrifice such a valuable tool to Zuberi's ire. "Bind his jaw, and splint his arm. Let Zuberi see that we tried to save him."

"A waste of my time and supplies," Galen muttered, but he turned to his slave and gave the necessary orders.

Nizam watched as Lucius's broken arm was splinted, his swollen knees wrapped in compresses. His jaw was realigned, and bound with linen strips, two reeds holding his lips parted to help him breathe. None of these efforts would save him, but they were visible signs of the healer's arts.

Lastly Galen mixed powdered herbs into a bowl of well-watered wine. Soaking the corner of a rag in the bowl, he wet the prince's lips, then carefully allowed a few drops to fall into his mouth. They watched as three drops became four, and then a dozen, but there was no sign of the reflexive swallowing that should have occurred.

Galen handed the rag and bowl to his slave. "Try again in half an hour, and then every half-hour after that. If his condition changes, send a guard to fetch me. I will be back to check on him myself later tonight."

The slave nodded, taking up his position crouched on the floor by Lucius's cot.

"I have done what I can, but it will not be enough," Galen said as they exited the cell. "If I had been called at once, I might have been able to stop the bleeding in his belly."

"Or he would have died under your knife, and you would have been held to blame," Nizam said. He did not believe in dwelling on what might have been. Facts were facts, and the past could not be altered. A wise man accepted this, and simply made the best of the present.

As Nizam intended to do. Whatever information Prince Lucius had held was lost to him, but there were others whose knowledge might prove equally valuable. He had preparations to make, and suspects to question. One way or another, the next time he saw Proconsul Zuberi, he would have information that would distract the proconsul from the issue of where to lay the blame for Lucius's premature death.